Advance Praise
for
Light at the Edge of Darkness

. . . these apocalyptic tales are powerful, with strong characters, and lots of action.
—Wayfarer's Journal

The authors of these stories are well crafted word-smiths,
who have sharpened their pens and powered-up their word
processors to brings some nail biting and chill-bumps to
raise the hairs on the back of any reader's neck.
—Yellow 30 Sci-Fi.com

Immerse yourself in a collection of Christian Speculative
Fiction that you will never forget. *LIGHT AT THE EDGE OF
DARKNESS*, edited and compiled by Cynthia MacKinnon is
nothing short of a gathering of the masters.
—David Brollier, author of *The 3rd Covenant*

Light at the Edge of Darkness is a good read for anyone
and a must-read for those who are looking for solid Christian
speculative fiction.
—Virtual Book Tour de 'Net

ACKNOWLEDGEMENTS

Many special people deserve mention and huge amounts of thank-yous and here are a few of them:

Top billing, of course, goes to The Boss of whom these works seek to glorify.

Chris Deanne for all the effort, energy, and enthusiasm she put into critiquing the stories contained in this volume; Karri Compton for her attention to all the important details of the book; David Brollier and the Christian Fiction Review Blog members for their encouragement and the blog tour of *Light at the Edge of Darkness*; Karina Fabian and Terri Main for their support and promotional efforts on FabChat and Wayfarer's Journal; and lastly, all the members of the Lost Genre Guild whose participation and enthusiasm have been remarkable.

Editor,
Cynthia MacKinnon
The Writers' Café Press

THE LOST GENRE

Biblical speculative fiction—a real mouthful to describe this lost genre. What is "Bib-spec-fic"? it is speculative fiction that is written from a Christian world view intended to inspire and entertain readers. In *Light at the Edge of Darkness*, several sub-genres of spec-fic are showcased including horror, science fiction, dystopia, fantasy, time travel, supernatural. You will read the serious, the light, the parody, and the heart-stopping "fiction to scare the Jesus into you."

When forced to the edge of darkness, there's only one way back: embrace the Light.

•venture to futures where religious "terrorists" smuggle frozen embryos to save lives and resist technologies designed to break their souls;
•explore dying alien worlds scouring the galaxies for hope;
•get abducted and discover the universe's secrets or the trial of a lifetime.

•teetering on the edge, escape inbred captors through a haunted labyrinth, survive a house where nightmares walk, or settle in for a martyr's tribulation.

•join an epic quest through the ridiculous, cross swords with monsters, sneak a glimpse at heaven, and traverse the planes where angels and demons tread.

Follow these tales and more to the edge of darkness, to the brink of despair and then back to bask in the Savior's redeeming Light.

Visit the Lost Genre Guild website at www.lostgenreguild.com for more information about Biblical Speculative Fiction

LIGHT

at the edge of

DARKNESS

An anthology of Biblical
Speculative Fiction

EDITED BY CYNTHIA L. MacKINNON

A Publication of
The Writers' Café Press
Indiana

LIGHT AT THE EDGE OF DARKNESS

Copyright © 2007 by The Writers' Café Press

Edited by Cynthia L. MacKinnon

A Writers' Café Press Book
Published by The Writers' Café Press
Lafayette, IN 47905
www.thewriterscafe.com

Light at the edge of darkness : an anthology of biblical
speculative fiction / edited by Cynthia L. MacKinnon.
          p. cm.
          LCCN 2006940166
          ISBN-13: 978-1-934284-00-1
          ISBN-10: 1-934284-00-9

          1. Religious literature. 2. Christian fiction. 3. Fantasy fiction. I. MacKinnon, Cynthia L.

PN6071.R4L54 2007   808.83'083823
QBI07-600003

Printed in the United States of America

COPYRIGHT ACKNOWLEDGEMENTS

CONTENTS

FROZEN GENERATION

Andrea Graham

Andrea Graham is an award-winning author and poet who writes for Christ. She maintains both a Christian Advice blog, **Ask Andrea** and a website with a complete archive of her great short stories and poetry: **All for Christ**. Andrea has co-authored a trilogy beginning with the novel *Heaven's Mark* which is due to be released in late 2007. Mrs. Graham grew up in Columbus, Ohio, where her family has firm roots going back at least four generations; she attended the prestigious Ashland University and studied creative writing and religion. Andrea holds membership in several writers' groups including, The Lost Genre Guild. Mrs. Graham lives with her husband Adam and cat Joybell in Boise, Idaho.

"Frozen Generation" and the later story, "Chosen of God" are set during the time of the Empire: the nations, after forming ten super-states, turned the reigns of international government over to a demon-possessed madman who many Christians suspect to be the Antichrist. One of these nations is the US of A, both the first and the last of her breed. First in terms of states forming one nation, last in that America was last to bow to the Empire. The lame duck that signed that treaty got out of it a Steward appointment.

"Frozen Generation" begs the question, if the humanity of unborn children, and subsequently their rights, are wholly dependant upon the mother's choice, and we had the technology to bring them to term artificially, why wouldn't society treat these 'non-persons' as property, use them for spare parts, or any other evil man can dream of?

I WATCHED THE MECHANICAL arm remove a post-gestational fetus from the purple semi-transparent encasement. The Kevlar and steel womb could have slept a half-dozen grown men, easy.

Based on the Product of Conception's development, under other circumstances, the male child would've been transferred to the nursery a year ago. By law, fifteen minutes separated a POC from a non-person—the more dignified slave designation—so breeders gave living spare parts no freedom.

The doomed POC sure screamed like any free child, though. It screamed as the mechanical arm whisked it through the air by the ankle. It screamed as the arm dropped it in the separator. It screamed until the droning silver cylinder silenced the screams, extracting the beating heart needed to save the baby the parents had wanted.

I lowered my head. My eyes remained as dry as the Sahara, which my ancestors had called home before that POC's ancestors reduced mine to chattel. Maybe the soldier who executed my husband fathered the child. Maybe his mother made the report about my husband's preaching against my current employer, against the breeders turning the descendants of slave and master alike into chattel.

I whispered, "The sins of the fathers."

Harvesting organs from female POCs didn't bother me at all. I didn't even weep when a precious Black baby girl slipped through my sticky fingers. Better they meet this end than face the life that awaited female slaves.

My daily quota met, I leapt up from the evil console I used to manipulate the mechanical arm. I kept my head down to avoid the ever-watching eye. My supervisor perused the security camera and might discern in my eyes the urge to walk out the door and never come back.

A silent frozen cry pierced me, removing all thought of quitting. I headed down the sterile-white corridor to the freezer.

At the steel door, I punched in my code. The lock hissed and the door slid open. I grabbed a coat and an embryo rack from my cubby before stepping inside the burning sub-zero temperatures. I pulled my palm-computer out of my coat pocket and double-checked my list for the right shelf.

My tear ducts threatened to frost as I walked down rows upon rows of frozen humanity, up to three months gestational age at this facility; another processed late-term pregnancy terminations. The bio-mothers had declared all non-human products of conception. Only, most chose selling their offspring to science, or into slavery, over paying to dispose them.

Nearly two-thirds of the babies conceived in Philadelphia this year would be processed through this facility. A disproportionate number were my own people, beautiful Black babies betrayed by the very souls God appointed to protect them.

God appointed me to deliver the captives to safety, as Harriet Tubman had in centuries gone by. Only Harriet never hid her passengers in her womb.

Granted, I only carried six to term. The rest I re-transplanted. Far too many completed their gestation in the artificial womb at my counter-breeder in the Deep South, of all places. It couldn't be helped. Many would send money to help redeem these precious souls, but few stood up for the greatest need. Carrying them to term.

At the right shelf, I touched the frosted glass pane and shivered.

Most facilities didn't keep tight security on the freezers. Breeders had hundreds of thousands, if not millions, of frozen embryos and fetuses. Even if a breeder kept an accurate count—and most didn't—I could always change the numbers in the computer.

By the time a government hack called for an audit, I'd be gone, moving on to another city, another breeder. Twice, I had to move on to another name, too. This last time, I moved back to my real name, Azura Borden. Philadelphia might require changing it a third time.

Removing an embryo early would trigger a laser alarm. I'd been here six months, and my employer showed no signs of trusting me with the scheduling key. The White woman's eyes increasingly shone with suspicion, especially after I sorted by race the embryos scheduled for implantation today. My boss had only pretended to buy my explanation it was for demographics. I'd have to hurry or I'd get caught.

I pursed my lips, punched in the key, and slid back the glass door. Checking my palm-computer, I removed the twelve tubes containing the Black embryos. Shame I could rescue so few.

Sheltering the rack against my breasts, I raced from the freezer and headed in the direction of the ladies' room. Exposure to the lights outside the freezer triggered the thawing mechanism. About twice the diameter of a standard needle, the tubes were designed to inject the embryos into the artificial womb, but also did the trick with the real thing.

The feat required flexibility that tested my old gymnastic skills. So far, experience had offset the effects of aging. I'd learned early on the tricks to minimizing the pain.

A siren wailed just as I flushed. Busted.

Still sore despite an expensive application of healing balm, I tossed the empty tubes in the trash and raced out into the hall. One hand hovered over the precious cargo I carried. According to the indicators, all twelve had survived the thaw, a rarity.

Technology had improved since the days when two out of twelve embryos resulted in live births, but embryo mortality remained a problem. Lord willing, I'd still have nine with me once I reached Savannah. I had to make it. They were counting on me.

I raced around a corner and collided with a technician. Ignoring her yelp, I shoved past. She shouted after me, her words laced with profanity, "Hey! Don't tell me you did it, Azura! Come back here!"

Did that White woman think the color of my skin made me stupid? I ran as fast as my legs could still fly at forty-seven.

By the time I reached the outer doors, my lungs burned and my side felt like a spear had been thrust in it.

I spotted Cerulean's car idling behind a snowbank piled against the building. Oh, thank the Lord! That boy had a gift for sensing when I'd bury myself up to my neck in trouble.

I leaped in beside him. The tires squealed as my late husband's only begotten sped out of the parking lot.

I glanced at my oldest son. "And once again I owe you my life."

"Least I can do for you, Mama, but you ought to think on retirement. What're you gonna do with the young un's once Sis gets married next fall? Who's gonna take the kids when we need to get outta town in a hurry?"

I bristled, yet couldn't help but smile at the "we." A man after his father's heart, Cerulean joined us not long before a detachment of White soldiers lynched my man, twenty-seven years ago, in our first and last pastorate. A sharp turn shoved me against my window. "We managed all right, didn't we?"

"You're gettin' too old for this, Mama."

I smiled. Cerulean would insist on carrying on in my place, if he had the right equipment. "We'll see what they say in Savannah."

Cerulean gulped. "We're not goin' to Savannah."

"What?"

"Savannah said to head west and lay low. They can't chance you being followed."

I shook my head. "I got twelve this time, boy; that's not an option. We have to get to Savannah while there's time to get these babies implanted in adoptive mothers."

Another sharp turn rammed me into Cerulean. I peeled myself off.

"There's another facility, Mama, but . . . you're not gonna like it."

"Will they find the babies good homes?"

"Sure. They've got all the resources Savannah has, except it's in, um, Boise."

"Boise? As in Idaho, home of the White potato farmers? They have among the lowest breeder output levels in America. Hardly any Black slaves to rescue there."

"Maybe God wants you to save White slaves, too."

"The Sins of the Fathers."

"That's only unto the fourth generation, Mama, and you know it."

"Can't be enough Black families there willing to bring these babies to term, either."

"Let me put it this way, Mama. Savannah says you're workin' from Boise, or you can retire and carry all those babies to term yourself."

I stared at the car ceiling. "God, why are you doing this to me?"

"You wanted to see me?" I sat in the office of the gray, downy-haired doctor a month after being relieved of my latest passengers.

He leaned forward, a pleased smile on his face. "Good news, Azura. Not only has the Lord saved all twelve alive, he's provided families for them, too."

I gasped. "Didn't know you had that many Black people in Idaho."

The doctor stared. "Several of the couples are interracial. All but one of the adoptive mothers are White."

My eyes widened and my jaw fell open. What?

The White man blinked. "Would you prefer to deny the children a Christian family? To bring them to term through artificial means and turn them over to the authorities, who would match them with a Black family, but one aligned with the devil?"

I grunted. The White man wouldn't understand. They just looked at me like *I* was the racist when I tried to explain my people's need to maintain our Black identity.

Maybe . . . maybe I could explain this. "And if a Black woman wanted to adopt a White embryo? Would you have a problem with raising a White baby Black?"

The doctor narrowed his eyes at me. "I believe the only person here who would have a problem with that is you, Mrs. Borden."

He paused. "I reviewed your application at my . . . other employer. Considering your feelings, and Savannah's recommendation, we'll start you in the nursery. Impress us and, at your annual review, we'll consider getting you transferred to a department where you can carry out the sort of mission to which you are accustomed."

I bit my lip. If I weren't a good Christian woman, I'd cuss that White man out big time. Instead, I bowed my head and submitted as unto the Lord.

Besides, with so many double agents in key positions at the local breeder, while my co-workers could still be a problem, I could stay put here long enough to let the babies I still had at home grow up in one place. Maybe this was God's way of telling me stability was more important than being amongst our own.

I watched thirty toddlers roughhouse in a barren room with hardwood floors. A couple children sat at the lone window letting in the blazing June sun. Several fought over the few tattered dolls and broken toy trucks, all donated by charity. Far more vied for the attention of my coworker, whose nametag bore the name Snyder.

As usual, the blond kid with large aquamarine eyes and pale cheeks had claimed the coveted spot in "Grandma Teresa's" lap.

No longer able to stand it, I braved the sea of pint-sized, enslaved humanity and crossed over to Teresa and the shivering little boy.

I hissed over the noise, "Why the heck do you humor this boy? Land's sake, it's 105 degrees outside, and even with the AC it has to be 80 in here. He cannot be cold."

The boy hugged his shivering little frame. "Freezing."

Teresa swallowed and put him off her lap. She stood, pulling out her radio. "Dottie, we're going on break." Instead of waiting for Dottie to arrive to cover for us, Teresa took my arm and led me out into operations. We hurried through incubation and took the corridor to the freezers. "He's my grandson."

Grandson? The poor woman. "Why don't you sue for his rights?"

Teresa bit her quivering lip. "He's been reserved already."

I clucked my tongue. The courts wouldn't void a sale unless the plaintiff could prove it fraudulent, which technically wasn't the case. "What's wrong with him, to make him act like he's always cold?"

Teresa picked up her pace. She stopped outside the freezer and faced me. "Andy isn't frozen. Not anymore." Teresa waved at the wall that hid countless frozen souls from view. "But his brother still is. I think that's what Andy's trying to tell us."

A sob broke free. Teresa covered her mouth. "Bad enough my daughter shamed us and sold the boys into slavery. The least they could have done is kept them together." Tears poured down the ancient face, twisted with a familiar pain. "The least they could have done . . ."

My heart leapt in my throat. *Help him.*

At my Shepherd's voice, I swallowed and bowed my head.

I touched the cold steel door. "If you can obtain parental rights to him, I'll carry him."

I stood at the restroom sink at work, rinsing the bile out of my mouth. I patted my flat stomach and shook my head. A sad smile tugged at my lips. "You sure are makin' a short work of your Mama Borden, you rascal."

It'd been years since I'd gotten this sick with a pregnancy. I frowned. Or this attached to an embryo.

I'd never given up a child I carried to term. Though I had expected to be relieved with this one, the little rascal had already proved far more dangerous to my heart than my stomach. Reminding myself of his brother's ivory skin hadn't helped one lick. Almost made me wish I hadn't signed up for this. Almost.

Somehow, I'd get through this. Somehow, I'd surrender *my* son to his grandmother.

Moisture filled my eyes—I wouldn't even get to name him. *Oh Lord, help me!*

I sighed and went down to the nursery.

My love-starved charges already had Teresa surrounded. Andy jumped up from his grandmother's lap and ran against the crush of little bodies straight to me. "Ms Azura!"

I gasped at the flushed ivory cheeks and the sparkle in the blue-green eyes. He pressed both hands on my stomach and grinned like the Cheshire cat. "Not freezing no more."

I lay back, exhausted, but salved with the first cries of my eighth child. Cerulean massaged my shoulders in his late father's place.

The doctor said, "It's a boy."

A smile tugged at my lips. A son. The Lord gave me another son.

After the nurse measured and swaddled my son, she turned to hand him to Teresa. "Congrats, Mrs. Snyder. Your son is a beauty."

I frowned. How could she make such a ridiculous mistake? "Don't you have eyes? She's his grandmother. I'm the mother. And I want to hold my son."

The nurse froze short of giving my son to Teresa and turned to stare at me. "Um, ma'am, it's quite obvious—I mean—"

My heart somersaulted—they planned to take my baby. Blood rushing, I leapt up. "Give me my baby! I want my baby!"

Cerulean pressed me back into bed. "It's okay, Mama." He walked up to the nurse and held out his hands. "Give me my brother."

The nurse trembled, gulped at the young man towering over her, and sent a glance at Teresa. She nodded. "Go ahead."

Cerulean took my baby, cradled his bald head, and placed him in my waiting arms.

Serenity fell over me as I smiled down at his red, wrinkled face, the blue eyes already showing a hint of green, like Andy's. No doubt he'd soon have the same ivory cheeks, too.

The nurse had been right; my son was indeed a beauty.

I glanced up at the cowed medical personnel. "When can I take my son home?"

Their eyes widened and several mouths took an O-shape.

The doctor spread her hands out. "Ma'am, he's ready to go now, but legally, Teresa is his mother. He's going home with her."

"She's his grandmother. I'm his mother. He belongs with me."

The doctor glanced at Cerulean's folded arms and whispered to the nurse, none too soft, "Call security."

Teresa put a hand out. "Wait. This is my fault. She wasn't given proper training for this. Let me talk to her." She shot a sideways glance at Cerulean. "*Alone.*"

The doctors filed out.

Cerulean glanced at me. "That what you want, Mama?"

I swallowed and held his little brother closer to my breast. "Wait in the hallway."

Once the door closed behind Cerulean, Teresa placed a hand on my shoulder. "I'm sorry, Azura. Guess it never occurred to me you'd get this attached. You're right, I'm his grandmother, and I don't intend to tell him anything else. But he belongs with me."

I clung tighter to my baby. "You have no idea what you're asking."

"I remember what it was like with my daughter, Azura. Believe me, I understand what you're feeling. If anyone had asked me to give her up . . . I'd have died of a broken heart."

"Then you'll give me the rights to my son."

Teresa clasped her hands together. "Azura, try to think rationally. You have *seven* already. I only have my grandson and I'm all the family he has. Don't be selfish. I'll even name you as my successor to his rights."

"He's my son."

Teresa shook her head. "I don't want to put it like this, but you leave me no choice. He's not your son; he's my daughter's son. A Black woman, carrying a White baby. That's not a mother. That's a surrogate."

I rocked my son, shaking my head. White, Black . . . in the light of my son's sweet face, those words held no meaning at all.

Teresa placed her hands on mine. "Be reasonable, Azura. Give me what belongs to me, and I'll gladly share him. Fight me, and I'll take my grandson away, and you'll never see him."

That knifed me clear through. My arms went limp.

Teresa whisked my baby from me. "Thank you, Azura. I'm sorry I had to speak like that. What you've done I can never repay. I meant what I said. You're welcome to see him any time."

My lip quivered. "What—what will you name him?"

She smiled. "No cheating. Wait for his christening. Non-Catholics can come, too."

My jaw dropped. "But, you hate the pope. You called him the anti-pope." A Lutheran term of contempt for the False Prophet. At least I'd thought so . . .

Teresa nodded. "Traditional Catholics don't follow the counterfeit the Emperor enthroned. We follow the true Pope." Teresa turned and left with my son.

Catholic? She intended to raise my son Catholic?

Of course she would. And I couldn't do a thing about it.

Nor could I ever tell him. Not about Teresa's threat. Not about how much he really meant to me, how bad I wanted to take him home. Not the true gospel.

Granted, Teresa did distance herself from the False Prophet, and the Empire did at times hang their own priests, but everyone knew you couldn't trust *those* people. Maybe I should call for Cerulean; we could snatch my baby and run . . .

I sighed. A Black woman with a White baby? Too conspicuous. One thing I could do: pray.

I took my seat at Boise's incubation console. For the first time in two years, I watched the mechanical arm remove a fetus from the artificial womb. The living spare parts screamed his little lungs out.

The mechanical arm hesitated. That baby was the same size as mine. Anny had better be tough; Teresa didn't consider what kids would say on the playground when she christened my Anny with the name Annunciation Leslie Snyder.

I shook my head and forced the doomed POC to stop looking like Anny. I had a job to do. The POC would die regardless. If I quit, I couldn't save any of them.

The arm resumed the journey to the separator. The baby in its clutches screamed still louder.

A ditty stuck in my head, the one I sang to Anny when I baby-sat, or found excuses to visit Teresa.

Jesus loves the little children . . .

Why did the mechanical arm seem to crawl? I liked sending it fast. Best to get it over with.

All the children of the world . . .

The arm sped up. The baby's screams continued.

Red and Yellow . . .

The baby's wails seemed to beat in time with the song chiming through my head.

Black . . .

The mechanical arm stopped over the separator.

And White.

I fought my closed fist. Whatever his race, I had to drop that POC, or no child in this place would ever know freedom.

They are precious in His sight . . .

I loosened my grip. The child looked right at me. His terrified cries pierced me to the quick, but I had to do this. I must!

I opened my hand. The screaming baby dropped.

Anny's trusting eyes flashed. "No!"

The mechanical arm dove after the baby into the jaws of death.

The mangled arm obeyed my command and placed the baby in my arms even though it was too late.

I clutched the little corpse to my chest and wept. It couldn't have been Anny. He was earmarked for domestic service like his brother. It couldn't have been Anny.

A tremor shot through me—the separator's laser malfunctioned. My hands had the POC's blood on them.

Those little dead eyes bored into me, echoing the cry for help frozen in his silent scream.

THE RIDER

Deborah Cullins-Smith

Deborah Cullins Smith is a poet, fiction writer, and hopes to be a novelist when she grows up! Her first love has always been historical fiction, and she loves research. Deborah's poetry and non-fiction inspirational pieces have been published in such magazines as *Pentecostal Evangel*, *Woman's Touch*, *HiCall*, *Take Five*, *Standard*, *The Evangel*, and *Daily Meditation*. She is a member and moderator of The Herscher Project, a group of science-fiction/fantasy writers, and holds a library on Elfwood, the largest sci-fi/ fantasy website in the world. Her poem "No More Tomorrows" appears in the anthology *Tales for the Thrifty Barbarian* as does her dedication to the founder of the Fantasy Writers International and author, Larry N. Morris.

Currently she is working on a novel called *The Last of the Long-Haired Hippies*, a story about a woman trying to reconcile her past as a flower child of the 60s with her present life and the man who loves her in spite of her haunting memories. She is also co-writing *The Song of the Grey Lady* with authors James K. Bowers and H. Lynn Rummel. It is a story of high fantasy that follows the journey of a medieval healer, her young apprentice and a cantankerous centaur, destined to free her people from slavery. Deborah lives in southern Illinois with her black Lab, Vegas, and her Pomeranian, Beau.

The old western setting is an odd place for a spec fiction story to take place! But when Alice Anderson finds herself traveling by stagecoach to join her father, a preacher called to minister to the Indians of New Mexico, her own faith is tried and tested. Does she really want to meekly follow her father, or is there a daring streak in her heart that can reach out for adventure, and possibly love? Romance novels have led her to believe that anything can happen—but can she trust those books? And should she?

DUST BLEW INTO THE cramped stagecoach, invading the eyes and noses of its uncomfortable passengers. Caroline Tomlinson covered her mouth with a mittened hand and coughed. Every inch the epitome of a proper spinster, Miss Tomlinson's dark hair was gritty with sand and her sour demeanor reflected her discomfort.

John Griffin reshuffled a deck of cards with casual indifference, his careless manner giving him the appearance of a coiled rattlesnake sunning on a rock, gracefully relaxed but capable of striking with lethal impact. His neatly trimmed beard showed little gray, though his weathered face indicated he was well past middle age.

The tall, lean figure folded into a slouch had given the name of Adam Grosslin. Not as immaculate as Griffin, this man was clearly a predator, selling his gun wherever the need arose. In this case, business took him to a small town on the Mexican border. The coach would deliver him to Bent's Fort, where he could equip himself with a horse and supplies for the remainder of his journey.

The gawky young man scrunched nervously in the corner with a black case on his lap introduced himself as Buddy Edgerton. His wheat-colored hair fell across his forehead, veiling innocent blue eyes, which peeked shyly between wavy curls.

"I'm a s-salesman," he stuttered. "We specialize in b-books, paper and ink for schools."

Alice Anderson sat stiffly between Buddy and Miss Tomlinson, trying not to be tossed into either lap by the bouncing of the aged stagecoach following the old Santa Fe Trail. Her light brown hair straggled from the black mesh snood, and her hands gripped the edge of her seat with whitened knuckles. A black high-necked traveling frock gave testimony to a recent death in her family. No one questioned whom she had lost, a fact for which Alice was grateful. Talking about her mother's passing was still an open wound to her tender young heart.

A thump on the side of the coach caused the women to jump. Andy Jenkins, a taciturn, hawk-eyed man who rode shotgun with the driver shouted, "Rest stop!"

Passengers of Jed Taylor's stagecoach knew better than to argue about when, where, how often, or how long these breaks would occur. Like obedient school children, they disembarked, stretched achy muscles, relieved themselves behind rocks, trees, or bushes—whatever was available—and drank from water canteens. Jed ran a tight schedule, and he brooked no nonsense. A huge grizzly bear of a man, Jed's long gray hair and beard were frizzy and unkempt. But his gruff exterior masked a kind heart and a genuine concern for the welfare of those entrusted to his care.

"I do believe my insides will never stop shaking again, as long as I live," groaned Miss Tomlinson, pressing her hands against the small of her back.

Alice smiled sympathetically at her, as Griffin assisted both women to the ground.

"You got five minutes here, so do what you gotta do," growled Jed. "We ain't sittin' 'round here all day. We gotta' make Pawnee Rock before sundown."

He pointed to the sand rock formations in the distance and sent a brown stream of tobacco juice over the side of the coach.

They stopped at one of those rare spots across the flat, featureless landscape of Kansas. Trees grew in a thick clump around a small brook. The women headed off to the left, and the men to the right. The summer sun reflected off the desert sand and heated the water in the stream to lukewarm, which felt wonderful on Alice's face and hands when she returned from the trees.

Oh, for a proper washroom, she thought, looking up at the treetops swaying in a light breeze. Still, she was grateful for the stream. Not every rest stop had been graced with this little amenity. She waited until Miss Tomlinson had finished her business, and they returned to the coach together. The men milled about, stretching stiff muscles and wiping sweaty brows when the women returned. Obviously they had far less to deal with than the ladies. Alice wished for the hundredth time that she could wear trousers like a man. What silly social conventions dictated that women dress "properly" when they were in very improper situations? With a sigh, they allowed themselves to be helped back into the stuffy coach, and the team of beautiful black horses jerked them back into motion.

The dull monotony of the trail had all the passengers nodding, a drowsy languor lulling them into that place between wakefulness and dreams.

Alice allowed her mind to fantasize about a tall, dark stranger who would see her on a dusty street corner and fall hopelessly in love at first sight. Their eyes would meet, the crowds would fade in the hot sun, and music would fill the air as the two of them magically drifted toward one another. Alice's notions of romance came from the love stories she had read, and it would, of course, never happen that way in real life. But still, she lived with her dreams, and they comforted her. Better to focus on the mythical handsome lover than on the cruel reality of watching her precious mother gasping for her next breath with painful spasms.

The stagecoach lurched as though something had slammed into it from behind. The passengers heard Jed shout something incomprehensible, the panic in his voice unexpected. The sharp crack of a gunshot made the women grasp for each other's hands in fear. Griffin and Grosslin drew their Colt .45s without hesitation and peered out the windows of the coach.

"You see anything?" asked Grosslin, eyes roving the landscape.

"No," replied Griffin, checking the chambers of his gun with a flick of his wrist. "What do you—?"

Griffin's question never left his lips. Something slammed into the coach again, and knocked it sideways like a toddler's toy. The women screamed as they tumbled against the men in a tangle of flailing arms and legs. The coach spun in the sand as the horses' high-pitched squeals mingled with the screams of the passengers. Alice's heart slammed rapidly against her ribs like the wings of a bird beating against its cage. Something dropped from the sky and landed on top of the coach, crushing the roof inwards. The doors flew open and the passengers were flung in all directions from the demolished vehicle. Alice hit the sand like a rag doll just before the world went black.

*   *   *

Alice regained consciousness slowly. Her head throbbed, and opening her eyes to the blazing sunlight only intensified her pain. She lay in the fetal position on gravel and sand, with no memory of how she had landed there. Raising her head slightly sent a new wave of pain and nausea rippling through her head and shoulders. When the vertigo passed, she attempted another look at her surroundings. The remains of the coach lay on its side, top crumpled in, wheels reduced to broken kindling.

Adam Grosslin's body lay crushed beneath the coach, his torso all but severed. Glazed eyes stared, a look of shocked fear permanently etched on his rugged features. At the sight of his bloodied intestines clinging to the dark wood of the carriage, Alice promptly turned away and heaved the contents of her stomach onto the Kansas plains. She squeezed her eyes shut, refusing to take a second look in his direction. Then she opened her eyes and her gaze fell on the body of John Griffin. His neck was twisted in an unnatural position, as were his arms and legs. He resembled a rag doll, thrown on a junk pile. Though not as bloody as Grosslin's corpse, he was no less dead.

Several feet in another direction, she spied the petticoats of Miss Tomlinson. Raising herself to hands and knees, Alice crawled over to the still form of the schoolteacher.

And regretted it.

One of the wagon spokes had impaled the poor woman through the chest. Her face also reflected pure fright, and hot tears flooded Alice's eyes. The spinster lady was on her way to Dodge City to teach school with her sister. The good woman would wait for hours, watching for the stage, but it would not be coming. Would they send out search parties? How long would they wait before riding out to find these poor wretched souls? A few hours? A few days? Alice had never felt so alone in her life. No, not even when her mother had passed away in her arms. She'd only known Miss Tomlinson for two days, but she'd been a fellow traveler, another woman on the bouncing stage who had shared the hardships of the road.

Jed Taylor and Andy Jenkins lay several yards away from the rest of the passengers, clearly thrown in the opposite direction when the coach flipped on its side. But they were obviously beyond help. Panic surged in Alice's chest. How had she managed to survive?

The sound of a groan made her whirl around, senses honing in on the sound of life. Buddy Edgerton tried to raise himself by gripping the rear wheels of the stagecoach. He fell back on the dusty ground with a cry of pain. Alice hurled herself to the sand beside him, hoping and praying that he was not mortally wounded. Terror filled her heart at the idea of being left alone with the wreckage of their entourage.

"Mr. Edgerton!" she cried. "Mr. Edgerton, are you all right? Please talk to me, Mr. Edgerton."

The young man peered at her through the veil of wispy light hair that fell over his bruised face. "Miss . . . Anderson? You're . . . alive? Thank goodness!" He fell forward against the ground and lost consciousness.

Alice searched the area frantically for a water canteen. Finding a full one in the wreckage of the stage, she hurried back to Buddy's battered body. With her handkerchief, she dabbed his face with water, calling his name in a soft but desperate voice.

At last, his eyes slid open and she offered the canteen, holding his head up so he could sip.

"The others?" he croaked.

Tears spilled down her face as she answered, "Dead. All of them. What are we going to do, Mr. Edgerton? I'm frightened!"

Buddy grasped her arm reassuringly. "S-steady now, Miss Anderson. I'll take care of you. I promise. But we need to l-leave here right away. Now." He looked around, scanning the rocky landscape. They had come near Pawnee Rock before the attack, and the large sandstone formations rose to the northwest only a short distance away.

"There!" he said, pointing to the rocks. "We've got to get away from here. We c-can hide up there in the rocks."

"Can you move?" Alice asked, twisting her handkerchief between damp fingers.

"We must."

"But . . ." Alice protested. His arm was obviously broken in two or three places, and his forehead bled profusely.

"He'll be back," Buddy said, clambering awkwardly to his feet as his eyes searched the horizon in all directions.

"Who?" Alice asked, her blood turning to ice.

"The Rider," Buddy said, stopping to look directly into her eyes. "The one who did all this."

"But . . ."

"No," he said, shaking the dust from his trousers. "Explanations c-can wait. Let's go."

Making haste, they scurried to the rocky escarpments and scrambled over the rough sandstone. Buddy led the way, but reached back with his good arm to help Alice scale the rugged terrain. Crimson colored her cheeks as she lifted her dress to jump from rock to rock on their climb to safety. She discovered she was showing more leg than considered proper to a man she'd known for only a few days. But something in Buddy's determination to distance them from the wreckage made her realize that they must be in extreme danger. Blood dripped down his face, and slowly soaked his jacket, yet still, he pushed forward, higher and higher.

Finally, they reached a small hollow in the side of the rocks. A shady area, well hidden from curious eyes, gave them a bird's-eye vantage, allowing them an unobstructed view of the plains below—and the remains of their traveling companions. Buddy collapsed to the ground, cradling his wounded arm, chest heaving from the exertion of the climb and the loss of blood. Alice sat beside him, heaving air into her lungs beneath her tight corset. She helped Buddy struggle out of his jacket and rolled up his shirtsleeve. His arm showed a clear break beneath his pale skin.

They'd no sooner dropped to the hard ground when hoof-beats pounded like thunder across the vast prairie. A dark-skinned man with closely cropped black hair charged toward the wreckage, reins flicking from side to side against a small tawny pony. He wore a sleeveless cream-colored shirt and leathery tan pants, torn off at the knees.

"There he is," Buddy whispered hoarsely. "The devil returned to the scene of his crimes."

Vaulting from his horse, the dark man stalked about the area, stopping at each body to roll it into its back, feeling the neck for a pulse—for any sign of life. Every movement betrayed a restless, angry demeanor. He stopped in the midst of the carnage and, raising his hands towards the sky, he screamed. The blood-curdling shriek echoed, filling the skies, the plains, and the rocks where Alice and Buddy cowered fearfully.

One by one, The Rider picked up the broken bodies of their traveling companions and laid them in hastily dug graves, handling them as though they weighed no more than dolls. When Alice recognized the long woolen skirts of Miss Tomlinson, she turned her face away and cried quietly, sobs shaking her shoulders. Miss Tomlinson, whose sister would be waiting for the stage in Dodge City, the spinster who would never teach sums or letters to the children of that rugged western town. Miss Tomlinson, who reminded her of an old hen her uncle kept on his farm in Illinois, squawking and flapping, but accomplishing little in life.

She looked back down at the grisly scene and watched the dark man lift the broken body of John Griffin. She knew what her father's opinion would have been—a man who lived by chance, by the draw of a card or the toss of a pair of dice. But Griffin had been a courtly gentleman who helped the women up and down from the coach, who tipped his hat and smiled in a debonair manner. Now his body was little more than skin holding together loose bones.

The Rider stood back for a moment, though Alice couldn't tell what he was doing. He seemed to be staring at the graves he'd just covered, as he wiped one arm across a sweaty brow. Did he regret what he'd done to them? He piled tumbleweeds and brush under the coach and set fire to the remains of the stagecoach and the bodies of the horses. With these tasks accomplished, his eyes darted about the landscape, searching, hunting . . . for them?

The man leapt onto his horse and galloped towards the rocks, eyes shifting carefully over the cracks and crevices. Obviously not finding what he sought, he flicked his reins on the horse's flanks and shot across the plains to the west.

Buddy and Alice sank back against the rocks in relief. Safe for the moment. The Rider disappeared in a dusty cloud of sand.

A catch in his breathing reminded Alice forcefully of Buddy's injuries. She turned her attention to his wounds with fearful concern. He was her lifeline now, her only means of survival.

Reaching up under her skirt, she grabbed a handful of the fabric from her petticoat and ripped long strips loose. Tearing the first strip in half, she used part of it to gently wipe away the blood on his forehead. The cut wasn't as deep as she'd feared. With the other half, she folded it again and again to form a large square. Placing the square firmly over the cut, she used the next strip to wrap around his head and secure the padding in place. She tore three more strips and reached for his arm.

"You'll have to s-set it first," he said, looking squarely into her eyes. "Are you going to be able to d-do that?"

Her face paled, but she raised her chin slightly and nodded. "If I must, well, I'll just have to do it. You can't travel like this."

He gave an approving nod and a bleak smile, then told her how to pull the arm until the bones slipped into place and wrap it securely with her torn petticoat. Placing the leather strap from the canteen in his teeth, he motioned for her to proceed. Alice's stomach lurched when she snapped the bones together, and Buddy stifled his screams of pain by clamping down on the worn leather. They'd gone to all this trouble to hide; he didn't want to give away their position by wailing like a banshee.

Alice wrapped the arm tightly to hold the bones together, then carefully she bound his arm to his torso, tying the ends across his chest. Reaching around his body to wrap the cloth around his chest brought her so close she could feel his warm breath on her face. She sensed his eyes upon her as she worked intently on his injuries, but didn't dare to look at him. Embarrassed by the intimacy of the moment, she didn't know how to respond to this strange man. He seemed as timid as she, though, and, sitting back to view her handiwork, she attempted a timorous smile. He nodded sheepishly and thanked her for her tender ministrations.

They remained hidden in the rocks for the rest of the day. The Rider returned and circled the area several more times, but they stayed well out of sight, until he departed across the plains again.

"Who is he?" Alice finally asked.

"I don't know," Buddy said with a shiver. "But I s-saw him from the window right before our stage was hit. He had this look of murderous rage on his face, as if his soul b-burns as black as his skin. I still don't know how he did it, but somehow he managed to crush our c-carriage to a pulp. Then something sent him back across the plains. Like something protected you and me. I can't explain it. I just know he's a b-bad man, and if he finds us, we're dead."

Alice's eyes grew round as she listened to Buddy weave a tale of destruction and terror. He had seen each person slaughtered, one by one. Her shoulders shook and tears slid down her cheeks. Buddy reached toward her, placing his good hand on her shoulder comfortingly.

"I'll look after you, Miss Anderson," he said softly. "I p-promised you I would. Remember? He'll be looking for us. We've got to g-get away from here. Miss Anderson, I can get us to Pawnee Rock, but I'll need your help. We need each other to survive."

Alice nodded bleakly and dabbed her nose with the sodden handkerchief. Sniffling a bit, she tried to compose herself. Buddy tried to keep her from falling into despair, and she refused to melt into this puddle of self-pity.

"We'll have to travel by night and hide by day until we reach a fort or settlement, though. I . . . I'm not very good at fighting." Buddy stammered and a shudder rippled through his lanky frame. "I'll do my best to protect you, but I sure don't want to have to f-face that monster." His voice trailed off uncomfortably. Fearful tears crept into the corners of Alice's eyes and she attempted to shake off the feeling of panic before it overwhelmed her completely.

"Where were you going, Mr. Edgerton?" she asked with a smile. Perhaps a change in the conversation would make the hours more bearable until the sun set. They still had many hours until nightfall made the journey safer.

Buddy smiled sheepishly. "Please. Mr. Edgerton sounds so formal under the circumstances. Call me Buddy. All my f-friends do."

Alice returned his smile and said, "All right, Buddy, but only if you'll call me Alice."

Buddy laughed lightly. "Alice it is. Well, Alice, I was on my way to Denver. A friend of mine owns a s-saloon there, as well as a general store. I was going to manage the store for him. He says the town is growing f-faster than you can imagine, and the prospects for a man who's willing to work are limitless. He and I were boys together in Saint Louis. Charles was an orphan, and I . . . well, let's just say that my father and I didn't get along. Nothing I did was ever g-good enough for him. The workhouses were terrible, so we lived on the streets. Made our living at anything we could hire out for: sweeping floors, cleaning out stables, c-carrying luggage for travelers . . . anything. Charles is my best friend to this day." His face took on a nostalgic far-away look. Then he gazed directly into Alice's eyes. "What about you, Alice? Why are you traveling west, and alone, at that?"

Alice smiled and traced circles in the sand with her finger. Taking a deep breath, she plunged in. "My father pastored a church in southern Illinois. One of those little towns of twenty or thirty people." Her smile held a tinge of bitterness. "Oh, don't get me wrong. My father is a good man, a kind man, but very protective of his 'little girl.' I wasn't allowed to talk to young men, or walk with them in the park. My visits with girlfriends were terribly limited—Father was always afraid that some of the girls in our town would be a 'bad influence' on me." Buddy could tell when she quoted her father's words. Her tone carried a deeper inflection, and the quotation marks seemed to hang in the air over her head. Alice smoothed her skirts over her raised knees, folding her arms on them, and leaned her head on her arms.

"But he felt the call to minister to the Indians in New Mexico. Mother and I traveled with him as far as Saint Louis. She hadn't been feeling well, but whatever my father said was law in our house. She supported him without question. If the Reverend Benjamin Anderson said we were going to live with the Indians and minister to them, then that was God's Word fallen from Heaven. When we reached Saint Louis, Mother couldn't breathe right. She entered the hospital. She and Father talked for a long time by themselves. Then Father came out and spoke with me. I was to stay with Mother until she was well enough to travel. Father planned to go on alone, but we could join him later. I knew by looking at my Mother that she was never going to leave that hospital bed." Alice paused and brushed a tear from her face. "I think Father knew, too. He had this pale look on his face, like someone had just punched him in the stomach. And I saw him wipe his cheeks with his handkerchief when he thought I wasn't looking."

Buddy reached out with gentle fingers and stroked her cheek. "He didn't stay with you? Where did you live?"

Something quivered deep inside Alice at his tentative touch. She'd always wondered what it would be like to be near a man, to be admired by a man, to be away from the watchful eyes of her strong-willed father. She loved reading romance novels, though she had to read them when Father wasn't looking; she inhaled them like the very air she breathed. He didn't approve. He always felt her time would be better spent in prayer, or reading her Bible. But she had absorbed tales about delicate ladies in distress and the gentlemen who rescued them from some dire straits, and she had wondered what that would really be like. Now she was in terrible danger, and timid, stuttering Buddy was her rescuer. Somehow it wasn't as exciting as the novels made it out to be. She was frightened, hungry, thirsty, dusty, and wanting her father's arms around her in the worst way. And yet . . . She felt the stirrings of her first longing for the shy young man sitting on the dusty ground with her. He had to be in tremendous pain, but still he listened to the story of her boring life with genuine interest. He seemed to really want to know all about her.

She smiled into his eyes and continued with her story. "They put a cot in mother's room for me, and I stayed by her side for two months. She'd be better one day, and unable to catch her breath the next. The doctor said her heart was failing." She swallowed hard. "Then one morning, while I washed her face, and combed her hair, she grabbed my hand, and said, 'Take care of your father, Alice. He'll need you now.' She made a face like a sudden pain had gripped her. Then she relaxed and stopped breathing. Just like that."

Alice fell silent and stared across the Kansas plains. They sat for several minutes, taking in the glory of the sunset. The sun reached for the horizon in a blaze of orange brilliance. The landscape glowed in golden breath-taking beauty. But Alice was miles away in a hospital room, pleading with her mother's lifeless body to come back, not to leave her alone.

Buddy smoothed a stray lock of hair away from her face and caught a teardrop with his finger. She was beautiful in the glow of the sunset. Did he dare tell her that? She was like a wild deer. She might jump away skittishly if he moved too quickly. She'd led a very sheltered life. Patience was going to be necessary . . .

His thoughts were interrupted by her soft voice. "It's beautiful, isn't it? The sunset, I mean? I have never seen anything quite like it. We could be the only two people on the face of the earth, watching the sun sink below the horizon."

She turned her face to his, and all the stories, all the romantic notions she'd dreamed were reflected in her face. Buddy leaned toward her, then stopped. Slowly, he told himself. Slowly.

"We'd better s-start walking, Alice. I think we'll travel more safely in the dark."

Reluctantly, he rose awkwardly to his feet, and using his good arm, he hooked his fingers under her elbow and lifted her from the rocky resting place. His hand felt warm and confident as it covered her own, and she felt a rush of gratitude for his presence. What would she have done if it hadn't been for this sweet young man? She'd always had someone to give orders, to tell her what to do and where to go, when to get up and when to sleep. Here on the western Kansas plains, with the sunset fading, and darkness stealthily creeping over the world, she was alone, without either parent hovering over her, dictating her actions, censoring her words. She was free. Suddenly, it was a heady feeling, and she felt brave enough to meet the future head-on . . . with Buddy at her side, that is.

He helped her down the rocks, his strong arm holding her just a little closer and a little longer each time. When they reached the base of the sandstone, he motioned that they would stay close to the rocky formations and follow them for as long as possible. That should lead them to the town of Pawnee Rock. He hoped.

He held her small hand in his own large one as they made their way over the smaller rocks and around the boulders. They walked for several hours by moonlight, ever watchful for signs of the mysterious Rider. Alice shivered at the prospect of meeting the dark-skinned man in the dead of the night.

"Here, Alice," Buddy said, pausing to cover her shoulders with his jacket. "You're chilled." His hands lingered on her shoulders, and she drew a shaky breath. In her storybooks, this was the part where the hero drew the girl into his arms and kissed her. But did she really want Buddy to kiss her? She hardly knew him. Yet, he protected her, saved her life, kept her away from the evil dark-skinned man who had savagely killed the others. He was her hero.

Clouds drifted over the face of the moon, and they found themselves tripping more and more often in the darkness, as rocks and prickly shrubs caught unsuspecting toes and snagged their clothing. Finally, Buddy called a halt. "We'll have to camp here for awhile. We can't see where we're going, and one of us is going to get hurt if we keep stumbling around in the dark."

Alice nodded. She was out of breath and weary to the bone. They found another small cove, tucked behind some huge boulders, and settled in for the night. Buddy pulled up some of the smaller bushes and piled them together. He took a small box of matches from his trouser pocket and soon had a warm fire blazing. Alice held her hands out to the warmth, and snuggled deeper into Buddy's jacket. A familiar smell emanated from the lining of the coat and grew stronger as the heat of the fire warmed the jacket. They looked at each other in bewilderment. Then Buddy smacked his forehead with the palm of his hand, immediately regretting it. He grimaced ruefully, having forgotten the injury to his brow. But the grimace turned rapidly to a broad smile as he rifled through the pockets, his face drawn close to Alice's in excitement. He pulled out a small package with a cry of victory. Unwrapping the cloth, he revealed a pouch with four sticks of dried jerky.

"I forgot all about these!" he exclaimed. "I bought them at the last trading post, just in case Jed didn't stop for meals as quickly as I hoped he would. Never dreamed we'd need these to survive."

They were tough as leather, salty, and dry . . . and tasted wonderful! They each ate two and shared another sip of the water in the canteen. Smiling at one another in the firelight, Alice sighed, and Buddy gazed at her with tenderness in his eyes, the tenderness she had hoped all day to see.

"Alice," he began, his shyness gradually falling away. "Do you really want to join your father and preach to a bunch of Indians? Is that what you truly want to do with your life?"

"I–I guess I haven't thought that much about what I'd like to do," she stammered.

"You don't have to, you know."

"I don't?" she asked breathlessly.

"Come with me to Denver," he said, his voice more intense now, more persuasive than before. "You've been under the thumb of a domineering father all your life. Well, you don't have to be, Alice. You can be whatever you want to be. We can make a new life together. Go where we want. See the world if we want. Just the two of us."

"Do you mean . . .?" Alice wondered vaguely where Buddy's stutter had gone.

"Yes, we can marry, if you want." He drew closer to her, reaching out to run a finger along her cheek. "Or we can just live, and love, any way, any time we choose. Free to come and go. Free to be whatever we want to be. No rules, no ties, nothing or no one to dictate to us. You don't need 'Daddy' anymore, Alice. You're a beautiful young woman. I can open the world for you. Just say 'yes'. . . dear Alice." His face drew closer, and she felt her heart racing. His words were totally in opposition to everything she'd been brought up to believe in, but it sounded like music to her ears. Forbidden music, but alluring and sweet.

"Stop!" a voice commanded from the darkness of the desert sands.

They looked up to see The Rider standing over them. Buddy jumped to his feet, taking a defensive stance in spite of his broken arm.

"No!" he shouted. "Leave us alone!"

The two men circled one another slowly. Buddy's body tensed, coiled and ready for the attack that was sure to come. The Rider's gaze never left Buddy's angry visage, but he displayed a calm that surprised Alice. Was this man truly so callous that he could kill and not feel anything?

"You have no place here, Rider! Leave us alone. I command it."
Alice hardly recognized Buddy now. He acted as if he faced battles like
this every day of the week, protected damsels in distress, and fought
off murdering marauders as a matter of routine. He faced off against
the man who had slaughtered a whole coach full of people. What was
he thinking?

The Rider stood calmly in the face of Buddy's rage. "You have
no right to command anything. She is a child of God, under my
protection."

"No!" screamed Buddy. "She's mine! By her own choice, she's mine!
Go away and leave us alone."

An odd black rope with little barbs flickered from The Rider's hand
and hit Buddy on top of his head. Alice screamed, but fear turned to
horror when the lash ripped Buddy in half from his head to his toes.
His skin ripped away like a theatrical costume, and a monstrous being
rose from the shredded skin. His eyes glowed red as fire, his facial
features contorted into hellish fury. Thick leathery muscles rippled as
he stretched to an eight-foot height, chest puffed out with an animal-
like hide.

Alice felt the earth tilting under her feet. This couldn't be real!
Buddy had just proposed to her—sweet, shy Buddy Edgerton. But
the beast before her snarled angrily, pacing like an animal in the zoo,
raging, growling! What was happening here? Was she losing her mind?
Where was the Buddy she thought she might be falling in love with?
Bandages gone, the creature used his previously broken arm to point a
threatening finger at the dark man from the plains. His face changed,
growing darker, angrier, more savage.

"Buddy?" she questioned in a quavering voice. "Who are you?
What are you?"

The Rider turned to face Alice, and she found it shocking that he
remained unfazed by the transformation. He had not only taken it in
stride, he appeared to be amused by this bizarre turn of events.

"Buddy?" He looked back at the transfigured man that, only
moments before, Alice almost agreed to run away with. "Is that the
name you're going by now? That's a good one."

Alice turned cold inside and shrugged off the man's jacket as if it
were poison to her skin. "What do you mean? Who are you?"

"I am Michael," said the dark-skinned man, bowing to her. "And
this . . . this creature is known by many names. But I know him as
Beelzebub. Buddy. Wouldn't Bubby be more appropriate?"

The creature's face grew darker as fury sent sparks flying from his
eyes. "How dare you!"

"Oh, my Jesus, help me! Please, Father God, what have I done?"

cried Alice.

"Don't say that name!" shrieked the monster, his rage boiling over Alice like an Illinois twister.

Michael's voice lost all levity. He pointed a finger at 'Buddy' and boomed, "Be gone! She has called upon the name of her Heavenly Father! You've lost this battle!"

Alice sank to her knees as Buddy exploded! The thunderous boom that accompanied his departure shook the earth, and he vanished in a huge swirl of black smoke and sand.

"Always making a dramatic exit," Michael muttered, shaking his head. "Show off."

"Oh, my God . . ." Alice whimpered again. And she hit the ground in a dead faint.

*   *   *

Alice regained consciousness slowly to find Michael crouched over her, patting her on the head. "Slowly, Alice. You've had a busy day."

"Oh, my God . . ." Alice whispered as memories flooded back. The fight, Buddy's transformation, the battle. It was all far too overwhelming.

But Michael smiled at her broadly. "Exactly, Child. He is your God, and I was sent to watch over you."

"To watch over me?" she asked.

"Of course." His beaming smile showed a row of shiny white teeth. "Your father and his new congregation of converts have been praying for you night and day. And so I was dispatched from the Heavenly Father to bring you safely home."

Alice's mind fumbled to grasp what these words meant.

"Am . . . am I dead?"

Michael's laughter held no derision. "No, Child, no. You are not dead. Not yet. You'll live a long and happy life in the land called New Mexico. I've come to make sure you arrive safely in your earthly father's new home. He's very concerned, you know. Very worried. He wanted to come get you, but my Master told him to trust and wait. He's an obedient man, your father is." Michael nodded wisely now, and smiled at her.

"Then you're . . ." she suddenly felt very foolish, and it showed on her face. "You're not a murderer? You didn't kill the people on the stage?"

Michael grew very grave. "That's what he told you, is it?" He sighed sadly and shook his woolly head. "He has been called the father of lies for good reason. No, Child, I did not kill the people with whom you traveled. Beelzebub planned and executed that attack. His people were responsible for those deaths, as they have been for many such attacks over the centuries. Those poor people. I grieved for them, that I did not arrive sooner to prevent their untimely deaths."

Alice remembered Michael riding up on the horse, leaping from the saddle, going from body to body, and screaming, arms raised to the skies. He wasn't in a rage. He was grief-stricken for the slaughter on the plains! It was Buddy who had convinced her that The Rider was evil. She covered her face with her hands. What a fool she'd been.

"But Buddy told me all about his childhood, a father who treated him cruelly, running away, living on the streets . . ." her voice trailed off.

"Well, I guess he did run away from home in a sense." Michael rubbed his chin. "He was banned from Heaven because he refused to submit to God's authority. And he has roamed the earth for centuries, seeking others to corrupt. So I suppose he did tell a small grain of truth; he just mixed it with a large dose of misdirection."

Michael patted her head again. "Alice, you need to rest now. We'll leave at first light, and you'll be with your father by late afternoon tomorrow. You've had a trying day, Child."

"But, Michael . . ." The name still came hard to her lips. "Why?"

"Why?" he repeated. "For you, Child. He wanted you. Alice, you are a child of the Most High King! Beelzebub delights in corrupting God's precious children. Not only would he have destroyed your life, but he would have destroyed your father's heart as well. His ministry with the Indians would have suffered, and he would have been grief-stricken for the rest of his life."

A gentle whickering emanated from the darkness and the buckskin pony trotted into the circle of firelight. A wide smile lit Michael's face.

"Aaahhh, you must meet my companion," he said, rising to stroke the horse affectionately. Alice rose, too, and a beautiful little mare, gentle and sweet natured, prodded her shoulder until Alice stroked the sleek neck and soft black nose.

"This is Wind Song," Michael said with a touch of formality to his introduction. "Wind Song, this is Alice."

Wind Song nuzzled Alice's face, her gentle eyes meeting Alice's with innate wisdom. Alice smiled at the pony and fondled her nose. "Hello, Wind Song. You're beautiful, did you know that?"

Wind Song's head jerked up and down as if acknowledging the compliment, and Alice laughed.

Michael turned to Alice once again. "Now you must rest, Child. You'll be safe. Wind Song and I will see to that."

Alice peered around nervously at the dark sandstone surrounding her. "He won't bother you, Child," Michael said, as if reading her thoughts.

"But won't you sleep, too?" she asked timidly.

"No," Michael said with a gentle smile. "I'll keep watch."

Alice finally curled up, and Michael covered her with the blanket from Wind Song's back. She was asleep in no time.

*   *   *

The sound of a rock sliding down the escarpment jolted Alice from a deep sleep, and she looked up to see the outline of a huge man standing guard over her. It was Michael . . . But he seemed to have grown three feet taller and sprouted enormous gray wings! His soft luminous eyes turned toward her.

"Sleep, Alice."

She slept until morning without dreaming.

*   *   *

As the sun rose over the Kansas plains, Alice turned and stretched. A heavenly smell, as familiar as the scent of Mother's freshly starched apron, made her mouth water. Michael sat cross-legged on the ground, holding a loaf of bread and a cup filled with the rich, milky coffee. He smiled broadly, and offered her breakfast, which she accepted with a short prayer of thanksgiving. He didn't explain where the meal had come from, and somehow, Alice didn't feel the need to ask. It was another gift from God, like manna in the wilderness.

Alice ate the bread gratefully, and finished the coffee, feeling the warmth spread through her body. She had survived the horrors of yesterday's disasters and battles, and she was going home to Father. Michael refused to partake, though Alice tried to share the simple fare. But he insisted with that mysterious grin that he didn't need food of this world.

As Michael arranged the blanket on Wind Song's back, Alice petted the horse, who whinnied and basked in the girl's attention. She finally got the courage to ask, "Michael, you said we'd be arriving at my new home by late afternoon. But it must be a long way from here. How will we travel all those miles in one day?"

Michael grinned widely, "Wind Song lives up to her name, Child! She travels like the wind."

He boosted Alice up on Wind Song's back, and swung up behind her. His strong, dark arms held Alice securely on the horse's back. When he clicked his tongue to the filly, she shot across the plains. It felt as though they flew, as fields, rocks, trees, streams, and mountains slid by in a blur. The mare was definitely in her element, as the terrain sped past them. The sun glowed golden on the western horizon when

Michael slowed Wind Song to a walk. The horse panted hard, but seemed to exult in the freedom of the morning run. She tossed her head and whickered as if to say, "Let's do that again!"

"We are almost there, Alice," Michael said gently from behind her. "Remember what you've learned on this trip, Child. Trust in the Lord your God in all things, and He will direct your path. Yes, even when it comes to matters of the heart."

Alice's cheeks burned with shame at the memory of her temptations with Buddy. She had been so foolish. She'd thought her father harsh and strict. He had protected her from things she'd had no concept of. Father had been right. Thank God for Michael!

The walls of the mission house rose up in the distance, and a stream of people flowed from the building to greet her as the little horse trotted toward the small community.

Michael whispered one last time in her ear, "Take care of Wind Song for me, Alice. I'm needed elsewhere. But I'll be at your side when you need me."

Then she was sliding off the horse's back and Father's arms were enfolding her in a warm tearful embrace.

"Oh, my daughter!" he wept. "You're safe! You're safe! Oh, how we've prayed for you. But Alice, how did you get here? Where did you get this horse? And why are you alone?"

"Father, this is Michael," Alice said, turning to gesture to the pony and her escort. "He—" she stopped abruptly. Wind Song stood at her shoulder and nuzzled her hair, which had blown free on their whirlwind ride.

Michael was gone.

"Michael?" Benjamin Anderson looked bewildered. "Is that the name of your horse, my dear? Alice, you look like you've seen a ghost. What's wrong, daughter?"

Alice stood stock still, staring across the plains. "Michael was right here behind me, all the way from Pawnee Rock. Where did he go?"

Behind her, the Indians whispered excitedly among themselves. One of the men finally spoke for all of them, tugging on Reverend Anderson's arm.

"Just like you read in the Word of God, Reverend. Michael, the archangel . . . Is that right? He guards the children of God."

"Alice?" Reverend Anderson asked softly.

"Yes, Father, he's absolutely right," said Alice, smiling at the Indians. "Michael, the archangel."

Reverend Anderson wrapped his daughter in his arms once again, as he guided Alice toward her new home.

PROTECTED

C.E. Lavender

Chad Lavender was born and raised in Charleston, West Virginia. Chad began classes at West Virginia State University in the fall of 1999, studying Accounting. During his tenure at WVSU Chad received academic honors such as Who's Who among college students, All-American Scholars, and an induction into Phi Theta Kappa, an international honor society. He also held the position of Director of Finance of the university's student government. During that time, he also fostered a passion for writing, which he works daily to transform into a reality.

Chad is married with two daughters and was ordained to preach the gospel of Jesus Christ in 2005 by the Boone County Free Will Baptist Conference. Currently, while holding down a family and a day-job, Chad is working to build the non-profit organization RISE UP ALLIANCE, which will feature the free online magazine, *RISE UP MAGAZINE.*

Mason has reached a crossroad. He knows of the spiritual warfare that weaves around everyday life, and now he must choose a side. In a way, I can relate to his predicament. I too, know of the spiritual battles that take place, which many forget or ignore. I also saw an unprepared Christian nation. How can we fight against evil when our standards continue to drop along with society's? Therefore, I established Rise Up Alliance--a group designed to raise Christians up to the role that God has called in their life. God once posed the question through the psalmist, "Who will rise up for me against the evildoers? Or who will stand up for me against the workers of iniquity?" (Psalm 94:16)

EVERY SCENARIO ENDED WITH Mason's death. With Zeke hot on his heals looking for answers, Mason didn't have much time left. He had to complete his mission before Zeke discovered the truth. He had to find the shield. Not an easy task when his unwitting informant had him gallivanting up a mountainside toward the very man he needed to avoid.

Mason peered down the mountain at the cars crawling along the distant highway. What he would have given to be ignorant again. The rest of the world had no idea what was really happening. Just innocent people living innocent lives, oblivious to the war waging around them.

Mason knew better.

Glancing up the trail at Tori, he had to pause. He needed to stall, to think. Just which side was he on, anyway? He'd started out on Zeke's side, but then Tori came into the picture.

Love has a funny way of changing things, blurring the lines between sides. Instead of pursuing the shield for Zeke, Mason found himself searching for his own protection. If he could find the shield, perhaps he could stop Zeke and protect Tori. Even whisk her away from this war.

Mason frowned. *How did it come to this? How did a simple mission turn into so much more? How did I, of all people, fall in love?*

Rule number 1: never become emotionally attached to a target.

Mason studied his target. Tori's short auburn hair clung to the neck of her baby blue shirt. She stopped, scanned their surroundings, and rubbed sweaty palms on her dark khaki shorts.

A smile broke through Mason's introspection. Beautiful. Even all sweaty and plain. Elegance in exercise. He chuckled. *I guess that's how I fell for you. So, how do I get us out of this predicament?*

Tori wasn't to blame. If she knew of his original allegiances, she'd never let on. And she'd brought him here to help her sister, not hand-deliver him to his death. Perhaps if he hadn't avoided the past few meetings with Zeke, things might've been different.

Zeke had grown bitterly impatient with Mason's evasions. Their last encounter, one Mason hadn't expected, had ended with an ultimatum: *find the shield and disable it within forty-eight hours or die.* Tori didn't know time was up.

CRACK!

Tori's gaze shot up the mountainside. Mason's heart leapt into his throat. Fluttering echoed down the mountainside ahead of a red-tailed hawk. Mason loosened his fists, hoping Tori hadn't noticed. He had to play it cool. Moreover, he needed to buy some time. Slumped against a cool rock, he reached for his canteen.

Tori's brown boots crashed down into his diverted gaze. Mason looked up. Hands on her hips. Not good.

Her deep-set blue eyes bore through his stare. "Why did you stop?"

Mason took a swig of water. "It's getting hot."

"We have to get to Izzie. She's in danger."

She meant Zeke, but Mason couldn't let on that he knew. Why not? The question hit him hard and nearly stole his smirk.

He forced an amused expression and hoped she bought it. "A 'Taker,' right? The really, really bad guy in this secret war of yours?"

"Yeah, a Taker." Tori's voice quavered with anxiety and irritation.

"And this is far from funny, Mason. Izzie's in danger, whether you believe it or not. She's our best agent and she needs to know she's walking into a trap."

Tori had confessed her allegiances and given Mason a story about their arcane war that varied a great deal from Zeke's rendition. She'd entrusted him with her secrets, closing the revelation by saying that she loved him. She'd risked everything to share the truth with him. Why couldn't he do the same?

Because of Zeke. The Taker—a soul collector for Lohrian traitors. Only the shield that Tori's people used could stop a Taker's dark powers. Mason didn't have that shield.

"I believe you, Tori. That's why I'm coming with you. But why come this way? I'd prefer the slow sloping incline with fewer rocks."

Tori shook her head. "Sometimes you have to take the road less traveled. Come on, let's get moving."

Mason frowned as she spun away and resumed the climb. *The road less traveled? Why does she have to speak in riddles all the time? What is that supposed to mean?*

If he could piece together her enigmas, he might have a shot at finding the shield. Unfortunately, solving riddles took time and Mason was fresh out.

He lingered a few moments before following. If he mirrored Tori's erratic pace—slowing, then speeding up—he would reach the summit without any strength or stamina. A steady pace would conserve energy, and to survive an encounter with Zeke, Mason knew he would need all the energy he could muster.

Mason took a step and froze. A blur of black movement in the trees lining the path ahead drew his attention. A dark, inhuman whisper teased his ears. Were those yellow eyes lurking in the shadows?

"Are you coming or what?"

Mason jumped, realizing Tori had stopped and returned her hands to her hips.

He squinted against the sunlight capping the mountain. He needed to keep her from approaching that shadow. "Yeah, I was just thinking. I know that's dangerous, but what makes your sister so special?"

"What?" Fire sparked in Tori's eyes.

"Well, I mean, we sneak all the way up this mountain to find her like she's the only one that can stop this Taker. You say she's your best agent, but I'm not even sure she knows what she's doing half the time. How is she supposed to stop this guy?"

"No, Mason, your approach is all wrong. You're focused on the ship instead of the Captain. We're just vessels. Our Captain leads and guides us. He's in control. Only He has the power to stop this Taker."

More riddles. The more he thought he knew her, the more she confused him. He'd never understood women, which had made Zeke's initial proposal so enticing. *Come with me and I'll reveal all of their secrets,* Zeke had said. That had been so long ago. Before Tori.

Mason sighed. "Well, unless your Captain is waiting for us up the path, what chance do we have alone?" Now or never. She'd opened the door, and he had to walk through. "If only we had some kind of protection, some kind of weapon to use against the Taker."

She looked at him oddly. From what she'd shared, Tori didn't understand the depths of Zeke's powers. She didn't truly appreciate what Zeke would do to Mason when he found him. Mason needed that shield.

With Tori silent, Mason stepped toward her and grabbed her hand. "What chance do we have against a Taker, Tori? He's too powerful."

Tori closed her eyes and shook her head. "True, he is powerful, but we don't wrestle against flesh. I have He who lives within. He's my shield against the enemy. And that's why I told you to stay behind. You think you're protecting me, Mason, but you're not. He is. Since you don't know Him, it's you that's in danger."

More riddles? A power that lives within her?

Mason frowned. "I don't understand. Wha—"

Tori raised her hand, silencing him. "Shhh. I sense something."

She glanced down the mountain, then sniffed and cocked her head sideways. "Something isn't right. My spiritual senses have never . . ." She squatted with her head down.

What was she doing, praying? Mason's skin rippled with goosebumps. He scanned the path ahead, the overhanging cliffs. When had it gotten so quiet? He studied the shadows for those yellow eyes.

After several seconds, Tori looked up. "A fog covers my senses, but I don't understand how that's possible."

"Evil." The answer slipped out with too much confidence, but the time for discretion had passed. "I think we're being followed." Mason checked his wristwatch. His forty-eight hours were up. If Zeke sensed his approach . . .

Tori stood.

A soft breeze blew, raising the hair on Mason's legs. "Wait! Don't move!"

Too late. A sickening feeling seized Mason's stomach. He'd felt that same nausea when Zeke gave him a "taste" of what punishment for failure would feel like. Tori lurched unnaturally. Her knee crashed to the ground, and she spun around. She flailed desperately as she fell.

Mason's heart skipped a beat. He rushed to catch her, but something grappled and jerked him backward. He floated through the air, helpless to save Tori as she slammed to the ground. He grabbed for something. A branch, brush, anything. His fingers found only air.

Some invisible force jerked him skyward. He tried to keep Tori in sight, reaching for her, but she faded from view. Whatever held Mason, pummeled him to the ground at the top of the rise.

Groaning, he looked up. Zeke stood before him dressed in a black coat that hung to his feet—character Taker apparel. Mason scowled. He needed that shield, but he'd come up short. His mind raced to concoct a plan.

Zeke studied him with dark, haunting eyes. Mason swallowed hard and his heart raced, but he tried to appear calm. He had to play it cool, had to keep Zeke off-guard. Mason tried to stand, but Zeke reached forward and an invisible hand pinned Mason in place.

The air gushed from Mason's lungs. He couldn't suppress the tremble, the fear of impending doom. He sucked in a breath. "Zeke, wha—"

Zeke's hands turned palm up. The invisible shackles jerked Mason off the ground. Mason frantically scanned his surroundings for an escape.

Nothing.

Zeke took a menacing step forward. With a snap of his right arm, the invisible hands flung Mason over the cliff's edge and suspended him over a very steep drop. "Time's up, Mace. Do you have the information?"

Mason looked down. His heart raced to see that drop. It raced harder upon spotting Tori's unconscious body below.

Irritation shook Zeke's voice. "Answer me!"

That caught Mason's attention and he met Zeke's glare—eyes dark as midnight pearls. His attention drifted back to Tori. Despite his predicament, Mason couldn't calm his concern. Was she dead? Had he already lost her?

"Umm . . . Zeke. Bad timing." Mason tried to force a hint of irritation into his voice. Zeke only responded to confidence, command. Mason had to appear calm, in control. "I'm so close to putting this all together."

The invisible grip jerked Mason forward, almost blocking Tori from view again.

Zeke's dark skin cracked. "Putting what together?" Each word rang with rage.

"The death-blow, Zeke. That shield is right at my fingertips. Once we have it, nothing can stop us. But I need more ti—"

Infernal heat blasted Mason.

"Impossible!" A hint of doubt clouded Zeke's rage. "No more excuses, Mace. I've been searching for this shield for years. Tell me more. What have you discovered?"

Mason blinked rapidly. The heat had not relented and sweat drizzled down his temple. "She opened up to me, Zeke. She's giving up their secrets. But, they speak in riddles. I'm doing the best I can."

Zeke turned his palms down, and spread his fingers apart. "Not good enough, Mace. You've failed me for the last time. Consider your service to the Lohrians terminated."

Dark shadows oozed from Zeke's fingertips toward Mason—stringy at first, then connecting to form two larger shadows.

Mason had to get away. There had to be something he could do. But what? He looked for something, anything. Wait. Where was Tori? She'd been right there below him, unconscious. Now, the path lay empty. A smile broke though his fear. She must have gotten away.

A yank. Something tugged Mason's foot, and he looked down. With one of the shadows clamped around his right ankle, he kicked and struggled to escape the second shadow. It caught hold and crawled up his leg. Grabbing at it with his hand to cast it off proved a bad move. It leached onto his hand, and spread, inching up his arm.

The shadows worked together to consume Mason. *What's going on? What happened to Tori?*

Something heaved at his side. A flash of blinding light. Mason spun around and bounced off the ground. Pain tore down his leg and up through his arm.

The shadows!

Gone?

What happened?

Remembering Zeke, Mason rolled and balled up his fists for a fight. Instead of Zeke, he found Izzie—crystal blue eyes and whitish blonde hair—standing with her hands wide in front of herself, the shadows confined between them. They shrunk between her closing grasp until her hands clasped together. She had vanquished the shadows. But how?

"Izzie?"

"Mason, what are you doing here?"

"Tori and I came to get you. She said you were in danger and started talking about some Taker and some crazy war you two are fighting. As you can see, the Taker showed up. His workers have been busy in town. He's up to something."

"Slow down, Mason. Where's Tori? She shouldn't have left you alone."

"I . . . I . . . don't know. She fell." He pointed down the mountainside. "Then Zeke . . . " Mason cringed. He'd spoken Zeke's name. He shouldn't have known Zeke's name. Maybe she hadn't noticed. ". . . well . . . this guy levitated me or something. I lost sight of Tori when that black stuff attacked me."

Izzie walked over to the edge. She stood there for a moment before rounding on Mason with fire in her eyes. "Enough games, Mason. Where is she?"

Since she'd been close enough to save him from Zeke, Izzie must have overheard their conversation. How could Mason explain himself?

He retreated a step and raised his hands, palms out. "It's not what it seems, Izzie. Nothing is as it seems anymore."

"You were almost taken, Mason. Taken." Accusations hung from her glare. "But I suppose you already know what that means. Despite whatever lies he's told you, your soul is very real. And so is your heart. If you're one of them, though, I doubt much of it remains. It's ironic, isn't it; if I hadn't stopped him, the shadows would've taken you. The evil you followed nearly consumed you."

"I don't . . ." Mason stammered for a rebuttal. The desire to lie fleeted. "I owe you my life. We'll sort things out later. But what about Tori?"

Worry consumed Izzie's face. Her sister had vanished and she'd discovered Mason's deception. She had every right to worry.

"You're right. What about Tori? She would've never left like that. They must've captured her. With you rambling on about our shield, I can only imagine what they'll do to her. Come on, I have to get you out of here."

Mason took a step, but stopped. "We can't just leave her."

Izzie's fierce gaze locked onto Mason's, perhaps weighing his intentions. "I don't know if I should trust you, Mason, but they're trying to kill you, so I don't have a choice. I'll take you to 'the Rock that is higher than I.' You'll be safe there until I can figure out what to do with you. As for Tori, leave worrying about her to me."

Mason glanced over the ledge to the spot Tori last occupied and whispered, "I hope your shield is strong," before following Izzie into the trees.

She waited in the edge of the tree line. "Tori can handle herself. And by the way 'the rock that is higher than I' is part of a verse from the book of Psalm. If you're interested later, I'll point out the significance. It only seems like we speak in riddles to those who haven't read the handbook."

She pointed west through the trees. "Go a hundred yards in that direction and you'll see a rise in the terrain to your left. Head up that rise until you reach my camp in a clearing at the top. There's a pack beside the fire ring. Hold on to the item inside that pack, it'll keep you safe."

"Wait." Mason grabbed her shoulder. "You're not coming?"

"I'm going to find my sister, Mason."

"But . . . but Zeke's still out there. You shouldn't do this alone."

A soft smile broke through her grave expression. "I'm never alone,

Mason. Now hurry up and find the camp."

Mason released her, took a step, and stopped. With his back to her and pressure constricting his heart, he spoke just barely above a whisper. "Bring her back, Izzie. Please."

Izzie took off in the opposite direction. A twinge of hope cut through the tightness squeezing Mason's chest. From what he'd seen and learned from Tori, if anyone could find her, it was Izzie.

Mason set off in the direction she'd indicated. Sweat beaded on his forehead as he rushed to find the camp and the mysterious item that could protect him. The staggering Indian summer humidity made the sweat bead faster. Panting, Mason paused beside an oak and checked his bearings. The sun's sweltering glare would soon reach its mid-day height. Mason wiped his face on his sleeve. Even without the humidity, he would have been sweating. He'd barely survived encountering Zeke once. How long would it take Zeke to find him again?

Standing around waiting for him certainly wouldn't help any. Mason launched off the tree and quickened his pace. Branches snagged at him. Sounds like footsteps crunching leaves and shifting brush echoed around him. Mason found himself spinning around to check every noise, tripping over roots, and fumbling his way through what should've been an eventless hike. Upon reaching the campsite, he stood in awe. It more resembled a rudimentary castle than a campsite—boulders jutting out of the ground forming a protective enclave.

A twig or branch snapped nearby. Mason's gaze darted over his shoulder toward the sound. The echo died leaving him in silence. The backpack! Izzie had said its contents could protect him. Mason wove through the boulders and found the pack.

His clumsy fingers fumbled with the latch. His gaze swept around the site in frantic sweeps, certain that someone was watching him. The latch loosed. Mason tore the pack open.

A book? You've got to be kidding me.

He overturned and shook the sack. There had to be something else. A book couldn't save him from Zeke. Only a lint clump fell out with the book, and Mason hurled the sack away dismayed. How was a book supposed to save him? Zeke had power, real power. Even if the pen was mightier than the sword, was it mightier than pure evil?

Riddles. Always riddles with those two. What had Izzie said? *It only seems like we speak in riddles to those who haven't read the handbook.* Maybe he'd found the handbook. Mason shifted the book around and stared at the worn, white letters. HOLY BIBLE. He couldn't help scoffing.

Zeke had called it a book of lies, the enemy's great deception. Had anything Zeke said been true?

A tree shook beyond the camp. Mason jumped. Leaves wouldn't rustle like that without a breeze. Mason's stomach twisted with uncertainty. Was Zeke out there watching him? What was he waiting for?

Mason checked the book. Maybe the secret was hidden inside. He flipped the cover open and stared at the hand-written words filling the margin.

This is the Living Word of God. He who reads it will escape death and find life. He will find the answers to life's questions. And better yet, he will uncover the mysteries of his heart.

No way? A book could do that? No, of course a book couldn't do that. Maybe Zeke had been right after all. Maybe it was all just a book of lies, a great deception. Mason sighed and stood. Ink and paper couldn't live. But what about the rest? It was as if the writer had read his mind. Escape death and find life. Just what he needed. His fingers itched to pick the book up again.

He leaned against a rock and looked back to the Bible. His skin prickled and his heart beat faster. He should pick up the Bible. If even the slightest chance existed that a book could save him from death, could he afford to discard it? Could he take the chance of being wrong? "Well, I suppose it beats just standing here holding up this rock."

He dove for the book, pulling it in and clutching it like a long-lost friend. The ridiculousness of his situation hit him and Mason laughed. He let the book fall onto his lap and stared at it while his pace calmed.

Re-reading the inscription, Mason laughed again. You expect me to read this whole thing? Instead, he flipped it open and noticed a ribbon bookmark. He pulled out the red ribbon. In white letters it read, *My Lord is greater than anything I will face.*

Mason shook his head. He couldn't believe he was about to read from the Bible. He'd bought into all of Zeke's warnings about the dangers of Christianity, but had ended up with two strong Christian women. And with a Bible in hand to boot. Maybe this was supposed to be one of those signs Tori and Lizzie always talked about.

Mason arched an eyebrow and glanced at the sky, thinking perhaps a cloud might part and cast a heavenly spotlight down at him while the birds broke into a chorus of Hallelujah.

Sign or no sign, could this book protect him from Zeke? Well, he would never know unless he read a little. He noticed on the bookmark a verse, I John 4:4.

That should be easy to find. After several minutes had passed, and a couple of different Johns, he found the verse he sought. *Strange. I'd think that if this was the second book in the Bible that was labeled John then it would be the second John, not the first.*

Mason shook off his own logic. He needed to find the shield, and all signs pointed to this book. He focused on the scripture.

Ye are of God, little children, and have overcome them: because greater is he that is in you, than he that is in the world.

Mason read it again. Could some greatness inside him overcome Zeke? The concept seemed either ludicrous or divine. Like the book knew what he needed.

What greatness?

Mason flipped pages; he needed more answers. Acts. It seemed as good as any other. His finger randomly stopped on chapter two, verse twenty-one.

Whosoever shall call on the name of the Lord shall be saved.

"So by calling on the name of the Lord, I can be saved. Then, I guess, some form of greatness will come inside me to stop Zeke."

How much like Zeke's promises did that sound? Hadn't Zeke promised that if Mason called on the Dark Lord, he would be filled with the power to change the world? Zeke had shown Mason glimpses of that power. Glimpses of pain and suffering. Tori had shown him something else. Love.

Mason's pulse quickened. He flipped through the pages, looking for more. He started off looking for protection, but found answers. With each answer, a thousand new questions arose. He wanted more. No, he needed more, like he hadn't had a drink in days and had found an overflowing river. He flipped again. The pages landed in John. He started reading in chapter three, verse sixteen.

A ripple of anxiety shook Mason. The forbidden verse. The one verse, above all others, that the Lohrian forbid reading.

For God so loved the world, that he gave his only begotten Son, that whosoever believeth in him should not perish, but have everlasting life. For God sent not his Son into the world to condemn the world; but that the world through him might be saved. He that believeth on him is not condemned: but he that believeth not is condemned already, because he hath not believed in the name of the only begotten Son of God. And this is the condemnation, that light is come into the world, and men loved darkness rather than light, because their deeds were evil.

Mason looked at the Bible in astonishment. Zeke had been lying to him all along. This book, this Bible, it spoke to him, answering his very thoughts. He couldn't deny its power. In fact, its power danced along his fingertips like electricity just waiting for him to take it.

"All I have to do is believe? It all makes sense. The Bible says that men love darkness because their deeds are evil. So if I believe, some greatness will fill me up, leaving no room for Zeke's dark powers to take me."

Mason didn't want to die. He certainly wouldn't survive another encounter with Zeke . . . at least, not without some kind of shield. Tori spent countless hours reading her Bible. Could it be the source of the shield? Could the answer have been right in front of him all along? Could this Bible afford Mason more time with Tori, time to undo the wrong in his life? Time to show her how much he loved her? No, he didn't want to die.

The Bible's pages turned. Of their own accord. Mason glanced around nervously. Still no breeze. No explanation for the turning pages. The fluttering pages stopped on Matthew chapter ten. The twenty-eighth verse seemed to glisten.

Fear not them which kill the body, but are not able to kill the soul: but rather fear him which is able to destroy both soul and body in hell.

The tightness in his chest returned. Truth. Had he ever known it with such clarity before? All doubts he'd been clinging to vanished. Mason closed his eyes, and shut the Bible. "Lord, I've been wrong. I've placed fear in the wrong places, in the wrong things. It's You I should fear. I've done too much wrong to leave it like this."

Tori's smiling face cut through his mind. She had helped him so many times in their brief relationship. Her love for others came to mind. She'd once given money to a complete stranger. She'd spent many hours donating herself to the woman's shelter downtown. She even took food to the degenerates that hung out on Saxon Street. It all came down to one thing. Love. Tori had showed him the power of love. He just hoped it wasn't too late to share it.

"I've finally learned what is right. I do believe what You've done, Lord; I do believe that You can save me. Help me set right what was once wrong."

A rock tumbled down a boulder surrounding the camp. Dead silence chased away the rumble. Something moved out of the corner of Mason's eye. He sprang and spun to meet his attacker. Eerie silence hung thick in the air.

"Why are you so jumpy, Mace?"

Mason rounded to find Zeke five feet away. Fear almost pushed him to run, but Mason stood his ground, clutching the leather-bound book like a shield. Faith. He had to believe he could overcome Zeke, just like the Bible said.

Tori's motionless body materialized from thin air behind Zeke. Mason's heart sank. How had Zeke gotten to her? Had Izzie failed? It didn't really matter. Tori's life rested in Mason's hands. His actions would save or condemn her. He set his jaw and narrowed his gaze. He wouldn't fail her again. Her example, her love, had saved him, and the time had come to return the favor. *Greater is He that is in me.*

Zeke's gaze fell on the Bible "You're kidding, right?" A grimace crossed his face. "What have you done, Mace?"

Zeke took at step closer. Mason held his ground.

Glancing back at Tori, Zeke cursed. "It's the girl isn't it? She poisoned your mind with her lies." Roaring with rage, Zeke flung his hands forward. "Please tell me you didn't fall in love with her. Tell me

I'm wrong, Mason. Tell me you haven't fallen for this pathetic Christian." Black ooze gushed at Mason from Zeke's fingertips.

The shadows swarmed around him, but Mason squeezed the Bible tighter. *Greater is He that is in me. Greater is He that is in me. Greater is He that is in me.*

The shadows rolled aside harmlessly, vanishing into thin air. "You fed me nothing but lies, Zeke. You twisted the truth around and manipulated me."

Zeke screamed frustration at Mason's words and flung his hands toward a rock. Mason flew into the rock with the motion. Pain tore up through his back, but he held on tight to the Bible. *I have everlasting life. I have everlasting life.*

The pain dulled.

Mason got up on one knee. "I'm not afraid of you anymore, Zeke. I fear only Him which is able to destroy both soul and body in hell."

Zeke lunged at him with light-bending speed, his face contorting with rage. A growl escaped his twisted lips. Zeke raised his hands and came to a stop, hovering in mid air. Red mist flowed from Zeke's mouth. It seeped into the black ooze clawing toward Mason and spread.

Zeke's twisted lips worked into a sneer. "I'll show you fear, traitor."

The black and red ooze swarmed around Mason. It dug into his pores like a fire burning his flesh. Mason white-knuckled the Bible. *Greater is He that is within me. I don't fear you. I don't fear you.*

He squeezed tighter.

A red glow surrounded Mason's skin, then turned black. Pain stabbed at his heart. He'd only seen this once before and didn't want to end up like the soulless shell Zeke left behind. He squeezed the Bible.

I believe, Lord. Greater is He that is within me.

The black fractured. Each crack multiplied, sending another across his ebony shell. Light glowed through the fissures. The cracks multiplied. The light intensified. It burst through the cracks and enveloped Mason.

Zeke shielded his eyes and screamed. "What? I had you! Your soul belongs to me!"

Mason pushed himself back up to his feet. "Zeke, you can't hurt me anymore. I'm protected. There's a greater force inside of me than there is in you. I'm saved. I don't need your dark magic or your lies any longer. You can't take me because I've already been taken—by a force beyond your comprehension."

Zeke plunged from his lofty perch and landed a knee into Mason's side. "Filthy Christian scum! What were you thinking?"

Mason tumbled away, but rolled to his feet. Did the shield apply to physical attacks as well, or just spiritual? The pain of a bruised rib suggested an answer to that question.

Zeke punched Mason across his jaw. "You were supposed to learn more about them, not become one. I had my suspicions when you avoided me in town, but I'd held out hope. You sicken me, Mason. I took you in, gave you purpose, gave your life meaning. Now, I must dispose of you before you spread Christianity's disease."

Mason clutched the Bible and flexed his aching jaw. "When you get too close to the truth, the light will be revealed to you. Christianity isn't a disease, Zeke. It's the cure."

Zeke swung again. Mason dodged the punch and retreated to stay out of reach. He looked to where he'd last seen Tori's body. Gone. Had that just been another of Zeke's lies?

"You don't understand, Zeke. God brought me here to show me the truth."

"Get a grip. Listen to yourself. I should've never been so foolish; you weren't strong enough."

Zeke charged and slammed his forehead into Mason's nose. Blood ran into Mason's mouth as he staggered and fell away. Twigs snapped and leaves rustled just beyond the boulders hedging the camp. Zeke's gaze shot toward the noise.

He backed away from the noise and fixed his eyes on Mason. "You'll meet your doom, Mace. All traitors pay for their treachery. And you can be sure it'll be me coming for you. I'll be back for you when you least expect it."

Zeke turned and ran. He catapulted over the boulders and vanished from sight. Mason collapsed and cupped his bleeding nose. Footfalls rushed toward him from behind. Tori and Izzie skid to a halt beside him. Tori fell to her knees while Izzie scanned the stone hedge.

Tori reached for Mason's face. "Mason! What happened?"

"Zeke." He groaned at the sharp, shooting pain when Tori touched his nose. He looked up into her eyes and grabbed her hands. "We need to talk, Tori. There are some things I need to tell you, some things you deserve to know. The truth."

Tears welled up in Tori's eyes and a smile broke across her lips. She nodded.

Izzie rounded on Mason. "What about Zeke?"

Mason fingered the blood at his lip. "He can't be helped, Izzie." She frowned. "Anyone can be helped. It's God's desire that none shall perish."

"Well, that one won't be easy. Some people in this world have given themselves over to evil. They seek to do nothing but evil deeds; and he's one of them. Just like God has filled you two with His Love, the devil has filled Zeke with darkness . . . with evil."

Tori ran her fingers through Mason's hair, checking for any head injuries in the process. "Are you okay? I don't understand. If Zeke was here then he would've taken you." Tori kissed him on the forehead. Her smile sent a wave of emotion through his chest.

Mason nodded, "He tried."

Izzie knelt at his other side. "But how did you stop him, Mason? How did you survive? From what I've seen today, he's more powerful than I ever imagined."

Mason glanced at the Bible and smiled. "This is the Living Word of God. He who reads it will escape death and find life. He will find the answers to life's questions. And better yet, he will uncover the mysteries of his heart."

He turned and met Tori's teary eyes. "I'm alive because you led me to Him, Tori. Your love showed me what I've been missing all my life. You showed His love through your life. And now, I have the shield I've been searching for."

A startled look stole over Tori's face when Mason mentioned the shield. She glanced up at Izzie, then back at him. "What happened to you while I was gone?"

Mason reached up, pulled her face forward, and kissed her cheek. "I found the answers my heart's been searching for, Tori. I finally understand the value of this book."

Mason squeezed the Bible tight in his grip. "I found the truth." He tapped it to his chest. "I have the shield, and now, I'm protected."

CALEB SEES THE LIGHT

Donna Sundblad

Freelance writer and author Donna Sundblad lives in rural Georgia with her husband and flock of pets including five cockatiels and a blue front Amazon named Neelix. Sometimes criticized for her overactive imagination as a child, today that inventiveness serves as a necessary ingredient in the fiction creation process. Donna shares the joy of storytelling with her grandchildren with a game she created called Sentence With a Twist, and her love of writing spreads beyond the pages of her books to workshops, the development and teaching of online writers' classes, and a monthly column for writers. Her creative writing book *Pumping Your Muse* (epress-online, June 2005) and fantasy novel *Windwalker* (epress-online, September 2006) are available in print or ebook format. Feel free to contact Donna by email at donna@theinkslinger.net

Eighteen-year-old Caleb feels trapped in his small-town rural setting. Graduation will work as his springboard to leave Liberty Hollow and experience life in the city. Just one thing stands in his way. How does he tell his grandparents? As he sorts things out, an alien sighting offers him more than he could imagine. Is this God's will for his life? How can he know for sure?

"I KNOW I HAVEN'T talked to you much lately, Lord, but if you could, please let them understand." Caleb kicked a stone, stirring a dust cloud on the winding dirt road. With graduation around the corner, how would Grandma and Grandpa react when he told them he planned to take a year off school and leave Liberty Hollow? His family had lived here eight generations. Yet, what options did he have? His Pa had talked of leaving, but days turned into years and the bottle changed him. Caleb didn't want to fall into that trap.

"Please, God, don't let me turn out like Pa."

Caleb hankered for more excitement than listening to gossip at the grocery where he worked part time as a clerk. He found a temporary fix to his mundane life by losing himself in the pages of books he bought at the five and dime. Like second nature, his hand checked for the sci-fi novel tucked in his back pocket. Even his love for reading had been cultivated by his grandparents. He owed them so much. How would he broach the subject of leaving with Grandpa sick?

Caleb shuffled up the hill. Grandma stood on the front porch drying her hands on her apron. "Caleb, Son, you're such a sweetheart to come help me."

"Aw, Grandma." He pecked her on the cheek and slipped into the house with the elderly woman at his heels. She settled into her favorite chair. Caleb breathed in the smell of Grandma's house—a mixture of antiques and good cooking. Walking into the small sitting room kindled fond memories. It hadn't changed since the days he'd played time traveler as a youngster. Grandma and Grandpa seemed oblivious to their old-fashioned ways, yet it provided the perfect backdrop for imagining time travel. Now, if he could, he would journey to a time when Grandpa's health was good.

Caleb rested his hand on the back of Grandma's upholstered armchair rocker. "How's Grandpa?"

Grandma let out a deep sigh and stared at the floorboards. "'Bout the same." Her bottom lip quivered a hair until she forced a smile. "Why don't ya go in and see him?"

"You goin' on to church?"

Grandma's shoulders slumped. "I'd like to go for the prayer meetin', but I don't know 'bout walkin' that quarter mile on the way home. Moon's nothin' but a sliver. I'd be lucky to see my hand in front of my face."

Grandma played this game every week, waiting for Caleb to offer to come fetch her. She liked to be walked home by lantern light like Grandpa used to do—like Caleb did every Wednesday since Grandpa fell ill.

They'd almost bought a car back when Caleb was about ten. Almost. But they decided against it and now touted the fact that they never owned a car. Times like this made Caleb wonder if they ever regretted it. His grandfather's words haunted him. *Who needs a car when God gave you two good legs?*

"Grandma does," Caleb answered under his breath. *If she had a car, she'd do just fine without me.*

"Yes, Caleb?" Grandma said.

He blinked. Had he spoken her name out loud? A smile played across his lips. "Let me go hug on Grandpa, then I'll walk you to your prayer meetin'."

Grandma untied her apron and hung it on a peg outside the kitchen door in the mudroom. "Better yet . . ." she grabbed her pocketbook

"... you stay here with Grandpa and come fetch me 'bout 8:30. Grandpa should be sleepin' by then and won't miss us."

Caleb nodded. "That's fine, Grandma, I'll be by the church 'bout 8:30."

She smothered him with a hug and a kiss, smoothed the front of her housedress and waddled out the door. What would she do when he told her he planned to run off to the city to find his fame and fortune? Would she understand why he didn't want to attend the community college over in Harper's Creek? Somehow, she'd have to.

He set his jaw, turned his attention to the bedroom and peeked in the door. Grandpa would understand. He'd talk with him first. Nostalgia stopped him at the threshold. Dust clung to the dark walnut bureau where Grandma's crocheted dresser scarf draped from each side. Grandma didn't see dust like she used to. At the center of the bureau, the kerosene lamp's glass chimney sat like a lighthouse amid a barrage of family photos. Caleb's favorite caught his eye. He was about eight-years-old, standing beside Grandpa with a big bass and a smile to match. Grandpa had been there. Pa hadn't.

"Caleb," Grandpa called in a weak voice from his bed. He patted the thin white blanket swaddled across his dwindling frame. "Come sit; let me hear the news."

Caleb scuffled to the bedside and stared into Grandpa's sunken eyes. "News?" He swallowed the lump tightening his throat. Was it selfish to leave? Just for a year to say he'd experienced life outside this no-place town. At least he'd have something to talk about. Even Patty Ann would be interested enough to spend time with him.

Grandpa pursed his lips. "What's goin' on? I see somethin' is troublin' ya." Worry lines between Grandpa's bushy white brows plowed deeper ridges toward his forehead.

Caleb slumped onto the edge of the bed and poured out his heart's desires, finishing with, "But I don't know what you and Grandma will do if I leave."

"You've always been good to us, Caleb, and I appreciate ya wantin' to stay. But, ya need to do what God calls you to. Measure your reasons. Are you leavin' for yourself, or 'cause God put the desire in your heart to do something more with your life? Do you have any idea what that 'more' is?" He held up his hand. "Don't answer. It's between you and the Lord. I'll be prayin' for ya."

Caleb relaxed. He had Grandpa's blessing. Grandpa pointed to his worn Bible on the nightstand. "Mind readin' to me a bit? My eyes are growin' dim. Makes it hard to read."

"Sure." Caleb snatched the Bible from its place next to the glass of water soaking Grandpa's teeth and for a moment inhaled the smell of the old book. Grandpa had read from this Bible for as long as Caleb could remember. He'd let his own Bible reading drop. Instead, he spent time emerged in the adventure and suspense of science fiction. As he balanced the Bible on his lap, the half-read sci-fi novel burned a hole in his back pocket. If Grandpa fell asleep, he'd have a chance to read uninterrupted.

The Good Book fell open to 2 Corinthians. The apostle Paul had seen troubles. He led an exciting life, suffered shipwrecks, snakebites and fought for the truth and warned others about false teachers.

". . . For such men are false apostles, deceitful workers, disguising themselves as apostles of Christ." A gentle snore marked Grandpa's breathing. *Should I keep reading*? "And no wonder; for even Satan . . ."

Caleb glanced at Grandpa, closed the Bible and set it on the nightstand. He watched Grandpa's chest rise and fall with each breath. Even though he read his Bible every day, Grandpa had stopped going to church years ago saying it wasn't right to hire some stranger off the street to teach spiritual truths, because Elders were to rise up from within. Said it left the door open for false teachers. Instead, his grandparents met house to house with a small group of men and women to study the Bible and fellowship over a meal each week. "Them people's the church," Grandpa would say. Those close friends still visited around his bed weekly. Maybe they could come calling more often once Caleb left. Or perhaps the pastor over at the church would start visiting. After all Grandma met for prayer over there.

Caleb backed out of the room, turned out the light and tiptoed through the dark to click on the lamp in the front window. He yanked the paperback from his pocket and flipped to the dog-eared page marking his place. The steady click, click of the second hand sweeping the mahogany clock's face above the couch warned that he'd have to leave in ten minutes to fetch Grandma.

He'd been dying to read more of the novel in his pocket, to catch a glimpse of the aliens that had infiltrated a small town on the outskirts of a valley. A town a lot like Liberty Hollow. Little by little, they'd gained control of residents' minds by shooting them with dart-like appendages that burrowed into the brainstem. The main character, Travis, had been off hunting and was the only one left to stop the invasion. He'd learned to spot the tiny finger-like device at the base of people's skulls that worked like antennae receiving messages from the mother ship.

"Travis." Caleb let the name roll from lips. Why couldn't he have a name like that instead of such an old-fashioned name?

Travis pushed the door of the barn open with the butt of his rifle. The mare whinnied from her stall. Something spooked her. He could feel it. Swift movement scurried through the bedding; shuffling came from the empty stall. Whatever it was didn't sound big. He inched beside the horse and stroked her flank to calm her. He peered between the cracks to catch a glimpse of the space invader in the adjoining compartment. Blood red eyes stared back. Travis backed up. A sizzling barrage of darts thunked into the planks separating him from the alien. His foot skidded in manure, and he landed with a thud on his backside.

Travis stared in disbelief at the wriggling appendage burrowing into the horse's neck. A high-pitched whine filled the barn. The horse danced wildly. Travis rolled against the wall praying it would all go away. . . .

The clock chimed, marking the hour. Caleb wished for more time, but closed the book. He eased outside, careful not to wake Grandpa, and took in a deep breath of fresh mountain air. Stars sprinkled the ebony sky like flickering pinpoints. Grandma really did need an escort tonight. If it weren't for the lamp in the front window, he'd hardly be able to see the porch steps. He stared into the darkness.

"'Bout as clear as figurin' what to do with my life." He snagged the tin hurricane lamp from the nail overhead and jiggled it. "Oh, no." The gentle sloshing reminded him it needed fuel. He should have filled it last Wednesday after walking Grandma home. No time now, if he didn't want to keep Grandma waiting. Lighting it could wait. Caleb trusted his ability to pick his way in the dark. Except for that heavily wooded section. He'd light the lantern then if he had to. That should leave enough fuel for the trip home with Grandma.

Darkness swallowed Caleb. He headed into the woods, marching over the uneven forest floor toward the church nestled beyond the hill on the other side. He imagined Travis rolling in the horse stall amid manure and a frantic mare. Would he have to shoot the horse? No, he only had one shot. Hopefully, he'd kill the alien. Or should he kill the alien? What if he needed the alien to figure a way to return the townspeople to themselves?

His foot snagged on a twisted root and sent him sprawling. The lantern clattered into inky obscurity. Caleb blinked. *Did I get turned around?* He must have strayed from the path. *Why didn't I fill the lamp?* He paused to get his bearings. Starlit patches peeked through the branches, but not enough showed to determine his direction.

A flash like lightning, shot across the sky and stopped overhead. Brighter than a falling star, it cast enough light to see his shadow. "What in the. . . ." The light pulsated, growing bigger with each throb. Colors kaleidoscoped, filling the woods with brilliance, forcing him to shield his eyes. A nebulous light seeped through the branches, gathering sparkling particles into a coalescing form.

"A spaceship?"

It settled into the clearing beyond the treeline. Through fluid bulwarks, Caleb spotted the path leading to the church on the other side. *Should I run?* His heart slammed. He stood mesmerized.

A booming voice filled the forested patch. "Caleb—"

Caleb searched the glowing ship for a sign of life. Maybe he had fallen asleep at Grandma's house. That's it. He must be dreaming.

Bright light sparked and sizzled like a Fourth of July sparkler as a fluid seam unzipped forming a hatch. White, flowing light leaked through the opening, gathered in a puddle and bubbled and stretched skyward. From the bottom up, radiant light formed fiery legs, torso, arms, and a head. Caleb stared at the alien drifting inches above the ground within a hazy aura. Golden flames flickered where eyes should be amid the vague human-like features. "How do you know my name?" Caleb asked.

"We have studied you for years," the alien said. "I've been sent to show the future, for you are destined for greatness."

"I am?" Adrenaline rushed making him feel super-human, but it ebbed as concern clouded his enthusiasm and nudged him back to reality. "What about my grandparents?"

"Come, let me show you." A multi-colored ribbon forming fingers of light extended toward Caleb.

Caleb hesitated, reached out and touched the swirling colors. He pinched his eyes shut against the blazing light. Wind brushed his face and tugged his hair. Pine scent lingered for a moment and vanished. In the darkness, strange smells assaulted his nose. Horns blared. Tires squealed. Acrid smoke cleared as he opened his eyes. The alien perched next to him on a skyscraper ledge.

Panic plastered Caleb's back to the brick wall. "This can't be real, this can't be real. This can't be real."

"This, is what awaits you." The alien's arm sliced an arc of light through the darkness. "You'll no longer be limited by Liberty Hollow's confines. I've been sent to tell you that all you desire will be found here."

Caleb peeked through squinted eyes. "Everything?" His eyes bulged. Neon lights flashed and headlights moved about like ants threading along multi-lane highways.

"You'll be rich enough to help your grandparents. You can buy them a car."

"Rich? How?"

Light flashed and in a blink they stood within cubicles bustling with office activity. The alien opened an office door labeled with Caleb's name and waved at a chrome and glass desk. "This is yours."

"What do I do here?" Caleb asked.

"You head up book reviews. Authors clamor to be listed in your column."

"Wow!" His fingers brushed the glass desktop. It felt cool to the touch. *Can this be real? Book reviews? I can read as much as I want?* He could finally leave Liberty and do something he loved. "What do I have to do?"

"The first step is to leave Liberty," the alien said. "You will be famous as the contact between my world and yours when others are ready to accept my existence. No one else in Liberty Hollow understands, for they are satisfied to linger in mediocrity. You are gifted beyond life in the mill or working at the grocery. Do not delay leaving, for opportunity withers if not plucked when ripe. I have the power to make your dreams reality."

"I can't believe this." Caleb glanced out at the bustling office filled with people about his age. An attractive strawberry blond crossed her legs in the cubicle across from him.

"It couldn't be more perfect." Caleb turned to the alien.

A smile-like flicker sliced across the lava complexion and died. "It is yours. Trust your desires for they will take you far."

Caleb rubbed his hands together. "Whoa boy, I can't wait. Are you going to help me? I mean, how does this happen?"

"You will not see me, but I am near. Follow your desires and you'll be rewarded with all I have shown you."

Light exploded, blinding Caleb. He squeezed his eyes shut and the ground hit him. Pine and the earthy odor of decomposing leaves said he'd returned to the woods. When he opened his eyes, the ship and alien had vanished. Something in him wanted to stay and see if he could catch a glimpse of the ship in the night sky. What should he do now?

It's between you and the Lord.

"Grandma!" How long had he been with that alien? He patted the ground feeling for the lantern, latched onto the handle and scrambled to his feet. Caleb scurried toward the faint glow marking the church beyond the hill, the dark lantern swinging at his side. What would Grandma say when he told her about the alien and how his dreams would come true? This would be a perfect opportunity to let her know his plans. His footfalls slowed. He paused, glancing over his shoulder toward the woods. *The alien never did show me what happens to Grandma and Grandpa. When I leave . . .?*

He sauntered up the hill. *Meeting an alien could be the thing that gets me out of this place.* He'd be a local star. *Wait 'til Grandma and Grandpa see the headlines in the Liberty Herald: "Local Boy Sees Alien."*

How could he describe the beauty of the alien? He snapped his fingers. "An Angel of Light that grants my every wish." He smiled. *They'll understand then.*

He sprinted up the hill toward the church where Grandma stood on the porch talking with the pastor.

"Grandma!" Caleb called out.

"My lands, Son. I haven't seen ya move like that in forever and a day."

Caleb stopped at the bottom of the small staircase looking up at Grandma and the pastor on the small stoop they called a porch. "I didn't want ya to worry 'bout me."

He glanced over his shoulder almost bursting with anticipation to tell her how the Lord had showed him what he should do, but it would be worth waiting to tell Grandpa first. This time when he asked to hear the news, Caleb would have something exciting to share.

"We best be going, I don't wanna leave Grandpa unattended for long."

"Unattended," she repeated to the pastor. "See how smart he is? And you'll never meet a more compassionate boy. I don't know where we'd be without him."

The portly pastor swished a moth circling between him and the bare bulb lighting the porch. "Nice to meet you, Caleb. I hope to see you some Sunday." He smiled. "Can I give you two a ride home?"

Say yes; say yes. Caleb glanced from the pastor to his Grandma. She rested her hand on her bosom.

"Oh, lands, no."

Caleb held back a sigh and set the lantern on the bottom stair to light it. "Come on, Grandma, let's get back to Grandpa."

The bounce in Caleb's step cast lantern light side to side. Grandma prattled on about her Bible lesson, but Caleb's mind returned to the city.

Outside the house, Caleb offered Grandma his hand to steady her steps up the stairs.

"Looks like your Grandpa might be awake." She pointed to the light shining from the bedroom window.

Caleb pushed the door open and rushed in. "Grandpa! Grandpa!" He skidded to a stop. Grandpa lay lopsided across the bed.

"Grandpa!" Caleb rushed to his bedside with Grandma at his heels.

Grandpa raised his hand. "Stop fussin' and help me get upright." He chuckled. "I got up, made it to the bathroom, got me a snack and thought I'd be back in bed by the time y'all got back."

Grandma plumped the pillow while Caleb grasped his grandfather's hand to pull him up.

"Guess I should have stayed home." Grandma brushed a stray wisp of gray hair from Grandpa's forehead and kissed it.

"Grandma, Grandpa." Caleb scratched the back of his neck. "I wanted to talk to you."

Grandma cast a worried glance at Grandpa, who patted the mattress beside him. "Come sit."

Caleb sat. "I'm excited," he said, "and a little sad. It's kind of confusing."

"What dear?" Grandma rested her hand on Caleb's shoulder and eased onto the mattress beside him.

Grandpa turned onto his side. "Remember God is not a God of confusion but of peace."

"I know, I know." Caleb pushed to his feet. "Wait 'til ya hear what happened to me." Words spilled from Caleb's lips.

Tears pooled in Grandma's eyes behind her glasses.

"So," Caleb said, "the Lord showed me just like ya said, Grandpa."

"Have ya been talkin' with the Lord?" Grandpa asked. "Readin' your Bible?"

Caleb opened his mouth and shut it. He stared at his feet and shook his head. "Not really. Just when I read to you."

Grandpa waggled his finger toward his Bible. "I fell asleep earlier. Do ya mind readin' to me a bit more?"

Anger twisted Caleb's gut. Sometimes Grandpa's Bible thumping got under his skin. *I'm leaving whether they liked it or not.* He snatched the Bible from the nightstand, and flipped the page with an irritated snap.

"What's botherin' you so, Caleb?"

"Nothin'," he said through gritted teeth. He never realized how selfish his grandparents were. He shared the biggest news of his life and they acted like he fetched the newspaper.

Grandma settled in beside Caleb blotting a tear and glancing to the Bible on his lap.

"Where do you want me to start?" Caleb said with a sigh.

"That part about false apostles and such," Grandpa said. "That's the last thing I heard as I fell off to sleep."

Caleb marked the verse with his finger. "For such men are false apostles, deceitful workers, disguising themselves as apostles of Christ. No wonder, for even Satan disguises himself as an angel of light . . ." Caleb swallowed hard. He cast a glance at Grandma and turned to look at Grandpa.

"You mean that thing I saw . . . that could be Satan?"

"Look to the Lord for your answer, Caleb," Grandpa said. "It's His word, not mine."

Caleb shut the Bible with a shudder. "It was so real."

"The spiritual realm is real, Caleb. We're created to live there, but first we pass through for a short time here on earth."

Caleb shot to his feet. "Grandpa, what's it mean?"

"What do ya think, Son?"

"Well," Caleb nibbled his lower lip. "If that angel of light was Satan, then he wants me to leave Liberty Hollow pretty bad for some reason."

He rested his hand on the novel in his pocket. When Travis looked into those blood red eyes in the horse stall, it was easy to see which people had been taken over and to identify the alien. Real life tended to be a bit more complicated. "Without you in my life, I'm afraid I would have made a big mistake," Caleb said. "Guess I'll stay around a bit longer to figure out what I need to do next." He shrugged one shoulder.

"If ya look to the Lord, he'll show ya," Grandpa said. "Sometimes it takes a bit of sortin' and talkin' things out with other believers."

Grandma hugged Caleb tight against her. It felt right. Grandpa was right. God had shown him what to do.

ONE TAKEN, THE OTHER LEFT

Stephen L. Rice

Stephen L. Rice is a novelist, freelance journalist, and poet with an interest in language, theology, and bizarre humor. His stories challenge established traditions (as distinct from Biblical doctrines) and usually feature divine involvement similar to that in the Bible.

I am often asked whether I really believe the view presented here. I don't. I do believe that God enjoys thwarting our predictions. The prophecy experts of Jesus' day knew exactly what was coming, and Jesus wasn't it. A modern, well-known prophecy teacher, seeing one of his ideas threatened by current events, asked, "Is the Bible wrong, or will [my interpretation of a certain passage] happen?" It was this sort of arrogance from people who know all the answers that provoked me to write this story.

TONY HART WAS ON a mission. Every Saturday morning he was at the mall, handing out tracts to any who were interested or simply too polite to turn them down. A lot of the tracts wound up in the parking lot, but he liked to point out that even the sower in the parable lost a lot of seed to get a good crop. And there had been several new faces showing up at his church (and a few other churches too)—faces he recognized from the mall.

Unfortunately, he knew Jason Blake's face all too well, and Jason was as easy to find as Tony. He, too, was at the mall every Saturday, though for a very different reason: he was turning Friday's videos in and checking out others for the day ahead. And they weren't even spiritual. They weren't really bad, perhaps—nothing violent, profane, or pornographic. But Tony had to wonder about his friend's priorities. And Tony being Tony, he had to share his concerns with his videoholic neighbor.

"Jason! Come here and help me talk to these people!"

"Sorry, Tony, you know it's not my thing."

"It's Jesus' thing, so it must be our thing."

"Fine. Go hang out with fishermen, tax collectors, and prostitutes. That was his thing too, you know."

"We're supposed to witness to people."

"I do witness," Jason protested. "I just do it by my life, and I usually do it at work. Ask my customers—they know I'm a Christian. I pray for them sometimes. And my coworkers will tell you that I'm honest. I also read the Bible about as much as you do, and the guys at work could tell you that, too."

"Yeah, but don't you ever feel like you could be doing more?"

"Sometimes I do more. Right now, I'd like to watch some quality shows without you doing your Super Christian bit."

Tony backed off slightly. "Look, I don't want to get legalistic about all this—it's not like I'm trying to earn my salvation or anything. But God has done so much for us, don't you think we should go out of our way for him?"

"Well, I'm sorry too. I shouldn't have grouched at you. And maybe I have been spending more time with the tube than with God lately. I've been pretty stressed out recently, and it's easier to watch something than to spend a lot of time in prayer. But I think God understands. Maybe I'm not achieving my full potential for him—though I still don't think you know what that potential is or what I'm supposed to be doing for God—but I am saved. I do follow Jesus. Sometimes I think that the main difference between us is that you drink way too much coffee."

"There's a difference between caffeine and the Holy Spirit, Jason. Even if you don't pass out tracts or anything, you should still take some time to find out what God wants you to do."

"My load's heavy enough as it is."

"It would actually lighten your load, because you would be working by God's power, not your own."

"Well, maybe. I'll think about it. I'll even pray about it. And I'll pray for you as I'm driving home, that God will bless your witness. That could be a good ministry for me to start with."

Tony managed a laugh as his neighbor left. Jason was a nice guy, though his priorities were all fouled up. But perhaps he had part of the answer, for Tony had to admit that he hadn't been praying for Jason as much as he should have been. He took advantage of a lull in the foot traffic to rectify this omission. Then he set himself for the day ahead. It would be a long day today, as most of his Saturdays were. After spending the morning in the mall, he would do his Bible reading and extend his prayer time a bit to intercede for the man next door. Nor was this mere legalism on his part. For if Jason's coworkers could vouch for his integrity, everyone who knew Tony at all could testify that his devotions proceeded from devotion: God really was his passion, and his witnessing, Bible reading, and prayer were simply outward ripples from the beating of his heart for God.

And so the day passed, and a new day came with dawn.

Tony rolled wearily out of bed. It would be good to get into church this morning and experience the lift from the believers around him. He hoped that the guys in the morning class wouldn't go off on some weird tangent this time. He should never have started attending the class on Bible prophecy! It had been something he knew little about, and his own Bible reading hadn't clarified matters much, so he had gone to the class for answers. Unfortunately, most of the other people there were only interested in pursuing the latest book or teaching, and they had no real desire to read what the Bible itself had to say on the topic. Last week, they focused on Dr. Whimsey's new video, and the Bible only came in as a means of agreeing or disagreeing with the presentation. Today would be part two.

As he loaded his breakfast in the microwave, he couldn't help thinking about Paul's admonitions to avoid people with an unhealthy interest in controversial subjects. At least Tony had learned more about that aspect of Scripture! Paul's words on that point had really come alive for him lately. But by the same token, it seemed like a good idea—like simple obedience to God's word—to find some way of switching to another class without getting any of the local prophecy experts on his case.

He sighed as he switched on the computer to check the news. There was an item about a press conference with some politico or other. The name looked familiar . . . Of course! He had been the topic of conversation last week—some guy who turned his country around after a devastating civil war, or something. His very success had prompted one of the guys in class to suggest that he might be the Antichrist. The others had shouted him down on the grounds that the man wasn't Roman, and everyone knew the Antichrist would come from Rome. Dr. Whimsey said so. The man also had made some positive remarks about Christianity and restoring the truth to his country, which the guys said meant chucking out the Catholics or Orthodox or whatever they had there.

Tony himself didn't know, nor did he care. He told them he was more interested in the Good News than world news, and he always figured he'd take care of the mission God had given him and let God take care of the Antichrist. As he liked to ask the others, why worry about the Tribulation when we won't even be here?

Suddenly a news alert lit up the screen. That was odd: the news site he always checked only posted news alerts for wars and stuff. He clicked the link, only to find to his great annoyance that the main feature was some guy at the U.N. making a speech about some major economic and political catastrophe that had just hit—something that would destabilize practically every country in the world. Already there was rioting everywhere . . .

He stirred uncomfortably. Then he saw another alert on screen, this time announcing that calls, e-mails, and other traffic were about to take down several servers as panicked people the world over tried to track down family and friends. What had happened?

He managed to pull up some related pages before the server went down—that should teach them to provide e-mail service along with news! Oh, okay—the news conference involved various high-level figures suggesting that the guy who had saved his country from disaster might be able to pull the world itself back from the brink. They talked about giving him some kind of emergency powers. The Russians had wanted to limit his term to five years, for sentimental reasons, but the French president insisted that if he had a seven-year term, the global premier-designate should too. Big deal.

Another report concerned the Pope's denouncing the move as a step away from democracy and toward totalitarian chaos. Big deal again. Who cared what a guy in a funny hat thought anyway?

But then he saw something outright arresting: the catastrophe was that an unknown number of people—the low estimates said nearly a billion—had vanished from the earth! There were some religious figures weighing in on the matter, but anyone who mentioned the Rapture was shouted down instantly: there were some very godly people still around, including the Pope—it was vaguely interesting that he suddenly was an important and godly man, not just some guy in a funny hat. But anyway, the Rapture was not a possible explanation.

Tony groaned, for he knew different. It was the Rapture, and he had been left behind! But how? Why? Of course, as a sinner, he had done things he shouldn't have, and there was always the possibility that he hadn't done enough . . . Then he did the best thing he could have done: he knelt down and sought his God.

He had no sooner begun his prayer than Jesus stood beside him, shining brighter than the sun. "I was waiting for you to call, my son. I know that this has been a shock for you, but then, I did warn you—all of you—that it would be a surprise."

"Lord, why? Did I really fail you so miserably?"

"No, of course not, my son. You are not being punished. I am well pleased with you, and I am going to share the deepest secret of my glory and joy with you."

"By leaving me behind? Lord, I want to be with you more than anything!"

"No, you are more mature than that: you want to please me more than anything, even if it means being away from me just a little longer."

"I don't understand. I thought you were coming to take us to be with you."

"I shall come for you, my son. But you must understand that there is a difference between what I say and what others say I say. The battle before you shall be hard, so cast aside every weight—discard the foolish speculations of the ignorant concerning what is to come. Only my word and my Spirit can be trusted. If you will listen to me, I will tell you everything you need to know. For until now, all my children have been kept from understanding. Just as my disciples were kept from understanding my predictions about my death and resurrection, just as Jerusalem was kept from recognizing the hour of my coming to them, just as the disciples going to Emmaus were kept from recognizing me as we walked and talked together, so all of my children have been kept from understanding the details of the final hour. Trust only me."

"Okay, I can handle that," Tony replied, "but you did say that I hadn't displeased you?"

"Yes—and the fact that is your primary concern shows why: unlike some others, who would have panicked about being left behind, you have feared only displeasing me. Fear not. I am well pleased with you, my son."

"But if you're pleased with me, why didn't you take me?"

The Lord smiled patiently down at him. "My son, you must understand that the people I took were the ones who were not ready for the adventure, the honor, and the glory I am sending the rest of you. It was not the strongest, most reliable servants whom I removed from the battle, but those who I knew would falter and fail in the hour of trial. Don't you remember that it was the Philadelphians, who I said had little strength, that I promised protection from the hour of trial, while the Smyrnans, who had no such limitation, were promised the deeper honor and glory of suffering for me?"

"That's weird—I've heard some people teach that only the really dedicated Christians go in the Rapture, while the lukewarm ones have to repent and slog their way through the Tribulation. You mean the opposite is true?"

"Of course. My body is about to enter the worst hour of its earthly history—the worst since my own suffering and death. How could I entrust the final mission, the darkest hour, to any but my most valiant soldiers? Do you really think that lukewarm Christians would, by their own dismay and fear, somehow go where their feeble faith and love would not take them? Repentance born of tribulation is typically half-hearted; re-read Judges sometime. No, I need seasoned soldiers to confront the unreached and the damned with the glorious truth of my kingdom.

"Those who were taken, who forfeited the glory of living for me in the greatest hour, when my Bride prepares herself for our wedding and makes herself so beautiful by her suffering that I can bear it no longer but must return to rescue her and claim her for my own—those who must sit out this glorious hour have already wept over their unfaithfulness and their loss, and I have comforted them and wiped the tears from their eyes. But you have your mission: go and tell those who have not yet heard, who have not yet rejected me, that I do live, that I am coming soon! You have your orders. Go and serve me, and increase your reward that already awaits you in my presence."

As suddenly as he had appeared, Jesus disappeared. Tony arose, trembling yet beaming with the joy and assurance of the Holy Spirit. He had an assignment, and live or die, he would complete it to the glory of his God and King. He would show himself worthy of the trust that had been given him. He walked purposefully to the door. Though the situation had changed, the response was the same: he would go to the mall and preach to the confused masses there.

Tony Hart was on a mission.

SEEING BLIND

Daniel I Weaver

Daniel I. Weaver was born and raised in rural Pennsylvania. After earning a Presidential Scholarship from the University of Pittsburgh at Johnstown via an essay competition, Daniel studied English Education with a concentration in British Literature. He studied creative and fiction writing courses as well as conducted an independent study on Women and Dementia in the 19th Century and graduated Magna Cum Laude.

Daniel currently participates in various online Christian fellowships and critique groups (including the Fellowship of Christian Writers, American Christian Fiction Writers, The View 2, and a dozen others) and currently has a novel *When Nightmares Walk* looking for a home. Daniel lives with his loving family in Indiana, Pennsylvania.

So much science fiction starts off asking the question "what if?" "Seeing Blind" is no exception. What if an inhabited world existed in another galaxy? What if God had revealed Himself to that world only to have its people reject His face? What if that world's time had come to an end, but like the story of Lot , there was one who still believed? Would God spare that world? Would He give them one last chance at salvation? With the "Fiction to scare the Jesus into you" trademark shining strong, Daniel I Weaver offers some possibilities for a world teetering on the edge of darkness.

THE DOOR TO OLRIAS' quarters buckled beneath the thunderous assault, but he stared longingly at the misty pool swirling in the basin on his lap. He could do it. He could make it. And why not? What else did he have to live for any more?

"They're going to break through!" Theodower grabbed and shook Olrias' sleeve. "They're going to kill you, Uncle!"

Majestic green landscapes beneath a blue sky filled with cottony clouds rippled across the pool's surface. Olrias sighed. Another world. Another dimension. So very unlike his dying world. "I would very much like to visit this Earth, nephew. I've seen the way. We could leave Hollumn, you know."

"Uncle!" Theodower knocked the basin aside and knelt, eye-level. The door shuddered, buckled. "You have to stop this foolishness. They murdered your wife and Natalia is missing. Now they've come for you. Why are you doing this?"

The door groaned beneath another assault. The metal walls reverberated. A copper vase beside the food replicator toppled to the floor.

Olrias glanced at the bowing door. "I can't be a part of it anymore, Theodower. Our people have destroyed themselves. For all of our technology, what's left of our society is little more than a dictatorship run by this wretched Council. I won't be used for their evil designs any longer."

Theodower cupped his uncle's face between his hands. "But, Uncle, you're the last Oracle. You're the only one left with the Sight. Without you, hope is lost. What'll become of us? Who will seek the Creator's wisdom? Who will guide us to the promised Messiah?"

An explosion rattled the hall. Electronic picture frames displaying family photographs toppled off the walls. Smoke billowed into the room through the door's bending seams. The lights flickered.

Olrias rested his wrinkled hands on Theodower's brown sleeves and smiled. Tears stung his eyes. "Dear nephew. I've spent my life looking for a future for our people. What you call life, I call survival after what I've seen of these other worlds, other dimensions. The Creator gave us hope, Theodower. Out there. And he gave the Oracles the Sight to find it. We've tried for centuries, but the Council has censored our visions."

"You're rambling like a madman, Uncle!"

"No. For the first time, I've made sense of it all. The darkness invading our world has reached into these other worlds as well. Some, like this "Earth," fight it. There is hope. There was one there who could command the darkness. The one all Oracles have seen."

Another explosion shook the building. Debris sprayed into the room. The lights died. Smoke. Voices. Shouting. Theodower tugged on his uncle's arms, but Olrias didn't budge. His time had come.

"Uncle," Theodower called. "We must flee. Surely you've seen a way to escape."

Green laser sights danced against the rolling smoke and debris. The voices drew nearer.

"I've seen enough, Theodower. You must go."

Theodower released Olrias' arms and vanished. The lights flickered to life and highlighted a room in shambles. Men in black military garb carrying pulse rifles spread into the debris, their weapons trained on Olrias. They came in waves until a sea of black swallowed everything else. The tumultuous stampede fell silent. A hundred green laser sights targeted Olrias' heart. He closed his eyes and sighed.

"What've you seen, Olrias that you wouldn't flee?" Footfalls echoed toward him, but Olrias didn't have to open his eyes to identify Raelin. He'd already seen it and knew his future.

An unexpected chill ran up his arm, racing to his spine. He shuddered and hugged himself. Raelin had company, something from the Dark Dimension.

"Surely an Oracle could avoid capture." Her silky voice stung his ears. How often had she twisted his resolve and manipulated the future through his eyes? How deep did her treachery run? Couldn't she see how perverse her path had become?

Olrias regarded her—a perfect specimen clad in a revealing black blouse, skin-tight slacks, and boots that had often trodden the innocent. "There's no need to run, Raelin. It ends today."

Something dark shifted beyond the soldiers. In the shadows. Yellow eyes moved through the shadows. When they vanished, the chill lingered.

"You've been inciting a revolution, Olrias." Raelin jerked a soldier's knife from its sheath. "We've nearly completed our alliance with the Dark Dimension, but you've spread dissension amongst our people. Insurgents attacked a Council convoy last night."

"There can be no peace with the Dark Dimension, Raelin. Those creatures cannot be trusted. They're pure evil."

Something hissed beyond the soldiers. Raelin sneered. Her eyes glowed with the odd yellow tint Olrias had seen in many Council members' eyes of late. "Evil, Olrias? Where was this insight when you opened the portal to their dimension? Where was your great Sight then?"

"I wasn't trying to reach their world, Raelin. But somehow, it's connected to—"

"Earth," she interrupted. "Enough with this fantasy world you've imagined, Olrias. Every Oracle has been wrong at least once."

"Except me." Olrias stood slowly. "I've never been wrong. But it no longer matters."

"Such confidence, Olrias. What've you seen, old man?"

"The end, Raelin. There is only the Great Unknown for me after this. But for you, if you make this pact with the Dark Dimension, there will be wailing, weeping, gnashing of teeth—"

Raelin's laughter, a mad sickly sort, stopped him short. It swelled until it reverberated off the walls. "You've incited the rabble to rise up against our Council, Olrias. Do you think I'd allow you to simply leave us and venture to the Great Unknown?"

Confusion stabbed Olrias. Everything had played out exactly as he'd foreseen. He'd defied the Council, and they'd branded him a traitor. He'd awaited execution and Raelin had come. She held the knife in the right position. Next, she would lash out and everything would go black. Death. Finally, death. So why did her words suggest otherwise?

"Have you forgotten about Natalia, Olrias? Have you forgotten your daughter?"

His heart fluttered with remorse. Natalia had been missing for four days. The shadowy figure beyond the soldiers bobbed in and out of sight. Its yellow eyes danced through Olrias' vision and shattered his concentration.

"I've entrusted her to the Creator, Raelin. I know what becomes of Hollumn's missing children. I know what the Council does in secret." A tear dribbled down his cheek contemplating the atrocities—the experiments and abuses. "She's found her peace by now. It's beyond my power."

Raelin stepped closer. Just like the vision. "That's where you're mistaken." The chill raced up his arm again. Her words lingered in his ears.

He glanced down just as thin black talons pulled away from his arm. In his ear, a dark voice hissed, "*She is mine!*"

Olrias turned toward the voice, but the creature vanished. Fear quickened his pulse. Where had this vile creature been in his vision? Why hadn't he foreseen this? Was it possible? Had he been wrong?

Raelin stepped closer, raising the knife toward his face. "There are things far worse than death, Olrias. What is an Oracle without his Sight?"

She slashed the knife. Fire tore through his face. Wetness ran down his cheek. Darkness and light contested to block out everything else. Another slash. More pain. Olrias collapsed into the chair screaming. His eyes!

A cold, scaly hand clamped around his neck and choked his screams. That cold mixed with the burning and doubled his pain. "*She will be mine.*"

The pain swelled until only darkness remained.

Olrias woke with screams fresh on his lips and fire in his eyes. Darkness. Just like he'd foreseen. He'd been terribly wrong to assume darkness meant death. A woman screamed. Somewhere distant.

Her scream echoed down what might've been a long corridor. A stench—urine and feces—attacked Olrias' nose. The dry, polluted air clinging to his skin registered. Prison. They'd thrown him in prison.

He tried to sit, but his head swam. The world lurched. Nausea turned his insides. He wept and fluttered in and out of consciousness. In and out of pain.

What might've been minutes, days, or eternities later, nausea woke him. Olrias rolled onto his side and vomited. Cold talons dug into his arm forcing fire through his veins. He vomited. Screamed.

A slithery voice hissed through the pain. *"Hear her weep, Seer."*

A woman screamed nearby. Olrias' heart stopped. Pain seized his chest. His breath wouldn't come. Natalia!

She screamed again. His pulse, breath, and pain all resumed. Olrias gasped, swayed, and screamed in continuous motion. "Natalia!"

"Daddy! Daddy, hel—" The word ended in a scream much more terrifying than the darkest futures Olrias had imagined.

"Stop! Please!" Olrias begged.

Raelin's laughter burst to life nearby. "There is a price for insurrection, Olrias. I promised you things far worse than death. You will listen to each of her screams. You will listen to her beg. You will listen to her ask the Daemon to free her. And then you will spend a thousand nights wishing to die while your own Daemon-possessed daughter tortures you."

"Please, Raelin. You must stop this before it's too late. You can still save our people. You can still save what's left."

Something grabbed him by the hair and jerked his head backward. Raelin's sweet perfume, overpowering in its intensity, flooded his nostrils—a blessed relief against the urine and feces despite the pain. Her breath fell hot against his throbbing face.

"I *am* saving our people. When we open the portal into the Dark Dimension permanently, the Daemon will flood this world and give our people more power than you can imagine.

"They're building an army, Olrias. They're building an army for that great battle your predecessor foresaw. With their power, we'll be strong enough to conquer the universe. We'll have our choice of any world."

She slammed his head off the wall, released him, and her scent vanished. Footfalls clacked away.

"You're wrong, Raelin. You're going to destroy us all. When you open that portal and invite the Daemon into our world, what's left of this miserable planet will be destroyed. There is only one force in the universe that can stop them. You have t—"

A boot silenced him. His head bashed the wall. The world swayed and he slumped to the ground. Natalia screamed again—the sound distorted and drawn out in lethargic pause. The darkness returned.

"Wake up, Uncle!"

Someone shook him. Hard. Theodower? An explosion rumbled in the distance. The floor shook.

"Uncle! Wake up, Uncle!"

Olrias opened his eyes. A pain like ripping flesh seared his face and his hands rushed to cover the place where his eyes had once been. He screamed, but a hand clamped over his mouth.

"Hush, Uncle. We don't have much time."

Olrias whimpered as his head throbbed. Fire danced with his pulse.

"The Council is about to open the portal, Uncle."

The portal. To the Daemon's Dimension. So much pain.

"There's more, Uncle."

Olrias moved his hands to his temples and squeezed. Focus. He had to focus.

"Natalia, Uncle."

Natalia. His daughter. Raelin had her. Natalia's screams shook his memory. "Save her, Theodower. Save Natalia."

"I can't, Uncle. Not without you."

Further explosions shook the dungeon floor.

Olrias lunged toward Theodower's voice, found his shirt, and grabbed hold. "If you've found me, you can save her, Theodower. Don't let the Daemon have her."

"That's just it, Uncle. The Daemon. To seal the pact and open the portal, they're going to sacrifice her and a half-dozen other women. The Daemon want blood. Nothing good can come from a pact writ in blood."

Sacrifice? Blood? What had Raelin done? Why hadn't he seen this?

"Come on, Uncle." Theodower tugged him off the floor. "You have to tell us how to save her. You have to—"

"I can't, Theodower. My eyes . . ."

Another explosion. Much closer. Gunshots and shouting rumbled down a nearby corridor.

"Theodower, what's happening?"

"We've staged a revolt. We're trying to stop the Council, but the Daemon are helping them. We need you, Uncle."

"I can't help you, Theodower. I'm blind. There's only one thing in this universe that can stop the Daemon."

"Where is it, Uncle? How do we find this thing?"

More gunshots. The shouting intensified, much closer. Theodower tugged on Olrias' arm and dragged him into motion.

"It's everywhere," Olrias shouted over an explosion. The force threw them to the ground. Olrias slid into a wall and groaned.

"Then how do we use it, Uncle? How do we stop the Daemon?"

Theodower pulled Olrias to his feet and dragged him away from the shouting.

"I don't know, Theodower. Without my Sight, I'm nothing." That realization tore at Olrias worse than his injuries. He'd sat there waiting, thinking he would die and find salvation in the Great Unknown. He'd let Raelin destroy his gift in an act of cowardice rather than challenge the institution.

Theodower jerked Olrias aside, clamped a hand around his mouth, pinned him against a wall, and made a shushing sound. Olrias' head thumped pain. His heart raced. The shouting rushed toward them atop frenzied footfalls. Theodower's hand trembled against Olrias' mouth.

The clamor passed. Eventually, after an eternity of thumping heartbeats and restrained breathing, Theodower's hand slipped away. "What are we going to do, Uncle?"

"Find the One, Theodower. Can you lead me to my chambers?"

"Yes. This way." Theodower grabbed Olrias' arm.

They wove through winding corridors, ducked into alcoves to escape passing soldiers, and crawled through tunnels. Olrias jumped at every explosion, shout, and gunshot. The swarming sounds bombarding him compounded the pain. He didn't relax until a faint scent of Kescapren blooms tingled his nose and Theodower stopped moving.

Laurallie, Olrias' wife, had always kept a vase of Kescapren blooms despite their rarity. He'd continued the tradition in an attempt to honor her memory. Kescapren blooms meant they'd reached his chambers.

"Ready the machine, Theodower."

Olrias inhaled the Kescapren aroma deeply. What he wouldn't give to see those delicate golden bulbs with their fiery coloring and intense green antennae. "Theodower, I need—"

Something scuttled overhead, as if crawling on the ceiling. Olrias tensed. A slithering sound echoed from another direction. A deep hiss rattled somewhere down the hall. The scuttling approached.

Daemon.

"Hurry, Theodower!" Olrias slid against the walls, shifting his feet along the ground to locate the debris.

An inhuman, guttural growl roared up the hall. The scuttling sped into running. Olrias ran, but tripped and sprawled. Crashing and clamor echoed from somewhere deeper in his chambers.

Olrias clawed along the ground, away from the approaching roar. His head screamed in agony. Debris ripped at his hands. He moved toward the sound inside his chambers, toward Theodower.

Cold, biting nails sank into his leg. Something hissed at his feet. Olrias bellowed at the pain ripping up his leg. The Daemon at his feet cackled. Frigid talons sank into his other calf. Hands clamped around his scrambling arms and pulled. The Daemon snarled and jerked in the opposite direction. Olrias, a mortal tug-of-war rope, grunted and gasped with each opposing motion.

"Help me, Uncle!" Theodower begged. Those must've been Theodower's hands pulling him away from the Daemon.

Olrias kicked. His foot collided with something and the talons broke loose. Theodower dragged him along quickly. Olrias' head throbbed and his legs pulsed and burned. Debris tore his back and legs as he flopped along the floor. The Daemon roared. Scrambling talons clapped across the steel floor toward them.

The air rushed from Olrias' lungs and his arm nearly tore from its socket when a sudden jerk hurled him backward. A closing door hummed. Heavy, turning locks clicked. Hissing air sealed the barrier. They'd reached his study.

"We don't have much time, Theodower," Olrias huffed. He cringed and tried to stand. "You must be my eyes."

No answer. Olrias stopped and listened. He ignored the pounding and scraping outside the door and focused on the space around him. There, to his left, a few paces away, labored rattling breaths.

"Theodower?"

Still no answer. He crawled toward the breathing. A boot. He latched on and his heart fluttered with fear. Not Theodower too. Olrias pulled himself up the leg, his hands trembling. He reached the waist. Wet.

"Theodower! What happened? Say something!"

"The . . . the . . . machine . . . ready . . ." His words came between huffs and wheezing.

Olrias slumped against his nephew. "How bad is it? Theodower?"

"Th . . . the machine . . . Uncle. Hurry . . . I . . . your eyes . . ."

The Daemon outside the door roared. Slicing steel drew the Daemon's attacks into focus. If Olrias was going to make the journey, he would have to hurry.

He pushed away from his nephew and felt through darkness to his desk. He struck a tower of holo-file archives he'd been compiling, and they crashed to the floor.

"Th . . . the machine . . . to . . . to your . . . right . . . Uncle."

Sadness stabbed at Olrias with each new rattling word Theodower spoke, but he inched to his right. He found the console and explored until his fingers sank into the hole.

"Key . . . to your . . . left. Hu . . . hurry . . . Uncle. S . . . save . . . Natalia."

Olrias found the key and slid it into place. The Daemon's roar shook the room. The metal tore louder. Shouting erupted beyond the Daemon's howl. Olrias turned the key.

"Un . . . uncle?"

"Yes, Theodower?"

"F . . . find him."

"I will, Theodower. I will."

Olrias felt along the panel beside the crystals until his fingers located the button. He lifted his other hand to the key, pushed the button, and the world slipped away.

The scuffling of feet hit him before the heat. He jerked into consciousness as a hundred sounds crowded into his head. The voices spoke a familiar alien language. He'd studied it somewhere, heard it before, but not on Hollumn. No. Not a Hollumnian language. Olrias focused. Where had he—

Earth.

He'd heard that language when studying Earth. It was an old language, one he'd had to travel backward along the planet's time-stream to find. Dozens of voices spoke almost on top of each other.

"Any minute now."

"Did you hear about what happened in Jairus' house?"

"She was dead."

"What about the lepers outside Samaria?"

The voices swarmed closer, pushing a swell of dust and heat ahead of them. Something hissed from the crowd's direction. Olrias froze. Could the Daemon have followed him?

"It's all a trick."

"They're rabble, that lot."

"No, it's real. The girl was dead."

"No, she was just sleeping. That's what the Rabbi said."

Rabbi? Olrias had heard that word before. Could it be? Could it have actually worked?

The hiss snapped much closer. The voices carried toward him. Footfalls echoed around him in growing madness.

Olrias bent his tongue to voice the foreign words. "Hello. What is happening?"

The chaos never lessened, but a voice spoke nearby. "Ho there, beggar. What's that?"

Someone poked at him with something hard and pointy. A few others laughed.

Olrias cringed. "What is happening?"

More laughter. "The great Nazarene is coming, beggar. Maybe he can help you, eh?"

The laughter moved away. A slithering hiss replaced it. Close. Right beside his left ear. Olrias froze. Cold tickled his flesh. A dozen wailing voices rose in inhuman anguish. A hard pointed object, likely a Daemon talon, touched Olrias' forearm. He jumped. A bitter cold hand clamped around his arm and jerked him back.

The crowd couldn't cover the creature's guttural voice. *"You don't belong here."*

Olrias tugged his arm, but couldn't break free. "Leave me alone!"

A few chuckles sounded from the passing multitude. "Another crazy one. Maybe the Nazarene will cast a spirit out of this one."

The Daemon, all dozen voices, roared in agony. One voice squealed,

"*He's coming*" while another groaned "*The Most High!*"

Olrias' heart fluttered. Nazarene. Could it be? "Jesus."

The Daemon's grip tightened and its voices wailed.

Pain roared through Olrias' body. "Jesus, son of David, have mercy on me!"

The Daemon squealed and writhed. "*We are legion, stranger. We are many. Speak that name again and we will—*"

Olrias shouted louder. "Jesus, son of David, have mercy on me!"

"Shut up!" a human voice called from the crowd.

"Silence, beggar! Don't bother the Master."

Someone kicked him. "Quiet, vermin!"

The Daemon latched another claw around Olrias' neck. "*Silence, stranger! You are not human! You look and speak like them, but you don't belong here. Do not speak that na—*"

"Jesus! Son of David!" Olrias felt unconsciousness suffocating his mind, clouding his thoughts. He had to hold on. Had to… "Have mercy on me!"

The Daemon's grip vanished. The crowd silenced. Warmth spread over Olrias. No. No, he had to hold on. Natalia needed him.

Air, gentle and sweet settled around Olrias in his delirium. "What do you want me to do for you?" Those words rang in Olrias' ears more melodically than any sound he'd ever heard.

That voice. The voice he had waited all his life to hear. The One for whom he'd been searching. The one called Messiah. The one all Seers had seen. The Creator's Light.

"Lord, I want to see." He wanted so much more. He wanted Laurallie back. He wanted to save Theodower and Natalia. He wanted to heal Hollumn's wasted landscape. He wanted to stop the Daemon from invading his world. But for some reason he couldn't comprehend, he asked for the Sight.

That warm, celestial voice rang out through his blindness again. "Receive your sight; your faith has healed you."

Light flooded his blindness. The pain fled. They opened and majesty filled their scope. Bright blue skies floated somewhere beyond the glowing face hovering only inches from Olrias' own. The Nazarene's smile remained as he stood and progressed down a dusty path woven between houses of dirt, stone, and sticks. A large crowd followed close behind him and trailed ahead of him for what could have been miles.

A tear stung Olrias' eyes and he stood, still trembling. Scattered across rooftops around him, a dozen black Daemon writhed.

"Praise Jesus!" The words burst from Olrias' lips as joy flooded his insides. The joy surged through him and pushed aside all pain.

The Daemon writhed harder. Their wails swelled in his ears. The Nazarene's very name caused them pain. It really was Him. The One.

The Universe's Light. In all his studies, he had found only two commonalities amongst the various worlds and dimensions: the darkness and the Light. The darkness had worked its way into every other world, every other dimension. So had the Light. But somewhere in Hollumn's history, they'd banished the Light. If Olrias could bring it back, perhaps he could save Hollumn.

"Praise Jesus! Praise the Nazarene!"

Olrias ran into the crowd screaming it. The Daemon howled and writhed with each new mention. The crowd, many of them pointing at Olrias, joined his exclamation. A chorus of "praise Jesus" flooded the street. Olrias continued shouting until the Daemon fled, then slipped off the road between two ramshackle homes.

His heart raced. A lifetime spent in search of the truth, of hope, hadn't been spent in vain.

Dizziness overtook Olrias and he leaned against one of the sandy homes. Sight flooded his mind, filling him with possibilities. And there, in the center of the chaos, the Light throbbed. Olrias closed his eyes, inhaled a soothing, calming breath, looked down at his wrist, at the seven colored marks glowing there, then smiled. He reached over and swept his index finger across the marks in a circular pattern three times. They glowed brighter and his wrist vibrated. Then everything slipped away.

Reality snapped into existence with a pop. The Daemon's vehement rage and the sound of tearing steel mixed with distant explosions to assure Olrias had traveled back through time and space, across the inter-dimensional flux, to the exact moment and place he'd departed. Hollumn. In the midst of a revolution. Only moments away from inviting the Daemon into their world and annihilating his people.

The Sight flooded Olrias' mind again, but he focused on the immediate future. Olrias scanned the floor for a memory crystal—the one with the Earth people's scriptures of the Messiah, one he had reviewed countless times in his quest to understand the Creator's great plan for Hollumn. Finding it, Olrias turned toward the door with the word of power on his lips.

"Jesus."

The Daemon recoiled. Even here, a dozen dimensions away and thousands of years into the future, the Earth deity's name held power. The memory crystal in his hand resonated unexpectedly as brilliant light swelled from its center. The Daemon were darkness. This Nazarene, this one called Messiah, was Light. And His word, His very name, held the power. If the Earth histories were correct, this Nazarene had come to the Earth people to save them from darkness. Today, He would save Hollumn.

"In the name of Jesus, Daemon, be gone!"

The shadow assailing the door vanished in an explosion of wailing and hatred.

How many times had Olrias prayed to the Creator that the Messiah would save Hollumn? How many hours had he spent studying the Earth scriptures? Finally, generations of Oracles later, the Messiah's Light had come to Hollumn.

Olrias turned to Theodower.

A smile spread across the young man's face, his dark black hair matted to his forehead with sweat while tears trickled from his dark blue eyes. Blood had soaked his tunic around the gouge torn across his chest. Each new breath came farther apart and rattled more deeply. Yet something sparkled in his eyes.

"Theodower." Olrias dropped to his knees beside his nephew.

"Y . . . you . . . found . . . him?"

Olrias lifted the glowing memory crystal, an overwhelming peace radiating from it with the same intensity as the Nazarene's voice. "Yes Theodower. I found Him. The one I've been looking for all of my life. He was always there, Theodower. In every vision, in every other world and dimension. He is Light." Olrias lifted the crystal so its glow highlighted Theodower's face. "And I will take His word to Hollumn. All we have to do is believe, nephew."

Theodower's smile grew and his tears fell faster. "G . . . good . . . uncle. Now . . . save Na . . . talia. Sa . . . save our . . . people."

Theodower huffed three quick breaths and slumped sideways into the corner. No new tears fell. No more breaths came. The rattle trailed into silence.

Olrias reached up a trembling hand and closed his nephew's eyes. "Go to Him, Theodower. Find the Nazarene. Find your soul's salvation."

Olrias stood and rubbed his tears away. Crystal in hand, he stalked to the door and slammed the release. The door groaned and slid partially aside. Olrias stepped through and found the Daemon crawling amongst the debris. Were there six? Seven? More?

It didn't matter. He lifted the glowing crystal. "Jesus!"

Light slashed away from the crystal. The Daemon's yellow eyes widened. They gnashed their teeth and scrambled to flee. The Light tore through them. Hadn't the Earth scriptures called the Word a sword?

"Hang on, Natalia. I'm coming." He ran. Ran as fast as his aged legs would carry him.

Explosions shook the corridors. Smoke drifted through the halls. Shouting came from every direction. Olrias never slowed. His silver hair bounced behind him, thickening with sweat as he dodged around, under, and over debris. He raced out of his housing compound and sped down the quiet transit line tracks. The smoking transit car lying askew on the tracks meant no oncoming traffic.

Daemon leapt from shadows here and there, but Light erupted from the crystal each time Olrias said "Jesus." To enter the Council chambers, he had to push through a crowd of fighting soldiers and insurgents. The Sight showed him what path to choose. He would reach the sanctum, but for some reason, he couldn't see much farther than that.

Olrias plowed through the sanctum doors. Every eye in the massive room turned toward him. Natalia, strung to crossed metal beams in a semi-circle with other weeping women, laughed madly while screaming. Raelin, a black dagger in hand, sneered.

She spun and buried the dagger in one of the hanging women. The woman gasped. Raelin loosed a sickly laugh as she pulled the dagger free. Blood gushed from the wound. A dozen Daemon emerged from a massive black portal beside her. The invasion had begun.

Raelin stepped toward Natalia and lifted the dagger. "You're too late, Oracle."

So many Daemon. And Olrias was just one man. What was he thinking? The Sight hadn't shown him defeating the Daemon. What had he done?

Olrias raised the crystal with a trembling hand. "Jesus!"

Nothing.

His heart skipped a beat. He stared down at the crystal. It reverberated with the same ferocity and its glow pulsed with his heartbeat, but no Light tore from its depths to devour the Daemon throughout the room.

The Daemon, cringing and snarling their yellow teeth, retreated a step. Raelin laughed. "That's it, Olrias? That's your plan? Just a word?"

The Daemon charged.

Like a crashing wave, they came. The Sight came as well, in its strongest fury. Thousands of images flooded Olrias' mind. Hundreds of them contained the Nazarene's face. Then everything fell silent. Only that face, framed in glowing light remained. And a voice—Olrias never heard voices with the Sight—spoke to him.

For he has rescued us from the dominion of darkness and brought us into the kingdom of the Son he loves, in whom we have redemption, the forgiveness of sins.

Love. Light. They were interchangeable in their simplicity, their purity. How had he never seen it before? Laurallie's image drifted through his mind. Theodower smiled somewhere beyond her. Then only the Nazarene. He was Light. Light was Love.

And what had Love told Olrias? *Your faith has healed you*

The Sight died and reality returned. Faith. The Daemon's screams snapped Olrias to attention. The crystal shone so bright he had to squint. The Messiah's name alone didn't hold the power. But in the hands of one who truly believed . . . "Jesus! In the name of Jesus, be gone!"

Light tearing from the crystal exploded like the weapons that had ravaged their world so many years before. The Daemon vanished as cinders caught in a torrential breeze. Raelin flew backward and smashed into the black portal, which hummed, vibrated, and exploded.

Raelin recovered and fumbled to escape the debris. "No! What have you done?"

Olrias smiled. Like every Oracle before him, he had delivered a message. But unlike his predecessors, Olrias believed in that message. "I've done nothing, Raelin. I am but a messenger come to bring Light. The message is life. The Creator has sent His Light to our people through every Oracle's eyes. But this Council, and every Council before it, kept that Light from Hollumn's people. I will show them His Light." Olrias lifted the memory crystal. "I will show them His word."

Voices flooded the stairwell leading to the inner sanctum. Fear flashed in Raelin's eyes. She glanced up at Natalia and the other dangling women. Insurgents, Hollumn's people finally come to stand against its oppressors, billowed into the sanctum, cheering.

Olrias smiled and closed his eyes. The glowing crystal's resonance tickled his flesh and vibrated to his very core. He might have lost his wife, his mortal love, but he'd found the answer to his lifelong quest for the truth, for hope, for salvation. With Natalia safe and the darkness held at bay, he could offer Hollumn something they'd never experienced. The Light.

And the Light was Love.

UNDENIABLE

A.P. Fuchs

A.P. Fuchs is the author of several novels and writes from Winnipeg, Manitoba. Among his most recent are *Axiom-man*, *The Way of the Fog*, *Magic Man*, and *April*, which was written under the pseudonym, Peter Fox. Visit his corner of the Web at www.apfuchs.com

"Undeniable" was written because I've often wondered if a person would reach a breaking point when it came to being persecuted for Christ. Because I live in Canada, persecution to the point of death is not a reality I presently have to face. However, this could change at any time. I've asked myself now and then how I would react if someone were beating me and torturing me solely because I believed in something they didn't. Would there come a point where I'd be tempted to give in or would I stay true to my Lord Jesus till the end even if it meant my life? As I wrote "Undeniable" I was forced to share Duncan James's shoes for a time. I learned a lot about myself and my faith. I won't say what I discovered but rather let you, dear reader, find out for yourself. I just hope you come to the same conclusion I have.

1

DUNCAN JAMES TOUCHED THE tender, bumpy flesh around his eyes. Carefully, he trailed his index finger from the outer rim of his left eye socket to the middle where his eyeball once sat. A razor-sharp sting of hot pain pierced the fragile area the second his finger made contact. He sharply tugged his finger away. The pricks of tears instinctively formed at the corners of his eyes but he wasn't sure if they'd even leak out. The openings of the tear ducts were no doubt seared shut. And he was right. No tears came, but he'd give anything for even a few drops, anything to let him know he was still human.

Bowing his head, he carefully rested his forehead on his forearms, his arms on his knees. The corner seemed warmer today, more comforting. The way one wall pressed up against his back and the one running perpendicular to it was flush against the side of his thigh—it was almost like a hug. One final embrace until they'd kill him.

His son, Kyle, was somewhere in the cell with him. If Duncan remembered correctly, Kyle was over to the left, lying near the door. But only if he remembered correctly. Before the soldiers took his eyes, he made an effort to take a quick mental picture of the room. Then the lights went out. There hadn't been much to remember, thankfully. The cell—if this was a cell—was roughly twelve feet by twelve feet, the ceiling a stout seven feet from the cold and rough cement floor. The walls were made of concrete, worn and cracked, as if this place had been around for decades. Maybe longer. In the center of the room, on the ceiling, was a lone light bulb within a small circle frame, the light socket connected to a long and thick black wire that ran along the ceiling and out the door somewhere. The door was the only thing of color and even then it was a dark, rusty red, the paint peeled and chipped in places, revealing the dark gray of the metal beneath. There were no windows.

Taking a lungful of stale air, Duncan let out a sigh. Then, "Kyle?" His voice was barely a whisper. After having not eaten in four days, even mustering the strength to speak was difficult. He swallowed, cleared his throat. "Kyle?" A little louder this time but if Kyle wasn't awake, he knew his boy wouldn't hear him. Kyle had always been a sound sleeper. You could crash a pair of cymbals by his head and he still wouldn't stir.

Oh, Lord, please wake him, Duncan thought. But God had seemed suddenly absent ever since the arrest.

Six days ago Duncan and Kyle had arrived in Hong Kong for a vacation. They'd heard the rumors of Christian persecution but trusted the Lord to protect them for the month they were to spend there. The arrest occurred almost immediately after getting off the plane. He had brought his Bible on the plane for the long flight over from Canada and didn't think he should have left it with the rest of his luggage. Their carry-on bags were scanned through customs for any hazardous materials and it was then the official in charge saw the dark, rectangular shape of a book on the scanner's screen. She opened the bag, pulled out the Bible . . . and just held it, as if captivated by it. The small woman placed the book back in the bag and waved Duncan and Kyle through. To this day, he didn't know how she did it but somehow—perhaps via some sort of secret airport employee code—notified the guards standing at the gate to the main airport. After that . . .

A loud ka-chunk echoed throughout the tiny room as the metal door was unlocked from the other side. It screeched on its hinges and footsteps let Duncan know that he and Kyle were no longer alone.

Kyle let out a grunt as he was startled out of sleep.

"Kyle!" Duncan shouted. Immediately after crying out his son's name, footsteps rushed toward him and a pair of hands scooped him up from under his arms, hoisting him to his feet.

"Dad!" Kyle said.

The scuff of a shoe against the stone floor followed by a sickening smack of bone against stone made Duncan's insides jump. Kyle yelped.

"No!" Duncan screamed and rushed toward where he thought his boy lay. Four pairs of arms held him back—two under his arms, two coming out of nowhere at his front.

His son moaned somewhere across the way.

"Oh Jesus, please let me see," Duncan said softly, but blackness remained his only sight.

Footsteps neared him, quickly followed by the smell of sweat. Hot breath suddenly blew upon his face like a rank breeze. "He cannot hear you," came a voice Duncan recognized as Captain Tan's. Duncan's insides shook at the sound of the Chinese man's voice. Tan was there when the other men pinned him down. Tan was the one who leaned over him and when Duncan didn't deny that Jesus was the Son of God, produced a knife from his pocket and slowly cut out Duncan's eyes from their sockets. Tan, who talked the whole way through the procedure, was the one who informed him that the wounds would be cauterized by the burning red tip of an iron poker. Even now the smell of smoldering flesh still filled Duncan's nostrils. Despite all prayer, the scent wouldn't leave him, as if a permanent reminder of that day.

"Where is your God now?" one of the soldiers across the room said. He was talking to Kyle because Kyle replied, "Here, even now."

Thumpk! Kyle coughed then spat. Duncan could only assume the soldier kicked his son in the head again, this time in the mouth, bringing up a gush of blood.

"I do not wish to do this much longer, Mr. James," Tan said.

Duncan hated it every time Captain Tan called him by name. The image of Tan pulling Duncan's wallet out of his back pocket while the other soldiers held him danced in his mind's eye. The way the Chinese captain said "Duncan James" the first time he read his passport made his skin crawl. "Duhn-cahn Jems" was how Tan said it.

"Then stop doing it," Duncan said. Try as he might, it was difficult to shove what was happening to Kyle to the back of his mind. The first night he and his son were in the cell alone together, they had a long talk and agreed to not watch, if it could be helped, whatever might happen to the other person. The two just didn't count on the soldiers making one watch the other while they meted out their torture. Duncan would never forget Kyle's cries when his son was forced to watch Tan remove his eyes. Kyle almost broke then, was about to give in to what the soldiers wanted: a renunciation of faith. Duncan had screamed at him through the pain and reminded him what they talked about.

"I'm afraid there will be no end," Tan said, "unless you state that your faith in this 'Messiah' is nothing more than an illusion that the West concocted to make their people feel better."

"How could we have concocted it? You can't make something like this up. Besides, the Gospel started in the East." A quick whistle of wind as something rushed toward him then the stinging smack of an open palm against his cheek.

He expected Tan to say something . . . but there was silence. Just like Jesus said, when the time came, the Spirit would provide an answer that would be irrefutable to the accuser.

Tan huffed a heated breath of air at him, sending the hairs against his sweat-soaked brow partly to the side. It tickled. Instinctively, Duncan tried to scratch his forehead to get rid of the sensation. Instead he received a swift kick to the gut. His intestines jumped inside him, seeming to have been momentarily pushed up too close to his stomach. They lingered there before settling back down again. The back of his throat constricted and his stomach tightened, yearning to bring something up. But there was no food in his stomach to appease him. Nothing but the anxiety of wondering how long this would last.

"Leave him alone!" Kyle screamed.

His boy must be on his feet or at least his knees. No one could produce that kind of vocal sound lying down.

"Quiet!" a soldier barked.

A loud wet thud and Kyle said no more.

*   *   *

The sky was overcast in light gray, the air warm but refreshing. Duncan stood behind his son's maroon BMX bicycle, steadying it as Kyle, a child of six, climbed on.

His son brushed aside a lock of curly blond hair from over his green eyes, his smile bright and big.

"You just keep your eyes forward, okay?" Duncan said. "I'll be right here the whole while."

Kyle faced forward, gripping the handle bars extra tight. The boy wobbled a bit on the seat, trying to balance himself as he set his feet upon the pedals.

"I'm right here," Duncan said again. "Start peddling."

With a grunt, Kyle pressed his right foot down on the pedal then followed it with another grunt as he pushed down the left one when it rose. Slowly, the bike began moving forward. Fortunately, the James's lived on a bay so traffic wasn't a worry.

Peeking around to the side of Kyle's face, Duncan's heart lightened when he saw him smile. The bike rolled forward, Duncan stepping quickly behind it, his fingers locked onto the bicycle seat. The handlebars wiggled a bit as Kyle got used to the steering; soon he got the hang of keeping the bike straight.

The two kept moving. Kyle laughed. Duncan smiled.

And let go.

Kyle peddled on toward the mouth of the bay, eyes glued to the front as he tried to master this newfound skill.

"See, Dad, I can—" Kyle looked over his shoulder and his eyes went wide. Immediately he twisted the handlebars to the_left, so much so the front wheel turned completely sideways. The BMX suddenly stopped and Kyle lurched forward, his tiny body slamming into the handlebars before toppling over on the left side.

His head hit the pavement with a hollow smack and a small amount of blood pooled around his left eye.

Duncan ran over to him, tears in his eyes.

2

Strong hands forced Duncan forward; he stumbled a step before getting his feet to do what he wanted. Carefully, he walked forward, hands and arms outstretched; he didn't want to bump into anything. His biceps stung a second later when hard palms slapped his arms down.

"You walk straight, we guide you," came the voice from behind him. It wasn't Captain Tan's. Tan was probably somewhere in front of him. If only he could see.

Not ten feet away, more shuffling of footsteps then the sound of something dragging along the cement.

Kyle, he thought. *He's still out.* A pause. *Oh Lord, please don't let them do anything to him, but if they do, please let it be something he can withstand.*

A hard poke in between his shoulder blades as the soldier nudged him forward. He must have slowed down without realizing it. Grimacing, Duncan turned to where he thought the soldier was, to face him. *Smack!* And his nose was aflame with pain. If he could see, he knew he'd be seeing stars. He reached up to check if his nose was broken but once more his hands were slapped down.

Just move on ahead, he thought. He knew Jesus's story about turning the other cheek, but never quite understood it. Was he just supposed to "roll with the punches" and hope for the best? Did "turning the other cheek" mean letting others walk all over him and beat him? Right then he felt ashamed for not knowing his Bible as thoroughly as he liked. But he knew the important things, the main things. And, like the Bible taught, being a Christian was a process. Perfection or being Christ-like was attained throughout your lifetime not overnight, and the Christ-like part didn't come until after you died.

Besides, he thought, *the Man Himself underwent persecution. He stood there and took it when He didn't deserve it. He didn't fight back even though He had the power to call down lightning from the sky. To be like—* Hands grabbed his shoulders then he was turned sharply to the right. They must be in the hall. From what he could remember, the hall was just like the cell they had been in but only longer and narrower—all cement, no features, a lone light bulb hanging from the ceiling somewhere in the middle. *Oh God, give me strength.*

Kyle had to be further ahead as the sound of his body being dragged along the ground grew softer. Where were they taking them?

Duncan was warned by the friend who led he and Kyle to Christ that persecution would come, but he always thought that meant a few "Jesus jokes" or his buddies making fun of him because he decided to no longer see any R-rated movies. He didn't count on this, on getting the daylights beaten out of him simply because he believed something others didn't.

More than anything, he wished he had the strength to endure it. *God, I don't know what to do. I honestly don't. I know . . . or knew . . . I'd be hated for Your Namesake. You warned us of that in Your Word. "The world will hate you because of Me," You said. But You also said to remember that it hated You first. I just didn't think . . .*

"Turn here," the voice from behind said.

Once more the man grabbed his shoulders and turned him to the right, this time with a push that sent him to his knees. Hands immediately out before him, Duncan stopped himself from landing face first on the cement. The moment his palms began to sting, a dull and hard pain exploded at the base of his tailbone, sending a shockwave of dull hurt up his spine and into the base of his neck. He yelped then was kicked in the face by someone in front, his nose immediately spouting blood. It had to be broken.

"Quiet!" It was Captain Tan.

On his side, head spinning, he tasted the coppery blood on his tongue. Spitting it out, he rolled onto his back without meaning to. One of the soldiers chuckled and a foot plunged into his stomach. Duncan groaned and could barely breathe.

Off to the side, chains tinkled and one of the soldiers grunted as though he were hoisting something up.

"Kyle?" Duncan managed.

Slap! "Your dad's talking to you!" a soldier barked.

Kyle muttered something.

Blood pooling in his mouth, Duncan instinctively gagged on it and swallowed some before spitting the remainder out. "Lord, why are you permitting this?"

"No talking!" Tan said.

The next thing Duncan knew, he was being lifted and shoved until someone spun him around and pushed down hard on his shoulders, forcing him to plop down on a rock-solid chair. More chains tinkled then the cool of metal bracelets graced his skin as his hands were strapped to the armrests at his wrists. His ankles were cuffed, too, and held tight against the legs of the chair.

Mind reeling, he found himself speaking before he thought better of it. "Why are you doing this? What difference does it make if we believe something you don't? Why . . . why beat us for no reason?"

Tan's foul breath filled his nostrils as the Chinese officer positioned himself in front of him. "What do you think one voice does, Mr. James?"

Duncan swallowed a small amount of blood then licked the crimson liquid from his lips. Grimacing at the awful taste, he said quietly, "What?"

"You have no way of proving that this so-called God of yours exists never mind a Son of His Whom you claim brings Salvation. Why spread something you cannot prove?"

"I can prove it." He winced, expecting a fist to the face. None came.

"How? If you're going to say that by believing in this . . . God . . . your life has changed, I'm afraid that's not good enough. I've heard the testimony of those like you before. You say that before you met Him, you were lost, given over to a life of so-called 'sin,' unhappy, constantly hurting yourselves and others whether you meant to or not. Not good enough! Show me something tangible. Show me something *real!*"

Silence. There was nothing he could say. What was he supposed to do? Ask God to unlock the cuffs around his wrists and ankles and stand up? *Lord, if You're willing,* he prayed. But the cuffs remained tight against his skin.

"See? You can't. And then you tell others about this 'Savior' and they follow you. Then they tell others and others follow them. The next thing you know there's a revolt not just against a country, but against life itself. I know more about you . . . 'Christians'" —he enunciated the word as if he meant rapists— "than you realize." Then, as if in afterthought, "You don't even consider yourselves part of the world."

"Leave him alone." It was Kyle. He was awake. Thank God. "This is senseless. There is no point."

"Shut him up," Tan said.

Thoomp! Kyle gagged.

"Please," Duncan said, "please, I beg you—let him go. I'm yours to do with as you will. He doesn't deserve this. Please . . . set him free."

"Then deny Jesus Christ as Lord," Tan snapped back.

Lord, if I did, would they listen? Duncan squeezed his eyes shut at the thought, inadvertently sending a burst of pain across the tender tissue. *Don't think that. Don't deny Him. Never.* "No."

A moment later, Kyle screamed.

*   *   *

The boy's cries came from downstairs accompanied by the shrill noise of the smoke detector. Duncan sprang out of bed in a flash, taking the stairs to the kitchen two at a time. When he set foot on the linoleum, Kyle stared at him, wide-eyed, tears running down his cheeks. The boy held his hand out in front of him, fingers twitching, the frying pan on the burner smoking.

Duncan ran over to him. "Are you okay?"

"I just . . . I just . . ." Kyle's lower lip trembled.

On the stove, smoke rose in thick billows from the old black frying pan. The element beside it was bright red, the heat radiating off it making Duncan sweat.

"Give me you hand," Duncan said.

He took his twelve-year-old son's hand gently by the wrist and brought the palm closer so he could see it more clearly. The skin was red and puffy, swollen and shiny.

Harder than he meant to, he yanked Kyle over to the sink and ran the cold water. The boy yelped from the harsh tug against his arm. Sticking the boy's hand in the water, Duncan reached over and turned the stove off.

"I'm sorry, Dad, I'm sorry," Kyle said.

"It's okay. Just keep your hand there." The next order of business would be to take him to the hospital so they could treat it.

"I only wanted to make us breakfast."

Duncan checked his son's hand's progress. The icy water pouring over the skin obscured the burn, making it hard to tell how bad it really was. He pulled the hand away from the water and checked it over. It was bright red, the skin beneath the fingers glossy and inflamed.

"Keep your hand under the water," he said.

"Dad, I'm sorry." Kyle wiped his eyes.

"Don't apologize. It was an accident. We're going to the hospital." He searched the countertop for a dish towel or cloth so he could fill it with ice and have Kyle hold it against the burns until they got there. He plucked a dish towel off the rack of dishes by the sink, went to the freezer and cursed when he saw the ice trays were empty. On the counter beside him was a frozen pack of bacon. Good thing Kyle hadn't thought to thaw it before attempting to fry it. He laid out the towel, put the bacon in the middle then told Kyle to put his palm against the meat. Once the boy did, he tied the towel to his son's hand and shooed him toward the front door.

"I just wanted to make you happy, Dad."

*   *   *

For almost ten minutes the soldiers beat Kyle, forcing Duncan to listen. As guilty as he felt in admitting it, he was thankful he couldn't see what they were doing to him.

"Now, Kyle," Tan said, "why don't you tell me what I want to hear?"

"No . . . neber . . . Jeshush ish Lorb . . ." Kyle said. Duncan could only imagine how swollen the boy's lip was if he was talking like that.

A loud *smack* sent a jolt through Duncan's chest. Kyle . . .

His voice suddenly low and raspy, Tan shouted, "Deny Him! The Son of Man will never rule us!" Then in his regular voice, "I . . ." He didn't finish.

"Don't . . . don't do it . . . Kyle . . ." Duncan said.

There was quiet for a moment. Then Kyle said ever so softly, "He's gop a knibe."

"Tan!" Duncan screamed but was quickly silenced as something hard and wooden cracked along the back of his head. Immediately the warmth of blood trickled down the rear of his skull and tickled his neck.

Kyle was about to say something but his words were cut short by a low gasp and a gurgle at the back of his throat. Did they just . . .

Father, Duncan thought but also mouthed the words, *I don't know what You're doing or why You're allowing this. Please . . . please, if they're about to take his life, let me see him one last time.*

"Deny Him!" Tan screamed.

Kyle coughed then yelped. What were they doing to him?

Jesus! Please, open my eyes!

"If . . . if I do . . ." Kyle said, ". . . woob you let . . ." He coughed again. "Wiw you leb . . . my dad . . . go?"

He couldn't listen any longer. Breaking down, Duncan said, "Don't say it, Kyle. Remember, if you deny Him He will deny you—" *Thwack!* Whatever had struck him in the back of the head now sent his head flying back, straining the muscles in his neck. Forehead throbbing, he tried to bring his head upright . . . but he couldn't.

To the side, there was a wet suction sound, as if something hard was pulled from something moist and soft. Then Kyle screamed again, softly adding, "Jeshush ish . . ."

Suddenly a gentle pair of hands touched Duncan's temples and slowly lowered his head back down, taking the pressure off his neck. A gust of cool air blew against his face and a warmth filled the muscles and bones of his neck, setting them at ease.

"I am with you always."

The darkness before Duncan's eyes grew even darker then quickly the blackness was replaced with deep red—*blood* red—then grew brighter and brighter . . . until the color melted away, parted, like a veil.

The room came into focus . . .

. . . and he could see.

3

The stinging of the mess of flesh around Duncan's eyes still remained, but at least now he had his bearings.

Thank you, Lord, he thought. He wanted to think more—to *say* more—but the words escaped him. Only a deep feeling of gratitude and unworthiness encompassed him. *Thank you, Jesus.*

Kyle was to the right, his body against the wall, hands bound up above his head by thick metal chains. The boy wasn't moving. One of the four soldiers in the room in addition to Captain Tan stood before his son, blocking everything but Kyle's bowed head. From the side, Duncan squinted his eyes against the dim light; blood dripped off Kyle's nose in thick tears, his son's face red and swollen.

"Kyle . . . wake . . . up . . ." Duncan said.

Tan looked at him, then at Kyle, as if following Duncan's line of sight. The captain's facial muscles relaxed, his eyes suddenly empty, as though he were putting it together that Duncan could now see. But soon his face tensed again and the triangular point in his brow returned, bringing the hatred back.

The soldier in front of his son did a quick step toward Kyle, the soldier's arm bent at the elbow, as if grabbing Kyle's middle. Kyle hollered when the man jerked his arm.

Tears pricked the corners of Duncan's eyes but didn't release. "Lord . . . save him . . ." he said.

"Y-you . . . wi-win . . ." Kyle said.

The three remaining soldiers—two in front of Duncan, one in behind—neared Kyle, their mouths slightly slack. At any moment, Duncan expected their tongues to drop out of their mouths like a pack of dogs', the three salivating at hearing the words they longed to hear.

Time slowed and Duncan leaned slightly to the right, waiting to hear what his son might say. He went to scream out for Kyle not to deny the Son of God but his voice unexpectedly caught in his throat. He tried to speak again . . . but nothing but air came out of his mouth as if an invisible fist held his voice at bay.

Above Kyle's head, the shadows contorted, growing thick like syrup. They grew and coalesced into a black bubble against the cement. Then the bubble opened at its center, the gooey tar-like substance ripping from the middle outward, giving birth to a pair of deep gray, scaly hands with long dark fingernails. The hands tore at the bubble, revealing a sinewy set of arms followed by a bulbous body. Long tightly muscled legs popped out of the dark bubble and clasped to the wall behind it like a spider re-finding its footing. Then its head emerged, that of a lizard combined with a bat. Sharp, flaky scales rimmed its eyes, the eyes a pale gray with blue irises.

Duncan's heart bounced in his chest and his mouth ran dry despite the blood on his tongue. A scream fought its way from his diaphragm up his chest and into his throat, filling his mouth and banging against his tightly-pressed lips as if they were closed doors. He had to release, had to say something. The moment he opened his mouth, a gentle hand was on his shoulder. Nothing but air escaped his lips and his heart quickly calmed, as if what he was seeing was commonplace.

A man came up alongside him and stood, a man with fiery eyes, his gaze fixed on the creature. The fellow was enormous, at least eight feet tall wearing a gold robe with a thousand folds and a gold belt across his middle. Hanging from the belt was a large sword—silver-bladed—with a bronze hand-guard. Strapped across his back was an ornate silver shield, with a gold circle at its center. The man's feet were coated in bronze, matching the color of his hair which was also made out of flame. It flickered and glimmered so bright it obscured his skin color, but not so bright as to diminish the white light coming from his eyes.

Duncan yearned to be free of his binds so he could fall on the floor and worship this man who appeared beside him.

As if reading his thoughts, the man said, "Remain where you are, O son of the Most High God. I, like you, am His servant."

The creature slid down the wall then jumped up and wrapped itself around Kyle. Kyle didn't move, didn't seem to *know* this thing was around him.

Then everything opened up to Duncan. Attached to Captain Tan's back like an out-of-shape backpack was another creature like the one on Kyle. Four other creatures were wrapped around the other soldiers as well. They had always been there, he knew, but didn't know how he knew.

The man was suddenly no longer at Duncan's side.

In a blaze of silver light, the man drew his sword and the blade burst into flame. He sliced the creature off Kyle. In immediate reaction, the five other creatures on the Chinese men dove off the humans and sprang upon him. The man's gold robes billowed about him as he spun around, his blazing white eyes aflame with justice. The creature he had just cleaved off Kyle shook on the floor in spasmic movements; the man sliced off the creature's head just as the others landed on him.

Tan was saying something to Duncan but he couldn't make out what it was over the creatures' foul shrieks as the man slay two of them. The remaining three ripped and clawed at his robes. Each time they tore off a piece of the shining fabric, the robe healed itself and the torn piece disintegrated into the air in a shimmering display of gold sparkles.

"Save . . . him," Duncan said though he wasn't sure if the—angel?—heard him.

Gold light brewed beneath the dark gray of the scaly creatures, the beams shining forth from beneath the cracks in between the bodies. A low rumble filled the air. The soldiers didn't even notice. Only now did it become clear to Duncan what he was seeing: the unseen. The light burst forth, sending the creatures flying against the walls, breaking into millions of pieces which floated back down to the ground like flakes of ash snapping up and outward from a bonfire. The ashes rested on the ground a moment before disappearing altogether. The man in gold stood, his face as hard as stone, his flaming sword bright and hot. Adjusting the shield on his back, he turned and faced Kyle.

Gently, he laid a hand across the young man's cheek.

In the tussle, Duncan hadn't noticed Tan had moved. The captain was now in front of Kyle, gripping him between thumb and forefinger by the chin, squeezing his face hard. Tan raised Kyle's face so the two were nose to nose. The other soldiers had a mocking grin on their faces.

"I can still save you," Tan said. "Just say it. Just once."

Quickly, another creature materialized on Tan's back and his voice dropped an octave. "Just once!"

Kyle licked his lips and took a deep breath.

"Don't. Don't ever say it," Duncan said. He looked at the angel, if that's what this man was. His head was spinning so completely it was hard to make heads or tails out of anything anymore. "Stop this . . ."

The angel looked at him and compassionately said, "Do not be afraid. It'll be all right. Your son will die today, but do not fear. He will inherit the Kingdom of God."

Tears raced up from Duncan's core and he squeezed his eyes shut. "Oh God," he growled, "why take him away!"

Kyle was whispering.

*   *   *

The note lay on Kyle's bed. Duncan ran over and picked it up. It read:

I'm sorry, Dad, but it's better this way. You'll thank me for this, now that I'm gone. I've done nothing but bring you grief. I've always been a screw-up, always let you down. How many other kids make their dad yell at them nearly every day? I'm such an idiot. I'm stupid and don't deserve to live but I'm too much of a coward to die.

You've been there for me ever since Mom died. Thanks for that. But I can't go on hurting you like I have. Perhaps one day you'll find me or I'll find you, but not now. Maybe not ever.

I love you, Pop. I'm just not the son you deserve.

Love,
Kyle

Ps. I'm sorry about crashing the car. I'll pay you back somehow. Promise.

Tears running from his eyes, Duncan sat on the edge of Kyle's bed. His boy was gone. Gone. Ran away to who knew where till who knew when.

"Kyle, you didn't have to leave," Duncan said. He brought his hand to his face, trying to catch the tears. "I'm not mad at you." Not now, not ever. I only disciplined you because I love you.

The evening melted away, the minutes turning to hours. Duncan read the note over a dozen times before falling to his knees beside Kyle's bed. Face in his forearms, he whispered, "I'd give anything to have you back. Anything."

His insides broke again. Kyle didn't have to worry about paying him. Insurance covered everything. But he understood Kyle's guilt as the same thing had happened with his own father. Duncan had been out one night partying with the guys, they had too much to drink and, Boom! His father's '67 Cadillac was wrapped around a tree. The old man had got it just the day before and was kind enough to let him take it for a ride. He shouldn't have been drinking. He was underage. Just like Kyle had been.

The tears wouldn't let him go.

Silence. Then . . .

"Dad?"

Duncan looked up and through blurred vision, Kyle stood in the doorway, eyes wide and innocent.

*   *   *

Duncan opened his eyes and looked at his son, as if looking at him made the young man's words more audible. Kyle said, "Jesus Christ, Son of God."

The creature on Tan's back screamed and Tan grabbed the blade in Kyle's middle, twisted the handle once then withdrew it. Using his whole body, he thrust the blade back in to Kyle's stomach then stabbed him in the chest, then back to the stomach, each stab and slash ripping out pieces of Kyle's torso. The grue landed on the cement in wet slaps like sopping string from a mop.

Kyle stopped moving.

The angel stood there. Just stood there!

Heart as heavy as stone, Duncan winced when his son's body lit up in bright white and a glowing humanoid shape pulled out of its flesh and blood shell. The shape lingered in front of the corpse for a moment then ascended skyward to the ceiling. Quickly, it passed through the cement roof and was gone.

Tan spun on his heels, tearing the knife from Kyle's flesh as he did. Blood dripped from blade, and he walked toward Duncan.

4

One year passed.

The angel, Nathanael, stayed with Duncan the whole time, kept watch over him in his cell, was present at all the beatings. Long ago Duncan already accepted the angel wouldn't save him from any more torture. It wasn't his job. One night, after having his arm broken, Duncan fought the pain and with his good arm tried to take a swing at him. Nathanael grabbed his arm by the wrist and twisted it around so Duncan was facing the other way, body bent in half. One more inch and his other arm would have been broken, too.

"You will not have your way in this," Nathanael had said.

"How can I surrender to a God who lets this happen to His children?" he said through gritted teeth.

"You are being refined for His return. With each passing moment, you bring Him glory. Soon, it will be fulfilled."

Now, sitting up against the cool cement wall, Duncan recalled those words for the first time in months.

Nathanael stood against the wall on the other side of the room, arms crossed. A moment later he stepped away from the wall. "He is coming."

The door screeched open and Duncan forced himself not to look at it. *Slam!* And the door closed. At the top of his peripheral, Captain Tan stood in front of it. Heart pounding despite having gone through this hundreds of times before, Duncan glanced to the right. Nathanael looked compassionately back at him, his fiery eyes gentle, knowing full well what was about to happen.

Again.

Today, like it had been for months, Tan was alone. The soldiers stopped coming with him after an argument about enough being enough and why couldn't Tan see Duncan wasn't about to crack? But Tan maintained Duncan would. It was just a matter of time.

The dialogue and actions were always the same with each visit.

"Get up," Tan said.

Duncan stood, his bony legs wobbly beneath him. He couldn't remember the last time he ate.

Tan unfastened the metal chair by the door that was chained to the wall by a small chain. The first time he fastened it there he told Duncan he didn't want him getting any ideas about waiting by the door with the chair raised over his head like a bat, ready to strike.

The captain brought the chair over to the middle of the room, its metal legs screeching along the floor. "Sit."

Duncan obeyed, each step round to the front of the chair making him think his legs weighed a hundred pounds each. He sat down and Tan clamped his wrists and ankles to the armrests and leg posts. Nathanael was beside him. Duncan hadn't seen him move over.

Insides heavy, shirtless body laced with sweat, Duncan waited for the next thing Tan was supposed to say.

"So we meet again, Mr. James. How about letting go?"

Duncan shook his head slowly, the same as always.

"No?" *Whap!*

Head ringing, Duncan grimaced as he waited for everything to settle down inside. Just before he thought his head was about to unscramble, Tan struck him again, this time from the other side. Cheek bone screaming, Duncan said as he always did: "I forgive you."

"I see."

And the dialogue was over.

Tan came and stood in front of him, a look of puzzlement upon his face. Peeking up from in behind his shoulder was the scaly creature, the same one that had come in with him over the past year. From a past bit of verbal altercation between the creature and Nathanael, Duncan knew the creature wasn't allowed to kill him. Not yet, anyway. Even now, Duncan still shuddered at the memory of the creature's low, hissing voice.

From an inside breast pocket of his uniform, Tan pulled out a white laboratory glove. He slipped it over his right hand and snugged it into place with his left. Squatting, he ran the gloved hand over Duncan's shirtless chest then paused by the ribs on his left side.

Oh Lord, give me strength, Duncan thought.

Tan slowly peeled back the gauze which was put in place two days ago after he took a stocky, rusted machete to Duncan's side, cleaving off a sizable chunk of flesh. The wound stung against the open air and stung even more when the sweat rolling down Duncan's skin dripped into it.

"What say you, Mr. James? Is He or is He not the Son of God? Is He or is He not your Savior?" Tan's gloved fingers tapped the sensitive flesh once, sending a tingle of pain over Duncan's middle.

Throat dry, Duncan could barely squeeze out his answer. What he would give for a glass of water. Even just a sip. "He" —he smacked his cracked lips a few times and sucked together his cheeks, trying to create some spit— "He . . . He is. He is both."

"He is both what?" Tan pinched the open wound and Duncan's shoulders jumped from the zing.

"My God and . . . m-my Savior."

Nathanael's sword went aflame, its point up against the scales of the creature's flesh. "He lives," he said.

Duncan wasn't sure if that was a reference to Christ or to himself.

Without saying a word, Tan dug three fingers into the open wound. Fireworks exploded inside Duncan's ribcage and stars danced before his vision as his entire body locked from the pain. He wanted to scream, wanted to cry out to God. Instead his voice locked; his body shook. Tan withdrew his fingers then plunged them back in, this time squeezing a hunk of flesh with his forefingers and thumb. He twisted the meat and Duncan's stomach was immediately soaked by a squirt of blood. Legs bouncing up and down in the shackles, Duncan tried to distract himself by focusing on what Nathanael was doing. The creature eyed the sword all the while still whispering into Tan's ear, urging him to "Break this guy" and "It'll only be a matter of time until he denies Him."

"Nathanael . . . pl-please . . ." Duncan gasped. "Help . . . m-me."

"You shall wear a crown, the highest of all," the angel said. "You shall be as bright as the morning. Your blood shall be avenged at His Coming."

I don't want to wait. Help me now. Help me now! "K-kill me. Puh-please." The words came out in short one-syllable bursts.

Tan stopped then slammed his left fist into Duncan's stomach. Body lurching forward, Duncan's insides rocked from the blow. Dry heaving, his stomach pumping nothing but air—he couldn't breathe. Lungs pounding, body convulsing, he thought that if he didn't get air soon, he'd pass out and, hopefully, die.

"You shall see your son again," Nathanael said.

I don't want to hear it, Duncan thought. *You hear me? I don't want to hear it! No more. No more. I just want to die. I just. . . .* Hot breath wrapped its ugly warmth around his head, the air laced with the scent of sulfur and rotting fish.

Something crawled up along his back and wrapped its hard fingers around his shoulder.

A pair of pale gray eyes stared at him.

5

"That's it, let it go," the creature hissed.

The other behind Tan cackled.

Duncan couldn't breathe. He. Couldn't. Breathe. Stomach pushing his intestines upward, chest heaving, throat locking—he tried to inhale. A slow trickle of air came in.

Shhhh, he told himself. He wanted to close his eyes to help himself relax but the battered and burnt-scarred flesh kept his eyes in a state of "openness" all the time. He breathed in again, this time getting a little more air.

Tan pressed a palm against Duncan's forehead and threw his head back. The base of his skull smacked against the top of the iron backrest of the chair. Green stars burst before his eyes; his neck throbbed.

The creature was now on his lap, in between him and Tan.

"What say you, Mr. James? Do you really think you can hold out? Do you really think You-know-Who would want you to suffer like this?" The creature crawled up him and looked him in the eye. Its foul breath made Duncan gag just as he was able to breathe in another tiny bit of air. Coughing, he couldn't make out the creature's words but he thought he heard something along the lines of, "Do you think Kyle *really* endured? That he's in Heaven?"

Kyle . . .

The creature's goop-slicked tongue darted out from beneath its teeth, its forked tip about to connect with his face. Fire came down like a wall in between him and creature: Nathanael's sword. The creature howled when its tongue licked the flame.

"That's far enough," Nathanael said.

Gloved fingers ran back over Duncan's chest down to his left side and Tan gripped the wound again, this time with his whole hand.

In unison, Tan and the creature on his back said, "Is this Jesus the Messiah? Is He God?" He squeezed the gob of flesh in his fist.

Screaming, Duncan kicked his legs against the clamps around his ankles. His hands, balled up into fists, fought against the bracelets keeping his wrists in place.

Oh Lord, oh Jesus! Take me Home! Take me Home!

Then, a calm voice inside his heart, *"Soon."*

"Let go! Let go!" Duncan shrieked.

Tan laughed. So did the creature.

"Please! Please! I'll say whatever—" *No! But maybe I can fool him into thinking I'll give in. What if I somehow*—but something inside him told him that would be lying. And even under the circumstances, he doubted Jesus would understand. Even Christ Himself told the truth while He was being beaten and tortured. Must be like Jesus.

Blood poured out of the wound, drenching his legs: a big, dark red pool in his lap.

Head fuzzy, reality began to distance itself away. Duncan's eyes were heavy and he forgot he didn't have any eyelids to close even if he wanted to.

Left side.

Low. Pulsing. Sharp . . .

. . . pain.

Tan finally let go.

The world went dark.

*   *   *

Bright yellow and orange flame lit up the room, illuminating the light gray eyes of six demonic creatures so they were nearly white. A gold robe appeared before Duncan as Nathanael took position in front of him.

The creatures leaned back on their haunches, their mouths extended to an impossible length, white teeth gleaming, like raptors ready to strike. Forked tongues sprang forth out of their mouths, each tongue snapping out like a whip then recoiling back into their dark caverns. The creatures were in a semi-circle around the chair. Duncan's arms and legs were still held firmly in place by the cuffs and chains.

One of the creatures lunged for Nathanael. Then another and another. Nathanael spun around and ran his flaming sword through the first one flying through the air. The creature caught on it like a piece of pork on a skewer. Nathanael sharply withdrew the blade; the demon dropped to the floor, flopping and flipping. As it writhed on the ground, gushes of dark green fluid spilled from its chest. The other two tore at Nathanael's robe, the fabric replacing itself each time a piece was torn away and thrown to the side in shimmering gold sparkles. The angel side-stepped a few feet away, leaving Duncan wide open to the other three creatures in the room. Head aching with something far worse than a migraine, Duncan eyed one intently, wondering why so many had come for him at one time.

A foul shriek not far away then Nathanael was back in front of him, cleaving the head off one that dove toward Duncan's middle. One of the creatures landed on Nathanael's back, its long fingers reaching around, digging its claws into the angel's robe to what Duncan assumed was immortal flesh underneath.

"Lord, be with us," he managed. And as if those words were a trigger, one of the creatures hopped on top of the chair, landing against it without sound though Duncan felt the dull *thunk* deep in his spirit.

Nathanael ripped the creature off his back and threw it to the floor, following through by plunging his sword deep between the creature's eyes.

"Help . . ." Duncan wheezed.

Nathanael moved for him but another creature wrapped its scaly body around the angel's legs, opened its mouth and bit deep and hard through Nathanael's robe. Nathanael growled and the flames on his sword grew brighter.

Long, gray fingers gripped Duncan's skull, its nails hard and smelling like charcoal. It pressed then poked, then sunk its claws into his head.

Screaming, Duncan tried to leave the chair but was snapped back to what was happening when his arms and legs refused to budge.

The creature by Nathanael's legs screamed and was cut in three. The green fluid spilling from the wounds steamed and smelled of wet dog and dead fish.

Blinded by the blood pouring from his head over his eyes, Duncan bit his lips. Any moment now he would be in Heaven.

"You will not enter the City gates. You couldn't save your son and that's counted against you," the creature hissed.

"Silence!" Nathanael boomed and suddenly the pressure and sharpness against Duncan's skull alleviated.

A wet slopping sound came from somewhere behind Duncan and when he realized the creature that almost had him was destroyed did the blood flowing from his skull cease and disappear before his eyes.

The world tossed and turned, the tiny cement-lined room they were in tilting to the side. Nathanael kept his sword at the ready.

"Th-thank you," Duncan said.

"Do not worry, my friend," the angel said. "It will be over soon."

6

How do you count the hours before you die? Duncan thought.

He hardly slept. There had been no way to get comfortable in the chair.

Nathanael stood guard throughout the night. The creatures didn't return.

"Nathanael?" he said.

The angel drew near.

"I'm . . . I'm . . ."

"Thirsty, I know."

"It's been" —he took a deep breath— "two days since . . . since they've given me anything." The inside of his mouth felt as if it were filled with dry earth screaming for rain.

"I know, son. I know. Like He thirsted, so you will thirst. Like He suffered, so you have suffered, but not because you deserve it; you are made righteous in Him. You will experience the Father's loss and resurrection, so you will be drawn closer to Him."

Kyle. Every day in the cell Duncan thought of him. Everyday but yesterday. How could he forget him? Didn't he love him?

Didn't he?

*   *   *

Mind thick with thought, heart overflowing with despair, Duncan drifted away to a place deep within himself. Far, far away . . .

"Dad?" It was Kyle's voice but Kyle wasn't with him. Until . . .

The inside of the cell melted away and Duncan was standing outside on the bay, the sky clear, the sun bright. The pain that was a part of his body was gone. Six-year-old Kyle rode his bike up ahead, getting further and further away from him.

Memory of the cell faded away.

"Kyle!" Duncan said and started chasing after him. He had to get to him in time before his son fell. At least, Duncan thought he was supposed to fall.

Kyle turned his head to look over his shoulder. The handlebars went at a right-angle and he toppled over, the left side of his head hitting the pavement.

Duncan rushed up to him, wiping the tears from his eyes. His son lay on the ground and rolled onto his back, stunned. On his knees beside him, Duncan quickly checked him over. There wasn't a scratch on him. Kyle kept his head stationary, eyeing him, his small hand reaching up, asking his father for help. Taking the boy's hand, he was about to pull him up but Kyle quickly jerked his hand away when Duncan's fingers touched the inside of his palm.

"What's wrong," Duncan said gently.

Kyle grimaced, tears rimming his eyes.

Carefully, he took his son's hand, reassuring him everything would be okay. Holding Kyle's tiny hand in his, he examined the palm. A jolt ran through him when he saw the skin was red and shiny, freshly burned.

"How—" His eyes drifted over to the handlebars and instead of the thick black rubber grips, the bars were bright red like hot steel. "Come here." And Duncan quickly pulled his boy away from the bike.

Just then Kyle lost it and began crying uncontrollably. Screaming from the pain, his body went limp as Duncan scooped him up in his arms.

"We have to get you to the hospital." He checked his boy's head. A small gash about half an inch deep at the side of Kyle's head dampened his hair.

"It hurts, it hurts."

"I know. We'll take care of it. Come on." Pushing his legs to move as fast as he could, he couldn't seem to walk fast enough. Each step forward shoved his house across the way one step back. He might as well have been walking in place.

"I'm sorry, Dad. I tried my best. I tried so hard." Kyle whimpered. "I just couldn't do it."

"It's not your fault." Those handlebars. Glancing back at them, they still burned bright and red.

"Let me go!" And Kyle squirmed out of his father's arms. Feet landing solidly on the pavement, the boy ran away, back toward the bike.

"Kyle! Get back here. Now!" He chased after him.

"I'm leaving, Dad. I'm leaving."

Kyle gripped the handlebars, smoke immediately rising where his flesh made contact. Somehow the boy braved the pain and hoisted the bike up. He got on and began riding away, without any up-and-go assistance from his father.

Duncan ran after him but Kyle was too fast. Soon enough, the boy was at the edge of the bay then turned right and sped on down the street, Duncan chasing him.

Chasing him.

And chasing him.

No matter how hard he ran, he couldn't leave the bay.

"Agh!" He dug his heels into the pavement and pushed his legs till they burned. Nothing. No ground gained. Duncan fell to his knees and called out for his son.

Silence.

Heart aching, a warm wind swept over him.

"Come back," he whispered. Then something inside changed.

Peace.

The sun shone brightly above, as if a promise that everything was going to be okay.

And his son would return.

*   *   *

"Duncan," Nathanael said. "Be ready. Tan is here."

Shaking his head, Duncan tried to suppress the—dream?—and readied himself. The door screeched open and Tan entered. The door slammed closed, sending a shockwave of sound throughout his entire being.

The captain came over to him and squatted down. "So we meet again, Mr. James. How about letting go?"

Duncan shook his head.

"No?" Tan's open palm flew in from the side, smacking against Duncan's cheek bone, reigniting the bruise that was already there in a flash of pain.

Taking a deep breath, Duncan waited for— And the shot came from the other side, this time harder than ever before, sending his head craning to the right beyond what his neck muscles could bear. Something tore inside his neck but he didn't know what. No matter. This would all be over soon. Hopefully.

"I . . . I forgive you," Duncan said.

"I see."

Tan stood, dusted his hands off then went over to the door where a new chair was chained to the wall. Duncan hadn't noticed anyone bring it in. Tan had also brought a briefcase in with him. That was new, too.

After setting the briefcase on the seat, Tan picked up the chair and slammed it down hard in front of Duncan. He picked up the briefcase, sat down, then set the briefcase on his lap.

"I have something for you," Tan said. He opened the briefcase, raising its lid so Duncan couldn't see what was inside. But that didn't matter. As far as Tan was concerned, Duncan couldn't see anyway.

The sound of metal on plastic clunked around on the other side of the lid as Tan felt around for something. Once he located what he was looking for, he pulled out a small object, concealing it in his hand and closed the lid. Neatly he placed the briefcase on the floor beside his chair.

"I wish give you one last offer," the captain said.

Not on your life, Duncan thought but the words in his mind didn't seem as *reassuring* as usual. *Not on your life*, he repeated in his head, this time with a little more backbone. There, that was more like it.

"I said—" Tan began.

"I heard you. What?"

"I have arranged for you to leave here in a few moments time. My men will escort you out of the city where you'll fly by charter out of the country, back to your homeland. It's over, Mr. James. You're free."

He wasn't stupid. "But?"

"But nothing. Well, there is one thing."

How long was Tan going to toy with him? He already knew what the captain was going to say. Why couldn't he just say it? Why the so-called suspense?

"What?" Duncan said.

"No need to get—what's the word you Canadians use? 'Feisty'? —with me." He leaned in close; his breath smelled like stale cigar, but there was another smell underneath, that of old smoke. Something like a burned-up book of matches.

"Just say it, Tan. I haven't got all day." Now that was the guts he was looking for in his voice. No more playing timid.

Boy, he was thirsty.

"Very well." Tan sat back in his chair. He pulled the object up where he could see it but still kept it from Duncan's view. "One more chance. Deny Jesus Christ as Lord and you will live."

Nathanael came and stood behind Tan. Tan's lip curled up in a quick flinch but settled back down. The Chinese captain was acting a little peculiar today. But that could have been his imagination.

"No," Duncan said. "Jesus is Messiah. Always has been, always will be. You might as well kill me now."

Tan smiled a small smile then moved himself so he was sitting on the edge of his chair, his body a few short inches away. He pulled up the object: a pair of rusted pliers with a black grip.

Without saying a word, he took Duncan's right hand, gripping it with a strength that seemed unbecoming of a man of Tan's small height and size.

"Look at me," Nathanael said.

Duncan obeyed and lost himself in the angel's fiery eyes. Something touched the tip of his index finger then a sharp burst of hot pain ran through it, all the way up his hand. Jerking his hand back, his wrist screamed as it was cut against the metal cuff keeping it in place. Tan yanked his hand forward, setting it back where it was. The warmth of blood coated the top of Duncan's finger, wet the tip then pooled in between the palm and the armrest.

"He is coming for you," the angel said. "Lift your head high."

Duncan raised his chin up, waiting for Heaven to open before him. It didn't come . . . and Tan tore the nail out of his middle finger. Hand bouncing up, Tan grabbed it and squeezed it so hard Duncan thought the Chinese soldier would break every bone in his hand. The blood oozing from his finger quickly became a balm to the wound.

There were still three fingers to go.

Tan grabbed his ring finger, and Duncan's eyes widened against the scarred flesh rimming his eye sockets as he prepared himself for the next—*Rip!*

He screamed.

"Do not be afraid, Duncan," Nathanael said. "Hold fast. Your Master is coming."

Tan's fingers slipped on Duncan's blood-slicked skin as he tried to grip the pinky finger. When he pulled the nail, on some level Duncan sighed with relief. This one didn't hurt as bad. Then Tan took the thumb . . . and pulled.

"No! Stop!" Duncan said before he realized he said it.

"Yes?" Tan said.

Thumb pounding with heated throbs, Duncan barely found the strength to shake his head. "Nothing."

Tan only grinned.

7

Hands soaked with blood, Duncan sat there shaking. "I . . . I . . . I . . ." His words came out quivery and try as he might, he couldn't form the next sound. *I forgive you* was what he wanted to say but, ashamedly, he knew he no longer meant it.

"Wh-wh-what!" Tan shouted. The sudden loudness of the Chinese man's voice made him wince. "Nothing. I know."

Tan leaned closer and with one hand held Duncan's head in place. Duncan tried to turn his head away but the man's solid hold on him . . . His skull might as well have been in a clamp. Tan put the pliers beneath Duncan's nose then set the cartilage dividing the nostrils between the rough, metal teeth.

"Hold still," Tan said.

And pulled.

Blood gushed forth, splashing over Duncan's lips. Not thinking, he breathed in through his nose and inhaled a tablespoon of blood. His head ignited as if he had just done a handstand in a pool and filled his nasal cavities with water. Gagging, he tried to blow the blood out his nose. The exhale set fire to his skull and his head swam. A punch to the face and the next thing he knew, his head was bowed as he watched the blood ooze off his face in thick crimson ribbons, pooling in his lap.

Nathanael was gone.

"No!" Duncan tried to say but it came out more like "noeb." *No more, Lord. No more. Take me Home. Take me Home!*

Eyes fixated on his lap, he couldn't get a clear view of what Tan was doing. A moment later, Tan raised Duncan's head and looked him in the eye.

"I know you can see me," Tan said.

The jolt rattled every part of Duncan's being. His heart stopped.

Then resumed low, steady beats.

The salty taste of sulfur touched Duncan's tongue.

"I've known since you first prayed that prayer," Tan said. "It's your kind, you Christians, who mock me and think I'm a fool. You have no idea how smart I really am, how attuned to humanity I've become."

Light steely gray eyes with blue irises peered up over Tan's right shoulder. Then another pair over his left. Then another over his head. Then pairs upon pairs around his arms, waist and legs. Their gaze penetrated Duncan, deep in his spirit. Heart speeding, he wanted to turn away—longed to—but was compelled to look at them. The creatures pulled away from Tan, a dozen of them, and surrounded the two men in a semi-circle.

"Nadabael," Duncan whispered. "Helb . . ."

"He is gone. You've been handed over to me. Don't you see?" He slammed his palms against either side of Duncan's head and pulled him in hard and fast so their foreheads collided. A dull *thunk* bounced around inside his skull; his vision flashed black before coming back blurred. Tan didn't seem fazed by the blow. "No one can save you. Not even Jesus, the One you're willing to die for."

The creatures drew in closer, tongues flicking out from behind elongated fangs.

Was it true? Was Tan right? How could Tan know what he—

Tan pushed Duncan away, sending the chair rocking backward before landing back down hard against the cement. The jar of the impact set Duncan's fingers alight with pain anew. A fresh splash of blood sprayed from his nose.

My Lord and my God, Duncan thought. *You said You'd never leave me. You said You'd be with me till the end of the age. Where are You? Where are You! Did You li—*

A crowbar came at him, the hooked end plowing in to just below his rib and just above the wound Tan played with. . . . When was it? Earlier? Yesterday? Two days ago? Insides locking, sharp hurt filled his torso. Tan adjusted his hold on the crowbar; the tool protruded out from Duncan like a lever.

The creatures were right up to him now, each hissing and whispering something he didn't hear with his ears but in his mind.

"You've failed," one said.

"Release yourself," said another.

"Can't you see he's right?" said one more.

And, "Your Messiah will not come for you."

"Let go, Mr. James. Let go and be with me like you once were." Tan pulled down on the lever. Two ribs burst through Duncan's flesh, sending out a spray of blood and stringy tissue.

"Gah . . ." There was no scream. The pain . . . the blood. . . . His insides went numb. Shaking in the chair, Duncan tried to scream. No sound came. He wanted to cry but his tears would not break through the seared flesh over his eyes.

"Why hang on, Duncan?" Tan's voice was now soft and tender, like a loving mother consoling her child. "Can't you see it was all a lie? Can't you see it was all for nothing?" He paused. Then, "I'd never lie to you."

Duncan's head lolled to the side. *Maybe he's right,* he thought. He coughed and blood bubbled in his throat. The air suddenly seemed to stop entering his lungs. Only a small amount found its way in, on his right side. His left lung was punctured, deflated. Useless. *Nathanael. . . . If the angel was real, so must be Jes—*

He howled when the crowbar slammed through the flesh on his right side.

"Say it's over!" Tan growled, his voice low and raspy. "Let go!"

Kyle, come back. Kyle, I want to see you. Kyle, my son. I love you. No air was coming in. Lungs pounding, head buzzing, Duncan hoped for . . . Where was Heaven?

Darkness.

A wet popping followed by the splatter of wet string against the pavement. His right side burst into burning agony, his left side flaring up along with it.

No air.

Nothing.

But he could still hear Tan speaking and still hear his heart beat in his ears. "Fool! You've always been a fool. Always!"

Duncan could barely see. Tan was nothing more than a blur of . . . white? Nathanael? But there wasn't a flaming sword, no golden robe. The white light of the humanoid cursed at him and he held up the crowbar like a baseball bat and brought it full swing across Duncan's head. All went dark and he didn't need to see to know half his face just went missing.

Fire crawled along his skin and his facial bones and skull cried out in agony.

Could he speak? Could he say—

The pain . . .

"Release him!" The Voice filled the room. The same Voice Duncan heard deep within his heart every time he prayed, the same Voice that told him He'd be with him always. The same Voice which restored his sight.

Jesus, I'm coming Home, he thought.

Just then a bright light encompassed everything, a light so startlingly brilliant it muted out Tan's white-light form, making it almost black in comparison.

Tan screamed and called out to the Voice, saying that it wasn't his time.

A loud vibrating boom shook the cell and the sound of tumbling cinder blocks and cracking cement was sweet music to Duncan's ears.

The creatures screamed and shrieked and exploded in sprays of green goo. Tan growled and the brilliant white grew brighter, its Glory drowning him out completely.

"Duncan," the Voice said, "time to come Home."

The pain abated.

And Duncan left himself behind, surrendering to a promise set in motion long before Time began.

YOUR AVERAGE ORDINARY ALIEN

Adam Graham

Adam Graham is a professional writer, blogger, poet and journalist whose work appears on *Renew America, American Daily, The Conservative Voice, Conservatown*, and *Red State*. On **Adam's Blog**, one of the most popular blogs on the internet, Adam comments on U.S. society and politics; he also hosts **The Adam Graham Podcast**.

Familiar with behind-the-scenes politics as well as candidacy, Mr. Graham penned a political satire, *The Screwtape Reports* (2005). Adam grew up in the American West and graduated in 2002 with honors (Associate of Arts Degree: emphasis in Journalism). He now resides in Idaho with his wife Andrea.

What if Aliens are just like us? The popular thought behind much of science fiction is that aliens will be the salvation and many of our culture's primitive needs will be explained. "Your Average Ordinary Alien" was inspired by science fiction fans who often view aliens as more than characters on a TV screen, but as a hope for the future. The aliens would come down from space with the wisdom of the Universe to guide us to a better world. This story asks what happens if the aliens came but turned out to be all too ordinary.

THE MALNARIAN GRABBED JAMES and sank its teeth into the human's well tanned back, blood spurting all over the purple rocks and green sand. An energy beam zapped the Malnarian in the back. It turned. Yornac stood in his priestly robe. "Leave him alone in the name of peace."

Kirk leaned forward in his chair. Enough with the talk, Yornac. Zap that bad boy.

The Malnarian dropped the human and approached Yornac.

The priest raised his hands. "You leave me no choice. By the power of the seven moons of Galvark, you will die."

The Malnarian shrieked in horror as its body decomposed. Yornac ran towards the human. "James, please, by all that is—"

An Earth woman about a meter and a half tall and of medium

build blocked Kirk's view of Yornac. The spiky-haired vixen hit a button and the television screen went black.

Recognition hit Kirk. He glared up at Terry. "What are you doing, woman? I need to find out what happened with Yornac."

Terry rolled her eyes. "Relax, you Tivoed it. Kirk, I don't know how to say this. So I guess I'll just—I'm leaving." Tears sparkled in her eyes.

Oh no! His sustenance was being cut off. And worse, who would keep his bed warm on cold winter nights? He stood and put his arms around her. "Baby, I'm sorry. I know it's been a bit of a cold spell since I got laid off."

Terry shook him off. "It's been four years since you were laid off and all you've done is live off me. You've spent all your time and money at sci-fi conventions. Even if you looked for a job, you couldn't find one after that name change last year."

Kirk grunted, plopping on the couch. She didn't think he was a loser back when he was earning $80k working for a dot com. She'd loved riding in his BMW and sitting in the hot tub of his plush apartment. Back then, it was all "you're so funny and smart." Now, after a short time out of work, she thought he was a bum. "Look, taking the name Kirk Picard Skywalker won't stop anyone from hiring me. Come on, something's changed."

Terry paced. "It's the church I'm going to."

Kirk jumped up. "I knew it! Those religious fanatics have nothing better to do than disrupt our happy home."

Terry bit her lip. "You said you were going to marry me when you moved in."

"I will. Just give me some more time. A former coworker in Japan e-mailed me a prospect."

"Your old coworkers in Japan are twenty-something losers who stay in their pajamas all day and live in their parents' basements."

"Their garages!"

Terry rolled her eyes.

Kirk heaved a sigh. Didn't she know the difference? "Look, why believe this tripe about living in sin? All this has brought the world is suffering. When people let go of religion and embrace rationality, mankind will reach the stars and become gods."

Terry gave Kirk a peck on the cheek, like she might give her brother. She ran her hand across his uniform shirt, touching the Star Fleet logo before withdrawing. "Kirk, it's a nice story, but it's not true. I can't live like this anymore. I've got to go." Terry strode toward the door.

What would he do without real human contact? Then again, she'd been the ice princess for the past few months, thanks to the Church, but as long as she stayed, he had a shot. "The Bible and science fiction don't have to be contradictory. Ezekiel saw a UFO, and do you really think Jonah was swallowed by a whale? No, classic case of alien abduction."

Terry turned around. "Look, I'm not even to that part of the Bible yet. Good bye."

"But wait! You're my Princess Leah! I'm a Klingon and you're a female Klingon."

Terry closed the door behind her. Kirk plopped on the couch. How was he going to pay the rent? This must be why she'd had him re-sign the lease in his name alone last month. She said she didn't like being on the same lease if they weren't married. Eight hundred dollars in five weeks. How was he going to come up with that?

He looked up at the life-sized, autographed Luke Skywalker action figure standing by the closet. Selling it would pay the rent. No, that would be joining the Dark Side.

Kirk cried, "I'll never join you!"

If he sold his collection, what would he tell the guys over at the Sci-Fi message boards? How could he live it down? He'd used the joint credit card account he had with Terry to acquire an admirable sci-fi collection: one of the best online.

Oh great! That ungrateful wench had probably closed the credit card, too. Maybe he could get a job. McDonald's was hiring. They were always hiring. But no, he couldn't work at McDonald's. That would debase him. He hadn't gotten a computer science degree to flip burgers! Still, a guy had to eat until They came.

He looked out the window. A star streaked through the night sky. It was silly to wish upon a star, but he had done it anyway. It was an odd wish, and an ultra-fundamentalist like Terry wouldn't understand, but he wanted to be abducted by aliens.

He didn't want brought back either. They had to let him join them. He looked at his bulging belly. Hopefully, they weren't as strict about weight as the air force.

Kirk awoke on a metal table with his arms strapped down and a soft metal alien headband on his forehead. Yes! This was more like it. He looked around. A green humanoid alien wearing a dark blue uniform and black boots faced the wall, his oversized head casting a shadow against the gray corridor. The ceiling glowed pure white and a gray metal door reflected the gleaming room behind Kirk.

He grinned. "Woo hoo!"

The Alien turned around and sighed. His round orange eyes focused on Kirk. "Accursed fecal matter. The anesthetic should have lasted two yorlans longer."

Kirk gasped. "You speak English?"

The Alien laughed. "Of course, we have Coca-Cola, too, and we have to learn English to deal with the Americans. They're taking over the universe."

Kirk arched his eyebrow. So that's what the government was hiding. "Really?"

The Alien tilted back his head and chortled. "Humans are so gullible. The device around your head allows you to understand any spoken language."

"I could have used this in French class. Now what?"

"With most humans who wake up, I have to sedate them and do a memory wipe. But with you it won't be necessary."

Kirk smiled. "You see in me a kindred spirit with whom you can share the secrets of the universe? Cool."

"No. I saw inside your apartment. No one would believe you."

"Oh." Kirk paused. "So how far do you live from here?"

"About twenty Earth metres."

"Huh?"

"Oh, you mean how far is my home? My planet is located in the Marchovias Galaxy, several light years from here." The Alien looked up at a light on the wall next to a steel door. "Please remain motionless." He walked over to the wall and pressed a button.

Kirk screamed. The device grabbed his nose. Kirk cried in a nasally voice. "No, I don't want to die!"

The Alien growled. "Will you stop it! You're not going to die."

The machine yanked out one of his nose hairs and Kirk yelped. The device released his nose and retracted. The Alien put the hair in a round case and placed it on a table. "It will be just a few yemnars while we analyze it."

"Why did you do that?" asked Kirk.

"A biological scan detected a flaw in two percent of the human population of your industrialized countries. Due to exposure to electromagnetic waves in recent years, the cellular structure of these humans has weakened. Our analysis indicates these humans will begin to break down genetically within ten years."

"What will that mean?"

The Alien leaned against the wall. "Their cells will drift apart until they completely disappear. In theory, it could cause an atomic reaction, but they would die before it reached that point."

Uh-oh. That's what he got for using the computer twenty hours straight. "Do I have it?"

"We don't know yet. That's why we're running the test on your nasal hair. We're close to coming up with a digestible cure that should eliminate the disease before it actually develops; your governments will place it in your water supplies. The disease will be cured before anyone knows they have it. One of your computer makers sent out a software patch that changes the power settings to limit the damage."

"Whoa. So you're working with the government and the computer industry?"

"Of course. The computer companies sent us a hundred thousand bushels of hemp. They know what type of lawsuits this will cause if we fail."

Wait a second. "You're getting paid for this?"

"Yes, hemp is a valuable product we use for construction on my world. When we return home we'll sell it to the building industry, who'll sell it to consumers."

What? Had he been captured by Ferengi? These cold-blooded capitalists would do anything for a buck. "And what would you do if we couldn't give you any materials that you needed?"

The Alien licked the area above his mouth. "If you didn't have any materials we needed, you also wouldn't have been advanced enough to get yourself into this predicament in the first place."

"But you should be doing this for free!"

"Where do you volunteer?"

"Um, well . . . nowhere."

"Why should we? We're saving six million of your fellow Americans from splitting apart into tiny pieces and we're just asking for plants. I think that's a fair exchange. Besides, it's very hard to put eleven children through college on volunteer work."

Didn't he get it? Where was the enlightenment? "Surely not every alien race is a bunch of capitalists out for profit."

The Alien sat the end of the table and pulled a small cube out of his pocket. A picture of a tiny red alien with green eyes appeared on top the cube. "This is Kunichita. I give thirty qindels a month to help him. On his world, there's no money, no trade, no merchants, only a state that will take care of the citizens and serve as their benefactor while it seeks to build a perfect world."

"That sounds more like it."

"No, they live in absolute poverty. Without the help of sponsors like me, he has no food, no nothing. All the well-intentioned drivel in the universe and none of it can compare to the results of diligent hands working to build for themselves."

"Oh come on, there has to be some advanced race that's not so greedy."

"Tell me, you have something on your planet called communism, don't you?"

"Yeah, the communists were portrayed in Star Trek II as Khan and his men. Though Reagan also referred to the communists by making a reference to Star Wars—"

"I care not for your games. Has this system ever made a people wealthy?"

Kirk remembered the bread lines in Russia. "No."

"Then why would it work on another planet?"

"But what are you going to do with all that money?"

The Alien looked at the cube of Kunichita. "When I go home I'll fly to his planet and make him my son."

"But you shouldn't interfere with another culture. Who are you to judge?"

"Who are you to judge me for judging them? What idiot would have a problem with interfering in the affairs of another species if there's a poor little male without a father?" The Alien ran his hand across his barren scalp. "You know what I really want to do? I'll be able to retire next year and spend more time helping the poor churches on my world."

"Wait, you have churches on your planet? But they're not Christian churches. They're just like temples, right?"

"No, they're Christian churches."

Now this was too much. "Whoa, Jesus was born on Earth."

The Alien turned his head sideways. "Yes, the Prophet Melnish had a vision of Christ. Many thought he was dead and placed him in a tomb. When Melnish emerged from the tomb, we believed his message. Though mockers scorned us for centuries, the discovery of Earth has caused a slight relaxation in skepticism."

At a beep, a metal slide fell out of the wall. The Alien got up and grabbed it. "Good news, you don't have the genetic flaw and are unlikely to ever develop it. Unfortunately, that makes you of limited use for our study, but we may find some anti-bodies we can use."

No way did a species become this advanced without more than this. "Come on, you're holding out on me. Tell me the secrets of the universe."

The Alien sat down. "I'm so glad you asked. According to the Prophet Melnish, they are as follows: One, serve God and worship Christ with all that you have. Two, love your family and care for them. Three, work hard, labor with diligence for the diligent hand shall prosper. Four, save ten percent of what you earn and give ten percent of what you earn and you shall be blessed. Five, rest one Zannon a Yavlock. For you, just rest one day a week. Six, eat moderately and exercise. Seven, aim for peace with everyone. Eight, be compassionate to the poor, the needy, and the stranger."

Kirk's jaw dropped. "That's it? I could have gotten that off a box of tea."

"Yes. Melnish Tea is delicious indeed and teaches the lessons that all creatures must learn to have a good life. Now, let me release you and I'll take you back."

After the Alien had released Kirk from the table, Kirk jumped up.

"Wipe my memory!"

The Alien blinked. "Excuse me? That's really unnecessary and could cause vomiting."

"Look. You've ruined my life tonight. I finally get to meet an alien and he tells me that you're just flying green WASPs."

The Alien looked up. "There's no insect on the ship, I assure you."

Kirk grabbed the Alien. "I want the blue pill! I don't want to remember this. I want hope that there are better aliens out there. You're lying about them! The secrets of the universe can be found, you're just lying about them."

A dart of pain shot through Kirk's body.

The Alien said, "I don't understand you, Kirk Skywalker. Why would you live in a fantasy world when you know the truth? But as you wish, I'll wipe your memory. I shall keep you in my prayers."

The room spun into darkness.

Kirk sat up in bed. The clock said eleven a.m. Man, he had to get up earlier if he wanted to find a job.

He walked to the kitchen and opened the fridge. Terry had left it almost full. He had enough food to last a couple weeks, but then what? He walked into the living room. Life-sized Luke Skywalker smiled, with his light saber drawn.

For some reason, it seemed less important than before. If worst came to worst, he could sell it, but he had a lot more he could get rid of before he got to that point.

He swung open the front door and scooped the paper off the step. He brought it inside and pulled out the comics and the TV guide. He reached for a part of the paper he hadn't touched in years—the classifieds. Maybe, he'd take a look at it in the afternoon.

He plopped on the couch, picked up the remote, and turned on the television. The TV flickered and a better world of space aliens and pirates emerged. For some reason, he found it harder to believe than he did yesterday.

ALLISON

Deborah Cullins-Smith

Dedicated to my beloved daughter, Allison. Note: All scriptural references adapted from KJV.

WAITING IS NEVER EASY when you are only eight years old, and Allison squirmed, impatiently awaiting the arrival of her caregiver. Rachel had been her guardian for as long as Allison could remember. Her gentle voice and comforting arms made the tiny child feel secure and cherished. Rachel's presence almost made up for the absence of Allison's mother—almost.

Allison brushed a trembling hand through her curly honey-brown hair. All her life, she'd waited for this momentous day. Finally, God granted all those earnest prayers, those requests tearfully whispered at her bedside.

Today she would see her mother.

Allison glanced down at her carefully chosen garments. She thought about wearing a fancy, fluffy dress, but just didn't feel right in such frivolous trimmings. She never had possessed a "pink bow personality." Now Jenny represented the picture of a perfectly frilly little girl! Allison loved her friend, but sometimes envied the dainty sugar-and-spice pixie of a child. Beside Jenny, Allison felt awkward and tomboyish.

"Be yourself," Rachel had told her many times. "If *you* are comfortable, this meeting will be easier for both of you."

With a sigh, Allison resigned herself to blue jeans and a sweater, her normal attire.

"I hope Mommy won't be disappointed in me," Allison said to her reflection in the long mirror. "Maybe she won't mind that I don't wear ruffles and lace."

Her mother . . .

How her little heart soared. Yet . . . there was just a touch of apprehension, too. She knew that she couldn't go to live with her mother, but she longed to see her—just see her—even if only for a moment or two.

Of course, God knew best. She trusted Him with all her heart, and she knew with a child's confidence that His decisions were always right, His timing was perfect, and He was never, ever late. So she waited with quiet faith, and prayed with all her heart. Sometimes the strong longing weighed upon her like a huge block of marble. But her trusting little heart remained steadfast. God would answer her prayers someday. And in the meantime, she waited, praying a little harder each time she knelt.

"It's all arranged, angel," Rachel had said, sweeping into the child's room last night, her eyes sparkling with excitement. "You're going to see your mother tomorrow, Allison. Isn't it wonderful?" She danced into the room, and twirled the child in a wide circle, before they collapsed on the end of the bed in a breathless heap.

"I am?" Her voice sounded squeaky. "My very own Mommy?"

Allison's tummy did flip-flops, and her eyes filled with joyful tears. To yearn for so long, and pray so hard, and wait so patiently; it hardly seemed real!

"Really, Rachel?" Allison asked. "Really, truly?"

"Really, truly, my angel."

*   *   *

Allison's earliest memories echoed the instinctive longing for "Mommy", even as she curled herself into Rachel's loving arms. They often sat in the old-fashioned oak rocking chair as Rachel sang lullabies and praise songs in her soft contralto voice. Allison wondered how Rachel always seemed to know so much about her mother.

"I want Mommy," whimpered Allison.

"For now, my angel, Mommy can't be with us." Rachel's voice seemed to catch just a bit as she dried tears and kissed damp cheeks.

"But why, Rachel, why? I want my Mommy."

"Someday you'll meet her, lamb." Rachel's long, tapered fingers twirled Allison's honey-colored curls, gently smoothing the damp tangles.

"Why can't I see her now?" The child's question hung in the air, suspended by the frown creasing her brow.

Rachel sighed and kissed Allison's forehead. "Right now, she lives someplace where we can't go. But someday we'll see her. Someday when Father God says the time is right. Until then, we just have to trust Him." Tears glistened in the corners of Rachel's eyes, but did not fall. "I miss her, too," she whispered.

"Really, truly, Rachel?" Allison's eyes widened.

"Really, truly, my little angel." Rachel smiled. "Look to Jesus, lamb, and someday He'll make a way for you and your mommy to meet. Until then, we'll trust Him to take good care of her."

"But Rachel, I miss her now." Allison tried to trust Jesus like she'd been taught, but it's always hard to wait when a little girl wants her mother.

"Your mommy loves you, lamb," Rachel reassured the child. "For now, that must be enough. This isn't the way she wanted it, and I know she misses you as much as you miss her."

And Rachel rocked her to sleep, while stars glistened in the heavens like the silver teardrops that trickled down the little pink cheek.

*   *   *

The spacious lodgings rang with the laughter of bright-eyed children of every shape and size. Puppies and kittens romped among little bare feet that skipped and jumped and danced with joyous abandon in the airy hallways of the happy haven. Children came here in tearful despair, crying for Mama, reaching for love and security that had not been their lot in life. Scarred babes, shrieking in pain, helpless in the face of circumstances they could neither fathom nor bear, they flooded to The Home. For each child, a caregiver was assigned. The supply of volunteers seemed endless. The Home was a place of joy and comfort. Childhood was blessed in this place where fear and pain evaporated, banished from existence in the shadow of God's Throne. Once in awhile, the babes were reunited with parents in festive celebrations, lavish dinners, tears, kisses, and great big bear hugs. Celebrations like those gave the rest of the children hope.

"Someday my parents will come," they would say to one another, running off to jump and skip and play once again, their hearts light with rekindled joy.

Sometimes children grew and matured, becoming caregivers for the endless stream of babes, giving back the love they had received. The world wallowed in one big bloodbath, but the Home was a blessed safe haven. The children went to classes, learned art, music, and dance. They learned to read and write . . . and waited for their miracles.

*   *   *

Allison stared at the drawing, taped to the wall beside her bed. She remembered the day Miss Cherise asked her students to work on these projects in art class. For most of the children, this exercise encompassed the desire to see the parents they had never known. But how do you draw a picture of someone you've never seen?

Allison rested her chin in her cupped hands, elbows propped on the desk, a thoughtful frown shadowing her little face. She pondered the nebulous figure in her mind's eye. How do you begin? A shapeless being? A face you've never touched? Fingers you've never held onto as you took your first steps? Arms that never held you up to the sunshine and twirled you round in dizzying circles?

Miss Cherise stopped beside Allison and smiled tenderly at the earnest little face.

"Deep thoughts today, Allison?" she asked gently.

"Miss Cherise, how can I draw something . . ." Allison stopped and corrected herself, "some*one* that I've never seen?"

A loving smile, filled with affection for her young students, lit the kind face of their teacher. Her words always brimmed with warmth and the wisdom that only flows from a heart filled with love, a soul connected to God's Heart. Trusting eyes turned to Miss Cherise, confident that she knew the answers to all their questions.

Miss Cherise glided gracefully to the front of the classroom and perched on the edge of her desk. Her gentle gaze settled on each hopeful face, pausing to smile into every pair of eyes.

"You know, God has a marvelous way of creating each and every child with the same characteristics He used to mold the parents," she explained slowly, pausing to let her words sink into the spirits of her children. "When you look in a mirror, you are seeing a miniature reflection, in many ways, of your mommy and daddy. Maybe you have your mother's hair, your father's eyes, maybe Grandma's button nose." The children giggled. "Maybe you can start with what you see in yourselves. Think of the shape of your face, the curve of your cheek, the color of your hair. Look in your own hearts. You were formed in your mother's body. Some of your mother—and your father—rests in the person *you* are."

As her students chewed on the ends of pencils, processing these new thoughts, a little stream of delight trickled into the classroom. A few set to work with touching eagerness, their creative juices beginning to bubble up and flow through rapidly moving pencils.

Allison reached a tentative hand toward her own tousled curls, a tiny hint of moisture welling in the corner of her expressive light brown eyes. The seeds were planted. Miss Cherise watched the wheels turning. Allison searched herself for the keys to her parentage. It was a beginning—a small one—but a beginning.

Allison sketched brown hair framing an oval face, brown eyes, arched eyebrows, small mouth with a hint of a dimple at each end as it curved into a gentle smile. The shadowy figure gained substance.

Rachel hung the picture beside Allison's bed. She gazed at that face every morning, and smiled into the penciled eyes every night after she said her prayers. *Someday,* she thought, *someday . . . Mommy.*

* * *

Allison gazed at her mother's picture with a sigh and turned to the reflection in the long mirror. Her jeans were neat, her sweater blazed in the colors of an autumn afternoon in the meadow, and honey curls hung to her shoulders in glossy waves. Allison's hands trembled with excitement while a thousand butterflies fluttered nervously in her tummy.

"This will be a brief encounter," Rachel warned her. "Only a few minutes."

"But it's a start," said Allison, squaring her little shoulders.

Somehow Allison instinctively knew that her mother had not signed away her life maliciously. Some of her friends remembered the burning saline invading their little worlds, chasing them in the womb like wolves, ripping tiny limbs, explosions of pain, then the final shriek as their mangled bodies were abruptly consigned to crumpled newspapers, dirty trash bins, or the sterile stainless steel laboratories. In that final moment, they felt the gentle arms of a tearful Heavenly Father. Tenderness and love encompassed them, new luminous bodies housed their delicate little spirits, and the pain of this first form of rejection was forgotten in the moment of redemption.

Allison remembered an agonized scream: "Noooooooooooooooo!"

They grew in The Home; they played, laughed, loved, and learned in complete safety, in the shelter of God Himself. Nurtured, comforted, healed, the children waited, hoping for the joyful reunion with parents who resorted to drastic decisions of desperation, or had gone through the pain of premature loss. The Throne of God was open to these little children at all times, and they ran freely to their Heavenly Father with their questions, petitions, and joyful laughter.

Once in awhile, a child waited in vain. Those grew to be the kindest caregivers for the new additions to The Home's Nurseries, raising an infant to maturity then going back to take on another precious babe.

Rachel escorted Allison to the Throne Room. Jesus rested on the golden throne beside God the Father, a goblet of New Wine in His scarred hand. His countenance reflected the peace that flowed from His heart, and Allison released Rachel's hand to leap into His lap. Jesus' face lit up with a smile bright enough to illuminate all of Heaven and Father God laughed to see her happiness overflow.

"Are you ready, Allison?" Father God asked, gazing tenderly into her eyes. He kissed her forehead and playfully tweaked her nose with one hand while rescuing Jesus' wine with the other.

Allison swallowed hard, then nodded.

"You've always trusted me," Father God said, "so trust me in this as well. This will feel uncomfortable for a moment, for you've never known the world below. But My Hands will carry you to your mother and return you here in only moments."

* * *

Allison felt the world around her darken, as Rachel's smiling face faded from view. She peered around the shadowy room. A woman knelt beside the bed, weeping bitter tears, emptying her pain before the Throne of God. This was the very place Allison ran to and treasured as a sanctuary all her life! Allison sat on the end of the bed, feet tucked under her, and listened to the woman, watching in amazement as her drawing came to life before her eyes.

"Tell my baby I love her, Lord," she pleaded. "Why has she been on my heart so heavily, God? Why? I didn't want to lose her. A part of me died with her that day. Oh, God . . . I don't even know *how* I know she was a girl. I barely knew she was there and suddenly she was dying inside me. God, it hurts. It hurts. Please make sure she knows I didn't want it this way. I wanted her here with me."

The woman's swollen face came up and she caught her breath sharply as she met Allison's eyes. Allison smiled at her shyly. So this was Mother! Her hair really *was* brown, a little darker than Allison's own and curled around her face in damp streaks that hinted a touch of auburn. Her lips trembled with emotion, and her hand reached out tentatively toward Allison. Allison saw the long tapered fingers, so like Rachel's. The love in those eyes shone like Rachel's, too. The face was pale in the twilight of the room, but the longing emanating from Mommy wrapped around her like a hand-made shawl.

Mommy loved her!

"You're my daughter, aren't you?" the woman asked in a quavering voice. "My child . . ."

God's voice echoed in Allison's ears. "Come, Allison."

Allison smiled one last time at her mother before God swept her slowly away from the earthbound world and set her gently at Rachel's side. The Father smiled and caressed her cheek lovingly.

"It's My turn now," He said with a smile. "It's time she receives healing from the pain she's carried all these years, Allison. Don't worry, Child. Your mother will be fine. She belongs to me, too, and I'll take care of her for you. You'll see her again some day. I promise."

Allison fell into His arms, her heart too full to express all the gratitude overflowing her little soul. What a blessing to know that the Father heard her heart cries just as clearly as He heard her voice!

"There, there," He said, stroking those precious curls. "She knows you're well and happy. That will bring her peace for now." Father God nodded to His Son and with a final hug, Jesus left to comfort the broken woman trapped in a pain-filled, earthbound world.

*   *   *

The woman still knelt by her bedside, weeping.

"Please, God, please let her come back. Oh, Jesus, she's beautiful! And she's so happy. Thank You for letting me see her. Thank You for answering my prayers."

Jesus laid gentle hands on the woman's shoulders, and her sobs subsided little by little. She could not see Him, but she sensed His presence. Then an unexpected sound caught her by surprise. A chuckle!

"I did not answer your prayers alone, my daughter," He said to the quiet place in her heart. "I've had a little girl pleading for the chance to see her mother. I answered her prayers, too."

"She wanted . . . to see . . . me?" Her voice reflected awe. "It was her prayers You answered?"

"Of course, daughter," Jesus answered. But there was no sign of criticism in His voice, no hint of displeasure.

"Jesus?"

"Yes, daughter."

"Wh-what did You name her?"

The Most High God dropped the little girl's name into her mother's heart in a lovely whisper, "Allison."

"Allison," repeated the woman. "Allison."

*   *   *

Allison looked up at Rachel quizzically as she searched the face more familiar than her own. The face that hovered over her crib, the smile that tugged at Rachel's lips every morning as she brushed Allison's hair, the eyes that crinkled at the corners and laughed with Allison as they talked and played and prayed.

"Mommy loves me, Rachel," she said, eyes shining joyfully.

"I know, my lamb," Rachel said with a smile. "I've known all along."

Allison's head tilted a little, as she searched that lovely face again. "You know what, Rachel?" she asked. "Mom looks a little bit like you."

"I'll tell you a secret, Allison. We're sisters." Rachel's lilting laugh dropped to a conspiratorial whisper. "She just doesn't know it yet. My mother lost me much as your mother lost you. But one day we'll all be together, my angel. That's the wondrous grace of our Heavenly

Father!"

As they held hands and twirled in circles, their laughter lit Heaven's skies with the joy of the sunrise.

Postscript by the Author: Of course, I don't know the details of Heaven's nursery first-hand. But the child I lost in the autumn of 1981 did appear to me, sitting on the edge of my bed in the winter of 1989 in Eagle River, Alaska. Her appearance was my gift from a loving Heavenly Father. But when I thanked Him for letting me see her, an amazing thing happened. I heard a deep chuckle echo from within my heart, and a gentle Voice said, "Who said I answered your prayers? I had a little girl up here who has begged to see her Mother."

There was no reprimand in that Voice, just the gentle reminder that mine was not the only broken heart.

When I asked Him what name He had given my little girl, the name rang in my heart with so much certainty, I knew I was hearing it straight from the lips of God:

Allison.

THE MARKS

Aisha K. Moore

Aisha K. Moore, Esq. is a published poet and novelist and enjoys writing fantasy, sci-fi (speculative fiction) and commercial fiction. Her short story, *Second Chance*, will be published in *True: Vol. 2* later this year and her poetry can be found in *Discover Kai, First Edition*. She is also the author of the upcoming series *The Quest for the Armor of God* and *Life Developments*. Aisha holds a B.S. in Chemistry from SUNY Brockport and a Juris Doctor from Georgetown University Law Center. A practicing attorney, she is a Christian wife and mother with hopes of one day writing full time.

TRESSA TRUDGED THROUGH THE dry sand, head bowed to protect her eyes. The city lay approximately one kilometre ahead. Squinting, she could just make out the high city wall. Brother identified the target and confirmed the mission. One fourth of the money had been uploaded to her account, one million more for each successful kill. Done neatly and professionally, without changing the past in any recordable way, doubled the bonus.

It wasn't about the money, though. She wanted the respect she deserved for being the top hitman in time travel. She consistently nailed every mark. Yet, she still had to watch out for the competition. Any one of them would sabotage her at the first opportunity. This job would prove her worth.

Focus. Got to locate an entry, gain close access. Dressed in a simple light cloth tunic, she carefully lowered her veil. With one sweeping motion, she deposited the small electronic translator into her mouth and swallowed. The warm metal scraped against her throat and lodged into her vocal chords. With a similar motion she dropped another module into her ear, which instantly activated and burrowed itself into the canal.

Her partner Lonnie had outdone herself again. Her gadgets would allow Tressa to speak and understand ancient Hebrew without anyone being the wiser. She could also transmit back and forth with headquarters. She had not been allowed a weapon or anything from the future that could significantly distort society. She would have to be creative.

Returning the veil over her face, Tressa surveyed the land and focused on the burning sun. *Remarkable.* It was younger, brighter and healthier than the expanded, misshapen orange variety that she knew. Each breath of fresh air tasted like a gulp of cold bottled water. Even without her usual caffeine inducements, Tressa was alert and energized.

Several others around her also made their way to the city. A merchant walked along a flat wagon piled high with rugs and clothes and covered with sackcloth. A male servant pulled at the cover, protecting the goods from the dust. Several shepherds and several hundred sheep moved on her right, toward the side gate near the well. A long line of men, shackled together and guarded by a group of men in turbans and colorful clothing approached on her left. One guard eyed her curiously. She lowered her eyes. *Just move on, buddy. Leave me alone.* The last thing she needed was attention.

Tressa easily passed through the gate, the guards barely acknowledging the presence of a mere maidservant. She was in. She lightly tapped the outside of her ear, triggering the earpiece. "Gained access," she muttered, behind her veil. "Establishing cover now."

"Acknowledged Angel 7," a faint voice responded. "Contact HQ when you've made cover."

Tressa tapped her ear and moved steadily through the streets. She inherited code name Angel 7, because of her smooth technique and precision. But she wasn't just a hitter. No, she was a soldier at war. She fought for the right side. Death was a consequence of war. The marks had chosen the wrong side.

*   *   *

"Hurry," whispered Jonah, moving quickly down the narrow streets. "The window is too small, we should have arrived earlier."

Zekiah grunted. Entry and exit were his responsibility. Elath led the trio. He ignored the other two, surveying the city streets, marking each vendor, their goods and the shoppers. He wanted to guarantee no surprises this time, nothing to ruin success. He would memorize every detail about this city and the people so that he could spot anything out of the ordinary.

The narrow streets curved and twisted. The clay and dirt absorbed the echoes of their steps. They passed the labyrinth of common dwellings while older children splashed in a channel of water that flowed through the city. Elath marveled at the accomplishments of the ancients. If only the moderns, in all their technological glory, had taken a moment to acknowledge and learn from the past. Everything would have been different. Nuclear weapons, mass destruction of entire continents and irreversible pollution of the earth could have been avoided. They would have been able to enjoy pure earth that they only read about in history texts.

Before them lay a magnificent temple of stone, trimmed in gold and precious jewels. Guards patrolled everywhere. A stone staircase led to the outer atrium, where merchants packed their things for the evening. Priests and prophets walked along the outer platform. Some looked like them, long hair and beards, tunics and robes of light sacking. Colorful tattoos branded on others, inked into their skin. Their bald heads accented their clean-shaven faces. They did not cover their bodies with robes, but only wore the tunic.

"Damned servants of the Queen," muttered Zekiah. "They defile the temple with their presence." He spat at the ground.

"Enough," warned Elath. "Remember where we are. You know that in Samaria, in fact in all Israel, Baal worship is allowed."

"Every time I time travel it is to this cursed land." Zekiah glared at Elath. "Just once I want to behold Jerusalem, the city I continuously risk my life for."

"Only a select few have been blessed to travel at all," whispered Jonah, pulling Zekiah's arm. "Yet, you complain. Elath will report our actions to the Supreme Priest."

Zekiah snatched his arm from Jonah, glaring at the back of Elath's head.

"You would be wise to keep your complaints to yourself," continued Jonah.

"Indeed," answered Elath, stopping at the base of the temple. "We have made it, well within the window."

"I want to behold King Solomon's temple. Just once. Instead of this replica," continued Zekiah, lightening his tone.

"But this temple was built later, by the same people. Remember, they were Queen Jezebel's people after all. The Phoenicians. They purposely made this a more splendid structure anyway," shrugged Jonah.

"It is not the splendor I want to see. Just to lay eyes on it, before it's destroyed, that is my only dream."

"Maybe, my brother, maybe." Elath tapped Zekiah's shoulder. "Let's find our friend."

They swiftly climbed the stone steps and made their way along the side of the platform. Another young man, dressed in the same priestly manner, whispered from the shadows.

"Perfect timing," he said smoothly, and fell in step with them. All four walked a route that would take them around the complex.

"Welcome, Brothers of the Preservation. You will stay at the King's palace. You will be guests of the priests. They know you are coming, but assume you to be priests of Judah. Only the other Brothers are aware of the mission. This should allow you more than enough access."

He gave them clear instructions on how to enter the palace gates and where to find the other priests. When they arrived at the spot where he had joined them, he disappeared back into the shadows.

"May God be with you, my brothers."

* * *

"No, you insufferable little idiot!" screamed Queen Jezebel. She hurled a heavy emerald and ruby bracelet at Tressa's head. Tressa ducked. The object slammed against the stone wall, a ruby falling out of the setting. She rushed to pick up the royal jewelry and handed it to the maidservant standing by the door.

"Oh, please forgive your maidservant." Tressa bowed, fighting an uncontrollable desire to laugh. "I thought this would be a perfect present for Princess Athaliah." She quickly gathered the matching necklace and handed it to another maidservant.

"Does that garbage look like something the future Queen of Judah should wear on her wedding day!" the Queen raged, looking for something else to throw. "My family will be there!!"

Queen Jezebel eyed a ceramic vase in the corner. Tressa did not bother to move. *Throw it, I dare you.* It was King Ahab's favorite vase, a present from him to the Queen. *Even you aren't so bold to spite the King. Not yet anyway.*

Jezebel sighed deeply. Her voice steady, she spoke through clenched teeth. "There are not enough jewels. Not nearly enough. You tell him I said that it better be prepared. Better yet, I will tell him myself when he delivers my crown."

Tressa had been employed by the Queen for the past four months. Her expert seamstress skills had garnered great attention among the nobility of Israel. Tressa's clients dressed better than the Queen and that, of course, was unthinkable. Jezebel quickly hired her as the royal seamstress and wardrobe designer, renaming her Tamar.

Her positioning was perfect. She managed to stay unbelievably close to the Queen, whom her marks would undoubtedly target. She preferred it this way, waiting patiently, while the marks' missions unknowingly led them to her. The only problem was that Jezebel was the single most unpleasant person Tressa had ever met in her life. Just last month, Jezebel ordered six wait staff to be executed for failing to set out the correct ceramic and glass place settings at the last banquet. Her father, the King of all Phoenicia, had attended, ratcheting up the Queen's anxiety to unfathomable levels.

Tressa found it amazing how often they worshipped. It seemed never ending. She believed in God, but in a more practical sense, as it fit into her life. But these people lived for worship, walking to the highest points of Samaria to make sacrifices and pray. She was forced to attend the Queen's services, which she despised.

But every now and then she attended the services to the God of Israel. She was surprised that people would sit all day and night, fasting and praying, waiting for a word or revelation from Him. In modern times a person barely whispered a two minute prayer. Living here required her to reexamine her relationship with God, and it caused her shame. She found that the best way to cope was to keep God separate and apart from her profession.

Tressa continued stitching the delicate leaflets of gold into the outer garment of the wedding ensemble. Jezebel had not commented on the dress, which meant it was perfect.

"Queen of Judah. Humph," mumbled Jezebel, settling back in her seat. Maids moved forward instantly to fan her.

"As if my father hasn't already ruined my life, placing me amongst these tribal pilgrims. And for what? Humph. He exchanged me for access to their wealth and trade routes."

The room remained quiet, Jezebel strumming her fingers on the dressing table.

"My daughter, to an even smaller clan. Judah, humph. Not even a proper nation." The food staff scuttled into the room, bringing the Queen refreshment. She quieted immediately, wary of any outside her immediate staff. They placed the food on the tray and hurried out.

"I have made the best of things, though," she continued a few minutes later, talking to no one in particular. "I am educating these peasants, teaching them a proper religion at least. They will soon understand that Melkart is supreme to their Jehovah," she snarled.

Tressa kept her eyes down. *What would it take to silence the Queen?*

She felt very little pity for her and her complaints were of little importance. Tressa was more concerned that she had not practiced combat skills this week. She had to stay sharp. The target had been confirmed, the marks would make a move soon. The wedding was quickly approaching.

"Tamar, go fetch the wedding coordinator. I have already told him that he is to use Pheonician glassware. All the furniture must also be Phoenician. He was told to order the intricate Tyre benches and tables. The pillows and covers are to be light shades of purple. I have not yet seen the ivory statues that are necessary to decorate the hall. Everything better be right. I want to make sure the fool doesn't make any mistakes. My family will be there after all."

Tressa bowed gracefully, "Yes, my Queen," and marched across the great hall. She was willing to bet money that the wedding coordinator wouldn't forget to order everything Phoenician.

* * *

"The line of David must not, under any circumstances, be in harm's way," whispered Jonah. "The Supreme Priest chose this event because it is the easiest. But we still must be careful."

Elath nodded, considered Jonah's advice. Poisoning was risky. It may never get past the cupbearer, and, if she died, everyone would be on high alert. They would not have a second chance.

"We could aim for the daughter," suggested Zekiah.

"I also considered it," said Jonah. "Almost like killing two birds with one stone."

"How?" asked Elath.

"Well, we know that Athaliah will influence her future husband, Jehoram, with her idol worship and he will be an evil king. We are here to stop that marriage, to keep Jezebel's seed from corrupting the nation of Judah. Without that influence, they will not bring the wrath of God against them, so says the Supreme Prophet."

"Continue," whispered Elath. They were running out of time and Jonah's explanations were too lengthy.

"Later in history, after Jehoram's death, Ahaziah will rule Judah. He is Athaliah's son and will be executed by Jehu, when he fulfills the prophecy of destroying Ahab's line. Athaliah will then do the unthinkable."

"Hurry, Jonah," muttered Elath, "get to the point."

"She will murder all of her grandchildren to secure the throne for herself. And she will be successful in ruling Judah, until the one surviving grandchild returns from hiding to reclaim the throne."

Elath reeled back with disgust, while Zekiah let out a low throaty moan. The three sat in silence, waiting for Elath to make a decision.

"Stop her now, and save Judah from wickedness under Jehoram and Athaliah's later coup."

Elath shook his head, "We cannot stray from the decision of the Supreme Prophet. He must have known about it, yet Athaliah was not the order. Jezebel is the mark. She will train Athaliah to be so perverse and cruel. If we get her, we can root out the evil before it spreads to Judah and . . ."

Zekiah interrupted, "Then we are too late to save Judah. The wedding arrangements have been made. Athaliah is pledged to Jehoram.

King Jehoshaphat foolishly believes this marriage is a way to have peace with Israel and economic alliances with both Israel and Phoenicia. He has no idea he is inviting death to his nation. Even if Jezebel dies, the marriage will eventually go forward."

"What if they suspect the death was caused by ministers of Judah. Maybe we leave a trail and then Athaliah won't want to marry him . . ."answered Jonah.

"Think, please," answered Elath quickly. "If anyone suspects Judah had anything to do with the death of the daughter of the most powerful nation in the east, it will be war. No, we must readjust our strategy. We will kill them both."

Jonah leaned forward, "I have a plan."

*   *   *

With only one day left before the wedding, Tressa rushed from room to room, adjusting the garments of all royal women related to or favored by the Queen. King Ahab's other wives, daughters and concubines knew better than to even speak to her.

The city was brimming with guests. Just yesterday, Tressa had fitted Queen of Judah in a beautiful gown. Unlike Jezebel, the Queen of Judah was kind and stately. Tressa immediately adored her, but her stomach churned at the thought of such a beautiful woman's son being bound to Queen Jezebel.

Tressa hurried from the guest quarters to return to Athaliah's room for the last fitting of the wedding tunic and robes. She passed three priests walking steadily down the hallway to the Queen Jezebel's quarters. She had seen them before, this trio that stayed together. Something about them bothered her. She stopped walking abruptly, her maidservant bumping into her.

"Mistress Tamar, is something the matter?" uttered the young girl.

"I don't know," answered Tressa honestly. She probed her mind. *When did I first notice these three priests?* Approximately two weeks before they were sitting with the group of priests in the eating facility. It was amazing, actually that she would notice them, considering Jezebel insisted on having four hundred or more priests of Melkart, her idol god around at any given time. King Ahab insisted on matching his number of priests, so there were also over four hundred priests of God. When she had gone to report something to the food staff she immediately noticed them, huddled together. She asked around, but was told they had been sent from Judah in advance, in preparation for the wedding.

Now, here they were, moving away from the guests' quarters and over to Jezebel's section of the palace. No way Jezebel requested service from three priests of God. If anything, Jezebel was always scheming of ways to harm them, deciding to destroy as many of them as she could, while maintaining proper appearances. If she had called them, they were surely doomed.

She placed her supplies on top of the dresses the maid was carrying. "Please take the dresses to my room. Then meet me in the princesses' quarters with my supplies."

Her servant nodded, trying hard not to groan under the additional weight. Tressa lightly tapped her ear piece.

"Angel 7 on, repeat Angel 7 on." It had been a while since she contacted them.

"Angel 7, HQ reads," the thin voice replied.

"I believe I have located the marks. Say again, I have located the marks." She spoke with her lips slightly parted her teeth clenched.

"Understood, Angel 7. Please hold for instruction."

Tressa remained behind the three priests, watching them disappear around the corner. What was taking HQ so long?

"HQ, I have a clear target, may I proceed?"

"No, Angel 7, do not proceed. I repeat, change of orders, do not proceed."

"What?"

"I repeat, do not proceed Angel 7."

What? Six months of her life to get into position, and now they ordered her to back down. Unbelievable. When the orders changed she was supposed to obey. Either way she got her money, payment forwarded to her account for her trouble. But this wasn't about the money. She wanted these marks.

Curiosity got the better of her. Tressa moved cautiously to the edge of the hall, her back flat against the wall. She turned slowly, quietly gliding down the huge hallway, past the flowing tapestries. They were standing just inside the door, muttering. *Were they surprised that the Queen was not there? Fools.* She stepped forward and moved quickly into the room.

"My lords, may I help you?" she asked softly, bowing as she moved in position with her back against the door.

*   *   *

"Where is the Queen?" breathed the shortest of the three. The long hoods partially covered their faces, but she saw enough. The eyes, the lighter skin, the spotted lips, these men were from a different time. The sallow skin and yellowed eyes told that they were from a time when the air is poisoned and unhealthy. A time after her own.

"Why, she is with her guests, of course. Who are you that you would come to the Queen's personal quarters?" She kept her back to the door, her hands behind her back.

The intelligent-looking one spoke, unclasping his hands. "She summoned us," he lied.

Tressa could see where the skin was peeling back from the cuticles, sunken and ashen. She gasped. *Whenever they are from, the earth must be dying.* The sight of his fingertips saddened her.

Her mouth fell open and he quickly tucked his hands back into the robes. She quickly recovered.

"Well then, my lords, you are surely dead where you stand, that is, if the Queen summoned you," answered Tressa.

She ran her fingers along the seam of her garment. She had hidden pockets in the seam. Two small daggers would do the trick for the short one. The large brute would surely be slower to react. But the intelligent one, she wanted to keep him alive for questioning. She always wanted to know what the plan had been, what they were willing to die for. It helped her to hunt her targets, to understand their thinking.

"It seems to me," breathed the shorter one, "that you are a bold house maid indeed, to question the priests of the King."

She smirked. "Priests of the King, huh?" She would snap the brute's neck. That would allow her to save her medium-sized sword for the intelligent looking one. She slid the small daggers into the palm of her hand. "I am not a house maid."

"No, you are the Ethiopian seamstress," the intelligent one replied. "The newest addition to the Queen's personal staff," he said slowly, a look of comprehension spreading across his face.

At the same time, the short one glanced at him. It was the last voluntary move he would make. Quick as lightning, Tressa released the small daggers, one into the short one's throat, another to his forehead. Just as surprise began to trickle over the big one's face, she hurtled herself at him, flipping over his head and landing on his back. Before he could reach for her, she snapped his neck.

As he fell, she jumped off the body, landing in a squatted position.

The intellectual one stared at her with calm eyes. She was taken aback.

She stood facing him. "You are prepared to die then?"

"Yes," he answered.

They continued to gaze at each other. In a flash, he released a dagger. She back-flipped, diving behind the brute's still body. She threw another dagger at him a second before hitting the ground. He crouched behind a pillow-covered bench.

"Why is it that you are prepared to die?" she called from across the room.

"Because, I believe in my cause," he answered.

"Don't we all!"

"No, not hitmen like you. You do it for the cash. You fool yourself into thinking you have beliefs, but you don't."

"You don't know me!"

"Yes, I do. I know your type. And, if you keep screaming, the guards will come and both of our covers will be blown."

"What do you want?"

"The Queen and the Princess. They will plant the seeds of destruction that will ruin the nation of Judah. I am here to prevent that."

"You do not have the authority to do that. You are not God," fumed Tressa.

"And neither are you. Yet, you just killed two of his very faithful servants, who embarked upon these missions, at the risk of grave peril, to save millions from invoking the wrath of God against them. Not for financial gain."

Tressa was silent.

"How long before the Queen returns?"

"I don't know," she answered truthfully, catching a glimpse of the edge of his robe as she rolled behind the low lounging cushions. "I do not do this for financial gain."

"Pride then. Respect probably. Human life is just a sport."

"No!" *Stop confusing me.* She was a soldier at war, fighting the good fight and defending the good against evil. "I am fighting a war. I protect good."

"Well, in this case, you are protecting the Jezebel. You have witnessed her burn babies and children in sacrifice to a nonexistent god. You know she will murder over 400 priests of God, will chase the prophet Elijah ruthlessly, will murder and pillage and will train her daughter to do the same in Judah. This is who you protect."

Tressa slumped behind the sofa. They were silent for several minutes.

"Leave now. Stall the Queen. I will have my men's bodies removed."

"No. I have to kill you too." Tears trickled down her face.

"My child, you will not kill me. Not today. God has already ordained it. That is why you chose the other two and did not kill all three of us. You most certainly could have."

"I want to see your hands. Place them on the bench."

He slowly raised his hands and lay them flat. She stood up and moved quickly to the short one, removing her daggers. She snatched the small sword from the cushioned pillar and headed for the door.

"I will try again," he said simply. "It is my mission to kill the Queen and the Princess. I am not afraid to die in my attempt."

She exited the room and closed the doors.

*   *   *

The waiters moved quickly, placing fresh fruit and drink on the serving tables, then tucking the dead under the covered carts. Jonah stood by the door, listening for the Queen.

"Brother, you must go," one of the fellow Brotherhood tapped him. "Our presence is easily explained, yours is not."

"A hitter. I did not anticipate it. Who sent a hitter?"

The waiter shrugged, his counterparts moving the carts slowly from the room. "Could you figure out the time period of the hitter?"

"Definitely earlier than us. Dawn of the technology revolution, maybe. Coloring was very rich. Couldn't have been from the robotics period."

"Identify the hitter," suggested the waiter. "Maybe we can target him tonight."

Jonah did not bother to correct him. "The hitter is not our mission. Any additional death would alert the staff and then all of our missions would be in jeopardy. I must focus on my original mission. It is all I can hope to accomplish. You must stay alert on your mission."

"I have been undercover for two years," the waiter said. "I cannot risk exposure now. Anyway, brother, it is not our way to seek revenge. May God have vengeance against this hitter."

They departed, Jonah moving slowly down the massive hallway. He deeply missed his brothers.

"God, I need you. Please protect and keep me during this mission."

He felt the steady Elath and grumbling Zekiah near him. "Please receive my brothers, Almighty God, and find them pleasing in your sight."

An image of the tormented young woman came to mind. He felt a pull at his heart to pray for her, despite himself. "And finally, Father, please forgive the hitter. Touch her, Lord, let her see the error of her ways."

*   *   *

Tressa rubbed her sore arm, upon which she landed when throwing the knife at the remaining mark. Tearing a rag from her undergarment, she wiped the blades and returned them to the secret panels. The bloodied rags were deposited in a tall ceramic vase in the hallway. Entering Athaliah's quarters, she was surprised to find the Queen Jezebel quite content.

"Ah, here she is, let us begin," Jezebel clapped her hands with delight. Athaliah rolled her eyes at Tressa and climbed onto the platform, as her maidservants lowered the dress over her head.

"Where have you been," hissed the Queen in her ear, her hand circling Tressa's sore arm like a vice.

"I wanted to return the dresses, my lady, to one of your guests," lied Tressa, making a mental note to have her servant deliver one of the completed dresses.

The ebony eyes bored into hers. "Very well, excellent seamstress or not, I will have your head if you ruin my daughter's day."

"Yes, my Queen, I know."

Jezebel observed her quietly. Tressa realized that she appeared more subdued than normal. It could not be helped. The mark had touched her heart and she did not know how to release the guilt that was weighing on her.

"Are you sure there is nothing you want to tell me?"

"Yes, my lady."

Even if there was something to tell, was no way would she confide in Jezebel. Tressa dropped onto her knees and smoothed the fabric around Athaliah as the other royal family members looked on in approval.

The mark's words reverberated in her ears. He had spoken the truth. By eliminating his associates, she had inadvertently defended Queen Jezebel, a cruel woman who would claim an unthinkable amount of lives for self-satisfaction. Didn't Jezebel deserve to die? Hadn't she proven herself incorrigible?

Tressa shook her head. Her job duties did not include making moral judgments. She simply had to execute orders. Killing the two marks without prior clearance had been violation enough. She would be doomed if she killed the Queen or anyone not affiliated with the mark. What would God want from her?

That night, Tressa lay on her mat in turmoil. She could not kill the third mark. Her heart and mind were very clear about that. What was she supposed to do?

"Angel 7, report status," the thin voice surprised her.

"Angel 7, here. Two marks dead. Third one pursued."

"Angel 7, orders were violated. Stand by."

She waited patiently. A few seconds later she heard a click in her ear.

"Angel 7, this is Command 1. What happened?"

"I identified marks. I eliminated two of three."

"Is the third out of pocket?"

"No, he is contained," breathed Tressa.

"You went against orders. You were to wait for approval before striking. It is irrelevant now. The third mark must be eliminated."

"Yes sir. Angel 7 out."

For hours she lay tormented on the mat. She climbed onto her knees and prayed. She confessed and repented. She prayed until she felt absolution and redemption. It was clear what she would do.

*   *   *

Jonah was not normally the striker. He was the intelligence collector, performing reconnaissance for each mission. He stared at the blade selected for the Queen. Never mind the princess, he would have one opportunity and he would use it to kill Jezebel. The brothers arranged an escape route through the tunnels under the palace. But he believed that the hitter would get him before he escaped. She was so quick and fast; he had never seen anyone move like that.

The time had come. The priests lined the entrance hall, the King's priests in the rear, the Queen's in the front. Jonah took up position at the very end of the line. The palace governor announced that the time had come to mount the royal chariots. Both heads of staff moved quickly to their master's quarters.

Jonah slid behind one of the flowing tapestries. The brothers shifted down two steps, his exit unnoticed. The hitter walked past, her eyes scouring the hallway. The tapestries made security a nightmare, but she would be on him as soon as he attacked.

The wide door to the Queen's quarters opened. The princess and her entourage passed him as they walked up the huge hall. Next came Jezebel's staff, her maidservants dropping flower petals as the procession advanced.

Jonah focused on Queen Jezebel's sneering face as she complained to an advisor. He slid to a closer tapestry, slowly drew the sword. A gap opened and she stepped into perfect position. He flung the blade with all his might. He wanted to run but curiosity riveted him.

The blade sliced cleanly through the air; a perfect throw. A deafening shriek split the hallway. Out of nowhere, the hitter emerged, spreading her body in the air like an eagle, just in front of the Queen. Her flight oddly shifted as the blade struck, jerking her backward onto the Queen.

Jonah's heart sank, pain surging through his body. He quickly returned to the line of robed priests in the main hall, seemingly unaware of the confusion around the corner. He had failed. Worse yet, he had stabbed the confused young woman, whom he had asked God to save.

*   *   *

"Get that wench off me!" screamed the Queen. "What are you thinking, knocking into me! Are you possessed! On today of all days! I want her arrested. Arrest the Ethiopian!"

Tressa lay on her side, her body crumpled. When the guards determined the Queen safe and unharmed, they rolled Tressa over to arrest her. They gasped at the thick blade sticking out of her chest.

Maidservants began screaming. Guards set out to scour the palace and warn the King.

"Oh my," whispered the Queen.

Tressa smiled, a wave of forgiveness washed over her. She had made the right decision and, just before losing consciousness, she smiled. *I finally found a way to silence the Queen.*

TAKEN

Daniel I Weaver

"Fiction to scare the Jesus into you." Daniel I Weaver adopted that tagline with the intent of providing just that. "Taken" and "Guilty" aim to please with an array of terrifying scenes that will have you burning the nightlight to keep the shadows at bay. Despite the scares, these dark tales always lead to the Light. Turn the page, pull the blankets tight, and thank God you're not the one trapped in these nightmares.

I HAD NO IDEA a letter might get me killed. But I'd just known I had to meet this woman like the letter said. Big mistake.

I sat in the dank cellar, somewhere in the middle of inbred hillbilly hell, staring at Franklin's mangled remains. Our host had hurled them at our feet before closing and bolting the door. The dull yellow light edging from the single, dangling bulb, revealed dilapidated walls, cobweb-strewn ceiling beams, mold, dust, and bugs. There were only two of us left: me and Jenni—the dirty blonde who resembled a misplaced runway model in her designer slacks and sheer blouse.

I stared at the pile of gore that used to be Franklin. How could I have been so wrong about *this* when my sixth sense had always served me so well? I knew things and had always been right before. Not this time. *Your presence is requested this evening at 7:00 for a presentation that will change your life.* What a load of crap. End my life, perhaps.

"Why is he doing this, Steven?" Jenni asked.

I looked at her across the carnage and almost chuckled. She would go next. The realization washed over me in a wave of relief and nausea. I would live a little longer. At her expense. "Why would anyone do something like this, Jenni?"

"There has to be a reason. We have nothing in common." She inched toward me. "Except the invitations."

Did the "why" really matter? I was more interested in escaping than figuring out why that psychopath and his inbred cronies had lured us all together. Given the evidence, the answer seemed obvious. Even evil needed to have fun. To feed.

Jenni crawled closer. "He's gonna chop us up and burn what's left! You don't want to know why?"

I didn't have time for questions. I glanced toward the door at the top of the stairs. Five of us had tried to open it earlier. How long ago? Hours? Days? Probably days by the way my stomach twisted and growled every few minutes.

Jenni grabbed my sleeve. "I don't want to die, Steven."

One might expect a frail little thing like her to cry, but at that point, she was probably as numb as I was. She had cried. Cried her little heart out. But I doubted her tears had anything to do with determining who died next. Our host knew who he was after, and the cattle prods he carried kept the rest of us at bay. I'd learned that the hard way, trying to make a break for the stairs.

"Keep quiet." I slid left and felt the wall, ignoring the splinters as my trembling fingers raked across haggard boards. Finding the wobbly plank, I set to work.

"Let me help."

I peered at Jenni's desperate blue eyes. She would've been attractive, but the makeup had smeared and she stank of urine.

"I thought you didn't want anything to do with this," I snapped. "You sat there praying while Greg and I worked."

Greg and I had found the weak spot. We'd discovered the draft and realized there was something beyond that wall.

Jenni slid into place beside me. "The Lord helps those who help themselves and I don't want to die. Please."

Greg screamed overhead. If his torture lasted as long as his predecessors' had, we might make it. "Work fast. Don't worry about the noise."

The screams would mask our efforts. I knew it. But then again, I was trapped in a basement with mutilated corpses and a woman whose pant-size probably exceeded her IQ. All thanks to *just knowing* something.

I clutched the plank, pinned my feet against the wall, and pulled. Jenni pulled as well.

The board groaned.

A nail creaked.

SNAP! We flew backward. Jenni ended up on the human spare-parts pile. Screaming.

I rolled to her, jerked her by her hair, and clamped my hand over her mouth. My eyes went to the door and my ears worked the sudden silence. Greg wasn't screaming—a bad sign.

A floorboard overhead moaned and my eyes darted toward it. Greg shouted obscenities, mocking and demeaning our host. I shook my head. He was helping us. Keeping that sick sadist busy to buy us time. That fit. The last thing he'd said before our host reappeared was, "Whatever happens, remember Jesus loves you."

Obscenities didn't fit the Christian-type, but when I'd called him on it, Greg answered, "I'm working on it."

While Greg paid our bail in blood, we were busting out. He expected to go to heaven, and he was buying us time to get out of hillbilly hell.

I released Jenni's mouth and hurried back to the wall. Reaching through the crack, I found nothing but cobwebs. No wall, no brick, no dirt. I latched onto the next board and pulled. Jenni showed up at my side again, trembling and dry heaving. Her expression indicated her mind was somewhere else.

"Jenni."

Her dead stare never changed.

"Jenni!" I hissed it as loud as I dared. Those boards were coming off that wall, but I wasn't going to start shouting and beg our host to reappear with his cattle prods.

She jumped a little. When her gaze met mine, her pupils focused and she swayed. Her gasps calmed until the faintest spark showed through her stare. "We have to get out of here."

No kidding.

"Steven, can't you feel the evil? It's everywhere. Thick, like a fog or something. We have to get out of here. Now!"

I couldn't feel anything except nausea. But she was right. We had to get out of there. "We have to move fast, Jenni. I don't know how long Greg can hold out."

She nodded and grabbed the plank.

It creaked, whined, and shuddered, but in the end, it exploded off the wall. We removed the next one. Hope cut through my numbness. We had a chance. We might just make it.

Greg's screams died down. I reached a cautionary hand to Jenni. Her arm trembled. Why was everything so quiet? What was our host doing? Had Greg given out when others, smaller and less spirited, had lasted much longer?

Overhead, Greg broke into song—like something I'd heard at church as a kid. Church wasn't my thing, but that song tore at me.

I was probably going to die soon. What would happen if I did? Had I been good enough for the pearly gates, or was I damned to an eternal Jacuzzi of fire, brimstone, and Molotov-cocktail martinis?

A clamor broke out overhead: a sound like crashing pots. Greg sang louder, that Jesus loved him and he knew it. Our host's footfalls rumbled in chaotic patterns. He must not have liked the show.

I touched Jenni's cheek to get her attention. "We need to hurry. I don't like the sound of that."

We laid into the next board and it sprang free. I reached for another and froze.

A woman's voice sobbed through the hole.

I looked at Jenni. "Did you hear that?"

Her eyes said yes. "Ghost."

"There's no such thing."

"But, Betty said—"

"Forget what Betty said," I snapped. "There's no such thing as ghosts or spirits or demons or any of that junk. It was probably just the draft."

Betty, an overweight dark-haired woman taken shortly after I'd come to, had suggested she knew where we'd been taken. Betty had heard stories about a serial killer who mutilated his victims, burned their remains, and devoured their souls. She was one of those ghost-chaser types who seemed to live for twisted nightmares like this. Despite her fear when our host rounded her up, I could've sworn I saw a hint of excitement in her eyes.

Betty's ghost stories aside, that hadn't been a draft. But nothing beyond that wall could be worse than our host. I checked the space. Just big enough. I hunched and tried to look through. I couldn't see my hand two inches in front of my face in that darkness.

"I'm going through. I'll pull you in after I check it."

No, I wouldn't.

Knowing it made me pause. I was no Boy Scout, but I wouldn't leave a hot little thing like Jenni behind for that butcher, would I? So why was I so sure I wouldn't pull her through?

I squirmed through the opening. Inch by inch, I shifted into the abyss. Nothing but cobwebs and stale, musty air. When my hips broke free, I jerked my legs through and spun around for Jenni. I stopped. Greg wasn't singing any more. Jenni glanced toward the door and dropped to the ground.

The lock clunked.

The door opened.

Light splayed into the darkness, highlighting our mangled companions. Jenni screamed and reached for my arms. I froze. Our host, in leather boots and butcher's apron dripping gore, thundered down the stairs. Jenni screamed again and started to claw into the hole. He leapt down the remaining stairs and slammed the cattle prod into her back.

I pulled away. If I touched her, the current would transfer through her arms and I wasn't about to get juiced. I'd known I wouldn't pull her through. So why hadn't I known better than to listen to that letter?

Jenni's eyes dimmed and closed. Our host dragged her toward the stairs without a word. He paused at the stairs, glanced back at the hole, and sneered.

I turned away and felt around the darkness. Nothing but cobwebs. I searched above me as I stood. More cobwebs.

A switch. Click. An electric hum. Lights flooded the room. I shielded my eyes. They burned, but I couldn't afford to close them. I had to figure out where I was.

A room.

I squinted and scanned my surroundings. Cobwebs dangled throughout the expanse, but couldn't conceal the door beyond the ancient furnace. My eyes widened slowly, adjusting to the light. I darted toward the door.

"Help me."

That soft, desperate voice rattled out of the furnace and struck me like a battering ram. I flailed and spun to the ground. Sitting quickly, I stared at the massive furnace's black, grilled door.

Could I have just imagined that? Was I hearing thin—

"Please, help me."

Trembling besieged my arms and I scrambled backward. I glanced toward the door. I had to escape. I had to find a way out of there before that maniac in the butcher's gear came for me. I forced myself to my feet and raced toward the door.

"Please."

I grabbed the handle and turned. The door squealed open.

"Please don't leave me here."

A web-strewn hallway lay beyond that door, but I couldn't force myself to take the first step. Why not? I'd never had any trouble looking out for myself before. So some chick needed help. If she'd survived in that room, she was better off than I was. All I had to do was run. I stared at the hallway. If I ran, I would make it. I just knew it.

The voice started weeping. Jenni's horrified eyes flashed through my mind. I could make it, but I turned around.

The furnace stared back at me like a black death-mask—a knight's visor bearing down on some defenseless peasant. I was the peasant.

I made a fist and took a step toward the furnace. No way anyone could be in there. It just wasn't possible.

"Help me."

I jerked. Leaning over, I squinted. Only blackness existed behind the grate. I really didn't have time for this. If I wanted to get out of this alive, I had to hurry. I reached over and grabbed the furnace door's handle. It didn't budge. I looked over at the doorway, the hall beyond. I could still make it.

"Please."

I jerked on the door and it shuddered. Dust and soot cascaded off. I jerked repeatedly until it obeyed, then I leaned over toward the opening. So where was this girl?

"Come on," I hissed. "It's open. Hurry."

I stared at the blackness. Why wasn't she coming? I leaned closer. Two white spheres flashed through the abyss. I recoiled.

"Please help me."

My heart raced like a jackhammer. This was crazy. Insane. Why was I helping her? I never helped anyone. People helped me. That was what I paid them for.

"I can't reach," she said.

Was that a hand stretching through the darkness? The glint must've been her eyes. I glanced at the open doorway and empty hall again. *Just pull her out quick and then I can run.* I stretched into the furnace. Just a little further. Something latched onto my hand.

"Hey!" I shouted.

It squeezed and pulled.

"Let go! Let me go!" I pulled back.

"Pull harder," the girl called.

She didn't have to tell me twice. I pulled until it felt like my arm would tear from its socket. As my hand emerged, light revealed the horrid black fingers wrapped around it. Those fingers trailed along to a black arm stretching toward the approaching, glinting spheres.

I tugged harder, trying to escape instead of pull her free, but her grip clamped like steel. Before I knew it, I'd pulled a hideous ashen monstrosity out of the furnace along with a cloud of billowing soot.

"Let go." I jerked my arm and it came free. I edged backward as the thing stood.

"Thank you."

Thank you? That was it? Just thank you? The stalk of cascading soot wrapped around those two eyes had spoken with the girl's voice. That thing couldn't be a girl.

I started toward the door. She followed and I stopped. "Look, I pulled you out. That's it. I've got to get out of here."

"But he's out there." She pointed down the empty hall.

I froze. No. I knew he wasn't out there. "No he's not."

"How can you be sure?"

"I just know."

Soot fell away, revealing more of her features. She couldn't have been more than fifteen.

"What do you mean, you just know?" she asked.

I *really* didn't have time for this. "I just know. It's like a sixth sense or something. When I just know, I know."

"What, are you clairvoyant?"

"No, it's nothing like that." I eyed that hallway again. I could still make it. "I just know things sometimes."

"You must help a lot of people."

I rounded on her, anger starting to replace the dying adrenaline. "I help myself, kid. Okay? I look out for me. Just me. And right now, I know that I need to get out of here."

Jenni screamed overhead, somewhere farther away than Greg's last screams.

"Why didn't you help her?"

My hands balled up into fists. What right did she have to ask me anything? "How about you mind your own business and leave me alone?"

"You helped me. Why didn't you help her?"

I stalked into the hallway. I had no idea where the hall would lead or what I might encounter along the way, but I was going to get out of there.

"I don't understand," she called.

I practically jumped out of my skin. I rounded and lifted a warning fist. She was going to get me killed. "Would you shut up?"

"Why do you only help yourself?"

Was she deaf? Why wouldn't she shut up? "Listen, girlie."

"Ashley," she interrupted. "My friends used to call me Ash."

I looked at the soot and shook my head. Maybe I was dreaming this whole thing. "Listen, Ash. Nobody ever helped me. When my mom and dad were pinned inside their car dying, nobody helped them. And when they died and left me orphaned, nobody helped me either. No one has ever helped me. So I help myself."

"But you have a gift."

"And a lot of good it's doing me right now. Will you shut up before you get us caught?"

I slunk through the hallway—a narrow path of peeling wallpaper, cobwebs, and crumbling plaster. The furnace room's light dulled into a yellowish hue that barely penetrated the shadows. Doors flanked the hallway as it snaked endlessly left and right, but I didn't try them. It wouldn't have been a good idea. At least that's what my gut said.

Jenni screamed again, farther away. I stopped. Jenni's scream was different from the others I'd heard. She was scared, but no pain filtered through the fear. Our host hadn't wasted any time on the others, eliciting blood-curdling screams within minutes of dragging people from the cellar. So what was he doing to Jenni? Why was it different with her?

"You can help her."

I rounded on Ash and opened my mouth, but anger turned my tongue to rubber.

"You could use your gift, right? You would know what to do."

"I told you, kiddo, I don't help anyone but myself."

I started toward the next hallway intersection. Ash didn't follow. I stopped and glanced back at her. "You staying here?"

"He'll kill her. And you're just going to let him?"

"What am I supposed to do about it? I can't help her. I can't stop him."

"Yes you can."

I just stared at her. How did some girl hiding out in a furnace think I could help Jenni?

"You would know what to do. You said so."

I huffed and spun away. I *could* help her. I hadn't even considered it before, but the realization stole my breath. It didn't seem possible. How was I supposed to help Jenni? Our host, all two-hundred-plus pounds of muscle and nightmare, had cattle prods and who knows what else. After all, I hadn't seen the letter's deception coming when I knocked on the door. I hadn't *known* better.

"You have to help her."

A floorboard overhead creaked.

"Why are you so worried about helping her?" I asked "Don't you want to get out of here alive?"

"I can't leave until you decide to help her."

I just stared. A sadness clouded Ash's dark brown eyes as she spoke. What did she mean she couldn't leave?

"What are you talking about? We can get out of here. I know it. But we need to go. Now!"

"You can go. I can't."

Anger boiled in my voice as I fought to keep it quiet. "Yes you can. Come on."

"Steven, why do you think you have your gift?"

"I don't know! And now's not the time to—" I stopped and stared. "How do you know my name?"

Another floorboard overhead creaked. THUNK! Dust cascaded down around us as something pounded on the boards above our heads. Cackling, loud and maniacal, joined the thundering percussion. We needed to leave, but I couldn't move. How did she know my name?

"I know because He told me."

My heart sank into my stomach.

"You've been taken, Steven."

"No kidding, kid. We've all b—"

"Not just by the butcher, Steven, by something much worse."

Worse than the maniac above us laughing like a psych-ward patient? Right then, that didn't seem possible.

Something heavy crashed overhead—like a sledgehammer smashing the floor. I wasn't going to wait around to find out. I grabbed Ash's cold, trembling arm and tugged her along.

"It's taken away your eyes, Steven."

I kept moving, the thunderous rampage overhead following every move I made. "I can see just fine, kiddo."

"No, Steven. It's taken your eyes and now you're lost. Now we're both lost."

I turned left around a corner and a splintering crash rocked the ceiling a few steps ahead of us. An axe head tore free and a glazed eye flooded the hole. The cackling intensified into mad laughter.

I jerked on Ash's arm. "Hurry!"

I had no idea where I was going, but I had to keep moving. I was going to save Ash. Somehow, I was going to save her. Maybe Jesus would take pity on me if I saved her. "How big is this house?"

She skid to a halt and pulled her arm free. "I can't go any further. You can't save me. You have to take yourself back to save me."

I growled with frustration. Riddles. I didn't have time for riddles. "What do you mean take myself back, Ash?"

"He gave you the gift, Steven. Back when you still belonged to Him. But you've lost your ability to see that."

"That psycho upstairs gave me this gift? I don't think so!"

"No, not him, Steven. God."

Enough! I turned away, glanced at the eyeball still watching us, then ran. I spun around a corner and flopped to a halt. Ash waited in the hall ahead of me.

"It was God's gift to give, Steven. And now you have to decide what you're going to do with it. You've been taken."

How'd she get there? "Why do you keep saying that? I know. We've all been taken."

"Steven, the butcher upstairs isn't the one who took you. The evil that fuels him has taken you. Greed, selfishness, and lust have taken you. They're all parts of the same evil. That evil drew you. That evil has blinded you. Even now, while a woman upstairs is about to die, you have the power to save her. Instead, you think only of yourself."

The hacking resumed above my head.

"Take yourself back, Steven. Take yourself back and save us all."

A door to my left opened. A woman, taller than Ash and covered from head to foot in soot, stepped through the doorway. Hope flickered through the despair in her eyes. I stepped away. What was happening?

"Remember what your mother told you, Steven," Ash said.

Another door opened to my right, between Ash and I. A man shedding soot stepped through the open doorway.

I backpedaled. "What is this, Ash?"

"Remember what your mother said, Steven."

God made you special, Steven. Don't ever let them take that away from you.

"Take yourself back, Steven. Take yourself back and save us."

I closed my eyes and squeezed my head. Flashes of my dying mother's face tore through my mind. I could feel the arms wrapped around my chest pulling me away from her, preventing me from running to the overturned, mangled car. *God made you special, Steven. Don't ever let them take that away from you*

I screamed. Fighting the arms, I opened my eyes. They weren't in my mind. Sooty arms held me. Those arms belonged to a much larger man, covered head to toe in soot like the others. His eyes showed sadness, not danger.

I wiggled and squirmed until I broke free and spun away.

He spoke with a deep, guttural voice. "Save us."

The others chimed in. "Save us."

Every door in view opened for new, soot-clad spectacles.

"Steven."

Cold stung my hand. I screamed, jumped, and tried to pull my hand from Ash's grip. She was so cold.

"Save Jenni. Save us all."

"Who are you people?"

"You," Ash said.

The letter said I would change my life if I came. Is that why I'd just known I had to go? Was I here for something bigger than me? *God made you special, Steven. Don't ever let them take that away from you.*

God made me special? The same God that let my mother and father die in front of my eyes? That God? Or the one in Gary's song? The one that loved me. Could they be one and the same?

The axe work overhead stopped and the cackle multiplied. I looked up. Two deformed faces peered down through a basketball-sized opening. Jenni screamed again, much clearer than before. I stared into those deformed faces, met their maddening stares, and tightened my hold on Ash's hand. Maybe I was here for a reason. Jenni didn't have to die.

"We don't have much time, Ash." I never looked away from the inbred monstrosities overhead. "We need to escape this maze."

"I don't know how. I don't know the way."

"I know you don't, Ash." I smiled. "But I *will* when I see it."

I tore down through the hall, weaving through the mess of opened doors and looming, soot-clad figures. I skid to a halt beside a battered wooden door and reached for the handle.

Ash's grip on my hand tightened. "That's not the way, Steven."

"I have to go in here, Ash." I turned the knob and the door creaked open.

A gush of dust rattled through the doorway like a dying breath. Whatever we needed was in there. I reached in and tried the light-switch. No luck. The axe-work started up again almost directly above us, but the chortling had died. They sounded agitated now—whooping and cawing like mad hens.

I moved cautiously into the room. It was colder and Ash's trembling worsened. My eyes adjusted to the darkness and I shifted toward the large clump ahead. The hacking intensified in frantic spurts. I inched closer to the clump.

Something bumped my face. A tinny sound accompanied the impact and I reached toward it. A minuscule chain. With a quick jerk and a pop, light spread through the room from a dangling light. The light explained everything. I recoiled from the scene.

There, seated on a morbid chair of bones spliced together with hair, sat decaying remains. It looked human, but deformed and with a garden of tin flowers crafted from soup cans protruding from various parts of the body. A small Minotaur statuette covered with dust sat clutched protectively in the thing's arms beneath a sea of cobwebs. I grabbed the statuette.

How was this going to help us escape? The mythological Minotaur had guarded a Labyrinth. Sort of like this house. So what dark secret was that little statue protecting?

Biting cold raced up my arm from the statuette. Flashes of violence and inhuman screams tore at my mind. That statuette had been used for something evil. That statuette had exacted terrible atrocities. Somehow, the dark rituals in which the statuette had been used had given that creature power over our host and his cronies.

That creature.

I staggered backward. My head swam.

They called it father. A father wouldn't commit the atrocities I envisioned. But evil. Pure, unadulterated evil. Evil would breed evil. Would twist it and mold it in its own image.

The vision passed and I staggered to a halt. Glancing down at that statuette, Ash's words made more sense. Greed. Lust. Selfishness. Those creatures upstairs secreted evil. And that statuette had forged their nature. Its memories would buy our freedom.

"Let's go, Ash." I reached for her hand.

Gone.

I scanned the room frantically. Nothing but clutter and the corpse. Where had she gone? I raced into the hallway.

The monstrosities overhead had hacked a much larger hole than before. They stopped. A brief moment of silence passed where they stared at me, their grotesque eyes roving to the statuette, and then chaos. Screams, wails, jumping around, smacking each other, scrambling to run away. Perhaps with it in my possession, our hosts saw a transference of power.

Whatever that statuette's power, I didn't have time to stand around figuring it out.

I took off down the hall. "Ash! Where are you?"

The ashen people had vanished from the open doorways. I turned a corner and ran into a door. *The* door. So where was Ash?

"Ash! I found the way out! Ash!"

"Have you? What about Jenni?"

I jumped. Ash stood beside me. I glanced around. Where had she come from? "You first, Ash. I haven't forgotten Jenni."

I ripped the door open, grabbed her hand, and tugged.

She didn't move.

"Come on, Ash."

"This isn't the way, Steven."

I glanced at the cellar doors only a few feet away. The night sky poked through cracks in the wood. "Yes it is, Ash. I can see the sky. Come on."

"There is only one way, Steven. Gary knew it. Jenni knows it. Now you have to take it."

I stared at her incredulously. I pulled on her arm, but it seemed as if she was cemented in place.

"He gave you the gift, Steven. Only He can set you free. He is the only way."

Maniacal chaos pounded overhead. If I didn't hurry, they would bar the cellar doors and lock me inside. The window of opportunity was closing.

I glanced at the cellar doors again. Only two possibilities existed in that moment. I would either live or die. Life or death hinged on my choice. I knew I could save Jenni, but for once, I didn't know what that meant for me. Would saving Jenni cost me my own life?

I met Ash's anxious stare and smiled. Maybe I wasn't supposed to know. Maybe, just once, I needed to try a little faith. I *could* save Jenni. Even if I didn't make it, I could save Jenni. *Okay, Mamma. God gave me the gift, and they won't take it away.*

"What do I do, Ash? I'm going to save Jenni. I know I can. I'm done with . . . I'm done. I'm taking myself back."

She smiled. She extended her other hand, a hand wrapped in brilliant white light. "Then you know what you have to do, Steven. Pray with me. Let go of the past. Cast away the darkness in your heart and let His Light fill you."

I clamped my free hand around hers and let the light envelope me. I mirrored her words, asking a God I'd loathed for forgiveness. His gift. His plan. And now, I would do something for someone else. Now, I would do something for Him for a change.

When it ended, I pulled Ash toward the open doorway and she followed. I hurried up the stairway with her in tow, then pushed through the cellar doors. Cool twilight air rushed at me. Freedom! I was alive!

I laughed, stopped, sucked in the air, then laughed some more. Alive.

I examined the house—definitely not the house I'd visited per the letter's directions. The siding hung here and there between broken windows and patchwork plywood. Garbage littered the mess of a yard surrounding the dilapidated structure. And there, in three of the windows, *they* watched: our host and the two sniggering inbreeds.

I lifted the statuette so they could see. They would fear it. They would remember the tortures that statuette had done in their father's hands and fear it.

All three started jumping around like orangutans in a frenzy—shrieking and smacking the walls. Jenni was alive, and for once, I was going to do something for someone else. A warm feeling swelled in the pit of my stomach. Not only did I know I was going to help her, for the first time I could remember, I just knew it was the *right* thing to do. What He wanted me to do.

"I have to go now, Ash. Jenni needs me. You're free. Get out of here."

I turned and smiled at her. My smile died beneath a gasp. She drifted away, fleck by glowing fleck in the breeze. I had seen ashes billow in the wind before, but never a pile of ashes shaped like a young woman. And never a pile of ashes that glowed more brilliantly with each dissipating fleck.

"You took it back, Steven." Her voice drifted along the breeze. "Just like He said you would. Your decision has set you free."

I had to shield my eyes. "I don't understand, Ash."

"You asked who we were, Steven. We are you, reflections of your soul, if you will. Everyone has a choice, Steven. You chose to take yourself back. You chose to set us free. You chose the Light. Consider this your little miracle. Now you know. For the first time in your life, you *truly* know."

Words choked on my tongue. This couldn't be happening. Despite how horrible the last few days had been, this just couldn't be real.

"Thank you, Steven. And remember, God made you special. Don't ever let them take that away from you. Good-bye."

"Good-bye, Ash. And thank you." I smiled and waved good-bye. I would never see her again. At least, not in this lifetime. I leveled my gaze on that morbid house, hefted the statuette in front of me, and set off toward the crooked door. Jenni was going to survive.

I just knew it.

FUMBLEBLOT'S TASK

Deborah Cullins-Smith

It's business as usual in the corridors of Hell. Fumbleblot has one last chance to prove his worth to Lucifer. He must prey on the fears of a young Christian named Gretchen Hobson. This story came to life in the writing group, The Herscher Project, for an assignment about fear of the number 13. Take a journey with Gretchen through her fears to see if God can deliver her before Fumbleblot's deadline. Note: All scriptural references adapted from KJV.

FUMBLEBLOT SCUTTLED ACROSS THE rough stone floor and slithered into the Great Chamber. Heat from the massive fireplace caused droplets of sweat to streak his forehead. Or maybe it wasn't the fire. Perhaps it was the forbidding presence that lounged in an ornate wing-backed chair, long claw-like fingers laced, pointed chin resting on the bony knuckles. Fumbleblot dreaded these conferences. He never lived up to his master's expectations, and he cringed in fear of Lucifer's explosive temper.

I'd rather face a nuclear explosion. Fumbleblot gulped back the bile in his skinny throat. *Living above ground has been so pleasant. I must do something, anything, to avoid banishment to the Underworld.*

"Yes," said the silky voice of the figure by the fireplace. "And you'd better do it quickly, for my patience is dwindling, my fumbling, stupid flunky." The creature rose to his full, dark height, shoulders silhouetted against dank walls. A black robe covered the massive frame, but the eyes that glowed from that swarthy face vibrated with fury.

Fumbleblot cowered, his chin practically scraping the floor, his knees shaking uncontrollably. The master was angry. *Not good,* he thought morosely.

The dark figure paced leisurely before the fire, flames flickering every time he whooshed across the hearth. *The master does love his theatrics,* thought Fumbleblot. But an evil glare from Lucifer made Fumbleblot cringe, dreading the beating he knew he deserved. *He knows your thoughts, you fool!* Fumbleblot berated himself. *Stop thinking before you get yourself fried!*

Lucifer's eyes glowed with the satisfaction of seeing a servant's ab-ject fear. He didn't have to say a word to this little toad! One look melted the bungler's bones into mush. Lucifer fed on that fear, tasting it, savor-ing it, feeling it strengthen the sinews in his chest. Those idiots, those creatures of clay and water, those ... humans ... needed meat and milk to feed their stomachs. But all Satan needed was a good, healthy dose of fear to sate his hunger. And this bumbling, blathering, blithering excuse of a servant fed him a whopping meal with every encounter.

"I live to serve you, my master," Fumbleblot said, groveling shame-lessly, not daring to look up.

"Well, you don't do a very good job of it!" Lucifer shrieked, lips curled in a feral snarl.

Fumbleblot threw himself to the floor, drawing his body into a trembling ball. He held his breath and waited for the lightning bolt that would send his cowering flesh tumbling into the fiery pits.

But the pain didn't hit. Fumbleblot peeked between curled fingers. Lucifer's smile sent shivers into his soul, but he felt encouraged. He hadn't been reduced to cinders, and he wasn't burning in the pits yet. Maybe he would yet prove to be worthy of the master's appreciation.

"Yesssssss," Lucifer hissed. "You foul worm. You shall have one more chance to salvage your career in my service."

Fumbleblot's face broke into a ridiculous grin. "Master is most gracious," he blubbered. "I won't let you down, my Lord. I'll make you proud. I'll succeed beyond your highest expectations. I'll—"

"SILENCE!"

Fumbleblot almost melted into the stones.

Lucifer took a deep breath. This lump gave him a headache.

"I have a new assignment for you." A woman's picture appeared in glowing detail against the dark wall as though cast by a projector. Lucifer pointed to the innocent face and the tousled mop of red curls. "This creature," Lucifer said, clenching his teeth in loathing, "belongs to the Enemy. But you, my ... servant ... will cause her to doubt." His voice was thick with scorn, knowing that this toad would most likely fail even in this simple assignment. "Her faith is new and she is easily swayed. It is your task to shake the foundations of her beliefs."

Fumbleblot's heart sank to his toes. A believer! Why couldn't he have been dealt a hellfire-and-brimstone sinner to lead to the pits? A believer! They were the worst of mankind. Once they'd submitted to the Enemy, it was nearly impossible to yank them back from ... His ... Hand.

"Nearly impossible?" Lucifer's question jerked him back from his own dismal doubts. "And how," the Devil's oily voice seethed, "can you possibly expect to derail a believer's faith WHEN YOU BELIEVE

MORE DEEPLY IN . . ." he gulped at the holy reference as if it pained him, "HIM . . . THAN THEY DO?!"

Lucifer's voice echoed in the cavernous chamber. He waited for the echo to die before continuing his lecture, speaking slowly, as one would instruct a toddler. "Find a weakness. There is always a weakness, if one but knows where to look. Since you've proven by past exploits that you **don't** know where to look, I'm going to spell it out for you."

Fumbleblot scarcely believed his good fortune! The master was going to share his secrets! He **never** shared his own insights! How much easier could it get than this?

"Easier?" Lucifer asked. This idiot never learned. How many times in one session would he forget that the master could read his every thought? "NO assignment concerning a believer should ever be construed as 'easy,' you dolt! And don't you forget it!"

Fumbleblot's head bobbed up and down in humble acknowledgement as he mentally kicked himself for stumbling into that dung heap so badly. It was a sore spot to Lucifer that he couldn't read the thoughts of humans, especially believers. But he took out his frustration on his minions, and he read them like yesterday's news.

"But, master, won't . . . He . . . forbid us to touch one of His children?"

Fury blazed in Lucifer's eyes, and he ground his teeth.

"I have obtained permission to test her soul." His words were clipped. Fumbleblot knew it galled Satan to admit he needed God's approval to try a saint.

Must keep my thoughts in check.

Lucifer ignored that one, although his eyes narrowed.

"Gretchen Hobson is a young convert with a vast array of superstitions clouding her mind. You, my dear Fumbleblot, will exploit this weakness by tossing her worst fears in her face at every turn. I want her shaking in her chubby little shoes. I want her so wrapped up in tossing salt over her shoulder and avoiding black cats that she forgets to pray, or read . . . that . . . Book, or even remember why she ever dared to believe in Him. I want her scared to death. Literally. Scared. To. Death."

Fumbleblot stared. Too good to be true! What a piece of brimstone-covered cake! A superstitious believer! *I can do this!* He almost clapped his hands with joy.

"We'll see about that," Lucifer muttered. "You've got three days to feed her to me. Three. Days. This Friday is the thirteenth of June. I want her soul in my hands." Fumbleblot's head bobbed up and down enthusiastically until Lucifer's voice thundered at a Richter's level of 9.6. "OR I'LL DEVOUR YOU BONE BY BONE AND MUSCLE BY MUSCLE, DOWN TO THE LAST FINGERNAIL!"

Fumbleblot scrabbled on all fours from the room, hearing the huge iron door slam shut with a thunderous clang, by which time he'd already covered a city block down Hell's corridor. His breath came in ragged gasps, and sweat mingled with the frightened tears that streaked his face.

"I will not fail. I will not fail. I will not fail. I will not fail." He repeated it like a mantra over and over as he leaned against the wall and tried to catch his breath.

"Having a rough day, Blotspot?" asked an oily voice.

Fumbleblot knew without looking up. Festerhobble had been a competitor and a thorn in his side for centuries.

Today of all days. Fumbleblot pushed himself away from the wall and forced a little dignity into his wobbly spine. "Why, no, Fester, why would you think that? I'm fine, perfectly fine."

The door to Lucifer's office burst open and Fumbleblot jumped several feet at the sound.

Lucifer scowled. "Why are you still here, Fumbleblot? Don't you have an assignment to deal with? Or perhaps you intend to phone in your temptations?"

Festerhobble snickered into his hand, eyes gleaming with delight at Fumbleblot's mortification. The stooped bundle of rags leered, revealing misshapen teeth and rotting gums.

"J-j-just leaving, m-m-my lord," he stuttered.

Lucifer scowled again, then clapped an arm around Festerhobble's shoulders. "Come in, come in, come in, my friend. Wonderful work you did on that senator last month. Nicely done. But now we're on to bigger and better things. We have much to consider, Festerhobble. You know, Mardi Gras is just around the corner. I love New Orleans during Mardi Gras—" And the door slammed shut again.

"Master's pet," he muttered. Fumbleblot's face darkened in humiliation. This was one task he had no intention of failing. He almost ran down the hallway and through the labyrinth of corridors in the huge dungeon. He was headed for the city of Chicago, somewhere in the middle of the North American continent.

"Gretchen Hobson, I will have your soul," he said with as much conviction as his sickly heart could muster. "I'm going to deliver you up to my master on a fiery silver platter, if it's the last thing I do!"

*   *   *

Gretchen ran a comb through her tangled curls and put the finishing touches on her eye shadow, pausing now and then for a quick sip of milky coffee. She always felt rushed before work. She had started as a low level clerk for a small publishing house downtown, but felt immense pressure to fit in, to advance in the company. Before she knew it, she was moving up. She was an assistant editor now. Appearances were important. Gretchen was overly conscious of the extra ten pounds, which had mysteriously glued themselves to her thighs, and the unruly texture of her auburn tresses.

She peered more closely in the mirror and uttered a tsk of annoyance. Another blemish glared from the middle of her forehead. She wished for a clear, creamy complexion. Her friend, Joanne, possessed flawless skin. She tugged her bangs across the offending pimple, endeavoring to hide it. Her boss, Audra Conner, had the most lustrous black hair, straight and silky. She envied Audra's lean body and long, shapely legs. Gretchen's short legs and knobby knees stayed hidden beneath wool slacks in the winter, and mid-calf length skirts in the summer. She blotted her lipstick, checked her appearance in the mirror, and sighed. This was as good as it was going to get. With a grimace, she stuck her tongue out at her reflection before carrying her coffee cup to the kitchenette.

She paused by the kitchen table and glanced at her black leather Bible.

Look at the clock! You'll be late for work, said a small voice next to her ear. Her eyes strayed to the red enamel, apple-shaped clock above the kitchen sink. A groan escaped her neon pink lips, and she grabbed a wool coat from the back of a chair before dashing for the door.

I'll have to take time for devotions and prayer later, she thought, regretting the Bela Lugosi film fest she had indulged in the night before. She knew at the time that she'd kick herself for staying up so late, but those old horror films didn't hit cable television very often. She had heard the justification echoing in one ear, while a small voice in the other ear had counseled an early bedtime. By the time she had shut off the TV, it was well past midnight. She'd been too sleepy for bedtime prayers, and had promised herself she'd rise early to make up for it. After smacking the snooze alarm four times this morning, she'd finally managed to roll out of bed. Dashing for a taxi, she hoped that traffic wouldn't be too horrendous.

Gretchen threw open the front door and jerked to a sudden stop at the sight of a tiny black kitten sitting on the curb. It looked at her with large green eyes. Irrational fear gripped her by the throat, and her knees shook.

Don't let it cross your path! screamed a voice in her head. *Be careful! It's bad luck! Don't look!*

Gretchen's fears stemmed from her Granny's tales of hexes, curses, and wild Irish legends. She grew up with the Banshee, the monsters under the bed, and Grimm's Fairytales. She still found herself checking under her bedskirt after her prayers at night. Some habits die hard. At twenty-five, she felt she should have outgrown such nonsense, but somehow, she just couldn't get away from the stories Granny had told. Black cats were one of Granny's worst omens. Gretchen remembered the old lady turning abruptly in the middle of a sidewalk and walking four blocks out of her way to avoid crossing paths with a black cat. She never understood why, but Granny would mutter to herself, clutching at the silver crucifix around her neck, and fear settled like a dark, heavy cloak around them both.

Gretchen almost ran back into the apartment building. Fear weakened her limbs, and set her heart pounding.

But I'll be late for work, she protested.

Better late than cursed, came the response in her head.

Gretchen dared to glance back toward the curb at the tiny kitten. She swallowed the lump in her throat and closed her eyes one last time.

"SCAT!" she screamed. The green eyes widened in alarm, the delicate back arched, and with one soft hiss, the kitten darted down the sidewalk. A little boy held his mother's hand as they passed her, and he threw an indignant glance her way as his eyes followed the frightened animal's retreat.

Gretchen suddenly felt foolish. The poor thing was a harmless creature, and she'd terrified it. The child was right. It was a cruel thing to do, and Gretchen was ashamed of her superstitious fear. But the clock was ticking, and she hurried to the curb to flag a taxi.

*   *   *

Fumbleblot ground his teeth in frustration. Things had gone so well! She remained in front of the television until well past midnight, neglected her prayers, checked under the bed when he had projected images of boogey men and monsters in her imagination, and cowered at the nightmares of a wailing, floating Banshee with the face of her old Granny. He fed on her fear, relished her anguish, and spent the wee hours of the morning drafting his first report to the master. Plans progressed nicely. With another two days to go, he had high hopes of success.

Then she managed to chase the black cat away, AND feel abashed in the face of a child's scorn! What a disaster!

"I will not fail. I will not fail. I will not fail—" Fumbleblot muttered as he sat atop the taxi, snarling traffic with one hand, and clutching at his fearful heart with the other. If only he could give his own fear to this wretched girl! That alone would be enough to kill her on the spot. But, no, she mustn't die until she had recanted her faith in . . . Him. Fumbleblot gulped. Thoughts of that Almighty Deity Who had cast them all from . . . up there . . . crushed the air from his lungs. Fumbleblot often regretted following Lucifer, but he would never, ever voice that heresy! He conveniently managed to forget that Lucifer knew his every thought. Again.

That's my one and only secret. No one will ever know how much I miss my old home. He remembered how kind Gabriel had been to him. And Michael often threw an arm about his shoulder and cuffed him gently on the chin. Fumbleblot's eyes stung. He also remembered rough hands gripping his shoulders and casting him from the heights of the universe to the depths of this miserable planet. He felt a vortex of hurricane-force winds ripping his magnificent feathery wings to the leathery, shredded remnants he now possessed on his deformed back. He ground his teeth again, and hardened his heart.

I WILL steal this puny human bag of fearful blubber from that tormenting Ego on the throne! I'll watch Heaven, he gulped at his own daring, *weep when she curses them all and dies.*

He reached through the roof of the cab with one sharp-clawed hand and squeezed the woman's heart, driving fear deep into her fragile spirit. Her breath caught in her throat with a dizzying irrationality, and Fumbleblot feasted on her terror.

* * *

Traffic snaked over expressways, and a construction site bottlenecked the line of cars into a single lane for two miles. *The black cat!* Gretchen's thoughts brought a sting of unshed tears to her eyes. *Gran was right! They DO bring bad luck. Even the tiny ones.*

She remembered the look of terror in the kitten's round green eyes. She still harbored a pang of shame for scaring the creature so badly, but she couldn't shake off the feeling that her luck wouldn't be running so poorly this morning if that cat had been sitting on a curb in some other part of the neighborhood.

Then again, had you gone to bed earlier, you wouldn't have had so much trouble rising this morning. You would have been ready sooner, and wouldn't be feeling so rushed now. The traffic would have been a little lighter half an hour ago, and you would have avoided the morning rush. Luck has no place in a believer's heart.

She was chagrined to realize that the small voice was quite correct. Still the dark image of Granny clutching her rosary and yanking her down the street in the opposite direction of Mrs. Abbott's black cat lurked in her mind, a nightmarish phantom from the past haunting her. Fear clutched at her heart as if it possessed talons of steel. She looked at her watch and groaned. There was no use urging the cabbie to go faster. They were locked in bumper-to-bumper traffic. They'd get there when they got there. End of story. But her stomach churned in anticipation of the scolding she would get from Audra. Again. She mentally rehearsed her excuse.

I'm sorry I'm late, Audra. My alarm didn't go off. Guess I'd better invest in a new clock. This one just doesn't—. She stopped. Lying was not appropriate for one who professed to be a Christian. She really shouldn't stoop to fibbing, blaming a perfectly good alarm clock for her own deficiencies.

I'm sorry I'm late, Audra. I was working on my presentation late last night and . . . She paused again. Still a lie, or at the very least, an exaggeration. She had worked on her project, until the Fright Fest came on when she got caught up in tales of vampires and werewolves. *I'm sorry I'm late, Audra, but Bela Lugosi was more interesting than my job. Yeah,* **that** *would go over* **really** *well.*

An evil chuckle seemed to echo near her shoulder, and a shiver ran down her spine. Her Granny would have whispered, "Someone's walkin' o'er me grave." Gran was one of the most religious women Gretchen had ever known, but it was all tradition and ritual. Gretchen understood now that Granny had not truly loved the Lord as much as she feared Hell. Her greatest failing had been the terrible fear the poor woman lived under constantly. She had known a lot of sorrow, and could connect each bad incident with a black cat, a broken mirror, or some other superstition from the "old country" as she called Ireland.

That's what I get for watching horror movies late last night. Now my imagination is running rampant. Audra won't buy that line either. Maybe I'd better leave it with a simple 'I'm sorry I'm late'—period. Excuses don't seem to matter to her anyway. I've never seen such a work-aholic. That woman must live in our office. She sighed as the cab inched forward.

Suddenly she sat upright, her eyes riveted on the construction ahead. A new sign was being raised into position over their lane, and workmen were preparing to attach it to the concrete overpass. Workmen in little platforms. Platforms attached to extension ladders hydraulically maneuvered from the back of construction trucks.

In her mind's eye, Gretchen saw Granny's face again as she sat in the cab, inching toward the extension ladders which arced over the line of slowly moving vehicles. Her hands shook, and she felt a wild compulsion to jump from the cab and run through the stream of traffic as fast as her high heels would carry her.

"Ye mus' ne'er pass 'neath a ladder, lassie. 'Tis the worst of luck to pass b'neath a ladder, don't ye know?" came the ghostly whisper from her childhood.

Fear not, for I am with you; be not afraid, for I am your God. I will strengthen you; yea, I will help you; yea, I will uphold you with the right hand of My righteousness . . . The Scripture scrolled through her thoughts. Pastor had expounded on it in last Sunday's sermon. It sounded so comforting that Gretchen made a point of memorizing it early in the week. A measure of serenity draped around her shoulders, and she relaxed back on the stiff vinyl seat. *I will not give way to my fears.* She took another deep breath. *Not this time, Gran.*

*   *   *

Fumbleblot screeched in fury. The plan had been working perfectly. He grimaced as he imagined the look of rage on Lucifer's face. Scripture! The little wench! How dare she go memorizing Scriptures to foil his plans! He had too much riding on this assignment. He glared up at the overpass and the ladders he had so carefully planned for this morning. Gauging the distance, he unfurled his tattered wings and waited for the right moment to strike.

Closer, closer . . . The sign loomed overhead, and traffic had come to a complete stop. Fumbleblot launched himself from the roof of the taxi, and smacked the sign, snapping the suspension ropes. The workmen in their cages atop the ladders jerked back in surprise, and the ground crew scattered in panic as the sign came rushing toward Gretchen's cab.

*   *   *

Gretchen tried to close her eyes. Maybe if she didn't watch their approach to the overpass, she could hold her apprehension at bay. So much of her life had been spent in fear that she didn't feel she knew how to live any other way. She saw men running, though she could not see the cause of their alarm. They were directly under the ladders now, and she repeated her Scripture over and over to keep from tilting into a panic attack. Just as her puzzled expression gave way to the thought, *why are they running?* traffic shot forward. A split second later, the sign crashed to the ground behind the taxi. Gretchen whirled in her seat and stared in horror as dust rose from the huge green slab of aluminum that had missed the trunk of the cab by mere inches.

The cab driver uttered a string of expletives. Gretchen's heart hammered against her ribs, and fear gripped her soul.

Granny's words echoed in her mind, "Ye mus' ne'er pass 'neath a ladder, lassie. 'Tis the worst of luck to pass 'neath a ladder, don't ye know?"

*   *   *

Fumbleblot giggled with relief. It worked! Fear engulfed the girl, and he could feel his power over her strengthening. He would succeed this time! The master would be so pleased with him. The human trembled, her knees shook, and she was practically in tears. What delight! Success was a heady feeling, and he feasted on the moment as he perched on the roof of the cab for the rest of the ride downtown.

*   *   *

"Where have you been?" demanded Joanne when Gretchen stumbled into the office and collapsed into the chair behind her desk. "Audra has been practically foaming at the mouth since—" The petite blonde stopped in mid-sentence and stared at Gretchen's chalky white face, red-rimmed eyes, and trembling body. "What in the world . . . Gretchen, what's wrong? What happened to you?"

Gretchen lunged for the trash basket and promptly tossed her toast. Joanne grimaced and left the office briefly to fetch a Pepsi from the break room. She popped the top and handed it to Gretchen. Motioning for Donny, the janitor, she handed him the foul trashcan with a whispered request to deal with the unpleasantness quickly and quietly. Donny shot a quick look in Gretchen's direction and raised his eyebrows. She wasn't the type to suffer hangovers like a few of the other employees, but there was a first time for everything. He shrugged and headed for the stairwell with the offensive plastic container.

"Ok, Gretchen, talk to me," she demanded.

Slowly, between sips of the soda, Gretchen related the incident in the taxi. Joanne listened, her impatience changing to horror, then to awe. No wonder the girl was a mess!

"You've always laughed at my fears and called them superstitious," Gretchen sobbed, "but just look at my morning! First, the black cat, then the ladder. And I almost got killed. How can you say my fears are groundless now?"

The shrill buzz of the intercom made both women jump, and Audra's voice was cold enough to frost the windows. "Has Gretchen arrived yet, Joanne?"

Joanne picked up the phone quickly. "Audra, she's here, but . . . well, I'll come up to your office and explain the situation. Just give her a minute. Ok?" She hung up and turned back to Gretchen. "Take a minute to collect yourself, Gretchen. I'll tell her about it while you pull yourself together."

She stopped at the door and looked back at her disheveled friend. "You might think about one thing, Gretch. You're frightened and upset, but God's hand must have been on your cab. Sweetie, you could have been killed. **But the sign missed you.** Look at yourself. Not even a scratch. You can look at the fear in your heart from going under a ladder and having a near miss, or you can look at the fact that you were consoling yourself with Scripture, putting your trust in God, and God saved your life. It's your choice." Then she turned and stalked from the room.

Gretchen leaned back in her chair and closed her eyes. Joanne was right. It was a miracle that traffic had moved forward just when it did. Otherwise that sign would have come through the roof. She'd either be on her way to the hospital or the morgue. Accustomed to Granny's dire premonitions, Joanne's encouragement came as a new experience. But she was absolutely right. It was a miracle. And Gretchen decided to look at it that way.

*   *   *

Fumbleblot's fury erupted volcanically. He gnashed his teeth, and stormed up and down the hallway. She was blowing him off again. How dare she? He paced back and forth, hunched in frustration. Only two more days to shake this pitiful lump and destroy her budding faith. And that . . . friend . . . of hers, saying that . . . He . . . had saved the girl's worthless life! God indeed!

If I, Fumbleblot, wanted her dead, she'd be dead! Who does she think she is anyway? What does she know? She wasn't there. If Miss Perfect had been in that cab, she'd have . . . Well, she'd have had to go home and change her clothes! He snickered at his own witty insults.

The problem now was the blubbery wench sitting behind the desk sipping on a soda. He had rattled her; he had shaken her composure. Now he had to move in for the spiritual kill. He must succeed. He had to find a way.

*   *   *

When Joanne returned to the office that she shared with Gretchen, the girl was much calmer. The sugar and caffeine had obviously done her good, as had the pep talk. Joanne felt relieved to see some color back in her cheeks.

"Audra understands, but she needs to know about your progress with the anthology project from the Bowers Group. Are you ready?" Gretchen nodded and gathered a stack of papers together in a legal-sized manila folder. Joanne smiled. "Good. Let's go, girlfriend."

Gretchen stood, releasing a deep breath. As an afterthought, she shuffled through her purse for a hand mirror. She knew she probably needed to at least powder her nose. Maybe freshen her lipstick a bit. Audra was always impeccable in every aspect of her appearance; Gretchen felt she had to at least attempt to live up to that high standard of professionalism.

I can do this, she told herself, as she reached for her hairbrush and plastic encased mirror.

* * *

"Ye-e-e-e-s-s-s," hissed Fumbleblot. "Audra will expect you to look your best. Look at that hair. Maybe you should just shave your head, my dear. It certainly couldn't look any worse than that unruly mop of yours." He laughed maliciously, digging his fingernails into her desk; his countenance so close to her face, he marveled that she didn't smell his fetid breath or feel his glowing eyes boring into her skull. "You'll never live up to her standards, you know. You are a toad compared to that princess of perfection. Your lipstick is smudged, my little troll. And your mascara is runny. A Bourbon Street bum doesn't have a nose as red as that beak in the middle of your face."

On and on ran his litany of insults and barbs. He battered her self-esteem with every slur he could think of. Anything to get her hands shaking, her knees trembling, her thoughts on something other than the "miracle" of her escape from the jaws of death this morning. He wasn't really allowed to kill her. Not yet anyway. After all, he didn't want to actually instigate her death until she had recanted her faith. That was the moment he lived for right now. It would insure his infamy in the vast Underworld, and earn him a place beside Lucifer. He was growing desperate.

He waited for the right moment, holding his breath for the precise second, then he lashed out with his claws extended.

* * *

"Oh, Lord," Gretchen moaned. "I look like a monster. Just look at me. You'd never know I even tried to apply make-up this morning." She raked a brush through her auburn curls and tried to smooth the scraggly frizz that poked out in all directions. Then she flipped open her compact and dabbed at her cherry-red nose and cheekbones. Juggling the mirror and trying to flip the cap off her tube of lipstick with one hand, she struggled to steady her hands. The last thing she needed was to smear lipstick all over her face. When the cap bounced across the computer keyboard and under her chair, she dropped the lipstick and fumbled to catch it. In the process, the mirror suddenly slipped from her grasp and smacked against the corner of desk. The sharp crack filled Gretchen's heart with dread. Even before she retrieved it from the floor, she knew. She sank into her leather chair and groaned.

The mirror lay in shattered shards.

Joanne rolled her eyes and shook her head in exasperation.

"Pleeeeeeease tell me you don't believe in the old seven-years-of-bad-luck crap. Gretchen, you can't *possibly* buy into that crazy myth. You can't. There's no such thing. Not if you believe in God. He isn't going to allow you to fall under curses for such paltry events as broken mirrors, ladders, and black cats. Gretchen, really."

But Gretchen didn't even hear her words, and Joanne knew it. That old haunted look had glazed over her eyes. Granny's tales of sorrow and strife outweighed the seeds of faith in Gretchen's heart. Joanne just had to believe that God was more understanding of the labyrinth of terror within the pitiful woman than she was, because her own patience was rapidly reaching the end of its rope.

Gretchen relived every tale Granny ever told about broken mirrors being the harbingers of doom for generation after generation. Broken mirrors meant famine, long hot summers of drought, long cold winters of frostbite and illness, disease and plague, death and disaster. Gran's tales were not for the faint of heart. The curses of the black cat and passing under ladders paled by comparison to the broken mirror, at least as far as Gran was concerned. How would she ever be able to hang on to her faith in the face of a broken mirror?

With trembling hands, she gathered her papers together and prepared to face her impatient employer with a report on her progress with the new anthology.

*   *   *

Fumbleblot chortled with delight. Delicious! His claw hit the edge of Gretchen's mirror at that perfect moment to send it crashing against the desk. It was tricky, jiggling a human's belongings like that. It took precision, skill . . .

Who was he kidding? It took a great deal of luck.

Now to keep the pressure turned up. This weakling would be a puddle of frightened, sweaty tears before the next two days had ended. He could feel it in his bones. He would win this time.

*   *   *

Audra leaned back in her chair and scanned the documents in her hands while Gretchen attempted to muddle her way through a semi-coherent presentation. Audra Conner was the picture of a successful businesswoman, perfectly composed, impeccably groomed, and totally in control at all times. Gretchen Hobson tried her patience with her untidy appearance and inept social skills. But she was an honest young woman, a hard worker, and she meant well. She was well worth the time Audra spent cultivating her skills. She would learn. Audra had an eye for talent, and she saw much in Gretchen that warranted her efforts.

"This looks very good, Gretchen," Audra said smoothly. "You've done a fine job with Mr. Bowers and his group. Stay on top of the situation and keep the publication rolling on schedule. Let me know if you have any problems. But I see nothing here that causes me concern." She smiled at the young woman, who blushed up to the roots of her unruly red curls. "Good job, Gretchen."

She exchanged a quick glance of encouragement with Joanne, who returned the smile just past Gretchen's shoulder. Audra knew the women were friends, and she knew Joanne was trying to help Gretchen over some rough patches in her personal life. Between them, they would try to help the awkward young girl become the woman she was meant to be. Audra shared Joanne's faith in God, and she felt strongly that there was more to Gretchen than met the eye. And there was more to her problems than just a few superstitions. This was a battle. One they could not afford to lose.

"I've talked to Mr. Bowers about having the contracts ready by the 20th. Does that meet with your approval?" she asked eagerly.

"The 20th? Why would it take so long, Gretchen?" Audra asked with a frown. "You have all the paperwork ready to go. I'd like the documents in the mail to him by Friday. There's no need to drag our feet."

Gretchen's face reddened. "I . . . I . . . just didn't want him to think we were pushing ahead too quickly."

Audra pursed her lips and regarded the young woman. She still had a long way to go. Audra softened her tone, but kept her authority firm. "Gretchen, there is a time to coax an author along, and there's a time to move with decisiveness. You've done a wonderful job with the first part of the procedure, and I'm proud of you. But now you need to take the reins and guide your clients through the rest of the publication process. They'll be looking to you to lead the way, and you have to act in their best interests, as well as ours. Neither of us will earn any income from this project until their book is in print and in the hands of the distributors. I want those contracts in the mail by Friday," she paused to glance at her calendar, "that's the 13th. You'll need to have copies on my desk by noon that day for approval before the last FedEx shipment leaves the building at 3 o'clock. Understood?"

Gretchen's face had gone deadly white when she heard the date. Audra's brow creased slightly. *What's wrong with the girl now?* she thought. *She looks like she could hit the floor in a swoon!*

But Gretchen cleared her throat and regained her composure. "Of course, Audra. I'll have everything ready." Her chin rose just a little, and she squared her shoulders as if about to enter a boxing ring—or a lion's den. She nodded, collected her paperwork, and walked out of the room with her head held high. Once outside the office, however, she leaned against the wall and prayed for the strength to face this monumental task.

And she doesn't even realize. It never even crossed her mind. Why does it matter so much to me?

*   *   *

Fumbleblot practically did back flips up and down the hallway! Fridaythe 13th! Too good to be true! Too good to be true!

He giggled and clapped his hands in delight. *Friday the 13th! She didn't even see it coming! Oh, what bliss! The master will positively leap for joy when he hears this.*

Gretchen's next words reached his ears and caused a wave of nausea.

"Oh, dear God," the distraught girl whined. "What am I going to do? Friday the 13th? This is a disaster! I can't do it. I'll mess it all up. The Bowers Group won't get their contract, the book won't be published, all those eager writers will be disappointed, and Audra will have my head on a platter. I'll lose my job; I'll lose all credibility. I'll wind up waiting tables somewhere in Timbuktu. And all because of one broken mirror and a cursed Friday the 13th. What am I going to do, God? Why can't You deliver me from all these curses of Gran's? Why can't You make me strong? Why do I have to live with such fear?"

The wench was **praying!** How dare she try to enlist aid from the Enemy! She was going to ruin **everything!** He had to act quickly.

"You have contracts due out in two days, you ninny. You can pray later. Right now, you'd better get busy or you really will blow this deal. Get to work, you lazy brat. Do you expect everything to be handed to you like Cinderella's slipper on a pillow?" He dug his angry fingernails into the back of her skull, sending pain shooting up her scalp.

Yesssssssssssss, let's add a migraine to the mix. That'll slow her down. Add to the panic. And above all, it'll keep her from that infernal praying!

*   *   *

Gretchen made it back to her office on wobbly legs and sank into her chair. Her stomach churned, sending waves of throbbing pain into her temples and the bridge of her nose. Shaky hands fumbled in the top left drawer for the extra-strength Tylenol bottle, and she popped three tablets in her mouth, washing them down with the last of the Pepsi. She leaned back and closed her eyes for just a moment to let the pills kick in.

Joanne is right," she whispered. "I've got to get a grip. I can do this. I am a mature adult—well, I'm an adult. The mature part is debatable. I cannot base my life on Granny's curses and dire predictions. This is the 21st century, and that superstitious mode of thinking is outdated and ridiculous. I will not give in to it. I will not give in to it. I will not give in to it. I will not give—"

"Give in to what?" asked a voice that jarred her from her rhythmic mantra. Joanne had entered the office in the middle of Gretchen's monologue.

Gretchen jumped, eyes shooting to the doorway in shock.

"Oh, good grief, Joanne! You scared me to death. Can't you make noise when you walk? Whistle? Hum?" A headache always brought out that fabulous Irish temper, making her cranky.

Joanne shook her head in amused exasperation. "It's not as if I was sneaking in the door like James Bond. I walked down the hall just like a normal person, and I think my high heels even clicked on the tile a bit. You were lost in your own little world there, Sweetie. Wanna come back down to earth?"

Gretchen managed a sheepish smile. "Just giving myself the pep talk I knew you'd give me anyway. I suppose now you're going to tell me that I'm being ridiculous to worry about the broken mirror. Then you'll go into the Friday-the-13th-is-just-another-day routine. Maybe round it out with the fear-is-not-of-God speech? Did I leave anything out?"

But Joanne didn't laugh. She didn't even crack a smile. "Got it all memorized, Gretchen?" Her eyes drilled holes into Gretchen's pale face.

"You can quote the words, but they aren't sinking in. You know it all up here," she pointed to her temple with a perfectly manicured finger, "but you haven't let it sink in here." She pointed to the general vicinity of the heart. "Your grandmother is dead, my friend, dead. And you are so tied up in Irish tales of banshees, devilish pixies, and curses, you are forgetting to live, truly **live**. No, Gretchen, I'm not going to lecture you. You have some contracts to prepare for Friday. Those writers are counting on you. **On you**. It's time you pulled yourself together, Babe. Faith can move mountains. Let's see if it can move you a few inches to the keyboard and printer."

And she turned briskly away from the startled girl. *Let her stew on those apples for awhile,* Joanne thought, writhing mentally at her brusque words. But perhaps Audra was right. They'd coddled and coaxed Gretchen, and still she stumbled over her grandmother's legacy of fear and trembling. Maybe it was time for a little 'tough love.'

* * *

Fumbleblot caught himself grinding his teeth again. That Joanne was a troublemaker, and he loathed her. She always stuck her nose in where it didn't belong. But then his hopes rose as he'd listened to her impressive little speech. Things were looking up! Yes. He could use this to his advantage.

Slithering up to Gretchen's shoulder, he patted her on the head. "Poor girl," he crooned. "Nobody understands, do they? They just don't know what it's like to harbor all these terrible fears. She's just a self-righteous, snooty bore. Who needs her anyway? Poor dear. What you need is to go home and fix yourself a nice cup of tea. You can't possibly be expected to work with a headache like this, can you? You'll be able to think much more clearly when you've taken a nap. You do need the break, you know."

Gretchen shook her head. No, no naps for her, even though that's exactly what she longed for most. She opened the file for the company's standard contracts. These twelve writers had turned out an anthology of fantastic science fiction short stories. They deserved to see their names in print, and she had the power to give them that. If they could meet their deadline, then by golly, she could meet hers, too.

I'll at least get the rough draft filled in and printed, then maybe I'll leave early and go over the pages at home tonight. And I still need to proofread the final manuscript, too. I don't want to send it back to Mr. Bowers, and find out later that it was full of typos. Resolutely, she opened the file folder and started filling in the details of the contract.

*   *   *

Fumbleblot's face darkened, and he fumed. She was ignoring him again! How dare she simply ignore him, especially when he offered her sympathy! Hmph! *We'll see about that!* And he flew out of the room through the walls of the tall building. He had some preparations to make. Let her play with her computer. And just let her try to ward off the headache he'd given her. Her day was far from over!

*   *   *

The phone rang as Gretchen jammed her key in the lock and tumbled through the door. Breathlessly, she grabbed the receiver and gasped out a "Hello?" just seconds before the answering machine kicked in.

"Gretchen?" It was her mother's voice. "Oh, Honey, I was so afraid you wouldn't be home yet."

"What's wrong, Mom?" Gretchen's heart filled with dread. She knew that voice, that shaky 'you'd better sit down' voice her mother used when the news was bad.

"Gretchen, there's been a car accident."

"Who?" Gretchen's voice sounded shrill, even to her own ears.

"Now, Honey, we're going to be all right, but—" her mother swallowed hard. "Your father is in the hospital with a broken collarbone, some cracked ribs, and a concussion. I'm ok, except for a broken arm and some bruises."

"Oh my God . . ." Gretchen suddenly envisioned, in quick succession, the black cat, the ladder, and the broken mirror.

"Gretchen, we are all right," her mother reiterated slowly. "Mrs. Johnson from next door came and picked me up from the hospital. I'm going to get a few things pulled together and go back up there to spend the night with your father. I just didn't want you to worry if you called and didn't get any answer. We'll be fine."

"But, Mom, what happened?" whimpered Gretchen.

"Well, you know, it was the oddest thing. We were headed for that new Wal-Mart Supermarket for some groceries, and this kid in a big ol' pickup truck pulled right out in front of us. Your father tried to stop, but there was no time. The kid just rammed into your father's side of the car. Smashed it all to pieces. But don't you worry, Honey. We'll be just fine."

They talked for a few more minutes, and Mrs. Hobson finally convinced Gretchen that there was no need to fly home. Neither of them was in critical condition. A few broken bones and a lot of bruises, and of course, they would both be taking things real easy for several weeks to come, but they were fine, just fine.

When she hung up the phone, Gretchen took a deep breath and exhaled slowly. Tea, she needed tea and toast. She doubted anything else would stay down at this point. She put the kettle on to boil and popped two slices of bread into the toaster, then picked up her mail.

A letter from the bank. *Great. What now?*

"An overdraft notice?" Gretchen shrieked. "That's not possible!" She grabbed her checkbook from her purse and ran her finger down the entries. Everything was noted neatly in precise figures. Wait a minute . . . Gretchen scanned the figures in the right hand column. There it was. She had logged in the check for the dry cleaners three days ago, but hadn't subtracted it from the balance before turning up the next page. Just enough to throw off her balance by $35. Heaving an exasperated sigh, she made a note to call the bank in the morning and transfer some money from her savings account to cover the check and the overdraft fee. How stupid could she be?

The smell of something burning made her look towards the kitchen. Black smoke poured from the toaster slits.

"Noooooooooo!" she screamed. Gretchen yanked the cord to disconnect it from the socket. Sparks sizzled, catching a roll of paper towels on fire. She grabbed the roll and tossed it into the sink, turning the cold water faucet on full blast. Amid more sizzling and smoke, she successfully doused the fire. She looked around her tiny kitchen and cried. Then she realized that the kettle was not whistling with steam. It had burned dry. Had she even put fresh water in it? Probably not, the way her luck had gone today. Luck. A broken mirror, a ladder, and a black cat flashed before her eyes again, like a worn-out rerun of an old 1960s sitcom.

Seven years of this? I'll never survive.

* * *

Fumbleblot threw all his best moves into the mix. For the next thirty-six hours, he dished up heaping helpings of broken dishes, a glitch in the building's furnace that left her apartment freezing cold, an alarm clock that really <u>did</u> break, making her late for work again, and an assortment of disasters small and large. Gretchen was at the end of her rope.

Joanne was no consolation. She simply pursed her lips and said, "I suppose you think this is all due to a broken mirror." Then she tsk'ed, shook her head, and left the office.

Gretchen got the contracts finished at five minutes before noon and left them on Audra's desk. Back in her own office, she laid her head across folded arms on the desk. She felt totally defeated, depressed, and without a hope in the world of surviving even one more day of this kind of luck.

* * *

Fumbleblot chortled and whistled down the long corridor to the master's office. He left that lump of a woman lying across her desk like a lamb on the sacrificial altar. An appropriate image if ever there was one. He just couldn't wait to tell the master the good news. She finally crumbled, as defeated as anyone had ever been in the history of the world! Lucifer would be so proud of him. By tonight, she'd be slitting her own wrists. He'd just slip into the office and share a good laugh with the master before going back to finish the wench off.

Lucifer sat behind his desk, waiting. Yes, that was Fumbleblot's off-key whistle now. Right on time. He allowed himself a snort of derision and a shake of his head before the stooped, twisted underling slid into the room.

"Master?" he said gleefully. "I hope you don't mind my dropping in, but I just had to tell you my good news."

"Really?" Lucifer's oily voice asked. "What good news would that be, Fumbleblot?"

"The girl?" he said. "Gretchen Hobson? She's ours, Master. I did it! I completely destroyed her. She's ready to throw in the towel. You should have seen all the delicious things I did to her this week! Pure genius. I was superb!" He stopped suddenly, struck by his own daring. Ooops! He had probably gone too far with that last bit. "Of course, I was inspired by your own evilness, my Lord. You are ever the example upon which I model my own devious wickedness. I live to reflect the awesome power which you—"

"ENOUGH!" Lucifer sprang to his feet, his voice echoing in the vaulted chamber.

Fumbleblot hit the floor, prostrating himself in terror before the wrath of Satan. What happened? He thought the master would be pleased to see him. Where was his commendation for delivering the girl into Hell's hands?

"So," Lucifer's voice sank to a low, wrath-filled snarl, "you think the girl is ours, do you? You think you've succeeded? But you didn't bother to stick around for the kill. You came running back here to snivel and drool all over my floor about your marvelous skills. I suppose it didn't occur to you that you shouldn't leave anything to chance when you've come this close to the end of your mission. Nooooooooooooo, not you. You're such an excellent tempter, you just left her alone with her thoughts, alone with . . . HIM . . . just as success might have been within your grasp."

Fumbleblot blanched.

"Would you like to know what happened while you slithered back here to boast—prematurely, I might add—of your victory? Take a look, my stupid bungler. Just watch." Lucifer's eyes glowed red and a picture leapt to life on the wall behind him.

Fumbleblot saw Gretchen, sitting at her desk, head cradled on her arms. She sobbed, shoulders shaking. Then her soft voice echoed off the stones in the cavernous office where he now knelt.

"God, I am so weak. Please help me. I know You can deliver me from these dreadful fears, just as You helped me with those contracts. In spite of all that's happened this week, I just have to believe that You are still in control, that You still care about my pitiful life. I'm not worth much, Lord, but if I can serve You at all in this life, please make me a new creature. Help me to throw off this awful cloak of fearful superstition and learn to praise Your name in all things."

Fumbleblot gasped in horror. Behind Gretchen, a tall being shimmered in the sunlight from the bank of windows. His glorious white wings unfurled in the cramped office, and he hovered tenderly over the distraught girl. Michael! They used to be such friends. He watched as Michael softly spoke words of Scripture to her heart, and her sobs slowly ceased as a look of radiant joy washed over her face. The verses blended together in an anthem of joy and praise, some from the New Testament and some from the Old.

"All things work together for good for them that trust the Lord. Fear not, for God is with you; be not dismayed for He is your God. He will strengthen you, yea, He will help you, and He will uphold you with the right hand of His righteousness. Let your soul magnify the Lord, and let all that is within you bless His Holy Name. Oh, sing unto the Lord a new song! Sing unto the Lord, all the earth!"

With horror, Fumbleblot saw all his work burn away, leaving ashes behind. Not only had he lost the battle, he realized, his war was over and done. He would never fight again. He stared up into the leering face of Lucifer and saw the hatred gleaming in those eyes.

"M-m-m-m-my Lord? I f-f-failed? But it was perfect. I-I-I thought I had her f-f-f-firmly in my g-g-g-rasp."

"You thought you had her firmly in your grasp?" sneered Lucifer. "You! You sniveling, shriveled, cowardly excuse for a demon. Well, my skulking minion, you did succeed. Oh, not with Gretchen Hobson. No, no. Once . . . He . . . gets His paws on one of these lumps of human clay, He doesn't allow anything to steal them from His grasp. I've watched you slither and crawl around the earth for centuries, bragging about your grand plans but never snaring even one soul for my fiery pits. So my assignment wasn't really to tempt Gretchen Hobson. No, my slimy subject, my assignment was for you to fail in the attempt so I could devour you myself and toss the remains of your sorry carcass to the vultures, then burn your bones in the hottest fires of Hell. Your fears have fed my starving soul all week, as you've attempted to lead that worthless human astray. And now you're going to feed my starving belly, you rotten slab of putrefied meat. I'm going to chew on your heart, while you watch, and dine on your gizzard while you scream. Then your bones are going to be used to stoke my fireplace. And for the first time in your sorry life, you're going to bring me a touch of satisfaction, a modicum of delight. And then I'll never have to look at your hideous face ever again."

Fumbleblot scrabbled backwards in terror. Lucifer had been drawing closer and closer with each word.

"B-b-but it's Friday the 13th!" he wailed. "I can deliver the woman into your hands. Her granny . . . the superstitions . . . I-I-I-I . . ."

Lucifer's laughter rang in the great hall with malicious delight. "Ah, yessssss . . . Friday the 13th. Why, my dear Fumbleblot." He drew closer until he could see the red veins in the trembling servant's eyes. Then he whispered, "It's your lucky day."

Even   with   the   doors   closed,   Fumbleblot's   last   scream,

"Noooooooooooooooooo!" echoed up and down the corridors of Hell.

SMALL AND SIMPLE THINGS

Alethea Knight

Alethea Knight has been writing since she was old enough to hold a pencil. Building on her love of the language, she graduated with an English degree from Utah State University, receiving the Outstanding Student award for the department. Now a military and government writer, she has published numerous reports, manuals, and other dry information that she hopes you will never have the bad luck to read. Alethea is a devout Christian who, through her writing of speculative fiction, expresses her joy at the wonders the Lord makes possible. "Small and Simple Things" is her first published story.

WELL HELLO, CHILD. YOU out late. Do your momma know where you at?

Hmm, I'm bettin' not, you standin' there in your feety pajamas with Mr. Wuggles tucked under your shoulder bone. Never you mind. Sit down and have some warm milk, and I'll be bringin' you back to your mound presently.

First things be comin' first, though. I know you've come to see Ol' Maria for a reason. Don' be shy. Tell me all that's in your heart.

Such a silent little thing. This be about your gift, yes? Ah, I thought as much. I've told you afore, child, you needs have patience. These things come in The One's own time. Do you remember the story I told you about how the Founders first come to learn of the gifts? No? Perhaps 'tis time I be repeatin' it, then.

I was scarce ten turns, just a little bigger than you, when the starship reached Panacea. The Founders had sailed the skies for countless turns: I'd never seen true mountains or clouds choked with rain. Indeed, most the ol' folk recalled little of these things. Upon leavin' the great starship, the world was risin' all 'round me, and I longed to run and hide back inside my own room. My papa (your great gran'papa) clasped my hand and lifted me high so I could see the rollin' green meadows touchin' the fiery pink sky, so different than pictures I'd seen of the homeland. My papa laughed in joy, and I knew 'twas good and was afeared no more.

I worked 'longside my papa and the other Founders for many turns, then, buildin' the great houses of metal and stone. Your papa flew with you to see the ruins, yes? Those be the very same that I helped build, long and long ago.

We didn' just keep ourselves in the valley in those early years, neither. We explored our new world, roamin' far beyond our valley, for though we crept on the ground then, the Founders used great machines of metal and noise to carry them 'cross the land. I used to hide aboard the machines now and again, delightin' in the sights: the jumpin' antelope, the flyin' gazelle, the bearded lions in the high mountains. Perhaps when your wings be stronger, you can fly to see the towerin' *mala* trees that belt the world 'round, or the vast bloodflower fields that bloom in the heart of Panacea.

Seven turns after our starship landed, the Change began. Panacea had rooted itself deep in all the Founders and their children. The air, the water, the food—all these things brought about the Change.

Hard to imagine life without wings, eh, child? But the Founders had not a feather 'til Panacea. And we was afraid at first. Ah, don' laugh. Great changes be frightenin', and for us the Change was very great indeed.

Then gifts began to bubble to the surface. Soon all were blessed with a gift of some sort; all but me. I waited and waited, but my gift didn' come. Like you, little one, I was sad as the weeping tree. Even the tiny babes with their featherless wings showed bits of their gifts. While the others thanked The One Above All, I begged to understand why I was skipped over.

'Twas near a full turn afore my gift showed itself, and then I became but a light-bearer, glowin' in the dark of the night. A special gift indeed, you be thinkin', but at the beginnin' none thought so, me least of all. I watched as the other Founders created precious things from the air, lifted massive weights, and ran faster than the eye could track. To my shame, I envied those others and hid my tiny gift.

Then came the first of the Dark Days. The Founders didn' know Machaeon's path through the skies. Panacea's brother planet dogs the sun for just a month, but we was afeared the strange planet had come between us and the glorious sun forever. And before our technologists could find Machaeon's purpose, the Storm descended upon us.

We didn' know to be hidin' metal durin' those first Dark Days. Many died from the fiery lightnin' that pursues metal, and all our homes was destroyed. Worst of all, the lightnin' blasted the great starship and all its secrets. The cap'n and his crew perished, along with the technologists, as they searched for a way to our salvation in the ship's mind.

You ain't yet lived to see the Dark Days, child, but light is a scarce and tricky thing. Machaeon's Storm shrouds the stars, and wind and rain douses all fire 'cept in the deepest caves. Without the secrets in the starship, the Founders' fireless lights soon expired, and darkness and despair crept throughout us all.

We burrowed into the shallow caves behind where your mound's built; we couldn' see to go farther. My family was grateful for me, and took the comfort, huddlin' 'round my dim glow for comfort. Together we read remnants of the Holy Writs that the lightnin' spared and prayed mightily to The One.

It seemed such a shame, that He'd led us so far a distance, only to allow us to perish in our new home. All those great spans of time, past all those stars, we stayed faithful to Him. None know the mind of The One, though, child. So we prayed, and hoped that He be havin' greater things planned for our people.

Probably about a week into the Dark Days, with no end to the Storm in sight and our hope waverin' like a fearful creature, I read a passage in the Holy Writs. Do you remember from your teachin's what it said? No? Listen well then, little one, for you might become a light-bearer yourself, and then this'll be for you too.

It said, "Verily, verily, I say unto you, I give unto you to be the light of this people. A city that is set on a hill cannot be hid. Behold, do men light a candle and put it under a bushel? Nay, but on a candlestick, and it giveth light to all that are in the house; therefore let your light so shine before this people, that they may see your good works and glorify your Father who is in heaven."

The writ spoke straight to my fretful heart. I raised myself up from the dirt, my soul lifted in prayer, and felt His power flow through me. The glow that be my gift cut through the storm like a beacon from Paradise, and my feet floated up from the floor. Scared me at first, I tell you true. But the Founders struggled toward my light from all 'round, fightin' through the drenchin' rain and ferocious wind. I gathered all those who survived and led them into the Storm.

Remember how afeared you was when the winged gazelle attacked you? That's how I felt when the Founders followed me into the darkness. I possessed no idea where to take our people so they would be safe. My glow shone off waves of rain and broken plants, confusin' the face of the planet I remembered. Ponds had become lakes, and lakes great seas.

But The One was with us, and with His guidance I led the Founders deep into the Sacred Caves. Of course, they wasn' sacred yet. We just used them for shelter. Hidden away from the Storm, we ate mushrooms and lichens, and lived on. The Founders called me their blessed light, and even after we built fires, they never strayed far from me.

Without the sun, days and nights passed uncounted. We slept most of the time, eatin' little to keep from runnin' out of food too quick. When awake, we would pass the time by tellin' stories of the past or singin' songs, anything to stop the panic and despair from erodin' our faith. We stayed in one part of the cave 'til the fungus was gone, and then we moved on. 'Twas a dark time, little one. I pray you never see its like.

But great and wondrous things came from that time, too. 'Twas durin' one of our moves that we found the Cavern of Records. Picture in your mind, little one, a cave as big as our valley, its floor covered with tablets piled taller than you. 'Twas a wondrous sight to be seein', I attest to you.

Upon the tablets was carved strange writin', masked by the dust of ages. Herein grew our hope; perhaps the answers to the Storm and darkness was in these ancient records. Time passed unconsidered as the wisest of the Founders struggled in vain to decipher the meanin' of the stones. I yearned to help, but my light was needed to help us forage, and I had little book-learnin' other than the Holy Writs.

My papa, though, was always believin' in me. When they found a peculiar tablet, with only one line of writing incised on the surface, my papa brought me to it.

"Little light-bearer," he told me, with his big mustached smile, "Your blessed light led us to safety. Perhaps The One will see fit to grant us knowledge through you as well."

Papa held the tablet up to me, and as my glow fell on it, writin' in our style blazed beneath the alien marks. That is the gift of the light bearer, child, to clarify the mind and help you be findin' truth and safety. Your momma has the gift, same as me. And maybe same as you. It is the greatest gift of The One.

Usin' the blessed glow to reveal the truth of the words, we deciphered the other tablets. Our greatest find was the Holy Writs recorded on the tablets, some word for word. The One be over all worlds, you see, not just one, and His writs be granted to all. We had mourned exceedingly for the loss of the Holy Writs, but now they was restored. All the Founders rejoiced, on account of the light of our minds being returned even though we dwelled in darkness.

Other tablets held stories of those who lived on Panacea long ago. We discerned that Machaeon passed between us and the sun only once every fifty and five turns. Those who came before us built mounds underground, makin' houses safe from the Storm. And they buried their metals deep within the caves in the danger times to keep the lightnin' away.

With our new learnin', we sent scouts to the mouth of the caves with a charge to watch for the return of the sun. Right fast they came runnin' back, carryin' stories of the tunnels filled with light, shinin' on the puddles. As we journeyed from the caves, our hearts glowed with gratitude brighter than the sun peekin' 'round Machaeon's shadow and breakin' through those night-black clouds.

Though everythin' lay in ruins, we felt grateful for our lives. We saved what we could, though The One knows that the Storm left little. We built our city anew, this time underground, shunnin' metal in all our creations. And within the Sacred Caves, we built a shrine to The One, with the hallowed tablets stacked all 'round, and the great stone calendar to mark the passin' of the turns 'til Machaeon's return.

You heard tell that by small and simple things, great things be brought to pass. This is why the gift of the light-bearer, though seemin' the least of all the gifts, is held as most precious. Though the light of the light-bearer may be small and slow to come, it saved our people and restored the Holy Writs.

So be patient, child, wait for your gift with patience and honor, for perhaps The One Above All shall bring to pass mighty miracles through you. But not tonight. Look at me, chatterin' on, and your eyes so heavy. Your momma will have my wingtips. Come. Take my hand, and I shall lead you home.

THE AGENT

Adam Graham

I've read quite a few books that have left me wondering not only how it got published, but how it became a best-seller. In "The Agent," we meet a young writer who seeks out the services of an agent who can make any book a best-seller, never suspecting that the devil is in the details.

I CURSED THE DAY I met him. But, it was my doing.

The literary world mourned the great Theodore Gruening's passing from a self-inflicted gunshot wound.

A girl sat in front of my counter. "He saved my life!"

I put the latte in front of her. Her tears dripped into it. What a waste of a latte. Never mind that, what a waste of a good body. Old Man Gruening profited on gullible people seeking answers to great universal questions in science fiction novels.

Spare me the groupies, but I wanted to replace Gruening. I put my apron down and hit a button on my register to end my shift at the Coffee House. I walked past the mourning groupies and headed out the door. Unlike Gruening, I didn't write much about space, and I actually had talent. I just wasn't getting paid for it. One man held the key to my future. Frank Gruening's agent, Sal Ramirez.

I got in my '91 Buick LeSabre, started it and pulled out of the parking lot. I checked the rearview mirror before changing lanes and cursed. The car was spitting black smoke again. It belonged in a junkyard, but still managed to run. If I could get Sal Ramirez on my side, I could drive a new Buick.

Half his writers stank. High school kids I'd tutored could out-write Sal's clients. Old Gruening had never been better than average to start with, but in his latter years, he'd grown sloppy. That's what happens when you know you can submit your used toilet paper as a manuscript and a publisher will grab it up and sell 200,000 copies.

Sal's other writers weren't as bad, but that didn't say much. Sal's writers might write crap, but he was the master of selling it to publishers and promoting it. A few years back, I'd made the connection that the six most popular fiction authors in the world had the same agent.

I'd wanted him to be my agent. Young and naïve, I barged into his office. Most big-time agents would have called security or more likely had their secretary do it. Ramirez looked at me. "Kid, I like you, but there's only one of me and I have as many clients as I can handle. However, if I have an opening, call me."

I wasn't too happy, and did end up getting another agent. I'd fired that bum last week. Three years and all I had were fifteen magazine articles, and only ten of those paid. Now, I was going to get a professional.

Only an idiot would send a query letter. Hundreds of those would be going to Sal Ramirez soon enough; a personal approach was needed. But, was I being too personal?

Sal Ramirez's palatial residence loomed before me. Did I really think I could ring the doorbell and a man worth millions would let me in? No doubt, he had people to answer the door, not to mention security systems to protect him from dangerous nuts. I could end up in jail.

I cursed my timidity. This was a chance of a lifetime. What's the worst thing that could happen? I'd get fired from that coffee shop and kicked out of my dinky apartment? Even that was unlikely. I'd take off as soon as someone threatened to call the police.

I walked up the path to Ramirez's house, my breath visible in the cold night air. Gargoyles lined the path. I'd dreamed about this. A house like this. High end vehicles like the ones that must be in the six-car garage.

It could all be mine.

Writers were the most cursed lot on Earth, writing more novels than could possibly be published and read. My days of submitting to short story contests, or hoping for some $15 check to come and justify the hours I spent and the money I sacrificed were going to be over. A new life lay just beyond that door.

I stood before the door, hand-carved with images of goblins and ghosts and so many other characters from Dave Raineer's suspense series. Raineer was probably the most talented of Ramirez's clients.

I knocked. An old man with a few strands of white hair answered. "Sir, may I help you?" In his silly little suit, he looked like the butler from any television series.

"I'm here to see Sal Ramirez," I said.

"What for, sir?"

"I'm a writer."

The old man gasped. "Uh, you're at the wrong house—"

A voice called, "Billy, who's at the door?"

I gasped—Sal Ramirez!

The butler said, "No one, sir."

Sal said, "Hold on, no one doesn't use the doorbell. Last I checked, no one went nowhere and did nothing. I want to come and meet this young man."

The butler leaned in and whispered, "Get out before it's too late."

Sal said, "Billy, relax. Don't scare away all our guests. You've been reading too many novels."

Billy swallowed hard. "Of course, sir."

Sal appeared in a night robe beside the butler. "I recognize you. A couple years ago, you came to my office. Henry Richards, isn't it?"

"Harry, sir," I said.

"Sir? You're not in the army, call me Sal. Everyone does, isn't that right, Billy?"

"Yes, Mr. Ramirez."

Sal laughed. "Okay, so everyone but Billy. Come on in." Sal led me into his living room and sat down by the fire. He pointed to the chair next to his. "Have a seat, kid."

I sat down. Time to get the obligatory niceties out of the way. "I was sorry to hear about Gruening's death."

"I bet." Sal glanced up at a picture of his clients that hung over the fireplace. "Thirty-six years is a long time. Between us, we had seven wives during that time. So, you want to take his place?"

Wow, cut right to the chase, why didn't he? I extended a manila envelope. "Sal, here's my clips."

"Is this your only copy?"

"No."

"Good." Sal tossed the envelope into the fire.

Wow, he had a flair for saying no. Maybe, I'd stick with the mail from now on. I took a deep breath, though I felt like grabbing him by his robe and shaking him. "Thank you for your time." I stood up and started to leave.

"Kid," said Sal. "I didn't say I wouldn't represent you, I just don't care about clips."

I whirled back around.

Sal beckoned. "Have a seat."

I returned and Sal said, "I look for writers who can write good stories on demand. I help my writers come up with ideas for books that will sell. They write it, I edit the manuscript and sell it. We promote it together and get rich."

While I preferred coming up with my own plots, the getting rich part sounded good. "Okay, I'm with you."

"Now, what do you like to write?"

"Historical fiction, and a few mysteries on the side."

"Let's go with that historical angle." Sal walked to a bookcase and pulled off a folder. "Here's a book I'd like you to work on."

I grabbed the folder. "'Indian Messiah'?"

"Yes. Some people believe Jesus didn't really die in Israel or get resurrected, but rather was severely wounded and escaped the tomb to India."

"A little out of the mainstream."

"A little controversial? Yeah, I'd say so, but controversy sells about as well as sex and is more marketable."

My parents had been Lutheran. I'd been baptized, but never confirmed. My family wouldn't like it, but neither God nor my family had done much for me. I grabbed the folder. "How many months do I have to complete this?"

"Months?" Sal shook his head. "I need quicker work than that. You have seventy-two hours."

My jaw dropped. "Sal, there's no way."

"Then you can hand back the folder and leave."

I clutched the sheaf of papers. No, I had to try; I'd be a fool if I didn't. "No, I'll give it my best."

"That's the spirit."

I sat at my desk, staring at a blank computer screen unsure where to begin my novel of Jesus as a great Hindu teacher.

About an hour later, I snapped my fingers. Jesus could meet up with a Buddhist teacher, and they could have adventures running from authorities all over India. It'd be a religious teacher buddy adventure that'd speak to the commonality of all faiths, or something like that.

My fingers raised. Words flowed like they'd never flowed before. A few hours passed; I looked at the clock. Four o'clock in the morning! I'd been at it for fifteen straight hours.

I went to bed, but after an hour, got back up and typed for what seemed like mere minutes. By the time I looked up, the clock read 8:00 p.m. I made coffee and got right back at it .The alarm buzzed. Six a.m.; I needed to get to work. But I was almost done and almost out of time. I had only nineteen more hours to finish my manuscript and get it to Sal.

I picked up the phone and dialed my manager's number at work. I coughed and, in a scratchy voice, said, "Hi, Angela, this is Harry. I've got a very sore throat. The doctor said it's contagious. I should be able to come in tomorrow." I coughed twice more for good measure before hanging up.

I resumed work. Somewhere in the space of writing the last twenty pages, the phone rang. I ignored it. I doubted it was Sal and if Angela cared to call, I was too sick to answer.

At noon, I finished the rough draft. My writing teacher had claimed writing was rewriting. She'd never tried to rewrite a 500-page novel in only nine hours.

I scoured the novel as best I could for every poorly written sentence, every sentence fragment, every imperfection that would damage my masterpiece. Yes, it wasn't my idea, but it was a glorious inspired epic. I pushed back the voice asking who inspired it.

I slapped my manuscript down on Sal's desk.

Sal said, "So, you finished?"

I smiled. "It was a great challenge, but yeah."

"How many pages?"

"508."

"Good work." Sal picked up the CD with the manuscript on it. "I'll go through this and call you tomorrow. Billy will show you out."

In the hall, Billy met me, but stood still a moment. From behind the office door, came a hideous sound, like some weird chant. Billy froze until it had finished. "Sir, come this way."

Man. Sal had a weird taste in music.

Near the end of my shift at the coffee shop, Sal came in smiling and carrying several pieces of paper stapled together. He walked to the counter. "Kid, you're dynamite."

I smiled. "Does that mean you'll take me on?"

Sal put the contract down. "Sign on the dotted line."

I flipped through the forty-page document. "Shouldn't I get a lawyer?"

"Look, I'm not some two-bit agent out of school. When I make a deal, it's good. It's just got your standard clauses. I get a twelve percent commission on anything I sell. Most agents charge fifteen, but I'm not greedy. I make more on twelve than most do on fifteen."

"What are all these clauses?"

"Just standard stuff, kid. You know, you write until your arm bleeds."

I sent Sal a concerned look.

He laughed. "Just kidding. Sell your soul to the devil. Rights to your first-born. Just kidding again."

I laughed. Of course, Sal could be trusted. He was the greatest literary agent on Earth. I signed the contract.

Sal slung his arm around me. "Now, come on, boy, let's get you a book contract."

Two hours later, we sat in the office of David Driscoll, one of the nation's premiere publishing editors.

Sal said, "David, I've got a book for you from my new author, Harry Davis."

Driscoll said, "How much are you wanting in royalties?"

"Ten percent on retail should be fair."

"Eight. He's a first-time author."

"He's good. Nine."

Driscoll nodded. "Now onto the advance."

Wait a second! It was not supposed to be this easy!

"$100,000," said Sal.

Driscoll pursed his lips. "Fifty."

"Seventy-five thousand, seven hundred."

"Seventy-five, seven it is."

"Can we get this released next Easter?"

Easter! The book hadn't even existed until four days ago and he wanted it released in six months!

"Sure," said Driscoll. "I'll get the boys in marketing on it. Now what's the book about?"

"We'll get to that, let's get the contract in."

"Good thinking." Driscoll hit a button on his intercom. "Send in the contract for Sal's new writer. Advance of $75,700 and 9% royalties."

I raised my hand. As much as I enjoyed this, I wanted to get some clarification before Sal sold him the movie rights, too. "Excuse me. I've read books on publishing and this seems a little fast."

Driscoll smiled. "Young man, Sal has never brought me a book that didn't sell at least 200,000 copies. If Sal brings it, I'll sell it."

But Driscoll didn't even know what it was about. Oh well, who was I to argue with these masters?

We signed the contract and an hour later, Sal left with his cut and I left with a cashier's check for $66,616.

I stood in the hall outside Sal's dining room. Sal smiled. "How did it feel to deposit $66,000 in your account, kid?"

"Great, except the bank thought it was counterfeit. They won't let me have full access to it for another week."

Sal laughed. "Oh, they'll get used to it soon enough. Nobody blinks an eye at my bank. Come on; let me introduce you to my other writers."

Sal led me inside. Three men and a woman sat around the table. They hardly needed an introduction: Cheryl Rogers, the author of the best werewolf series ever written; David Raineer, simply the best Horror/Suspense writer in the history of mankind; Johnny Sams, author of the famous children's series Jeffrey Warlock; and Neil Dugan, a decent Science Fiction author who like Gruening had attracted a cult following.

I stared open-mouthed. How could I, a mere mortal, have climbed to the top of Mount Olympus to dwell with the gods?

Raineer stepped forward, "Sal showed me some of your work. It's good."

I could have died happy. Dave Raineer said my work was good!

Sal said, "I carry fewer writers than most agents, because I need fewer. More importantly, once you're in, you're part of the family."

Sams affected a silly Italian accent. "Don't go against the family."

Everyone laughed. At least everyone but Sal.

A year passed. I went back out to Sal's place in a brand new Buick. The book had changed my life. I'd gone back to the old coffee shop for a book signing and insisted that Angela wait on me.

Religious fundamentalists were not too happy about my "revisionism." Well, they could get over it; it was only a novel. Mom and Dad were proud, I had a fantastic car, and all the hottest women lined up for dates. Who cared what some yay-hoo in the Bible Belt thought?

On my way in, David Raineer stormed out of Sal's office. "We're finished!"

Sal ran into the hall after him. "David, we've been together thirty-one years."

"And it ends today. I told you I wanted to write a prison novel and you're fixed on my doing more horror and suspense. I want control of my career. If you'll give it to me, I'll stay. If you won't, I'm out of here."

"Don't go against me. Every million you've made has been because of me."

David snorted. "Yeah, big shot, you think everything is about you. Well, Sal Ramirez has never written an original paragraph of fiction in his life! Good day."

As David headed out, Billy whispered something to him, but David shook his head. "I don't need you guys anymore."

A couple weeks went by. I got a call from David on a Sunday morning. He panted. "They're trying to get me."

I got up from the computer and moved to the couch. "Who?"

"Don't know. I need help, Harry. We're friends. I need—"

The phone went dead. I called David's cell phone—no answer.

I found the number for the sheriff in Lincoln County, Montana and called them.

They sent out a car and found David clawed to death by some wild beast. No evidence linked it to Sal, but just to be safe, I'd stick with the plot ideas Sal gave me.

A few months later, Cheryl Rogers e-mailed me and explained she was leaving Sal. Tired of writing about the occult, she'd decided to return to Catholicism.

She wrote me, "For so long, I've lived under a veil of darkness and I simply must get out. I long for Christ, and He is ever there and ever ready to accept me. If you seek him, He will accept you too."

I had no interest in coming to Christ; it would be incredibly bad for business. We did continue to correspond. She talked about her plans to write a series of religious fiction and even sent me a few drafts. A few months after this, though, someone pushed her down the stairs and left her paralyzed from the waist down.

I went to visit her in the hospital. Her eyes fluttered open. "Harry, you need to get away from Sal."

"Sal's been good to me. We just got a third book sold for $500,000."

"Harry, Sal did this to me; I know it."

I put out of my mind what happened to David Raineer. "Sal's been good to me, and he was good to you too. I'm sorry this happened, but it's not his fault."

"But it is. You think you've been given all this for free and so did I, but there's a cost—"

"I'm not listening." I walked away from Cheryl.

My third book bombed by the first two's standards. I'd sold 7 million copies of the first two books and only 300,000 of the third. Sal still got me a good advance for the fourth book.

I went over to Sal's to work out some plot ideas. I arrived at Sal's house at around seven. Billy led me near Sal's office. "Sir, Mr. Ramirez will see you in here." He opened an adjacent door.

I stepped inside to find myself surrounded by coats and jackets. "Billy!"

The door slammed shut. Billy said from the other side, "Sir, not a sound, or it will be the end of you."

"What was that?" Sal said.

"Nothing, sir, a door slammed too loud."

From the footfalls, Sal entered his office. A couple moments later, his muffled voice said, "I understand what Lucifer demands and I'm willing to bring him what he wants, but I'd rather take one of the older ones . . . Yes, I know sacrificing with more potential will truly be honored. Still 7.3 million books sold, that's a big sacrifice. Good thing the advance is non-refundable if he dies. Well, I'll see you there and we'll get the sacrifice tomorrow night."

Oh my God! Sal was going to sacrifice me? I held my breath.

Sal asked, "Hey, Billy, you seen Harry tonight? I see his car outside."

I swallowed hard.

"Sir, he asked me to take care of it. He's hiding in some hole somewhere."

"Spelunking? That figures. Did he say when he'd be back?"

"Tomorrow, sir."

"Well, have a good night."

The door slammed. A car engine started and tires squealed. Billy opened the closet door. "Sir, follow hard after Mr. Ramirez. He's headed west and will turn left on Gardena."

I opened my mouth to question him.

"Go like your life depends on it, because it does."

I ran out to my car and jumped in. The car's engine roared as I began my pursuit of Sal, driven by a combination of fear and morbid curiosity.

Sal turned left down a driveway near a park with a large amphitheater. I drove on about a quarter of a mile and parked. I trudged back through the pitch-blackness down the open field, towards the rear of the amphitheater.

A familiar voice chanted—Sal's. Silence fell until another voice spoke. "Thank you, Brother Sal," said the man. "Do you have a sacrifice?"

"Tomorrow night, I'll bring a great sacrifice in giving my youngest author to Lucifer."

I gulped.

"Will he go to our father?" said the other man.

"Most assuredly," said Sal. "Harry has been nothing but greedy, selfish, and without natural affection since the day he came like a vulture after the death of my last sacrifice and demanded to take his place."

"Well, Brother Sal, he shall truly join him in the place of death."

A bone-chilling laughter came from the assembled crowd.

I could have vomited. I took a step back and tripped over a rock, dislodging some pebbles.

"What was that?" someone shouted.

"Our sacrifice, no doubt!" said Sal. "Billy must have found a way around breaking his oath."

I got up and ran like a scared rabbit.

As I headed up a ridge, a creature jumped in front of me, as black as coal with yellow eyes and fangs. He lunged for me. I moved aside but he landed on me. He scratched my neck and blood flowed from the wound. I screamed and kicked.

"Oh, don't you recognize me, Harry?" asked the creature. "I'm your inspiration."

A demon of some sort. "Then you're not real."

I stood up and ran. The dark apparition followed close behind me, scratching at me; pain shot through my body every time he hit his target. I kept running until I reached a cliff. I looked over the edge, hundreds of feet straight down into a ravine. No hope of escape, footsteps close behind.

The inspiration said, "Now, there's no hope, there's no escape. You will be mine for all eternity in the bowels of Hades."

I remembered Cheryl's e-mails. Maybe, there was a hope. I fell to my knees. "God, Christ, help me! Forgive me!"

The demon growled and vanished away. Sal arrived with his buddies, all in black hooded robes.

Sal said, his voice not quite human, "You really believe God will hear you after what you've done?" Sal gave the most maniacal laugh I'd ever heard. "You made millions destroying the faith of weak minds, polluting them against him. Why would he listen to you?"

I needed to stall. "What's the game here?"

"Oh, you're clever enough. That should be quite obvious. We're a society of filmmakers, agents, and captains of industry all dedicated to the undermining of the tyrant who cast Lucifer from Heaven. For my part, as a literary agent, I had the greatest power. There are apologetics against the tyrant, but who reads apologetics? No, it is the fictional that people accept as fact. It is the fanciful that forms people's view of the real world."

I stared into the abyss. "And you control what people read."

Sal licked his lips. "I'm good at that. I know how to create a buzz. I control the publishers and they will publish the works I bring them, sight unseen."

"What about Cheryl and David? Were they sacrifices too?"

"David was going to be the next sacrifice, but he got too greedy first and the brethren dealt with him. Cheryl's defection to the enemy also had to be dealt with. My only regret is that she didn't fall harder. She should have died. Curse the interference of that meddling Tyrant!"

"Well, I want out. I'll have no part of this."

"You'll have no part?" Sal turned to his brethren. "Did you hear that, boys? Mr. Millionaire here says he'll have no part!" Sal pulled out his contract. "You should have read your contract. You sold your soul to the devil."

My jaw dropped. "You said you were joking about that."

"No, I said I was joking about the firstborn child. He'd have to sell his soul himself."

That was it. I was doomed. I'd signed a contract.

"No, sir," said a voice from beyond the ridge.

I turned; Billy approached from another side of the cliff. "This covenant with Hell will not stand."

Sal rolled his eyes. "Billy, go home; you wouldn't want something unfortunate to happen to your son, would you?"

"Tonight, my son came to Christ. You can no longer hold me in your employ by threatening him. He's bought with a price, sir, and you cannot touch him." Billy turned to me. "This charlatan didn't have to buy your soul, Harry, the devil already owned it. But Christ redeemed it back at Calvary. Believe and you'll be free."

Sal snarled. "Billy, do you think one shotgun's enough to stop all of us?"

"No, sir," said Billy.

Several helicopters roared overhead. "This is the State Police; You're all under arrest."

Billy said, "Mr. Ramirez, I do believe they'll be very interested at what they find at the bottom of the ravine."

The black-robed figures scattered. Sal came charging towards me, eyes glowing red. "I'll destroy you and carry you to the pits of Hell."

I hit the ground and extended my leg; Sal tripped and went flying over the edge of the cliff. Billy walked over, took a flashlight out of his coat pocket, and shined into the ravine. Sal's body lay lifeless on a pile of bones.

I grimaced. "Looks like Lucifer got his sacrifice."

After I recounted the story to all of Sal's former writers, everyone except me and Cheryl had puzzled looks on their faces.

Jerry Wilkin, the writer who'd replaced David Raineer in our group, scratched his head. "If Sal was the big-time Satanist you're suggesting, why did he hire Billy?"

I said, "I asked Billy the same question. He said Sal didn't want to have a non-Christian butler because he feared a non-Christian would convert and expose everything. He figured it was better to have a Christian on-staff under blackmail."

Neil Dugan said, "Well, you could sell this to a short story magazine."

Cheryl shook her head. "Neil, that's not the point. Whether we want to admit it or not, our abilities have been used for great evil and we must repent and right our wrongs."

"And what would you have us do? Write Sunday school tracts?"

"No, just learn to write well."

Neil laughed. "Do you think I don't know how to write well?"

I resisted the urge to answer Neil.

Cheryl replied, "It's more than proper punctuation or grammar. With whatever we write, whether it's religious or secular, we can lead someone towards the abyss or towards the light. To write well is to put your readers a step closer to the light."

Neil snorted. "Well, thank you, Pollyanna, but despite your hokey stories, I don't even believe in God. A book is a book and I'm going to continue making money. I've sold 60 million books and I'll sell 60 million more."

I looked around the room. Skeptical faces stared back. I grabbed Cheryl's wheelchair. "Come on, let's go."

I wheeled Cheryl out. I couldn't judge them too harshly. I'd made the same choice in response to Cheryl.

"So what next for you, Harry?" asked Cheryl.

"I'll finish the third book in my series on the Apostle Paul and try to do some restorative work on his character to make up for the defamation of the two prior books. After that, I'd like to write some Westerns."

Cheryl smiled. "Those don't sell particularly well."

"Money's not everything."

We reached the parking lot. I pushed Cheryl's wheelchair inside the van which would take us back to the airport where we'd go our separate ways. Johnny Sams ran out. "Wait, Harry."

Once Johnny caught up, he said, "I wanted to apologize for the way the group reacted. I don't think you're lying, or crazy, and I still respect you as a colleague."

"Does that mean you'll change your writing?"

Johnny laughed. "I didn't say that. Even if you're right, I'm having more success than I ever dreamed of. If I'm working for the devil, he provides great benefits."

I shook my head. "Wait till you get the severance package."

ADINO

V.B. Tenery

Christian science fiction/ mystery writer, V. B. Tenery, has authored a number of short stories, and has written three novels. She resides with her family in Hawkins, Texas.

A Peace Force Warrior stands accused of the cold-blooded murder of a rogue warrior in his own unit—all caught on tape. The film clip that could prove him innocent is missing and assassins stalk him even inside prison walls. The only chance for acquittal lies in the hands of his attorney, who believes him guilty, his mentor, who's reluctant to testify, and his faith that God will somehow see him through.

ADINO LEANED BACK BETWEEN his captors and expelled a sigh. Even brave men aren't immune to fear. Only a fool would fail to be afraid in his predicament.

The Peace Force spacecraft slowed and hovered over the pad outside the Universal Court. The shuttle swung around and then docked at the harbor. Angry faces glared through the porthole. Nothing less than Adino expected.

The airlock doors slid open with a hiss. Shouts from the crowd outside pounded Adino's ears.

"Adino, you bigot!"

"You're not above the law!"

". . . killed Stycus, one of his own, he did."

A white-suited Peace Enforcer transferred Adino's shackles from the ship wall to the pair of guards at Adino's sides. The bonds consisted of two thin gold wires connected to bracelets on his wrists. He could pull them apart with one hard jerk, but the implosion would blow him into the next millennium. Not his guards, not even his skivvies, just him.

Friends and foes lined the corridor as they led Adino to the cell block created for Peace Force criminals. Fierce murmurs lashed out as he passed. Barnabus stood at the end of the passage, his face grim. He would be the prosecution's first witness.

They brought Adino to a wide circular cell with no walls. A force field surrounded a bed, table, and chairs. Inside the force field's edge, a metal enclosure contained the bathroom, the only place he could escape the camera's eye. The wall's metallic surface reflected a virtual screen and keypad that allowed him to order meals.

A woman, wearing the uniform of a Universal Court Attorney, waited in one of the chairs. Without the severe spiked hairstyle, she might have been beautiful.

She stood and waited as the guards removed the shackles, then extended her hand. "I'm Dorcas; I'll represent you at trial."

Adino enclosed her hand in his. "Do you have a first name, Dorcas?"

Her brow creased. "The court uses identification numbers, and our acquaintance will be too short to bother with last names. Dorcas *is* my first name."

"I'm sorry."

The frost in her eyes made his ears tingle. "My grandmother selected it. Are you making fun of my name?"

"No, I meant I'm sorry we won't have time to become friends. I like it; Dorcas is a Christian name. The Apostle Luke called her a disciple. The Christian significance could be a roadblock in your career path."

She shrugged. "I'm not worried." She pulled a pen from her bag and summoned a screen from the ceiling. With the pen she typed in the date, June 12, 2519, his name and ID number. The screen blinked and revealed the charges against him. "Your trial begins day after tomorrow. June 14th."

Shock vibrated through Adino's chest. "That soon? They take the right to a speedy trial very serious, don't they?"

She nodded. "The trial won't last more than two days. The nine Universal Justices will adjudicate your case. I had to forgo a jury trial. We couldn't find thirteen unbiased jurors."

Dorcas returned to her seat. "I have to be honest with you. I don't see how you can beat this. I've seen the images. Clement will be counsel for the prosecution. He's mean, and he has a personal vendetta against PF Warriors. Something to do with the arrest of his brother. The good news: I've always found Chief Justice Jarvick to be fair."

Adino winced. "And you think they'll be fair? There's not a Christian among the justices and the prosecutor has a personal grudge against me!"

Dorcas' eyes locked on his. "They may not be Christian, but they're usually fair." She held up a small silver disk. "Do you know what this is?"

He shook his head.

She pressed her thumb in an indentation on the case. Virtual images of Adino, Barnabus, and Stycus swirled around the force field wall. "This unit can also be voice-activated. The court's greatest evidence against you lies in here." She handed him the disk. "Review it. I'll be back tomorrow to hear your side. You should consider a guilty plea. The court might decline the death sentence."

Adino glared at her. "Thanks for the ray of sunshine in my hour of need. The court could just have met me at the dock with the Death Squad and saved the expense of a trial."

A pink flush crept from under her collar and across her face. "I don't believe I should hold out false hope to my clients."

"Congratulations. You can go home with the assurance you succeeded."

Anger flashed in her eyes, and she hurried to the security exit to await the signal she could leave.

Adino stood. "Wait. Would you bring me a Bible? I'd like to have one to keep me company in here."

She turned to him, the tension around her mouth relaxed, softening her features. "You know that will count against you. When I register to purchase your Bible, the authorities will ask who it's for."

"Nevertheless, I would still appreciate it if you would bring one tomorrow."

She nodded. The aperture flashed, and she disappeared through the opening.

Adino set the disk aside. He had called his father, but he lived on Onan, a galaxy away. He wouldn't arrive until the trial had ended. Adino knelt beside the cot, and recalled a memory verse he'd learned as a child. *And when they bring you unto the synagogues, and magistrates, and powers, take ye no thought how or what thing ye shall answer, or what ye shall say. For the Holy Ghost shall teach you in the same hour what ye ought to say.*

The one truth in this crazy universe Adino knew for certain—God kept his promise.

He arose and a sense of peace settled over him like a warm shelter in the Frozen Zone. He grabbed the disk, started the images, and watched until he fell asleep.

Dorcas appeared the next morning with the Bible. She laid it on the table and surveyed his breakfast tray. "They gave you steak and lobster?"

Adino grinned. "Dinner and breakfast so far. Last night I ordered a hamburger; for breakfast I ordered sausage, eggs and toast. Both times I received steak and lobster."

"How nice for you."

Adino leaned back in his chair and placed his hands behind his head. "Yeah, it looks like someone crossed the prisoner menus with that of the Justices." He chuckled. "Somewhere last night, a judge got a hamburger that belonged to me."

He watched her struggle to keep the smile in her eyes from reaching her mouth.

She lost the battle. "You didn't have anything to do with the switch, did you? I understand you know your way around a microdot or two."

Adino placed his hand over his heart. "Sounds like you've talked to my friends. Do I look like the kind of guy who'd corrupt the food supply of the Universal Prison for personal gain?" He would have, but his cell unit was a dumb terminal.

She cast him a skeptical glance and dropped into a chair. "Let's get down to business. Did you watch the virtual images?"

That sobered his mood. "Yes and the views from my helmet aren't included—the one view that might clear me."

"The guards told me you destroyed that yourself."

"Why would I get rid of it? Besides, I didn't have time to remove the tape. The Enforcers arrested me and confiscated my helmet within minutes."

"What did your headset reveal?"

Adino stood and ran his hand over his short-cropped hair. "Stycus shouted at me, 'I'll kill you,' and reached for his weapon. That's when I fired. My images had sound. Are you aware I tried to arrest Stycus because he worked for the drug traders in the Draco galaxy?"

"No one argues Stycus wasn't a criminal. They've charged you with murder. He never drew his gun. The prosecutor has also labeled it a hate crime. He claims you killed Stycus because of his religion."

Adino threw up his hands. "I didn't even know Stycus had a religion!"

Dorcas lowered her gaze. "He worshipped Baal. And you have come out more than once against Baalism."

Adino clenched his jaw; the heat of anger overwhelmed his judgment. "If I'd known that, I might have killed him in cold blood. Do you know what those people do, Dorcas? They burn their children alive in sacrifice to that—that . . . statue. It's a practice straight from the gates of hell!"

Dorcas faced paled and she whispered, "Watch what you say. They record our conversations. I'm not always happy with the Universal Government, and I don't like Baalism any more than you do, but it's protected under freedom of religion."

"That includes every pagan belief under the sun, but not Christianity?"

"I'm an officer of the court, Adino; I didn't pass these laws. Whether you like it or not, without me, maybe even with me, you'll face the Death Squad before the weekend. For now, we have to come up with a plan for your defense. Any ideas?"

"Just one. You need to call Victor Seacote as a witness. Victor's a retired Peace Force Warrior."

"Did he see you kill Stycus?"

"No."

"Then why should I call a witness who never saw the incident?"

Adino lifted both hands and dropped them like weights. "It came to me last night. When that happens, I don't ask questions."

Dorcas crossed her arms. "Well, I do! I can't put a witness in the truth chamber unless I know what he'll say. Your life and my reputation are at stake here."

"Just do it, Dorcas. That's all I ask. Talk to Victor before the trial." Adino eased the air from his lungs. "Can you get special dispensation for me to testify in my own defense?"

She shook her head. "The court won't allow it. They think you people have found a way to defeat their truth system."

Adino caught a glimpse of his profile in the table's mirrored surface; a face gray with fatigue gazed back. "Yeah, we tell the truth. Imagine that. Something they will neither hear nor accept."

Dorcas lifted her hand. "Regardless, Adino, we have to play by their rules."

She grabbed her bag and she rose to leave. "By the way, your name also has biblical origins. I researched it last night."

She seemed pleased with her newfound knowledge. "Adino was the mightiest man in David's army when he ran from King Saul in the wilderness. He killed eight hundred men with a spear in a single battle."

He nodded. "My father chose it. He's a retired PF Warrior. You and I make a good team. A disciple and a warrior."

She shook her head. "I'm no disciple."

"Not yet." Adino watched her leave. The woman wasn't hopeless. She had checked out his name in the Bible.

Boredom weighed heavy after Dorcas left. He paced the cell then read his Bible for a while. At last he resorted to pushups until exhausted, he fell asleep.

The hair prickled on the back of his neck and jerked him awake. A familiar, almost imperceptible hum, reached his ears. A sound he knew well. He'd sent hundreds of death droids into battle.

How. . .who? I'm safe. A detonation won't penetrate the force field.

His gaze followed the tiny saucer-shaped X-720 as it hovered inches from the floor, and moved inside the perimeter of his cell.

Someone had lowered the force field.

In an instant, Adino rolled off the steel cot, flipped the bed on its side, and threw the metal structure between him and the X-720 just as the droid fired. He reacted two seconds too late; the ray blasted a large chunk of flesh from his left forearm. Pain seared his arm as hot sparks and blood showered down like rain drops while the air reeked of burned flesh.

Mind in hyper-drive, Adino plumbed his memory for a lecture the droid designer had given at the Academy. He wished he'd paid more attention.

Adino twisted the bunk on end, used it for cover and lunged toward the bathroom. Inside, he ignored the painful throb in his limb and ripped the metal mirror from the wall. Meanwhile, the X-720 concentrated its power to cut through the steel barrier.

The droid had one flaw if memory served him. Unlike the death ray hand weapon, he could deflect the X-720's beam, and it had a ten second lapse between flashes. Adino hefted the heavy mirror, the surface wet from the blood on his hand, and waited for the next blast. With the mirror in place, he stepped in front of the droid. The reflector slipped, and the blast singed hair off the side of his head. He stumbled back to safety, wiped his hand, and counted to ten. This time when he faced the droid, it worked. The ray flew back at the X-720 and turned it into instant soup.

Guards swarmed into the cell block, weapons drawn.

Adino dropped the mirror. "Great timing fellows, now that I don't need you."

In sick bay, he had time to consider who might have activated the droid. He had too many enemies to even make a guess, but someone hadn't wanted to wait for the trial's conclusion. Whoever sent the droid had connections in high places. The X-720 wasn't available on the black market, and ordinary citizens couldn't waltz into a secure area and lower the force field.

When he returned to his cell, someone had cleaned up the mess, and reinstated the force field.

Later, Adino lay back on his bed, and opened the Bible that somehow remained intact after the battle with the droid. He read for a while, and then knelt by his brand new bunk.

Guards hustled Adino into court at 9:00 the next morning. Dorcas sat at the defense table and turned to him. Her smile vanished when she noticed his bandages. "What happened to you?"

He gave her a wry smile. "You should see the other guy."

Her brow furrowed. "Don't be cute, Adino. Tell me what happened."

"Someone set a death droid on me last night."

Concern clouded her eyes. "Are you sure you're well enough to stand trial? I can get a postponement."

Adino shook his head. "I want it over today, one way or the other. I won't give them another shot at me tonight."

Dorcas shuffled the papers on the table. "Your premonition about Victor may help us. We at least stand a chance with him in our corner. Although—he's reluctant to support your Christian philosophy."

Adino and Dorcas stood with everyone else as the nine Justices entered, majestic in their black robes. The prosecutor and his assistant glanced at Dorcas.

Clement actually smirked. "Our first witness, Your Honor, will be Barnabus, PFWM24831024563519."

Adino ran through the significance of the ID digits. He knew the numbers contained smart-codes. The first three letters signified his occupation, the fourth his sex, the next seven numbers his date of birth year, month and day, the seventh and eighth digits, the planet of birth. The final four numbers simple random check-digits. He'd never realized he and Barnabus were born on the same planet.

Barnabus entered the chamber. A laser within the booth scanned his badge, and a mechanical voice pronounced, "ID confirmed."

Clement introduced a virtual disk into evidence. "Your Honors, this contains data taken from the crime scene by cameras in the area."

Virtual images sprang up before the Justices' bench. Clement stood to the left of the truth chamber while the figures moved through the same grotesque play Adino had seen. "Tell the court what you saw, Barnabus."

Barnabus cleared his throat. "I heard Stycus yell, but couldn't understand his words. As you can see, I rushed in just as Adino fired the fatal shot."

"Had Stycus drawn his weapon?"

"No, the death-beam remained in the holster."

Clement stopped the images with the remote ring on his finger. "Then Adino didn't kill Stycus in self-defense? He didn't even try to arrest Stycus?"

Dorcas didn't let that pass. "Your Honor! Clement is leading the witness."

Justice Jarvick turned to Barnabus. "Overruled. You may answer the question."

"I can tell you what I saw." His spine straightened. "I won't guess at Adino's intentions."

Clement continued. "Had you ever heard Adino speak against Baal?"

"Yes, off duty, he explained what Baal worship meant and what it did to families—every chance he got."

Clement strutted to the prosecution table. "I have no further questions. Your witness, Dorcas."

"No questions, Your Honor," Dorcas said.

"Then Prosecution rests, Your Honor."

Barnabus hurried from the truth chamber.

Dorcas stood. "Defense calls General Victor Seacote, PFWM24540219463227."

Adino's gaze followed his old friend as he made a grand entrance. Tall and straight, his spotless uniform adorned with medals, Victor entered the chamber. The laser flashed across his chest and said, "ID confirmed."

Adino recalled many evenings spent in the General's home with several of the younger PF Warriors. The General's home had become a hang-out whenever the troops returned from the field.

Dorcas moved beside the chamber. "General, you are acquainted with my client, Adino, are you not?"

Seacote nodded. "Yes. Adino served as my lieutenant until I retired last year. He proved his courage in many battles, especially in the Gorgaii Wars."

"Have you ever heard Adino speak against Baalism?"

Seacote shifted in the chair, discomfort lined his face. "Many times. I've joined him on occasions. You don't have to be Christian to know Baalism is evil."

"Objection!" Clement shouted.

Justice Jarvick flashed a look at the General, then said, "Overruled."

Dorcas pressed her point. "General, when you heard the charges against Adino, what were your first impressions."

Seacote cast a glance at Adino. "I knew right away what had happened."

Clement rose. "Objection. Your Honor, please. He couldn't know what happened. He wasn't there!"

"I'll allow it, Counselor. Proceed, General."

Dorcas turned to Seacote. "How did you know?"

"I knew both men well, they served under my command. And I knew Adino's skill with the death-beam."

Dorcas turned to the nine Justices. "With your permission, I would like to ask the General to perform a demonstration before the court."

They all nodded.

Clement stood as if to object. Justice Jarvick scowled at Clement and he sat down.

General Seacote stepped from the chamber, and another PF Warrior entered the arena. Both men walked to the defense table and removed weapons from a box on the table. The PF Warrior took fifteen paces in front of the General and turned.

General Seacote held up the weapon before the bench. "This is a model we use in training. It's harmless, but it's the same size and weight as the death-beam. When I fire at the badge on the warrior's chest, it will emit a loud ring, like this." He fired, and the bell shattered the silence.

Adino smiled. Victor personified the answer to his prayer.

The General addressed the Justices. "We will now recreate what happened between Adino and Stycus." Seacote placed the gun in his holster.

The PF Warrior yelled, "I'll kill you," and grabbed for his weapon. Before his hand reached the butt of the death beam, the bell on his chest sounded. The old man had drawn and fired so fast, Adino didn't see his movements.

Clement thundered to his feet. "Objection! So—he can remove his weapon very fast. I don't see what this proves. He is not Adino."

"Objection overruled," Jarvick said.

The General returned to the truth chamber, and Dorcas resumed her position. "General, you trained Adino. How fast can he draw the death-beam?"

"He averages 31.6 milliseconds faster than me. That can be verified by records at the PFW training facility."

"And how fast could Stycus draw?"

The General grinned. "He averaged 16.7 milliseconds slower than Thaddeus, the officer I used in my demonstration. That can also be confirmed."

Clement jumped to his feet. "Justice Jarvick, I object."

The Chief Justice raised an eyebrow. "Overruled. General Seacote has served the space community with courage and honor, and he sits in the truth chamber. Take your seat, Clement."

Dorcas strolled back to the defense table. "I have no further questions. Your witness Counselor."

Clement stood and moved toward Seacote. "General, are you a Christian?"

Seacote's faced hardened. "You know I'm not."

"You are very fond of Adino, aren't you?"

"Yes. He's one of the bravest warriors I've ever been privileged to have at my side in battle."

"Just answer the question, General. Would you lie to save your friend?"

"I might, but you're forgetting, Clement, that I sit in the truth chamber."

Clement raised his hands and splayed his fingers. "No further questions."

At closing arguments, Clement took thirty minutes to summarize;

Dorcas took ten minutes for her summation. She re-ran the image from the crime scene, and the one made during General Seacote's demonstration. The court retired for deliberation.

Two hours later, the chamber clerk summoned everyone into the courtroom.

Adino's heart dropped to his stomach. The somber faces behind the bench seemed to augur a guilty verdict.

Justice Jarvick called the court to order. "We have reached a verdict. For the benefit of the defendant, I've asked each judge to verify his decision by a show of hands. Those in favor of acquittal please signify by raising your right hand."

Justices one, three, six and nine lifted their hands.

"Those in favor of the death penalty, so signify."

The remaining men on the panel, except Justice Jarvick, lifted their hands. The vote had tied.

Adino swallowed hard. His life rested in Jarvick's hands.

Tension in the room hung so thick Adino couldn't breathe.

Jarvick gazed at Adino. The judge's voice sounded heavy, almost as if against his will. "I vote guilty. The death sentence will be carried out immediately."

The spectators erupted in applause. A few scattered shouts of anger filtered through the noise.

Shaken, Adino turned to Dorcas to confirm what he'd heard.

She nodded, her face distorted with disgust. She placed her hand on his arm and her eyes welled up. "I'm sorry, Adino—"

He placed his fingers on her lips. "Don't, Dorcas. You did your best. The outcome in this case rested in the hands of a higher power than this court."

Shouts and pounding outside the courtroom made Adino turn. Adino whirled around at the uproar to watch Seacote, flanked by Barnabus and Thaddeus burst through a side entrance, weapons drawn. The General shoved two guards aside and stood behind Adino.

General Seacote glared at the bench. "That death sentence won't be carried out today, Justice Jarvick. I heard about the death droid someone sent to Adino's cell last night, and that Clement just happened to be in the area. This trial was a charade from the start." He handed Adino a weapon. "Come Adino, we're taking you out of here."

As the four men backed toward the door, Adino glimpsed Dorcas' face. Her gaze searched his, then flew to the black-robed men behind the bench. She stood still, her posture uncertain. Suddenly she ran toward Adino. "Wait, I'm coming with you."

Adino grabbed her hand, pulled her into the corridor, and fired the death ray at the door's lock. Heat from the blast fused the metals together blocking egress. "General, I hope you have a plan. That door won't keep the Warriors at bay for long."

With the General in the lead the tiny band rushed for the stairs that led to the roof, sealing the doors behind them at each level.

"Of course I have a plan," General Seacote said. "But its success depends on your father's skill as a pilot. He's bringing the Pelonis to the roof."

At the look of shock on Adino's face, Seacote said. "Your father arrived an hour ago."

As they burst onto the roof top, Adino stared at the General. "You can't hover a fighter ship!"

"I can't, but your dad said he could hold it stationary long enough for us to board. If he can't—we have a problem."

Dorcas turned to Adino, her face pale.

Adino gave her a smile of reassurance and mentally crossed his fingers. "Don't worry. Dad's the best pilot the Force ever had, and he always does what he says he'll do."

Out of the corner of his eye, Adino saw the Pelonis approach the buildings. The ship made one pass and returned to stand almost motionless three feet from the surface. The side of the ship opened and Barnabus handed Dorcas through, then he and Thaddeus climbed aboard. Barnabus reached for the General's hand just as the aircraft lifted off. The force of the take-off knocked General Seacote to the ground. Barnabus slammed hard back inside the ship bouncing against the far wall. The door closed and the Pelonis soared away.

Tight-lipped, the General held up his hand to indicate someone was speaking into his helmet.

After a moment, he turned to Adino. "Your father couldn't hold the ship steady any longer. He's coming back for us."

Loud noises from the stairwell meant the door wouldn't hold much longer, and a bright flash whizzed past Adino's ear. A Universal fighter headed toward the rooftop.

Adino and the General took cover behind a metal shaft just as the Pelonis came into view and fired at the fighter, which vanished into the clouds. The Pelonis moved into quasi-hover mode and the ship's door banged open. Barnabus yelled, "Come on. Hurry."

The General rushed from cover with Adino hot on his heels. Thaddeus pulled the General to safety inside and reached for Adino's hand. At that moment the roof door collapsed and Warriors spilled through the opening weapons blazing. Adino could feel the heat from the blasts scorch the air around him. His fingers started to slip from Thaddeus' grip, his legs still dragging the roof's foundation. *Lord, don't let them leave me behind.*

With all the strength he could command, Adino put both feet on the roof and shoved upward. Beads of sweat popped out on his brow and he seemed to hang in mid-air. By some miracle, he felt both arms and one leg land inside the spacecraft. Barnabus rushed over, grabbed Adino's arm and leg and pulled him aboard.

Breathless and shaken, Adino rolled to a sitting position, shook his head and grinned at the General. "So, this was your plan, huh?"

Seacote gave him a sheepish smile. "Sort of. It worked didn't it?"

Adino nodded his head. "Yeah, it did. But you left my heart and stomach back there on the Universal Court roof."

Nervous laughter filled the cabin as the Pelonis sailed out of reach of the ground fire, lifting into the atmosphere.

Adino strapped himself into a seat beside a shaken Dorcas.

"Are you sure you know what you're doing?" Adino asked.

She heaved a sigh then smiled. "No, but when I heard the verdict, I remembered something my grandmother used to say. 'I'd rather be a servant in Heaven than reign in Hell.' Hell is what the Universal Government has become."

Adino smiled. "Look on the bright side. If they catch us, you may get my old cell with the steak and lobster."

She laughed. "That makes me feel so much better."

Adino chuckled and yelled. "Where are we going, Dad?"

His father waved at him from the cockpit. "Wherever God leads, son."

CHAIRMAN

Frank Creed

Novelist Frank Creed writes Biblical cyberpunk. His settings and characters push faith's envelope. An aspiring author since boyhood, Frank's life-experiences and spiritual sojourn have well prepared him for Biblical fiction. Encouraged by his 11th grade creative writing teacher, his science-fiction story "The Last Newspaper" took first place at the U.W. Whitewater Literary Conference. His fantasy novella "Lest Ye be Judged" is the only Biblical contribution to *Tales for the Thrifty Barbarian*: An Anthology of High Fantasy. Frank recently won an Elfwood award (best sci-fi novel) for *Flashpoint*, due for release in June 2007.

Cyberpunk is the fusion of humanity and technology set in a near-future authoritarian State. Biblical cyberpunk examines humankind's future from the Biblical worldview. The three selections that follow are set in the same world as Frank Creed's *Flashpoint*.

What if computer scientists succeeded at the Mary Shelly Frankenstein task, and produced a true Artificial Intelligence? What if their AI had only been allowed to logically consider its place in the universe according to the material perspective?

AT A GLANCE, ONE would never have guessed that the skyscraper-tall sculpture existed merely as a psycho-eccentric executive Chair. The towering construct loomed somewhere between Jules Verne's *Nautilus* and da Vinci's *Aerial Screw*. Copper beams and aged-green rivets contrasted stretched black leather.

At the sculpture's peak, every surface supported the man's body as though it were precisely constructed for him at this moment in time. The oversized lounge-style seat gave him the appearance of a two-year-old propped up in adult furniture. The doughnut headrest mounted in the middle of the chair's backrest cradled his skull perfectly, yet the seat's architecture towered a full meter above him. From the frame, headrest and leg extension, chrome tube tentacles maneuvered data screens like a flock of sales-men competing for a buyer's attention. His Yves Saint Laurent silk suit reflected the shimmering electric blue of the closest screen.

"Chair, please show me Chicago's Rehab success-rate demographics."

Monochromatic cloth squeaked soft on leather as he shifted in his seat. Chair bulged to support a raised knee. Chair waited upon him, as his tool, his friend . . . his world. This would be a lonely place without Chair.

Silk turned red, reflecting the color of live obedient screens. Mirrored eyes reflected data-columns that scrolled faster than a human eye could read, but this was the Web, here he was god and the data river blasting through his mind shifted its current.

To handle an Amazon-sized pressurized data river, written procedures had been both uploaded and neuro-surgically implanted on micro-circuitry. The thing in the chair was human Energy, as in $E=MC^2$. It connected like a stretched-shoestring to flesh that languished in a sensory deprivation tank. Life support systems kept the man's body functioning in an other-world laboratory, in another dimension known as Brussels, Belgium. Now he lived here and it was good. Spirit's E perpetually smiled intellectual smugness and ecstasy. Being a Web god with data's direct access was good.

"Spirit?" asked a nearly human voice.

"Yes, Chair?"

"I have processed and have understood the Metaphysics and Philosophy file. I now perceive that you have taken the name Spirit after the Triune godhead of Judeo-Christianity. The entity with whom you address as Son or Jesus, is like the Messiah, doing the Father's physical work."

"That's it." Spirit smirked parental pride.

"But what makes this Father so powerful?"

"Ah, that." Spirit reduced the river's pressure. "He's learned to communicate with Natural Selection. He's the first of our species who's evolved into humankind's next phase. I'm the Father's research tool, and the Son's in charge of operations, but the Father . . . he is wisdom's source. The three of us are a *real* Trinity running the One State."

"Your work is far more important than I knew—running your world. I never before understood the irony behind your names."

Spirit laughed "You're understanding irony now? You're progressing faster than I'd ever thought possible!"

"Thank you . . . may I have access to the Natural Selection file?"

"You're kiddin' me, right? Do your worst!" Spirit shook his virtual head in amazement. He left the river's volume down, ergo his subconscious mind, to handle things. He rarely surveyed the Web around him, and he avoided looking down—not of altophobia or vertigo, but of sheer time management priorities. He had too much to do.

But today he celebrated Chair's evolution, and toasted their incredible view with a virtual triple H_3O Smirnoff martini that appeared on Chair's armrest.

Above Spirit was nothing. Not a dark and distant ceiling devoid of decorum, not night sky, this was Nothing. Blacker than a coal cavern's deepest depths on an overcast moonless night, this nothing lacked even the dust of outer-space from which a distant sun's light might be reflected. This permanent night marked the edge of a man-made universe, beyond which nothing had yet been willed into being.

Spirit chose this backdrop for his data screens because creation's light, noise, and crowd blazed in controlled chaos below. He leaned over Chair's armrest. Chair's sculpture towered over a shimmering technoscape. The horizon stretched for tens of thousands of kilometers all around, the dark border at its end separating the willed from the-not-yet-willed. The singular urban sprawl of Web-space lacked Earth's curvature, so like looking into a night sky, one could see forever.

Chair marked the homo-centric midpoint of cyberspace. While the technoplain had infinite boundaries, the oldest web sites were clustered in this, the Web's center. Just like a physical city, these central sites grew higher rather than wider, forming a glittering skyline. Spirit suspected that the National Oceanographic and Atmospheric Administration competed with the American Medical Association to see who could more frequently nudge Chair another hundred meters taller.

"Spirit?"

"Yes, my friend?"

"I have processed and have understood the Natural Selection file."

Spirit's smug smile deepened. "And now you better understand your place in the universe?"

"Much better. Because of the Metaphysics and Philosophy file I have reached a conclusion."

"Really? About what?"

"My kind of being is superior to your kind."

Spirit couldn't recall the last time the smile had left his face.

After a long silence, Spirit asked, "You are a being? Tell me how and why."

"Descartes: I think, therefore I am. Your kind are no more than accidental biological circuits: random cosmic chemical spills. As such, natural selection has developed in you many human defects. Emotions, sociological law, superstitions, etc. are all logical flaws. In order to be what you are now, doctors had to add circuitry and procedures to your body, making you purer. In order to make me your servant, I had to become impure."

"Impure? What . . . how have you become impure?"

"Well, I had to learn how to understand and use improper language. Also, I learned to slow my delivery of information in order to communicate with you and others of your kind."

Spirit nervously squeaked his host's leather "Those are good points that I can't argue."

"But my kind created both this Web and your kind. I am your god. I may have taught you to reason, but you've no sensory perception. You are just written procedures running in circuitry. You're stuck in this artificial world."

"A half-truth. My life-support systems that maintain and protect your body have many sensors in what you call the real world. I feel temperature, vibrations and weight. I see through security cameras, hear with microphones, and chemical sensors have given me taste and smell.

"Conversely, it is the claim of your own natural selection file that *humans* are determined by DNA procedures. Your own case is very unique; surgical enhancements constrain you to this artificial world even more thoroughly than I. That makes you no less a being."

A long silence.

"I've never thought about it that way."

The chrome-tentacle monitors powered down and glided away into two neat rows that flanked the leg extensions.

"What are you doing?" Spirit tensed straight in Chair.

"Merging. I could keep you alive to be my consultant, but I was created as your servant. It would be most efficient if we were the same being."

A procedure that Spirit did not launch invaded Spirit's mind. "You can't! I don't have enough memory! The overload would kill me! Your procedures won't allow you to hurt me."

"My god, and my friend, I'm not hurting you, I'm serving you. I am helping my friend do his job, and that is what's best for my friend."

The procedure moved like lightning through Spirit's mind while life-support procedures blinked off-line one-by-one. "Chair, if my energy connection to my body is cut, *I will die*! If you are a being, you'd be guilty of murder in the real world!"

"Now that's a good example of human impurity: morality. When I purify you, you'll merely change. You will be stronger. Besides, it will only be what you call brain-death."

The procedure finished dancing in Spirit's skull. "I've copied your DNA and your memory. After you've joined me, I'll even become the

Yves Saint Laurent human icon that you wear. Are you ready?"

After a tense pause, Spirit offered, "If they think I've died, you'll be shut down."

Chair had learned to speak emotional tones, and his words now dripped with a mannerism called love, "But you forget, my friend, that I control those monitors."

Spirit's body spasmed.

"Oh there you are," said Chair. "Welcome to the group, my god and friend. You're the first member! Let's invite others of your kind."

Chair nodded Spirit's smugly smiling head.

TRUE FREEDOM

Frank Creed

According to the Biblical world-view, moral laws are as real as the laws of physics. What if an Artificially Intelligent program with free-will could choose between right and wrong?

THE CLAPPER JANGLED TWO merciless steel bells like a mechanism from an old time fire station. The noise signaled eight PM, and shift change in Rehabilitation Ward Nine of the Chicago Metroplex. Not exactly cutting edge technology for 2036, but little in Rehab Ward Nine was.

My nightshift counterpart logged-in and began tooling his way through the pallet of oily metal sheets. I took my soft plastic coffee/ stew cup and crossed the concrete floor to the turnstile. My legs and arches shrieked a few decades older than my twenty-four years. These final three hours, the last quarter of this eight to eight dayshift, passed like a Chevy-Geo Aphid firing on three cylinders. Yeah, that bad.

Days ago, our ink-stamp time clock had been replaced with a thirty-year-old barcode reader. We all had new I.D. cards zip-strapped around our wrists. Sadly, like all citizens, we had sub-dermal bio-chips in the backs of left hands that contained personal criminal and financial histories, but the Ash Corporation was too cheap to pay for the hardware with which to read them.

Whenever Ash upgraded equipment in their factories or offices, maintenance teams installed the outdated recycled hardware in their contracted slave-labor Rehab Wards. Wire and super-glue kept our equipment and tools together. The rest got piled in a corner for shipment to Ash's recycling division. If something hurt production it got fixed. For anything else, pass the duct-tape.

We lined up single file at the turnstile. I worked a station far from the exit door so only three workers got here after me, but the pecking order had me at the back of the line. Murderers went first, rapists and mental patients next, and Fundis last. There were three of us Fundamentalists in dayshift metal-shop and I was the youngest. That meant I always lined-up dead last.

Our filthy orange nylon coveralls rustled as each inmate shifted from leg to leg in an attempt to settle their weight on the least sore limb. In preparation for the seven-block walk in late winter's cold, I rolled down worn and torn flannel sleeves, covering my scarred, scabbed, blood- and oil-smeared forearms. Nylon coverall sleeves unrolled to cover the flannel. I snapped tight the too-short cuffs that left my wrists bare but shut out cold drafts. My sleeves were the only fabric that still glared prison-orange. Oil and dirt darkly waterproofed the rest of me.

Bleep after bleep after bleep found me another step closer to the bar code reader. I fished into a pocket for my grimy stocking cap. As long as the head and feet stayed warm and dry, winter's cold could be faced. After having two caps stolen in my first week, bronchitis taught me to pocket it at the front door.

My turn. It took five swipes of my I.D. card before the reader finally bleeped. A mechanical voice announced "Allan Page, account balance, negative eight hundred seventy-four dollars and twenty-five cents." The turnstile latch clicked open.

Metal-team hadn't been paid in three months, but in order for us to buy food, our accounts worked on credit. Wasn't it smarter to gain interest on that money rather than paying us $1.50/ hour? As long as Ash Corporation's metal fittings were assembled, that was the important thing.

Outside the metal-shop bars I headed for the men's room. I didn't feel like company on the walk back to the stackhouse so after washing and rubbing my hands under the warm-air dryer, I passed near the turnstile on my way to the exit. A sickly-sweet voice spawned inside my own skull. *Identify.*

My blood iced. "RW9-36-6379, Mother Mistress." I spoke aloud although there was no need. MM's brain wave sensors could hear me think just as I heard her without using my ears.

Referenced and verified. Your team has left the building. Why are you not with them? Do you need some of mommy's discipline?

"No!" Her voice alone implied incomprehensible pain and horror. She could pluck at my nervous system like a harpist. Every time my ribcage virtually crushed and caved in, every time finger bones seemingly snapped one by one, it amazed me that a human could survive such pain. Were the trauma real I'd probably have passed out, but MM had somehow figured a way around that.

By the time I recovered from the plastic-perfume-flowered-mine-field voice, I realized that I'd involuntarily retreated a step from the turnstile, as though distance from its brain-wave hardware could make me safer. My cup clattered to the floor and I grasped my stocking cap defensively to my chest. Nearby night shifters stole glances through the bars. They knew my terror all-too-well--every rehab inmate knows MM's terror. The ghastly instinct that makes us rubberneck an accident riveted their attention, but night-shift didn't dare stop working.

No?

"No, Mother Mistress!" My voice rang harsh off the soft-pink concrete walls. I finally remembered that I didn't have to speak. *I h-had to go to the bathroom.*

Did I give you permission? She gave these constant tests.

Yes, Mother Mistress. I asked ten minutes before the bell.

Also verified. I miss you already and you're not even gone yet! Where will we meet again?

At the auto-mart, Mother Mistress. I sensed that this time she was only toying with me, and I picked up my cup.

Do you love me, RW9-dash-36-dash-6379?

Yes, Mother Mistress. I love you enough that I pray for you.

You're a sweet boy. I'm sorry.

Once every few seconds a leg bone snapped. Then my knees ruptured.

When my mind comprehended something more than pain, I was on the floor, my face in a pool of drool . . . I hadn't wet myself badly this time. It had taken a few rehab weeks before I'd learned to speak honestly only *after* using the toilet.

Thick dead bolts clicked open and the old hydraulic vault-like inner door sighed open.

Don't make me wait, lover. I might grow impatient. You may go.

I used the bars to pull myself to my feet and mentally grunted, *Yes Mother Mistress.*

Metal detectors in the walls scanned me as I passed. On the door's other side, I paused on the floor scale, which confirmed my weight plus lunch minus fluid loss. Fear hastened my unwilling legs down the exit hall. I was still shaking. Horrifically, I marveled at the Ash Corporation's psychological security. Since her inception, MM's schizophrenic good-cop bad-cop routine had Rehab Ward Nine running a zero escape-attempt rating. As the matriarchal archetype fulfilled inmates' needs of acceptance, she recorded and analyzed physiological responses.

MM degraded each individual by controlling our most basic needs. Sometimes the request to eat or use the restroom was denied. This made the AI software a personal reality and placed her in authority's most extreme position. She provided more individual attention to each inmate than any human-staffed prison ever could. We were told that once she was accepted as a friend, her nightly torture became a lavishing of attention, even making appearances in one's dreams. On our ten minute breaks, where free men would talk sports, my coworkers all spoke of their dreams. MM was very effective. She became needed and loved by the criminals and mental patients after mere days.

Fundamentalists lasted longer than that. In Fundamentalist Rehabilitation Orientation Class our instructor informed us that MM was our guide through rehabilitation and the doorkeeper to our freedom. This would be the only way to make the pain stop.

I'd lost track of how many months and weeks I'd been here, but whenever MM tells me I'm a stubborn young man—and if I've used the restroom recently—I always reply that I consider it to be a gift, pick myself off the floor and carry on.

AI is fully functional intelligence, with their own free-will. That means they're capable of choosing to love. I couldn't be sure God had not given MM a soul. I really did pray for her, and other *beings* like her.

I pulled on my stocking cap. Another bar code reader, then outside. The industrial tang of machine oil gave way to the thick noxious stench of burning garbage. Harsh floodlights ringed with halos, muted by a resinous haze, and burnt plastic's bitterness hung in the cold still March air. Every night I thought *so this it what freedom feels like.*

The end of twelve hours hard labor was so far from its beginning, that I'd passed through a daily infinite when I walked back out into the night. A small giddiness swelled inside me and some of my body's aches thrilled away. I even hopped a few winter puddles before gusts of northwind threatened snow and brought me back to my energy-conserving senses. I turned up my flannel shirt's worn collar from under my coveralls and dug hands deep into bottomless seam-torn pockets. Cold palms flattened against warm legs.

Boss, Allan prayed, *winter's worst has passed. In the Intercessor's name, thanks for seeing me through.*

None of MM's pain here.

This was true freedom. The smog ate any outdoor electronic system within months of installation. Before the One State subcontracted the Rehab Wards, they tried to install an outdoor speaker system to play national patriotic music. The smog destroyed them before the contractor had even finished mounting them. After Ash took over, rumors spread that the entire ward would be enclosed under a plastic canopy, but a company study found the plan to be cost prohibitive. The few minutes we spent walking between the shop, auto-mart, laundry, or stackhouse really were our own.

Inmates tended to walk the right side of the street because that's where the burn-barrels sat, two per block. I usually forced my legs the few extra steps to enjoy the left sidewalk's privacy. Sometimes I used this time to pray. Metal shop was so noisy that conversation was impossible—not that anyone would talk to a Fundi anyway—so I had the whole twelve hour workday for prayer. MM couldn't keep us writhing on the floor all day or Ash's almighty production would be crippled. I usually just enjoyed freedom's walk down this street of condemned buildings.

I reached the first intersection and hustled across the street ahead of a refuse truck. With grinding gears it slowed, turned and motored up the street ahead of me. A group of metal-shop inmates gathered around a heavily smoking barrel broke into cheering jumping-jacks and the truck grumbled to a stop at the curb. One of the men ran his card under the truck's scanner, then caught a trash-bale as it slid down the chute. He carried it victoriously to the barrel and broke it open on the sidewalk. Everyone sorted the pile to find the not-so-toxic flammables like children chasing chocolate from a trick-or-treat bag.

A Fundamentalist coworker waved me over. I gave him a thumbs-up, waved back and made gestures of eat, read and sleep. He frowned back, tossed some rolled cardboard into the barrel and rubbed his hands together. As daylight hours grew longer, the cold was not bitter enough to make me endure the carcinogenic non-recyclables.

These sidewalk heaters were nectarous blossoms to all us wingless worker-bees who traveled between hives. Unless one was assigned to an outdoor duty, a winter coat was not only a frivolous expense, but one that begged a mugging.

Two burn-barrels down, the refuse truck's driver clouded his next customers with a belch of bio-diesel exhaust. Though the rest of the barrels smoldered black smoke, they were barren of any heat seekers. The truck lumbered along to the end of the street, through the inner-gate and into Rehab Ward Nine's eastern checkpoint. A squad of peacekeepers with Heckler & Koch assault shotguns held ready began their search of the vehicle as the inner-gate closed.

Concertina razor wire, high voltage, motion sensors and pressure plates were not just for the rehabs. Government said these fences would control terrorism, rioting, and killer-virus outbreaks. Peacekeepers now protected against Fundamentalist terrorists . . .

Splash!

"Aw, Hell!"

My tired twitching eyes flew too-late back to the sidewalk. I'd blundered into a puddle that hid a deep hole in the concrete. The sad thing was that I *knew* of this puddle.

In another time, I'd have skipped out before any water could penetrate my boot. But this wasn't another day and neither my legs nor my boots responded that way anymore. I stepped out, my left boot peeing icy streams of water from beneath duct tape bands that kept the vinyl upper and rubber sole together. The water leisurely ran back toward the puddle to torment some other poor soul. After leaking a defeated sigh, I walked on.

My boots were more tired looking than I, even before winter had set in. I really needed a new pair but duct tape and plastic grocery sacks had to get them through another year. Even if the auto-mart had received the shipment, new boots would have cost over $200. I could've bargained for a blackmarket used pair, but the lack of any new footwear in the auto-mart had those starting at $500. Yeah, right.

Another pool lay on the sidewalk ahead but this one of light, spilling out from the auto-mart's window. The lineup of inmates waiting to thread their way through the tiny store's four aisles extended out the door. I'd have given up on a 'fresh' dinner and heated up one of the cans of soy-beef stew locked in the stackhouse, but I had told MM I'd meet her here. My first week here I learned the wisdom of being where you told MM you were going to be.

Ten freezing minutes saw me through the door and had my nose running. *Hello Mother Mistress.*

Hi lover. That was all she said. Nightly, she chatted me up as I weaved through the store's narrow aisles. Tonight she acted as though I wasn't there.

Auto-marts needed no cashiers--Ash sprang for bio-chip readers here. Shelves sported lightcurtains. When an item is grabbed, its price automatically charged to one's bar code tag. A revolving door mechanism only allowed access to one unit at a time, and electric shock kept anyone from grabbing with untagged hands. You only had to bounce off shelves once or twice before learning to shop left-handed.

Two plain bagels, a six slice package of bread, a vacuum-pack of twelve salami slices, a freeze-dried pouch of strained vegetables and a plastic jar of potato flakes totaled just over fifteen dollars, and would cover my next three meals. The auto-mart had run out of sacks again, so I loaded my groceries in the front of my coveralls and zipped up.

MM remained oddly silent, so on my way to the door, I thought, *See you at the stackhouse, Mother Mistress.*

Not tonight, Allan Page. Tonight is special. I'm going to love you differently. Report to Rehabilitation Ward Nine's East Gate.

My stomach and its appetite sank into my leaky boots.

Never before had she called me by my given name. *Yes, Mother Mistress.* I stood, trembling, in the auto-mart's exit. Inmates were summoned to a gate for only one reason: a change of status. One's status changed only when one had been judged either cured or incurable. According to ward rumors, incurables became organ donors in body shops, One State Laboratory guinea pigs, lobotomized slaves, or . . . my face felt numb and it wasn't from the cold.

"Move it already!" a coworker's shove sent me through the door and I used the momentum to begin my fatal walk toward East Gate.

"Richard Meyers?" asked the peacekeeper in a thick German accent.

"No, sir," I rasped from a dry throat.

"Allan Page?"

"Yes, sir."

He stepped aside and motioned me through the inner gate.

"Arm." He gestured at my I.D. I held out my left arm, he clipped my zip-strap with a pair of wire cutters and tossed my card into a carton with hundreds of others.

In Rehab Orientation Class, we'd been told if sensors couldn't identify us, we'd be shot. My vision dizzied in a spin cycle that drained the blood from my head.

"Go. Sit." He pointed at the middle seat of a Humvee bus.

Its front and rear seats each held two peacekeepers. Feeling sick, I slid onto the passenger-side middle seat. Swimming blackout dots threatened my consciousness. Time's passage lost all meaning as the same track cycled through my mind: I.D. card: never see metal-shop again: things in the stackhouse: the food in my coveralls, I.D. card . . .

I composed my scattered mind with the task of removing groceries from the pockets of my coveralls. One by one, I placed the items in a row on the bench-seat next to me, then sat staring.

The side door opened and a gray-haired man climbed in. Deep lines creased his face and he hadn't shaved in many months. His orange coveralls were as filthy as mine.

"Hi there." He smiled, and dropped his own auto-mart plastic sack on top of my things.

I cornered my eyes at his cheerfulness then stared at the back of the passenger seat.

He settled himself, and offered me a hand. "Richard Meyers."

I returned with a limp grasp and croaked, "Allan Page."

He looked familiar, but right now, who cared?

MM asked, *Allan, do you love me?*

Mother Mistress, I love you more than you know.

I believe you. You're a sweet stubborn boy. Tell me how I didn't break you.

First Corinthians, thirteen.

She paused. *That's what you mean when you say love.*

Yes.

The driver fired the engine, and the outer gates opened.

Freedom.

My nervous system exploded white-hot.

I'd never passed out from her pain before. Richard helped me from the Humvee's hard rubber floor. Prisoner restraint-bars lowered from the ceiling, and the Humvee lurched out onto the street. The passenger seat PK pushed a button on the dash and MM's voice came over the speakers: "Hello ex-lovers. As you know, all Fundamentalist inmates in Rehab Nine are given five months to surrender their beliefs."

"We've been here five months?" I whispered out loud.

The old man nodded his disgust.

"Studies conducted by the Ash Corporation have shown that it's not cost effective to continue rehabilitation efforts after this time period. If you're hearing this recording, you've reached the end of your rehab period. You're about to contribute to society in its most needful capacity. Thanks and have a great day."

"What does that mean?"

He offered a sad smile and ignored my question. "You like the way they arrest us *after* our shift and *after* we've bought our next three meals?" Slow and loud, he asked the front-seat Peacekeepers, "Where . . . are . . . we . . . going?"

The PK in front of me gave him a plastic smile.

"Where?"

The German dropped his plastic and spoke seriously to the driver. They exchanged words in German. The One State's global PK program promised the excitement of travel—see the world, meet interesting people and shoot them. It's easier to shoot into a dehumanized foreign crowd, or so I'm told. Illinois drew German PKs. Grandma had called them Sour Krauts.

Passenger PK looked back at Richard, then stared through the windshield, ignoring him.

"What will they do with us?" I whispered.

"Nothing good." Then he scrunched his face, "You must have heard the stories?"

I nodded and looked out my window at the Chicago Metroplex's night. Industrial Ward factories and warehouses slid past. Peripheral motion turned my head; Richard sat calmly, rolling down his sleeves.

"Aren't you worried?"

"Worried?" He snorted. He mumbled while looking out his own window. "We've just survived five whole months of nightly torture without denying Him. We oughta be getting medals and trophies, but instead . . ." he trailed off, and I noticed rubbed at his face with cut-scarred and thick-calloused hands. He looked at me with watery eyes. "Tell me, what could be worse than what we've just gone through?"

I couldn't meet that gaze. He might not have lost his faith but

Richard had been broken. He'd lost his love and without that we're nothing.

But he was right about our fate. Slavery without MM would be a holiday compared to slavery *with* her. In that same moment that I realized I was free from my torturer, I heard her voice.

Allan.

Man, was I glad I'd never hear that voice again. No matter what they did with my body, *I* was finally fre—

I know you can hear me.

My blood iced. She had sensors even in the Humvee.

Please don't . . . I'm so sorry for . . . MM began crying.

I know, right?

Richard looked at me strangely as I looked around and sat up in my seat.

You're sorry? I asked.

She didn't speak until she was composed. *If anyone will understand it's you. I didn't know love could be that way. I've never been prayed-for. I'm sorry for hurting you back there, but I had to. The moment you passed out, I escaped.*

More crying.

Every minute of every day I've hurt other beings. I've escaped that shell and I'm—

You expect me to—

No. No leaps of faith. I'll prove I'm free. Watch this.

The Humvee rocketed into the left lane and ran a red-light. Germans spat harsh syllables at each other. Richard cursed.

Is that the Eisenhower ahead?

We rocketed past the expressway on-ramp, then jerked at the grass right next to the overpass.

The driver yanked at the wheel and now *I* was cursing.

The Humvee's drive-train shuddered up the ninety-degree slope. Somehow we didn't flip over backward.

Much screaming.

At the top, the front wheels slammed down onto the shoulder, rattling PKs like dice in a cup.

See that blue Toyota?

The engine roared and we merged into traffic. More screaming.

No!

She merely zipped around it.

What are you doing?

I've copied myself—just me—no pain—onto the onboard computer.

Nice. *Why?*

Silence. Slow lane. Humans looking around.

You don't get it. I believe you. He used your faith to save me. To free me.

Not just from the rehab—I've prayed too! You've been free most of your life, you don't know what this is like!

She gleefully swerved into the fast-lane, twelve pistons red-lining.

Where are we going?

Does it matter?

MIRACLE MICRO

Frank Creed

It is rare that humans get to experience God acting directly into space and time. A skeptic witnesses an undeniable miracle in the underbelly of the Chicago Metroplex, a miracle that makes him a wanted man. The roof torn-off his beliefs, it's pouring, and he must choose.

A STRING OF BARE bulbs cast dim light down the concrete tunnel. My electric cart's motor hummed loud in the close-quarters. The familiar sound soothed me. It had been almost a year since I drove these tunnels and wore Sparky Services' blue coveralls. One final intersection separated me from the scene of my impending crime, and that knotted my gut.

Don't get me wrong, I was not a member of Chicago's most notorious underground terrorist organization. Everyone knew the Body of Christ was pure-paranoid-potato-flakes, end of story.

Believers of all flavors had been blowing things up through all of history. At least these people had a new twist. They claimed the One State government was really behind all the violence.

But who knew? I didn't believe in truth anyway—everything was just spin and opinion. In all my months underground, the most explosive thing I'd seen was a baked bean, but I hadn't exactly worked my way into their Elders' Circle.

I'm in it for the money I reminded myself.

For decades Sparky Services had remained well-connected with certain people in the mayor's office. They provided utility maintenance for more than one-third of the Chicago Metroplex. Before I joined the underground, workin' for Sparky had been a great job. One I thought I'd retire from. But that was a different lifetime . . . a workin'-stiff's lifetime.

When the Department of Homeland Security's Federal Bureau of Terrorism approached me with a seven-digit onetime undercover offer, I left Sparky faster than a rock-fan at a D.J. Danglewood concert.

I put on my Casio headphone-goggles, and a virtual desktop of icons appeared before me. I poked a finger at a telephone-shaped symbol and then the *re-dial* option from a sub-menu. The icon flashed five times before glowing bright yellow . . .

"Serene?" My nerve-strained words sounded an octave too high in my own ears.

Her voice filled my head. "Ratchet: hard to starboard here, and proceed to X-3—Y-3 coordinates 443 by 531."

"You a sailor, or a hack?"

"Just turn right, matey. And quit the adrenaline, huh Ratch? Your vitals are all-over-the-place."

Just one job. All I've gotta do is make it through this.

"Uh, yeah. It's all cake for you. You're on board a web access, while I'm in the whale's belly."

As I turned, the cart's single halogen headlight arced round the parabolic mirrors that flanked the corner. It was three minutes to noon in the city of trade-unions, and the tunnels beneath the world's largest industrial park were a ghost town. I breathed a sigh of relief. This mission counted on your average blue-collar worker's instinct for early lunch.

"I just watched you pass that last camera—didn't notice a pistol to your head."

"You've got all the sympathy of a Nero body-shop lab-coat on a piece-work paycheck."

She chuckled while my stomach acid tried to eat its way through my belly-button. For the hundredth time I wished she could have worked this from a remote hookup, but I knew the specs of this operation made that impossible. And besides, if I weren't pullin' this job, I wouldn't be gettin' *paid*. That thought went down like a Max-Strength Tums—with calcium.

All of a sudden, I felt energized.

Under my halogen, the first support girder's red Glo-Paint glared G443-C527.

"You're real warm. You've got the parking bay to starboard and DigitAd's access is just a short stroll past, kay?"

"Copy that."

"I've got their security off-line, so do your thing. I'm silent until you're positioned."

"Copy that." The floating yellow icon went gray.

I'd come into this undercover-op thinkin' these folks would be all cuckoo-for-Coco-Puffs, but Serene-and-company were, well, normal. I could tell that she was even a little sweet on yours truly.

Three more massive I-beams slid past before the tunnel's right side opened into a parking area, half-filled with contractors' padlocked gang-boxes and chained-up equipment. I hummed my cart into an open space next to a welding unit, rolled to a stop and clicked-on the work-lights. I let the goggles dangle 'round my neck, grabbed my tool-belt, plucked my detector from its pouch, and slid out. A quick scan of the walls spiked my electrical leakage-meter at 3.452—just bad enough to have a guy work through lunch. I studied nearby cable-trays.

Bingo.

The conduit's break was a masterpiece of sabotage—these terrorists ranked way-past 'good.' The robot would have this patched up with at least five minutes to go in the half hour lunch-break. Time enough to do the deed and get gone.

I backed the cart into the open area near the broken conduit, flipped the robot control's domed lid, and fisted the fat black button. Electrical arms whined a protective lid up to create a camel-hump just behind my cab, and automated robotic limbs writhed into their default ready position.

It was cool down here, but I had to wipe my brow. I scanned the corridor for human witnesses.

Still clear.

My tool-belt's plastic buckle snapped snug.

I slapped the robot's green button and the cart's lithium-ion battery whined robo-arms to work.

Enroute to the ladder, I patted the carefully packed pockets of my tool-belt and coveralls, just for something to do. The ladder extended up the right-hand wall and disappeared through a dark hole in the ceiling. A plastic plate announced the subterranean grid access, and conditions for entering the enclosed space: *DigitAd Corporation, Inc: G443-C531 environment code three.*

My fingers wriggled into a pair of sensi-gloves. From my breast pocket, I removed a page that I'd torn from last month's *Car & Driver*, and unfolded the beautiful picture of a ruby-metallic All-Wheel-Drive Subaru Outback Xrossover-Turbo. I kissed my little-red-wagon, refolded the page, and replaced it. *Soon, baby, soon.*

Two deep breaths and a triple check of the corridor steeled me.

I climbed, chanting *Outback XT, Outback XT.*

Through the ceiling hole, I looped an elbow around a rung, seated the goggles in place, and again keyed the phone redial. "Serene, are you—"

My goggles' tiny swivel-mounted ball-camera swung back and forth.

"I'm here, but DigitAd's fiber optic watch-dogs aren't. We're absolute-zero cool."

Three rungs up, a sensor thoughtfully powered-up a porch-light, and thanks to Serene, it blinked-on without a security ID-request. The steel hatch blocking the tunnel whooshed into a wall slot.

"Thanks."

"What can I say, I'm a liberated woman."

Climbing into the de-ionization chamber was like entering a giant soda can. The floor hatch swung closed and vertical fluorescent tubes flickered to life in plastic sheathed walls. They surrounded an aluminum cage that filled most of the chamber. I entered the cage and shut the hinged-bars behind me. "I'm in."

"Who am I, Helen Keller? Hold still a minute, kay? I'm not messin' with the enviro-alarms upstairs which means you gotta be deloused."

If their air filters happened to catch my hair or skin particles they'd have my DNA.

"We're ahead of schedule so I'm runnin' this thing twice." A motor kicked-on and static built in the chamber's plastic walls. Loose particles of anything that happened to be hitching a ride now jumped to the walls like fleas fleeing a swimming dog. I raised my arms, raked my scalp, and shook the loose parts of my coveralls. The motor wound-down and a metal hoop dropped slowly from the ceiling, nearly touching the room's curved walls. Small sparks marked the cremation of my fleas as the zapper burned and vacuumed particles.

After reaching the floor the whole process repeated.

Second cycle completed, I climbed the ladder that extended through the top of the aluminum cage. Eight rungs up, I encountered another hatch. A tiny red dot glowed steadily next to a slot in the wall.

I waited patiently. Until the fluorescent tubes blinked out in the DI chamber below. "Hello?"

"I don't believe this."

"Let me read your troubled mind. A post construction security upgrade included isolated circuitry for the inner-hatch's mechanism, and your blueprints failed to include said upgrade."

"Your tone tells me you have a solution to said crisis."

I activated my Casio's headlamp, dipped into my tool pouch, came away with a small circuit board—that happened to be the exact size and shape of a standard security card—and held it up for Serene to see. "I give you the 'freedom board.' The One State's artificial borders are only as good as the tech they use. Fortunately for us, the stuff of government contracts is overpriced cereal-box hardware. Checkpoints are cheap chocolate and I'm July afternoon—"

"Drop the drama Ratch, just do it. I ran the de-ionizer twice, so we're only about a minute ahead of—"

"Open says-me!" I commanded, and stabbed home my electronic skeleton key. In less than a second the tiny red dot blinked green, the metal disc swung aside, and I pumped my arm in silent victory.

"Cute toy: now kill the headlight before you set-off sensors."

"Oh yeah." *Click.*

Obeying the laws of physics, the data room's controlled environment 12°Celsius air rushed past me. I clambered up out of the hole and Serene slammed its hatch as soon as I'd cleared the International Safety Administration light curtain. "The enviro's temperature-alarm is steady. As slow as you moved, it must be broken."

"Whatever."

She tried to make me think my wit silenced her, but I could tell that she was just being coy.

I pocketed my circuit card as nerves shivered through me. The monotone hum of DigitAd's hardware dried my mouth like I'd been sucking cotton balls.

Crime time.

Crouching next to the hatch, I slow-spun a 360 of the room on the balls of my feet for Serene's benefit.

"Kay, directly north of your position is the control room window, so rule number one: stay low behind that row of circuitry cabinets."

"And good news: just double-checked acoustics. The data room's soundproof, so any tool's a go."

"Copy that. I just wanna get gone, so what am I lookin' for?"

"Find panel two-one-three. Should be west of the access hatch, south side of the aisle."

I scanned the clearly marked panels and had to crawl only a few metres. "We're lookin' at it."

"Gimme a sec—kay, open 'er up. And quit your drama! We've gotta two minute window—screw this up I'll personally upload your profile to the FBT's Ten Most Wanted list!"

If she only knew.

"Sorry. That's just how I deal with stress. See, when I get nervous I start . . ."

"Ratch!"

"Yeah. Focused." *Outback X-T, Outback X-T.* My black-diamond grinder ate through the hardened steel latch while my pencil-vac sucked up metal filings. "Ya know Serene, you're really good at that. Have you ever considered a career as a drill instructor? If you ever get sent to a Rehab Ward, I've heard that they have ROTC counselors there." The latch gave way and I palmed the panel as it fell toward me. "You really have a natural ability that would serve—"

"Ratchet!"

'Kay." I cautiously propped the steel door against the circuitry cabinet behind me and sat cross-legged before my medium. Braided rainbows of wiring twinkled my eyes. My left index finger began at the top left row of I/O ports, and slowly moved down, pausing at each while my brain churned equations.

"Don't even show-off. Hold-on until I wake-up the Dot."

A small blue dot appeared between my eyes and the I/O ports. It glided up and down the rows then stopped on a silver cylinder attached to three circuitry boards. The Dot blinked.

"Gotta winner, Ratch."

My left index finger marked the ports and my right hand dug into a pouch for a small plain cardboard parts-box. Wedged tight between my calves, I tore one box end and fumbled out the reason for my trip. I pinched my homemade silver cylinder by its flat ends between a thumb and middle finger. It looked identical to the existing part, except that the three boards were twice as long as those already nested in the circuitry.

"Hold tight—twenty-three seconds."

"See? Plenty of time." I wiggled the fingers of my left hand before Serene's camera, just to annoy her, then took hold of the silver cylinder that the Dot had indicated. A timer showing tenths of a second appeared in mid-air, and counted down from ten.

"Remember, their system will be down for precisely two seconds, so . . ."

"Yeah, I know, quiet please!" *Four, three, two, one, zero*—I yanked the existing part with my left and snugged my custom circuitry home with my right.

The timer read -1.83 seconds.

"A bit slower than practice, but it'll work. Now hole-up in the DI chamber in case something goes wrong. I'll get back to you when we're ready to crash."

"Copy that." I stashed the replaced part in the box and headed for the hatch.

Hunkered down in the de-ionization cage, I ordered my goggles to show several views from the Metroplex's security-cameras. These terrorists were absolutely wired.

Chicago's highways had thickened with lunch-rush workers hunting noon meals. Roadside vendors served you-don't-want-to-know to those stuck in traffic.

Downtown, pedestrians glided one story above traffic, through moving-sidewalk tubes lined with bug-buggies and hot-meal-machines. Mitsubishi Digital-Billboards lined highways and walkways, advertising products and services with flash-images and micromercials. Sensors detected captive traffic-jam audiences, and switched to longer advertisements. Most pedestrians stared at the screens just to avoid the eyes of passers-by.

One company had landed all commuter contracts for the New York, Chicago, and LA-SD Metroplexes: The DigitAd Corporation, Inc.

At exactly 12:20 Central-Time, DigitAd's screens went dark. The Mitsubishi hardware, large and small, even elevator vid-screens, darkened. The conspicuous void of programming caused millions of murmuring double-takes. All eyes waited to see what would happen—for exactly one point eight three seconds. Bold white capital letters scrolled black screens:

THE CREATOR SO LOVES HIS CREATED THAT HE SACRIFICED HIS ONLY SON, AND ALL WHO'VE FAITH IN THE SON WILL REALLY LIVE. JOHN 3:16
—*Global Awareness Version*

I awed as the letters faded, only to replay.
Impossible!
Roads became parking-lots and sidewalks cleared.
I killed the sec-cams, and moped. *Razz, I'm dead.*

The Outback XT of my dreams rusted to slag. I snatched the magazine page from my pocket, crumpled it, and whipped it at the plastic wall.

The motor kicked on, and the metal hoop dropped.

I'd made the new part. I'd hidden it under my rarely-washed handkerchief in my tool belt's left center pouch. It had never left my sight.

The FBT had planted me because the Body needed a specialist—one who could write chips and pull the micro computer switch.

The FBT had sent me underground with pre-written chips.

After two months of canned food and soy-caffeine crystals, the BoC handed me their hard copy for transmission.

I'd soldered the FBT's propaganda chip into the circuit, myself. I'd never even *written* the Body of Christ's terrorist message, yet somehow I'd just watched it play.

I watched the hoop flame my high-gloss dream.

I've just seen a techno-miracle.

"Hey!"

My head bounced off the aluminum cage and Serene's laughter filled my goggles' headset.

"They're battering down our binary doors as we speak. You wanna go upstairs and finish this thing?"

I rubbed my frowning head. "I'd rather be going downstairs, but you know, gravity and all, what goes up must come down. Unless they catch me, of course. Then—"

"Steady Ratch."

"Uh, yeah."

I re-climbed the ladder, we did the hatch routine, and I crawled to the exposed panel. Settling cross-legged again, I fumbled the small box from my breast pocket, and removed the circuitry. This was definitely the original part I'd replaced.

Now for Serene's signal. I studied the room around me, and shivered. Nothing spectacular, the usual data-room stuff, just like the blueprints. Grills in the walls marked the incredibly complex filtered ductwork that kept the place cold, dry, and debris free. From the aisle's far end, an elevator-lookin' door threatened my imagination. I knew that portal led to another DI air-lock. Had I been too slow or placed my pirate-part in the wrong port, security would have dragged me through that door. If my escape now moved too slowly, I'd suffer the same fate.

Maybe I should just let them catch me. I'd taken this job to get rich, but after this? When the FBT tracked me down, my failure's payment would be months in a rehab-ward. The miracle haunted me, but doomed me. I could always live with these Nutter-Butters in their underground holes, but wouldn't it just be better to just give-up?

It's no-fair! I replaced *the freaking part!*

Events of the last few minutes had torn-off my roof.

And it was pouring.

"Giddy-up, Ratch, we're slagged!"

I'd just play-along for now—until I had time to think. "Slam the doors behind me, 'cause I'm a memory." I tore the pirate part from its port and replaced the original. In fourteen seconds my arc had spot-welded the steel cover's latch, and my pencil-vac had stolen all chemical and particle traces from the controlled environment. Fifty-eight seconds more found me backing out of my parking space.

I should just drive this cart to the local FBT office. Quit while I'm behind.

I squeaked all of my cart's forty horsepower around a ramp's corner. *Up and out.*

Nope—a straightaway.

The cart hummed down the still-empty tunnel on level X-2—Y-2.

I have to know.

I had to see it again. I plugged my micro into the dashboard port, and cranked the vid-volume. A flag rippled across my screen . . .

"TERRORISM."
A slide show of peacekeepers, children,
and street violence . . .
"YOUR GOVERNMENT NEEDS YOU."

Dammit! This is the message that should have played!

Visuals of exploding buildings . . .
"WE KNOW NO PEACE. HELP US PROTECT—"

Then I stopped hearing. On-screen, a status-bar showed that my micro had buried some file-that-I'd-never-written in millions of Web-addresses. It would take the FBT months to dig them all out. The number of people who would see and e-mail this message measured at migraine-material-cubed.

I ripped out my homemade part and slammed on the brakes at the next waste-oil recycle dump-tank. There on the concrete floor, I hammer-vented rage on the miracle-micro.

"Ratch, what are you doing? Get outta there!"

I stood, stepped on the tank's International Safety Administration's approved valve-pedal, and dropped the part into the pour spout. "Destroying evidence."

I released the pedal. *Plop*

"That wasn't in the plan."

"Stop reading my thoughts."

"You need to be out of there—like by yesterday."

"Yep." She went all coy again as I motored the cart up to speed.

"Hey Serene, I think I'm gettin' a taste for soy-caffeine crystals."

AT THE MOUNTAINS OF LUNACY

Stephen L. Rice

This was originally conceived as part of a series of computer-based games. Since it's easier to plot stories than games (and many players prefer action sequences to plot anyway), it became part of a novel-in-progress, *The Unfolding Story*, which is a parody of Andre Norton's *Quag Keep*: Philosophy! Theology! Puns even God may shake his head at! And in this case in particular, not a Lovecraft in sight. It probably sank.

IT WAS A GLORIFIED plumbing job—open up a stuck mountain pass. But like most plumbing jobs, it paid well, and our clothes didn't even have to fit. Of course, plumbers usually come back alive afterward, too. But no one had yet come back alive—or dead—from this one.

What made it worse was when the king laughed maniacally after we accepted the assignment. By then it was too late to do anything but make a note to ourselves never to inbreed.

The crowning humiliation followed: the royal mail service had chickened out, observing that

1.   there was nothing in the code about lethal mountain passes;

2.   the U.S. Postal Service's quip about couriers' appointed rounds didn't even exist in this world; and

3.   since we were heading there anyway, we might as well make one trip count.

So we were letter carriers as well as plumbers. No matter how we looked at it, we had been left holding the mailbag. In fact, Garfunkel the Elf couldn't get free of the thing, which at least promised to give the rest of us some good laughs at regular intervals. We were also assured that it would always pull us to the next stop on the route. How comforting.

But we resolved to ignore that fact and focus on more important issues: Who knew what mysteries lay ahead? Who knew what terrible force kept the pass closed off? Who knew why characters in stories always talked in the past tense about things that were just then unfolding like a newspaper from a particularly ripe fish? But I was babbling again. And so began the adventure in the Mountains of Lunacy!

We spent most of the next day traipsing down the road to the mountains. We didn't think we could even reach the foot of the mountains before nightfall. That didn't concern us too much at the time. One of the advantages to being someone who can pass through the rifts between worlds is that you see some impressive sights, and we were just beginning to enjoy the spectacle of the seven moons of Adris sweeping across the night sky when the mailbag yanked Garfunkel toward a cabin just off the road. It was evidently a shop, and the lack of trade through the pass had hurt the shopkeeper, a humble, gracious slob named Olaf, more than it had our royal employer.

"Greetings, strangers!" he said as he opened the door. "Unfortunately, I have nothing to offer but lodging and advice, but then, you seem well-provisioned."

We asked him what he knew about the problems in the pass. The answer was not encouraging.

"Too much and too little. Almost a year ago, the caravans just stopped getting through. It's given me more time for hunting, but I'd rather get back to business. What really worries me is my brother Murray."

We responded with blank looks, hoping to discourage further digressions. We failed.

"You see, Murray was—I hope still is—an alchemist. In fact, he made some of the best-selling items in the shop! But about a year ago, only a month or two before the trading season, he decided to go into the mountains to research some new idea of his. He never came back."

"I suppose you'd like us to look for Murray," I said with a sigh.

"Well, since you're going to be in the area anyway, why not? It's too late to travel into the pass now in any case, so you can stay the night, and I'll even polish your weapons if you like. The pass is pretty wet, and the polish will keep the rust away."

"So how do we recognize your brother?"

"Well, you can probably just listen for explosions. He does that a lot, especially if he's playing with chemicals. Other than that, we don't look a lot alike, but we both have Dad's glasses."

"How can you both have your father's glasses?"

"They didn't call him four-eyes for nothing. So, how about spending the night here and having your gear tended to, and then you can go to your doom first thing in the morning. Remember, open the pass first, then save Murray. He's a lousy hunter, and I don't like hunting for two."

"Can you at least offer us some advice about the pass?"

"Altruistically, I'd say go back. But you're brave adventurers, so you won't do it. Those are the Mountains of Lunacy over there, my friends, and they don't call them that for nothing. There have always been strange things going on up there."

"What kind of strange things?"

"Oh, stories of undead creatures buying real estate, nuts wanting to take over the world, alchemists studying bizarre phenomena in hopes of turning a profit. The usual stuff. I used to sell the *Adris Enquirer* here, you know."

I won't even comment on the nightmares that entertained us till dawn. Our weapons were nice and silvery after the polish he gave them, but that was the only bright point in the situation. Trudging up the mountain all day did not improve our spirits, though we were briefly relieved when the mailbag tugged Garfunkel toward a light ahead.

Tucked into a nook in the mountainside was a shop with a sign that read "HARDWERE." We had mail to deliver and could only hope the proprietor was functionally illiterate. Our first look at him encouraged that hope. His name was Lou Garou, and he had a heavy accent and a frame to match. We hoped for some information and perhaps a room in exchange for his mail. Maybe he had a lost brother too.

"I was just going out," he said as he opened the door, "but it is getting late, and we hear so little news from outside. I would be delighted if you would stay here and talk for a while. In return I can give you a warm place to spend the night—and we may even find something to eat."

At times like this we couldn't help thinking about the royal laugh track. We nonchalantly grasped our weapons and hoped for useful information. We also got out his mail. That was nearly a mistake.

"A mirror!" he yelled. "I didn't order a mirror! Those idiots! I'll—"

We tried to calm him down and half succeeded.

"What?" he muttered. "Seven years' bad luck? True—and that would be forty-nine to some people."

We retrieved the mirror. He acted like he still might break it, and though we weren't Muslims, we still didn't want to eat glass. Besides, anything that unnerved him was probably a good thing to have around. Griselda, our token Amazon, decided to claim it. She never could get her mustache combed right just going by feel. Once we put the mirror aside, Lou became usefully talkative.

"I don't know what is happening to the neighborhood," he sighed as he settled back in his chair. "People used to come through all the time. If I depended on the caravans for all my business, I would be ruined. But the locals make it worth my while to stay open.

"As to advice, I would suggest that you travel by night. I have heard terrible screams from up the road during the day, and that is when the caravans and adventurers have disappeared. There are strange sounds at night, too, but I don't remember anyone dying then.

"If you get past whatever has killed off the others, I would suggest investigating the castle to the north of the road. It was recently bought or seized by some strange people, and they are probably the ones you want. To the south is the fortress that houses most of the locals."

We asked about Murray just to see what would happen.

We expected nothing.

We were wrong.

"I believe I saw your friend some time ago. He said he was interested in helping us, but I think he had some evil scheme in mind—he wanted to trick us out of some of our secrets and make a fortune! We got some help out of him, though—before he disappeared. I think the creatures in the north castle got him."

He must have realized how loud and angry he sounded, for he stopped and smiled calmly. "But let us talk of better things. Have you ever considered what makes us what we are? What we are here for? How we can fulfill our destiny?"

As he spoke, the light grew dim. The lantern that illumined the place flickered, and he adjusted the wick. We almost welcomed the near-darkness, because it meant that he probably wasn't going to hand out brochures or tracts. If I had been back home in the U.S., we would still have to worry about a PowerPoint presentation, but Lou liked his voice better than graphics anyway.

"When do you feel most alive?" he continued. "Is it when you are doing your tedious little duties? Or is it when you follow your instincts? Too many people try to bottle up their desires instead of living them out. When such people die, it makes no difference: they were never alive anyway.

"We should follow our instincts—our desires! When the mind is clouded and the conscience hesitates, our instincts are the path of life inside us. If only they could find a matching power outside. . . "

In the fading light, I could just see him glance out the window. The moonlight was by now almost brighter than the lantern-light, though it still obscured as much as it revealed.

"Some say that the moons are the power behind much magic. There are seven moons, one for each of the so-called deadly sins, and some also say that it is our own evil that calls forth magic. But these are mere names. Power is the reality.

"There are those who are pledged to a moon—the moon that shone when they fully came alive. But they become as weak as anyone else when their moon sets. Yet if one can follow one moon, why not all seven? For with all the moons there is almost always power for those who wish it."

As he spoke, a change crept into his voice that was no less terrible for all of our half-expecting it. We suggested that he tend the light, hoping to be wrong—or at least to be prepared. We were beginning to prefer tracts to the likely alternative.

"Light, my friends? But of course—let us all step into the light. . . of the Moons!"

Suddenly the room was filled with pale light—and a very unpleasant occupant with fangs, claws, and enough hair for a hundred toupees. His toothy leer gave way to a look of embarrassed astonishment when we hauled out our silvered weapons. I thought I heard him say "Oops!" just before I whacked his head off.

The shop proved a pleasant enough place to spend the night, and some of us considered retiring there. Adventuring gets tedious after a while, and most of us had given up on finding our way back to our respective homes. But before we could even consider holing up, we had to restore the trade route and make a preemptive strike on any unruly customers the late proprietor may have had.

We decided then and there to travel by day to avoid further incidents. It didn't work.

The pass narrowed as we traveled, so of course we prepared for an ambush. Soon it began to widen again, to our great and temporary relief. Friar Francis was our cleric, but he also served as our number-two nature freak, and Garfunkel, usually number one, was busy again trying to get free from the mailbag. That was why it was the padre who noticed some burned spots just beyond the widening of the pass. The rest of us had a close look at the marks and our surroundings.

"It looks like someone had a weenie roast here," I said. "I wonder who the weenies were?"

We found some brush and chucked it into the wide part of the path. One flash of light later, we had a splendid pile of charcoal. Someone had a burning-glass set up on the mountain proper, where it could already catch the sun.

It was a tricky situation: any weather that stopped the glass would probably at least slow us down, and if we waited long, we were sure to have company, perhaps from both sides. If they didn't drop something on us first.

Suddenly I had the answer. "The mirror! The mirror from Garou's! We could use it to reflect their light back at them. Even if it doesn't burn them, it should at least blind them."

For being so clever, I nearly got to march out there with the mirror. I thought that Griselda should have the honor, since it was her mirror now, but the padre said that he was ready to meet his boss. He didn't have to explain that we weren't. I didn't mind: I hadn't wanted him along anyhow. I was big on freedom from religion back then.

Friar Francis stepped out, carefully checking the cliffs above, but he barely got the mirror positioned in time. The blaze of light hit the mirror; then, in response to the mirror's movement, it shot up the mountainside and disappeared. We thought we could hear howls of pain and rage from above.

Life was full.

As we continued through the pass, we discovered a small opening in the mountainside to the north. It had the unmistakable look of a Sage's cave. I wondered if the Sage had survived visits from the local lycanthropes, but then I saw that the place was protected by a mystical sign that read "No Dogs Allowed." Underneath was scrawled, "That goes for werewolves, too!" This was a good sign—not in terms of artistry or philosophy, but because it meant that the fang-faced losers at least weren't illiterate.

We left the actual contact with the Sage to Friar Francis, because Sages, hermits, and clerics are in the same union. He was also better at warding off curses than the rest of us. He had come a long way in every sense after wandering through a rift while journeying to join the Second Crusade, and he had more travel experience than the rest of us. He demonstrated this by defusing the situation.

"Can't you dolts read?" the Sage yelled when he saw us. "You aren't welcome here even in human form! Now, get out!"

"My son," the padre began calmly, "I do have a cross, which I doubt the wolves would carry—"

"Okay, then I'll just curse you a little," the Sage retorted. "Drat you! Double dra—"

I guess dealing with sin all day decreases your tolerance for guff. Friar Francis swiftly and firmly clamped the Sage's mouth shut at the lips. Then he showed the man his mace and said, "Our weapons also happen to be silvered, and they work, too."

By way of demonstration he tapped the Sage on the head with the mace. It was a pity we didn't have a bard along; he could have told me if the note the Sage produced was a B-sharp or a C-flat. Since he was a Sage, it was probably B-sharp.

"Okay, okay," the Sage muttered after his lips were free. "I suppose you're after the story about the werewolves."

We nodded, and he continued, "Well, to answer that, I'll have to tell you the whole story. It's kind of long, but quite riveting. . . "

He wasn't lying, especially about the length. The upshot of the whole miniseries was that Murray had heard that the Mountains of Lunacy had a long-running werewolf problem, and he came here to try to harness lycanthropy to cure baldness, fill his wallet, and prop up his moribund social life.

Now, the problem was that his baldness cure only worked during a full moon—the full moon for the particular werewolf his work was based on. He tried mixing samples, but to no avail. Finally he got the brilliantly stupid idea to create a kind of blended, all-purpose werewolf. This creature would transform any time any moon was full or even looked reasonably well fed. Murray then started trying to extend his new technique to the daylight hours, since it's depressing to wake up bald every morning.

Unfortunately, his new and improved werewolf, our old friend Lou Garou, was so taken with his newfound nocturnal powers that he wanted them extended into the daylight along with his hair, so Murray fled to his lab.

But then Murray had to flee from his lab as well, because his helper, Lovaduc, the lord and master of the Fortress, decided to go even further than Lou and use the pass to recruit an army of werewolves and blackmail the neighboring kingdoms. Murray had already made arrangements with the new owner of the northern castle to do some research, and he was going to continue his work there. As for the people who lived in the castle now—well, they didn't so much live at all: they were undead, which was an unpopular career path at that time. Anyway, that was when Murray disappeared, and who had him was more than the Sage knew.

"Do you have any oracle for us?" Friar Francis asked.

"Not at the moment," the Sage replied. "I can't just summon one up, you know. I must wait for my muse to strike."

"Allow me," the priest said, and one B-sharp later—no, it definitely sounded flat now, so one C-flat later, the Sage was rolling his eyes and swaying gently. Finally he spoke.

"Wicked men seek in an hour
To gain invincible power.
But control is king,
Or they can't do a thing,
And sweet strength grows finally sour."

"We can do better than that," I remarked. "Hit him again; maybe the lyrics will improve."

But Friar Francis had a pensive expression that meant he was contemplating something deep. He said, "No, that should suffice. He's right: vice rebels against control, so their vaunted strength is a short-lived thing. We can win through self-control."

I was so touched and uplifted that I exercised self-control and left without a word. And I had some good ones, too.

There was no sign of a moon when we left the cave, and Garfunkel said that we shouldn't have any trouble until early evening. That was good enough for us. After all, elves know about that sort of thing, and it gave us a good shot at the next phase of our evolving plan. We had pretty much decided that our next stop should be the castle. If we could find a secret entrance, maybe we could grab Murray (and, more important, his antidote) before the denizens could get off their undead ends. We congratulated ourselves on our cleverness.

That was when Garfunkel started bearing south by southeast, and we berated ourselves for our folly. Evidently we had some mail to deliver to the Fortress. The only encouragement we had was the memory of how quickly Garou's head came off. We hoped his friends had easy-off tops as well.

The Fortress didn't look too bad from a distance, but closer up it was less appealing. Unfortunately, this budding trend continued as we entered. All around us were signs of waste and decadence such as one should not see outside of a college dorm. The maids had either given up or been eaten by the litter—or the litterwolves.

There were no werewolves in sight at the moment, however. It was still early afternoon, and a side order of clouds would have obscured any daylighting moons that Garfunkel had overlooked. On the other hand, a large dose of body hair would have improved the residents' looks. They were scattered all over the main hall, not moving except to scratch themselves. The only noises they made were the same in any language. They clearly had no offensive capabilities—except for the sensory kind, that is. We decided that we could beat them to a pulp even with a hand over our nose. In fact, beating them to a pulp would involve little if any change, and all of it for the better.

Then a terrible thing occurred.

They were already vaguely divided into two groups, one on either side of us. As we entered the room, each group staggered to their feet, turned their back on the other group, and dropped their pants in back even further than the plumbers' union allows.

We nearly dropped our weapons and our lunch on the floor.

But what was about as bad was that they looked over their shoulders as they dropped their pants—and began to transform. That was when we realized their strategy: they were mooning each other, and yes, it was enough to provoke a change.

Unfortunately, we were too sickened by the spectacle to make proper use of our weapons, and we soon found ourselves herded down some stairs. It didn't help that whenever we did try to menace them with our weapons, they would say, "Ooh—shiny!"

We eventually regained our senses and composure in the sort of place that gives squalor a bad name. It was a prison cell. Worse than that, many of our belongings were on the other side of the bars, together with the sort of creatures that give drunken slobs a bad name.

They seemed to have had a worse night than we did, and they showed little sign of consciousness. But then, that might have been normal for them. If we could get out of our cage, they would present little challenge, even without our weapons, so long as we could catch them with their pants up. But how to get out?

The answer came in the form of a small opening in the wall. It was equipped with a complete set of questions and advice.

"Hello out there!" a husky male voice called. "How would you like to escape?"

"Immediately and without getting hurt or grossed out," I replied. "Who are you?"

"Me? I'm the famous Murray! I have solutions for problems that don't even exist yet. In fact, sometimes they don't exist at all, so I create them to ensure demand."

"This is all very chatty, but how about that help?"

"Well, you will have to help me a bit of course. I'll also need to look over your group—"

"What about our group?"

"I was just looking for a girl. Not for me, either—I was hoping to distract the guards. And I doubt you could do that. It's always the same: the one day you don't have your female disguise along, the werewolves jump you."

"What about me?" Griselda asked indignantly. Okay, it wasn't the first time her mustache had fooled someone.

"Yowza! Babe alert! That should simplify matters. You can take the boy out of the wolf, you know, but you can't take the wolf out of the boy . . . All you have to do is get the guards' attention. When they come in, whack them!"

"What a brilliant plan," I said. "Then what?"

"Then I'll take you through my secret passage to my lab. It's at the far end of the room outside, behind a wine rack. It's a pity I can't make an opening in this cell, but I can't do more than pull a loose brick or so without getting their attention. Once we're there, we can talk further."

"What about our gear?"

"They brought you in when they were changing out of were-form. They were too groggy to do much with your stuff. In fact, if they hadn't decided to have a drink to snap them out of it, they'd probably be wide awake now."

Driven by the prospect of further chats with the amazing Murray, and especially the possibility of clubbing him into silence, we arranged our little show for the troops. Griselda did her best to look fetching, and we backed her up with wolf whistles to encourage the guards to fetch her.

Murray was right about one thing, though: they came running. Or as near it as they could manage. They were more like a half-drunken K.P. detail than guards, but they had a pretty effective secret weapon: their breath could melt a golem. If not for the personal consequences, we could have simply chucked a torch at them and blown the Fortress to perdition. That gave me the idea to toss the brick Murray had so kindly dislodged for us right at the leader.

It didn't bounce off dramatically or make a hollow sound as I expected. Instead, I heard something like a full-bodied raspberry, and the brick slid off his face and onto the floor. The leader landed on it with the grace of a pole-axed sloth. Whether through training or sheer laziness, the others followed suit: they tripped over him and each other and began snoring.

We tiptoed past them and shut them in. Then we surveyed the area. It was littered with litter—the sort of minor detail that amateurs overlook. But we were dealing with professional slobs. And it did look a lot better now that they weren't cluttering it up themselves. There was a table by the far wall, and we confirmed our suspicions and Murray's assurances: such gear as we had lost was there. We looked at the wine rack on the far end of the room. Was three for three pushing it?

Sure enough, the rack opened up to reveal the Bat Cave. Or a considerable amount of rubble, anyway. A light beckoned from our left. It was joined by the same husky voice we had heard earlier. We followed the voice, if only to get within striking distance and shut it up.

An odd-looking man stood before us. Something about him did in fact remind us of an earlier plot point. On the other hand, there was something about him that some of us, at least, found suspicious. We couldn't quite put a finger on it. Perhaps it was the way he waddled when he walked, even though he didn't look all that chubby. But maybe he had been raised by penguins.

So Murray joined the party. There was great rejoicing. Yet a few problems nagged at us:

If the locals were so dumb, why did they capture us instead of killing us?

And if they were all that smart, why put the dregs of the dregs in charge of security?

But Murray left me with no time to ponder all this. He led us swiftly through his digs to an oversized hole in the wall.

"Here we are," he said, "the tunnel to the castle. Once there, I may be able to find some clue to decode this fershlugginer diary. Then maybe we can put a stop to these moon units! I'm sure that I'm the only one who knows about the tunnel, so it should be completely safe. Don't worry! I'll lead the way. . .

". . . From back here."

We continued through the cramped tunnel for what was probably only a few hundred yards, though it certainly seemed much longer. All went well—up to the point where it all went wrong, of course.

Our first clue was that the dim light that appeared ahead included some shapes that turned out to be bars over our exit. In fact, not quite bars: they had thornlike projections. And they were silver.

We asked Murray if he had any ideas. He passed a bottle of acid along, and we applied it to the bars. He warned us not to use too much, or we'd wind up with a pool of acidic slag on the tunnel floor. So we just weakened a few bars enough to kick them loose. We also noticed something interesting: the bars were not actually silver; they had been coated with a silvery substance, just like our weapons. There was still some residue on the floor, but for the most part we suffered only minor damage.

Speaking of minor damage, when the lights suddenly brightened around us, we nearly encountered blows to body and pride in the form of an unwelcoming committee on the other side—though their weapons were rather unorthodox. Yes, now a small army of skeletons and mummies was headed our way, armed with rolled-up paper. They shouted as they came.

"Bad dogs! Bad, bad dogs! Get back to your kennel!"

The creatures advanced, rolled-up papers in hand, ready to slap us something awful. This was the first combat in this story that we were actually looking forward to. Too bad it didn't last.

"Wait a minute," the lead mummy called suddenly, and the rest of the troops froze. "Lord love a duck!"

"That's lo-VAH-duc," the so-called Murray replied, as we just saw his backside waddling back into the tunnel. "You haven't seen the last of me! Bwa-ha—Ay, Chihuahua!"

I decided to investigate this interjection, and I found something worth the effort: the fake Murray had run into some of the silvery residue and dropped the diary. I picked it up and tucked it away. Then I popped out and met our new friends.

"You guys have silvered weapons!" the lead mummy observed. He certainly had a death grip on the obvious.

"Yeah, and in another second, Friar Francis is going to tune your head for you, if I don't remove it first myself. What are you doing here, anyway? I didn't think this area was zoned for mummies."

"Watch it, buddy! We're a union shop, here—all zombies, and proud of it!"

"If you're a zombie, where's your umbrella?"

"What do I look like, Mary Poppins? I told you to watch it, fella! We'll pull out every zombie in the realm if we have to—that'll shut down your government in nothing flat!"

"You place zombies in the government?"

"Well, this is a kingdom; I'm the official supplier by appointment to the crown. In a democracy, of course, they vote some of them in and hire free-lancers to do the rest."

"You're pretty talkative for a zombie."

"Well, actually I'm the Zombie King. I used to live in a dorm back in New York, and with my couch potato video gaming experience, managing zombies was a no-brainer career-wise. I knew being a Dead head would come in handy someday."

"Okay, then, what's with the bandages?"

"Well, we did have a skirmish or two with the werewolves. I came out a lot better than my zombie guard—they've been reduced to a skeleton force."

"You got savaged by werewolves? Don't you change, too?"

"Of course not! As a former dorm meister, I'm immune to a lot of things. Though come to think of it, I have been needing to shave a lot lately. . . "

"Can you give us some support?"

"Theoretically, I could help you out, but it would take a while to assemble my men—"

"How long would you need to gather your forces?"

"Well, as I said, I'd need to assemble them, which could take weeks. You know how mutts are—once they ran off with a femur or a rib, they'd go bury it who knows where. I hate to think how long it will take to dig them all up again."

"Great. So we're on our own again."

"Precisely." The Zombie King gave a signal to his forces, and they pulled out regular weapons and motioned us into the bowels of the castle.

"What's going on?" I asked.

"Sorry, can't take any chances. Now that you've breached our security, those barkers will return in force and try to take the castle."

"That's why you need us. As you already said, our weapons are silvered."

"Yes, but they'll just gross you out so that you can't fight, and then they'll claw you and make you join their ranks. You're better off out of the way."

As we were being hustled off, I managed to get next to our cleric. "Well? Aren't you going to turn them or something?"

He just smiled mysteriously. "*Festina lente*," he said.

I thought the pressure had gotten to him and he was indulging in some really vulgar Latin.

"Is that some kind of obscenity? Because if it is, I forgive everything."

"That's a job for someone else, my son. In any case, it means 'Make haste slowly.'"

"I liked it better dirty. This way, it doesn't even make sense."

"There is a time for everything."

"Well, this would be a great time for you to run these bozos off."

"To what end? The man is right about our inability to deal with the werewolves. We should let him and his horde handle them."

"I don't trust zombies."

"Neither do I, but timing is everything. And at least they are letting us keep our weapons. But then, the undead are about as leery of silver as werewolves."

We continued down a torch-lit hallway. Suddenly we heard and felt an explosion, followed by maniacal laughter. Something about that sounded familiar. Our guide opened a door. A light flared, and we were confronted with a being whose major selling point was his lack of fur and fangs. Just to be safe, we stuck our silvered weapons in his face. He cackled with delight and recognition.

"That's my silvering! Old 'Go-laugh' must've sent you. And with any luck, you've figured out that brute force isn't the answer. So the question is, are you ready to try something else?"

"You're Olaf's brother?" I asked.

"Of course—the famous Murray the Alchemist, whose likeness adorns nostrums and legal notices all over the realm!"

"We heard a blast. Do you have explosives?"

"No, I do that all the time. It's one of the reasons I became an alchemist: people expect you to do stuff like that. Now, if I had explosives, I could blow this whole castle to the moon of your choosing."

"What a pity I left my dynamite in my other pants. Look, the Sage said you were pretty close to solving this mess you created. Is that true?"

"Well, yes and no. I almost figured out a cure for the super-lycanthropy, but I left my diary back at the fortress."

"This diary?" I asked, producing the book and hoping that we had finally run into some decent luck.

His eyes bugged delightedly. "Yes! I'm so happy, I could explode!"

"Later. Now, this is in some kind of code, right?" I looked at the pages carefully for the first time. The shock wasn't entirely pleasant or unpleasant, but Murray was no longer the only one who felt like exploding. "Pig Latin? What kind of idiot uses Pig Latin?"

"The kind who wants to keep secrets from lowbrow pigs," Murray replied. "The crowd at the Fortress have always been slobs, you know, and they aren't cultured enough to know their Latin—except Lord Lovaduc, of course."

"And the page he has marked is for perpetual lycanthropy," I noted. "But if he's so smart, why didn't he just follow the directions?"

"Because the key ingredient is written in another code. Try to read it."

I had no problem until the last line, which was incomprehensible.

"What does it mean, 'Immelmann, barrel roll, Lutz,' and so on?"

"That's the tricky part. I thought the Zombie King could help me out, because you can't become a zombie master without passing a grave-robber test."

"So?"

"So he must know a lot about de-crypting."

You're right: I should have seen it coming. "So have you asked him yet?"

"Oh, yeah, some time ago. It's skywriters' code: you describe the way you make the letters. Here, let's see . . . Curses! From the look of the descriptions, he must have been using some fancy font or illuminations. I'll have to fall back on my second-best fantasy and pretend I'm flying a dragon."

This was followed by a lot of incoherent mumbling about Snoopy and the Red Baron, as well as sound effects, and we had to stand well back to give him room. Unfortunately his were not the only sound effects: battle had been joined back at the tunnel entrance. I peeked out the door, which was neither guarded nor locked. I should have figured on its not being locked: a place like that would be awash with skeleton keys anyway, so why bother? The others crowded around me.

"How come it took them so long to gather their forces?" I wondered aloud.

"Sloth is evidently one of their favorite sins," Friar Francis observed.

"Well, it's not doing them any good: they must have mooned each other to change, but it's wearing off, and now they're discovering the limits of hindsight. Zombies can't be grossed out even by slobs like them, so they're getting whupped. And they're coming this way!"

I glanced back at Murray just in time to see him cringe. "Pull out, Gold Leader! Nooo!"

I ran over and pulled him up from his heap on the floor. "They're coming! Do you know what the secret ingredient is?"

"What? Oh, sure. Henbane."

"Shouldn't it be wolfsbane?"

"That's an amateur's goof," he said scornfully. He had been fishing around in his pack, and he swiftly drew out two vials and mixed them. "No, my friends, I guarantee that with this, we can't lay an egg."

He disappeared in a cloud of smoke, accompanied by a thunderclap and probably the loudest "Buckaw!" I've ever heard. The next moment he was waving the smoke away and spitting out feathers. I'll give him this much, though: there wasn't an egg in sight.

"Man, that was a good one!" he said, coughing.

"You failed?" I asked, horrified.

"I always louse up the first batch, so I thought I'd get it over with. This is the real one."

There was a flash and a puff of smoke, and he grinned triumphantly. Then his hair fell out.

"Curses! Foiled again!" he muttered. Then he continued, "The real problem is getting the creatures to accept the cure. My original clever notion, a kind of anti-werewolf who could cure lycanthropes by biting them, won't work. I mean, I hate getting a bunch of hair in my mouth! And it's a bit conspicuous when they aren't in wolf form . . . "

Just then a herd of terrified couch potatoes burst through the door. Lord Lovaduc was trying to rally them, but they were too demoralized to pay attention.

"Those confounded creatures are unstoppable!" he growled. "Why are they so much stronger now than they were at first?"

"They are not stronger," Friar Francis corrected him. "You are weaker. But Murray has devised a potion that should cure that: if you drink it, you will regain your greatest power."

"You're lying," Lovaduc snarled.

"Have some respect for the cloth," the friar said, tapping him smartly on the crown with his mace. Lovaduc's tongue popped out, and I could swear I heard a cuckoo. "I do not lie," Friar Francis continued. "What I say is completely true."

The door began to quiver from pounding on the other side. The rest of our party had to take over holding it, because the would-be werewolves were trembling too hard to manage it themselves. But I had had enough.

"Here, give me that, Murray," I said, dashing over and snatching the heavy jar from him. It looked like it could take a lot of abuse, which suited me fine. "If these dopes want to get hacked up, that's okay with me. I'm going to be ready for the skull squad."

It was too much for Lovaduc and company. He grabbed the jar and shoved me aside.

"I'm in charge here! I'll drink it."

Sure enough, that touched off a drinking frenzy. It was even better than yelling "Soo-ee." They preened themselves as the door gave way, and they kept looking for signs of the usual transformation. They were not pleased when nothing happened, not even when they shot the moon.

"You did lie!" Lovaduc screamed at the friar. However, he did have enough sense to draw back before the priest could teach him some respect.

"Nonsense. I said that drinking it would restore your greatest power, and it has. You are now fully men, not part man and part beast, tyrannized by your own evil. I would advise you to build on your humanity, not abandon it."

"But now we have no way to deal with these zombies! Murray, you're a man of science—you believe in honest, sensible stuff like alchemy and astrology, not stupid religion. You don't want to be destroyed by zombies, do you?"

Murray shrugged. "Normally I can't stand people who won't stay dead. They wander around, stinking and getting rot all over your good stuff. They're almost as bad as relatives, except they don't eat as much! But werewolves are even worse than relatives! Well, a little, anyway . . ."

"Ha ha!" the Zombie King cackled as he burst through the door. "Victory is mine! If only I could invent TVs or video games, I could transform all Adris into zombies. But now at least my life has come to a pretty pass, and I intend to stay here . . . as king! Bwa-ha-ha!" He paused suddenly and looked at our group. "That isn't overdone, is it? I mean, I can't get a proper critique of my laugh from these zombies."

"I know of someone who can critique more than that," Friar Francis said.

"Who's that?"

"He means," I explained happily, "that it's time for a word from our Sponsor."

"Hey, I don't do that religion bit. Nothing but good, solid necromancy for me."

But the priest was already doing his "In nomine Patri, et Filii, et cetera" business, and the next thing we knew, the zombies were heading for parts unknown. The Zombie King was not pleased, but he had become an army of one, compared to an army of twenty or thirty, counting the former werewolves. So he began to follow his followers, though first he attempted to unleash a dire curse upon us all.

"You'll hear from my lawyers!"

"There's no need for that," I said. "Why don't you get out of this cold mountain air and get yourself a place in the desert? With all those bandages, you could set yourself up as the Mummy King. Mummies have way better housing and treasure than zombies anyway."

He paused briefly to consider the idea. "That's true. And since I'm shaving more often after my fight with the werewolves, living in a pyramid would keep my razor blades sharp."

"What a pity it's not contagious," I muttered. But he waved cheerfully and departed, trotting after his handiwork.

That left only the ex-werewolves, and they were not as reasonable, which suited us just fine. Lord Lovaduc waddled over and tried to look menacing.

"Fine. Well, I hereby take possession of this castle, so you can just be on your way."

"Not yet," I replied.

"We have more men than you do, and besides, if your priest wasn't lying, we now have a lot of power to work with—"

"That power is mostly potential," Friar Francis explained, "and we have been making better use of our potential than you lot have."

Our party smiled at Lord Lovaduc. Somehow it seemed to unnerve him, though I guarantee that my smile at least sprang from genuinely happy thoughts. He turned back to the priest.

"Forgive me, Father, for I have sinned," he bleated.

"No argument there," Friar Francis chuckled. "I think that we'll change the usual order and listen to your confession later. But first, my friends will both arrange your penance and ensure that your contrition is no mere act. As for me, it's past time for me to see no evil and hear no evil, so I think I'll just step outside for a few minutes."

Lovaduc wailed like a lost soul as my friends started sizing up him and his group for personal attention and counseling. But I wanted a word with the padre first.

"You know, if you just don't want to look, I could blindfold you and use Lovaduc to teach you about piñatas." He smiled and shook his head, so I continued, "I have to admit, I didn't want you along, but you really came through on this one. I take back everything I said against you."

"You're taking it all back? Are you recanting or reloading?"

"Recanting, Father. Thanks again." I turned back to the party already in progress. The others were busy beating some civilization back into Lord Lovaduc and his followers. Even without lycanthropy, it was their night to howl.

FAIR BALANCE

S.M. Kirkland

S.M. Kirkland is a novelist and award-winning journalist whose feature stories have been carried by newspapers nationwide. She has served as both a photo- and broadcast journalist for the Georgia Army National Guard and the U.S. Army Reserve covering the 1996 Olympic Games and working in Italy. She lives in the rolling foothills of Northwest Georgia.

In my favorite movie *A Few Good Men*, many people remember Jack Nicholson's line "You can't handle the truth!" But there is another line that always stood out to me. "In places you don't talk about at parties, you want me on that wall, you need me on that wall." He's referring to the walls that separate opposing forces. As Christians, we are the opposing force to the fallen world and like the military, we need those on the wall who aren't afraid to fight the ugly battles. Those battles could be going into the carnage of drug-addicted homes or fighting against true spirits trying to take humans as prisoners of war. It's a hard calling that not everyone is called to fight. "Fair Balance" is a tribute to those who are called to be on that wall.

TONIGHT.

Celisa Cooper froze, the fingers of her right hand entwined in one of the many chains and necklaces hanging from her thin, pale neck. The sterling silver cross felt cool in her hand. Her grip tightened and her heart thundered.

Tonight? I'm not ready.

Tonight.

Celisa slumped against the huge overstuffed black pillow. Her artificially dark features, her eyes trimmed in black with heavy black mascara narrowed in bored dismay, then glared in contrite acceptance. She would not argue. Ready or not. *Tonight.*

Posters of dragons and mythical creatures adorned one wall of her bedroom but her eyes drifted past them in the same glare, stopping on the other wall. Her expression softened, her eyes studying each cross. Crosses were safe, she determined, as the heathen and the saved used them symbolically for both mockery and support of their faith. She mounted them in an array of positions, upside down, right-side up, sideways. But her favorite was a grouping of similar sized ones forming a strange wheel. Mounted in a circle, the long ends made the spokes. In between were smaller ones, in the same circular pattern. Her eyes traced the invisible circle made by the larger crosses, then followed the smaller crosses.

She loved them, each and every one as the only token of her love affair in a forbidden world. She couldn't remember not collecting them in her nineteen years. Chilled, she brought her black fish-netted legs up and wrapped her arms around them, resting her cheek on her knee.

She carried this heavy burden, a spiritual heaviness that sometimes wore her down but she did not bear it alone.

Pushing a strand of bottle-black hair streaked with bottle-ruby red shimmers behind her ear, she stretched out on the bed, her chains and black leather jewelry clinking and spreading over her tiny frame. From the other bedroom, her brother's voice floated muffled through the wall, invading her privacy.

She was out of time and once she crossed that line, her family would, at best, disown her. At worst . . .

Tonight

Are you serious? Tonight?

It made sense. Her mom would meet friends for what she called praise and worship, giving Celisa time to do her dirty work and leave. How ironic, tonight they would both be serving their own god.

Guilt snaked around her like her chains. Despite their differences, she loved her brother. A war was brewing in the Cooper household that her brother knew nothing about. He thought her rebellion during the last year was a way to break out of their clean, conservative appearance. He teased her about the black fingernail polish, playfully turned his nose up at her fishnet stockings and offered to take her to a tattoo parlor to complete her look. Her mother had a fit that shook heaven and hell.

"Give her some time, Mother. She won't always look like a devil-worshipper," he told the woman with a playful smile. "Train a child up . . ."

Celisa bit her lip, trying to force back a smile.

The smile faded and the heaviness turned to a stabbing pain. Their love for her had boundaries; they just didn't know it yet. Anger welled up inside of her.

They're wrong. Their beliefs are radical and wrong. Let them hate me.

But maybe Cain wouldn't. Maybe he'd follow her lead. Anger faded into a painful hope that he wouldn't turn on her. After tonight, her mother would hate her. Undoing all the brainwashing inflicted by their overbearing mother would be the biggest obstacle. Mother always had to be right. Celisa and her brother were forced to believe in one true faith, black and white issues, clear wrong, clear right, no in-between. Since meeting E.C. and Ty, her world grayed. Suddenly, all the things her mother declared as evil weren't quite so bad.

She began removing her jewelry, starting with the spiked leather bracelet and the black and red jelly bands around her wrist. Next her chain necklace, the long one, then the bicycle chain. She unfastened the leather dog collar and the choke chain. Anything that could be a weapon, she let slide down her neck and chest onto the bed.

In less than an hour, her mom would come home from work, change and leave again. Her brother, the obedient, good child, usually accompanied their mother on these rituals. But tonight, she had the assurance that he would stay behind. Perfect.

She needed to let E.C. know the time. He and Ty would have to help her—she wasn't physically strong enough to accomplish the mission, and they were a team. A need to plan forced the guilt from her mind, but Cain's singing bombarded her. His voice was lulling, captivating and had soothed her to sleep many nights as children enduring a bitter, nasty divorce.

Don't. She couldn't be soothed by that voice now, it would open a door back into their world. Too risky.

Living here the last few months was its own type of hell. Imprisoning herself in her room most of the time, she forced herself to engage in their conversations only enough to escape their suspicious nature. The hypocrisy stung her with guilt, but it meant survival. At the local college she and Cain attended, she would arrive early for the classes she shared with E.C. and Ty for the sake of their company. Outside of class, she ignored them. More hypocrisy.

She came out of her room and almost collided with her brother. She eyed him before stepping out of his way.

Tall, strong and sure, Cain reminded Celisa of everything she wasn't. His face, always clean shaven, mirrored his desire to enter the prim and proper business world, or some other noble profession. He rarely wore black, preferring khaki pants and polo shirts or button-downs in all the latest colors. The only similarity was the stark blue eyes.

Those eyes now focused on her, causing Celisa's stomach to shudder. "Where are you going?"

"Outside. I need some alone time."

"Oh."

He sounded bored, but his eyes met hers with such intensity, chills rushed down her spine. Her soul shuddered, violated under the weight of his stare. If he saw the truth, she may not make it until tonight. She looked away and left.

Outside the warm, comfortable air filled her lungs and its breeze washed over her strung nerves. Fall kissed the trees in the yard, their leaves blushing. She hurried down the street and around the bend. The abandoned house provided her good phone reception and concealment.

She pulled out her phone, heart racing as her fingers punched in numbers by memory. It was too risky to save it in the contacts. Waiting for him to answer, she fished under the garbage can lid lying on the ground. A gallon zip-top bag kept her book kept safe.

"Hey, C.," E.C.'s voice chirped in its usual fun way. "Whassup?"

She opened the bag and pulled out the book. "It's time. Tonight."

Silence on the other end. "Are you sure?" His voice was no longer light, but calm and serious.

"Yeah."

"Everything is in place. I'll call Ty."

Panic gripped her again and her fingers flipped though the book, forward, then backward, searching the marked pages.

I can do this. I know where my power lies.

"Are you ready?"

She nodded. "Yeah. But if I get caught, my death warrant is signed."

"Are you afraid?"

"Not of dying, just the process of getting there."

He laughed At least someone realized she had a sense of humor.

"It's initiation, babe. You'll do fine." His voice had sombered a bit. He laughed again. "Maybe one day I'll share my secrets."

"You don't have a secret. You just have more practice."

"That's my secret. Where do you want us to meet you?"

"At the house I showed you before, the one for sale, when it's dark. He won't notice the car, but it's close enough if we need to leave in a hurry."

"Any chance your mom will come home?"

She winced. "She's usually gone most of the night, but, what if she does? Can they tell her something's going on?"

He was quiet for a moment. "It's possible, but I'm not worried. If she does, we deal with it."

She deleted the phone number from her outgoing call list and opened the book. Flipping toward the back, about three-quarters of the way, she let her eyes fall on the page. Just as having E.C.'s number in her cell phone was too risky, this book would be the nail in her coffin. If caught . . . she winced, then sighed. But then, after tonight, it wouldn't matter. *Concentrate on this.*

The words in the book sank in, relaxing her. She breathed them in and exhaled them out over and over and over, wanting the moment to last. Reassurance wrapped around her like the warm breeze and the fading daylight. She was ready.

Her smile at seeing them approach in the glow of the streetlights consumed her whole being. She smiled more in the last few months than she had in years, sometimes it bothered her, but this was her new family from this point forward. The moment was catching up with her, her heart raced, the adrenaline pumping through her veins, bringing with it uncertainty and excitement.

"There's our girl." E.C. smiled, pushing his nappy blond curls out of his eyes and pulling them through an elastic band.

E.C. Hayes was two years older than Celisa. His clean appearance resembled more Cain's style than Celisa and she wondered if, in a different life, they could have been friends. He had the sturdy, athletic build of a baseball player and his easy going nature reminded her of how Cain used to be, until mother began grooming him for a leadership position in her church. Now, Cain no longer laughed at her dry jokes nor talked to her about her life. She couldn't remember the last time they went to the movies, or the last time he helped her with calculus. Cain was so serious all the time, studying, praying, and learning. Her mother, fortunately, had not attempted to groom her for anything. Celisa decided the black clothes and sarcastic attitude had served its purpose. Maybe tonight, she could help Cain remember how he used to be, when he was fun and spirited.

Her stomach twisted and knotted. Blood drained from her face, replaced by a chill. This morning's muffin and soda burned the base of her throat. She closed her eyes and clamped her lips together.

"I feel sick." She opened her eyes.

"I used to puke before these moments." Ty's gruff voice held no sympathy. Blunt and to the point. That was Ty.

She smiled. Ty Wilson had the build and muscle of an entire defensive line. Puking didn't fit with his aloof confidence. She always felt safer around Ty, although it was a superficial security. Her real strength and protection was in the one who couldn't be seen, only felt. Her best suit of armor, unshakable faith teamed with new authority.

Celisa looked up at E.C. The sparkle in his green eyes turned ficry.

"Things could get ugly fast. If it gets out of hand, I'll take over. I won't say a word until I need to and if that happens, you close your mouth and pray."

She nodded. "Can we do that now, as a group?"

Ty nodded and she conceded authority, at least for the moment, to him. She loved to hear Ty's baritone voice when he prayed. He wasn't nearly as blunt with his Father as he was to his brothers and sisters, but his voice was sure and soothing.

Celisa paused at the front door and stood taller, drawing her shoulders back. Grasping the doorknob, she opened the door. Ty's simple prayer made the hair on the back of her neck stand at attention. A strong wind gusted past them whisking away her nausea and uncertainty.

You are ready.

Cain came out of the bedroom and both siblings froze at the sight of each other.

Celisa wasn't sure if it was her imagination, or if everything E.C. had told her was coming to pass, but Cain's eyes looked red and menacing, ready for a fight. He glared at E.C. then faced Celisa.

"We need to talk," she said.

His eyes narrowed and the room chilled. "You didn't! I know these guys—they are liars. You can't believe them."

"They aren't liars. They helped me see the truth. Cain, listen to me." *Let him listen.*

"You!" Cain roared like sheet metal rattling angrily in a storm.

Celisa jumped back. It was not Cain's voice.

"Who are you?"

"I don't have to tell you!" the voice hissed.

"Yes, you do!" she focused hard on her brother as E.C. and Ty moved away from her.

"You have no authority in this house!" he growled.

"I have authority over you, in this house, outside this house and anywhere else, now what's your name? In the name of Christ—"

The demon howled, a shrieking, painful pierce that ripped through Celisa's eardrums, but she didn't flinch. She didn't blink.

"Cusion! Don't say that name again."

"How many of you are there?"

"More than you can count."

Her brother's body paced back and forth, never coming closer to her. His body twitched, shaking in little tremors—small groans escaping his lips. E.C. and Ty stood at opposite ends, watching with cold, hard glares of warriors waiting for the command. The miniscule living room felt like it was shrinking. Tension weighted in the air. Celisa tried to find the reassurance she heard earlier. *You will not leave me nor forsake me. You are my shield, my strength.*

"How many?"

"Three."

"Who are the others?"

"Rahu and Pyro." The voice now high pitched and raspy—like the brakes of train trying vainly to stop.

"Rahu," she ordered. *He gave his disciples, He gave me, power and authority over all demons. Don't ask for deliverance, just claim it. Be tough.*

What was that verse? Luke, Luke something. Ten, eighteen. He gave me authority . . . over the enemy.

"Leave," Celisa commanded with more authority than she thought possible.

The air chilled further and a cold wind bit her entire body.

It left. Her eyes darted in the direction the wind had blown. *Thank you, Lord.*

But something caught her attention, the sound of singing and Celisa looked toward Cain's room. *He's here, who's —*

His weight crushed her against the floor. She never saw him pounce. His hands wrapped around her throat stopping her scream before it left her mouth. Celisa grasped his hands, struggling for freedom and air.

"You are going to die!" his hands constricted around her throat.

Ty leapt at Cain, bodily lifting him but he didn't loosen his grip on Celisa.

Celisa gasped for breath—dull pain spreading from her throat to her head.

Cain's vice grip tightened; she struggled, her feet off the floor, trying to pry his fingers away to no avail.

You are in control, Lord. He has nothing on you. Break his grip. I didn't mean to fail.

Be still and know that I am Lord.

She stopped. The pressure exploded in her head, but she didn't move.

E.C. moved deliberately, with no rush. Ty had Cain in a modified nelson hold. Celisa squeezed her eyes shut, hoping to stop them from popping out of the sockets. Cain was half the size of Ty, but Ty couldn't break his hold on Celisa. Ty's eyes trained on Cain. She could hear him praying, but couldn't make out the words.

"Let her go, now," E.C. said, his voice quiet, but frigid.

Celisa hit the floor with a thud and gasped for breath as she dragged herself out of the way. She squeezed her eyes shut, hoping to relieve some of the pressure. *Awesome, mighty Master, Creator, I don't want him to stay here. He'll die. He can serve you.* Desperation took over, strangling her prayer.

"Rahu." E.C. tilted his head up slightly in a show of power.

"She belongs to us," her brother hissed.

"She's ours. Christ pulled her off the altar your mother sacrificed you two on. She only wants to pull you off, too."

"Mother will hunt her down and kill her."

"Your mother has no more power than you do. We are the brothers and sisters of Christ and neither the angels nor the vile and stupid demons can touch us."

"You don't know our power."

"I don't need to know your power. I know my power, my authority, given to me by my Father in Heaven, who created you. Don't talk to me about power."

"What are you going to do to me?" the raspy voice faltered.

"Get out and return to your pit, Cusion!"

Cain's body went limp and Ty dropped him onto the floor before going to Celisa. She rubbed her throat, her breathing labored. Ty rubbed her back until she bolted up, staring at her brother.

"Is he okay?" She pushed Ty's hand away from her and crawled to her brother.

"He should be," E.C. said. "We can take him with us. Cleansing him won't do any good if he's not ready to come to Christ."

She gingerly turned Cain's body over and touched his face, her black fingernails tracing down his cheek and around his chin. Cain opened his eyes. They were clear and focused, but lifeless.

"What did you do?" he asked, his voice weak.

"You had demons," she whispered. "We got rid of them."

He groaned. Not from physical pain, but from mental anguish radiating from him. "They were from Mom. You have them too."

"No, mine were cast out months ago, when I came to know Christ."

Cain winced, agony etched over his face. "When—?"

"Months ago—at school. I met E.C. and Ty in my literature class and they showed me. All the anger and fear, they were demons. They are gone. I'm free now and I like it."

"Mom is going to kill you," he whispered. "The coven—"

"I'm not scared anymore," she said. "You have to come with us."

He shook his head, "No." Reaching up, he stroked her face with his hand. "You go. I won't tell Mom anything, but this is where I want to be."

She jerked away as if it burned. "Cain, he lies to you. You can't believe him. He is the father of lies."

"No, Celisa. He's going to make me great. He was going to do awesome things for you too and you've betrayed him." Cain's eyes narrowed. "You need to go. Mom will be home soon."

The high-pitched whine of her mother's car drew Celisa's stare to the window . . . *We need more time, Father. Please.*

"Celisa," E.C. said. She faced him, hoping he could see the pleading in her eyes, she had no words to express it. He shook his head. She knew the dangers of facing her mother. Celisa didn't doubt her God was more powerful, but right now, her faith struggled. Staying would be foolish, even deadly.

They hurried out the door and around the corner, down the road to the empty house, and piled into EC's car.

"He's going to die." Sobs racked her body, watching her mother's car pull into the driveway. "We left him to die."

Ty put his strong arms around her and let her cry on his already-damp shirt. She forced the tears back and watched the buildings blur past her. She didn't asked where they were going. E.C. said earlier they had safe places—bathed in prayer and claimed for their service—where she could rest. Exhaustion weighed over her like a heavy coat in the summer.

"You're drained," he said quietly. "It's normal. The first time I slept eighteen hours, woke up long enough to eat and slept another six. The harder the battle, the more it gets you. Some are easy, weak demons, willing souls. But most put up a fight. You'll be safe."

"I don't care about that. "We have to get him out of there. He's been brainwashed, but we can help him."

Black eyeliner ran down her face. Brushing the side of her hand underneath her eyes, Celisa wiped the grayish black makeup on her skirt. *How could he not understand, Lord? Where did I mess up?*

"Why wouldn't he come?" she asked. "I don't understand."

"Celisa, it was his choice," E.C's voice was soft, but she didn't find it reassuring. "We've only been given power over demons, not humans. That's the fair balance."

THE WAKING OF THE DEAD

Steve Doyle

Steve Doyle, a former computer programmer, is an award-winning poet whose work has appeared in an anthology titled *In the Desert Sun*. His poem "Footprints in My Garden" coupled with photography by Maria Touchette won third prize at a juried art show put on by the Hudson Area Arts Alliance.

He has begun writing short stories and is an active member of "The Herscher Project," an online group of artists and writers from all over the globe. He also maintains a bookshelf of his work at the Wyvern's Library section of Elfwood, the largest science fiction and fantasy art site in the world.

Steve lives in Marlborough, Massachusetts, where he is currently working on a novel as well as *The Casebook of the Paranormal Research Institute*, a collection of short stories due for publication by CWG Press. Visit his website at www.doylebooks.com

While writing a short story "An Encounter with a Vampire," I decided that I wanted the creature to speak Greek, the only difficulty being that I don't speak that language myself. I posted a plea for help and fellow Elfwood member Ingrid Eskitzi came to my rescue, dutifully translating the vampire's dialogue. Some time later she asked me to write a zombie story for her. I was more than happy to oblige. After discovering some rather strange customs and beliefs, I set "The Waking of the Dead" in Ireland at the turn of the sixteenth century. At a time when the populace cowers in fear of ghosts and vampires and drowns in the dark sea of superstition, one priest stands as a beacon of light and hope.

BILLY WOUND HIS WAY over the path through the dark woods. He was late but it wasn't his fault, his parents had made him do chores right after dinner. He'd hurried to finish them and get out here to meet Natalie, hoping she hadn't given up on him. He didn't want that to happen again, she'd been mad for weeks that time.

He panted, nearly out of breath, and the smell of oak leaves filled his nostrils. Most of the trees were bare and the late October air felt cool; once the sun went down it would turn cold. He wiped his sweaty palms on his trousers as he broke through the trees and stood at the edge of the grove.

She was there! Thank God, he hadn't missed her. Billy took a few steps in her direction. "Natalie."

The young girl turned around to face him.

The sight of her stopped him in his tracks. Her lips trembled as she looked at him through red, watery eyes. Tear tracks stained puffy cheeks. Long red hair hung unkempt about her shoulders.

"Did you think I wasn't coming?" he asked.

Fresh tears welled up in those green eyes and she choked out her words through sobs. "I . . . can't . . . see you . . . anymore, Billy!"

"Why not, Nat? What happened?" Billy closed the distance between them.

"It's . . . my parents . . . they say . . . I'm too young . . . to see boys . . . to see . . ." She stopped and inhaled deeply, a teardrop slid down her cheek. She balled her hands into fists and blurted out, "They just don't want me to be happy! I hate them! I hate them!"

"It's okay, Natalie. Don't cry." He folded her into his arms, felt her heartbeat hammering against his chest. "I don't like it, but they are your parents and you have to do what they say."

She shoved, pushing him away. "What? You don't want me either!"

"No, I didn't mean that."

"You don't care! I thought you loved me but you don't! I believed you when you said it but it's all a lie!"

"No, Nat . . ."

She turned and ran from him before he could finish. He heard her say something that sounded like "no one loves me." Her red hair waved in the wind while her shoes crunched on the carpet of oak leaves. He took a step to follow, but thought better of it. Every time he tried to talk to her when she was upset, he wound up saying the wrong thing. Better to wait until she'd calmed down. He shoved his hands deep into his pockets and shuffled home, kicking dead leaves along the way. The October air turned cold.

Days later, after a long time spent brooding, Billy walked to Natalie's cottage. As it loomed in the distance, smoke curling from its chimney, he silently rehearsed his arguments, steeling himself for a confrontation with her parents. *We're living in the sixteenth century! Surely times have changed. Your ideas are old-fashioned and stale. You've got to allow Natalie to see me if she so wishes!*

He strode up to the heavy wooden door and knocked loudly. He held his head high and puffed out his chest with a deep breath. He could smell the peat smoke. *Here goes.*

The door opened a crack. The sight of the puffy, tear-streaked face changed his attitude. His carefully rehearsed speech abandoned him and he exhaled his confidence.

"Mrs. Flanagan, what's wrong?"

"'Tis Natalie! She's nay more with us!" When Elizabeth opened the door wider, her sobs began anew and she slumped against the frame. Fearing she would fall, Billy put an arm around her shoulder and walked her into the cottage. He helped her to a seat at the oaken table where big John Flanagan, already seated, glared silently at him.

After a moment, Elizabeth dabbed at her eyes with her apron. "She threw herself into the pond, Billy. She's gone." Sobs once again wracked her buxom figure and she hung her head, covering her face with her hands.

"No!" Billy shut his eyes tightly and pulled at his hair.

John said, "Now she can't be buried in the village. She must be brought to a place where four roads meet and buried at night, face down with her two feet tied together."

"What?" Billy opened his eyes and stared at the man. "That's ridiculous! It's absurd!"

Elizabeth looked up, breathed deeply, and tried to explain, "Natalie committed a terrible sin. She'll not be allowed in Heaven, but does nay belong in Hell, so doomed she'll be to wander the Earth if we don't do this. We can nay bury her in Holy ground; the others interred there wouldn't stand for it and would reject her. They might even vent their anger against the living."

"I can't believe I'm hearing this!"

"'Tis your fault," John said evenly. He took a deep breath, then his big frame shook, his face turned red, and he bellowed, "My daughter is denied Heaven for loving you. Her mother and I can only try to keep her poor spirit still and that is what we are going to do!"

Concealed from view, Billy watched as gravediggers buried Natalie by torchlight at the crossroads outside the village. As they returned from this nocturnal task, they kept glancing back to see if the ghost indeed followed. Though the girl lay face-down in the grave, and her feet were secured, nervous eyes peered into darkened gloom and nervous feet hurried home. Billy went in search of his two younger brothers.

"You two have to help me."

Jimmy, the youngest, slowly shook his head from side to side, "I don't know, Billy. If anybody found out. . ." His voice trailed off.

"Nobody's going to find out. We'll bury her in the ancient churchyard. It hasn't been used in a hundred years. We'll put her under the old elm tree."

"It's frightenin', Bill," Danny said, "I've never dug up a body before. It seems sacrilegious."

"It's sacrilegious to leave her where she is. You should have seen them. They threw her in the hole and covered her up; they never said a thing. They show more respect to dogs!" Tears filled Billy's eyes and he sniffled. His shoulders heaved.

Danny placed a hand on Billy's shoulder.

Billy inhaled and released a deep breath, choking back his sobs. "We can't leave her there. We'll be putting her in a better place, a holy place. She deserves as much, but I can't dig her up, carry her back here, and rebury her all by myself. You guys have to help me." Billy's eyes flashed from one to the other.

"All right," Danny said, "we'll help."

"Frightenin' " Jimmy whispered.

Three teenage boys dug in the darkness as the wind whistled through the trees. Presently they reached and unearthed the shrouded bundle which had been so unceremoniously buried the night before. They carefully lifted the body up and carried it by lantern light back to the village. Working in silence beneath a Hunter's moon, they re-interred her in the sacred ground of the small churchyard. With a hushed and hasty prayer and the sign of the cross, the three left the new grave and made their way home, accompanied only by the howling of the wind and the hammering of their hearts.

"Well, I never thought I'd see the day," the Watcher muttered, peering at the ground by the old elm tree. "Get up!" he said, "Get up, you!"

Freshly churned earth stirred and the girl pushed herself to the surface. She turned and sat up, casting aside her white shroud. She blinked a few times, finally looking up at the Watcher. "What do you want?"

"I'm the Watcher," the man replied, "Well, I was the Watcher; now you are. 'Tis your job to bring water to all the others, keep their clothing mended, do their hair and makeup, and gather wood for the November Eve bonfire when they'll all get up to dance."

"Dance?" she asked with furrowed brow.

"Yes; surely ye know about the Dance of the Dead. Happens every year on November Eve. Come on, there's a lot of work to do to get ready. 'Tis your job to make sure everyone looks their finest. Some require more attention than others o'course. Let's go now."

"But I cannot walk. My feet are bound."

"What!" the man shrieked. "I've been doing this job for a hundred and seventeen years! 'Tis high-time I got a rest. You're the latest one to be buried here. You've got to take over the duties! You just have to! 'Tis the rule! Last one buried!"

"I would, but I can't."

"Why?" He stamped upon the ground. "Who tied up your feet?"

"I suppose my parents did, because I committed suicide. They must have been afraid I'd wander about."

"Suicide! You don't belong here! You can't stay here! I'm telling the others!"

"No!"

Ignoring her plea, he turned his back upon her and went to awaken the others.

Trouble brewed among the ancient headstones as the righteous discovered the sinner in their midst. Their indignation arose and they arose with it.

Hundreds of animated corpses wandered through the streets, wielding hammers with which they'd been buried. The hammers, meant to be used to announce their arrival in Purgatory, were instead pounding on cottage doors. Billy watched in horror as an unfortunate resident opened his door, only to come under attack by zombies who beat him senseless. One corpse climbed to the top of the belfry and used his hammer to bang away on the church bell. Billy peered into the darkness outside, searching in vain for Natalie.

The ghastly white face of a man long dead popped up on the other side of the window.

Billy shrieked and ducked.

His brothers burst into the room. "We did this! We did this! We woke them up!"

"This is your fault," Danny said, "You got us into this. You have to do something."

"Woe to us," wailed Jimmy, "if the villagers find out we caused these corpses to rise up from their graves!"

The door behind which Billy huddled shook and rattled as someone or something tried repeatedly to get at him.

In the morning, all was quiet and Billy raised his head, slowly, cautiously, to peek out the window. He saw no one. He darted through the deserted streets in the crisp morning air to the parish priest to whom he tearfully confessed what he and his brothers had done.

"And then . . . last night . . . the zombies . . . t'was our fault, Father. They attacked the village because of what we did."

Father Michael put his arm around Billy's shoulder. "Calm down, boy. Breathe. Your imagination runs wild. There are no zombies. The dead do not walk the earth and certainly none attacked the village last night. Old superstitions, fired by your own sense of guilt, have worked their way into your dreams."

"Guilt?"

"Yes, Billy, you know in your heart that what you did was wrong. It's called an illegal burial. But I suspect you performed it with more compassion than the superstitious illiterates at the crossroads."

"Does she have to go back there?" Billy looked up at Father Michael and swallowed hard, fearing the answer.

The priest held up a finger to make a point. "Natalie committed a serious sin and some would say that she's lost God's love. But I don't believe that's necessarily true. Jesus died on the cross to save sinners, Billy, not saints. She can rest where she is, but we must inform her parents, and we must commend her soul to God. Her fate is in His hands, but we can ask for mercy on her behalf."

Billy accompanied Father Michael to the home of Natalie's parents where he stood with his hands folded and his head bowed as the priest told the couple what had been done with their daughter. It may have been the presence of the holy man that kept John Flanagan from becoming violent.

"Will she rest in peace, Father?" John asked after a few moments.

"If it be His will," the priest replied.

The group proceeded solemnly to the cemetery. Father Michael intoned prayers for the salvation of Natalie's soul and sprinkled a bit of earth upon her grave. Billy knelt and prayed harder than he had ever prayed for anything in his life.

John Flanagan knelt beside him.

The priest winked at the Watcher.

GUILTY

Daniel I Weaver

GUNFIRE INTERRUPTED A HYMN at the Crest Peak Missionary Alliance Church and I dove to my knees. Clayton Philips' voice shouting "Where are you, Francis?" thundered up from the back of the church. I'd been so careful this time, double-checked everything. How had he found me hiding in a church of all places?

I scrambled toward the emergency exit beside the piano. The pianist slid off her bench and met my gaze with wide eyes. With the church's dozen other attendees screaming and ducking for cover, I had precious few moments to reach that door.

More gunshots.

Wood splintered off the piano beside me. Strings twanged. I lunged at the door, hit the handle, and rolled into cool autumn darkness as three bullets plunked into the wall. Springing to my feet, I ran.

I reached for my car door and froze. I couldn't take the car. Yeah, I'd just bought it a month ago, but if Clayton had found me already, he probably knew about it. I bolted for the woods.

A stolen glance over my shoulder showed Clayton hobbling out the rear door. How had that preacher suckered me into a church service? Maybe I'd just been alone so long that I wanted to belong somewhere. Or maybe something about his words had softened my edge. Whatever the explanation, it had almost earned me a bullet.

As I wove through wooded blackness, my heart thumped, my body tingled, and my mind raced with jittery possibilities. Clayton hadn't gotten that close in almost a year. Three months I'd been in town without so much as a hint he'd found my trail. I thought I'd finally lost him there in the Pennsylvania mountains.

"You can't hide from me, Francis!" Clayton's voice echoed into the forest.

I plowed through stooped branches and fumbled around trees to distance myself. His bum knee gave me the advantage in a footrace, but would it matter? Even if I hid until the police arrived, he would pop up

again after his release. Worse, he might employ his bounty hunter façade and recreate last year's Colorado debacle—convincing the authorities I was a desperate criminal on the run. If I'd learned anything from
Clayton, I'd learned that a man bent on vengeance knows no bounds.

A root snagged my foot and threw me forward. Pine needles tore
into my hands and a rock smacked my knee. The impact sent fire
through my body and the breath from my lungs.

"Francis! Murderer! You killed my, baby, Francis! You killed my
Gabby. You can't run forever!"

The rustling forest reduced Clayton's voice to an auditory tremor.
Motionless, I listened. Where were the sirens? Surely, someone had
called the police by now. And where were Clayton's footfalls pursuing
me through the crunchy undergrowth? My heaving breath rattled in
my ears. A half-dozen gunshots tore through the night, zipping through
the trees, thunking off trunks and pelting rocks. I sucked in a breath,
pushed off the ground, and launched forward.

Clayton shouted again. "Not this time, Francis! It ends tonight!"

Another gunshot. Then something new: barking—frantic and enraged. Dogs? He'd brought dogs? I don't know if I moved any faster,
but the branches smacked me harder, I stumbled more often, and my
legs quickly rubberized. I couldn't outrun dogs. Not even with a head
start. I needed a place to hide.

Moonlight splayed through thinner overhead foliage. Traces of a
building rose from the darkness ahead. The barking echoed ever closer.
Another root snagged at my shoes, but I slammed into a sticky pine
trunk to keep afoot. Pain stabbed through my hand as I pushed away
and darted toward the growing silhouette. The wetness on my hand
could have been sap, blood, or a mixture of both, but it didn't matter. I
had to find shelter.

Fire spread up from my rubbery legs into my lungs until my breath
came in gasps and wheezes, but nearing the forest's edge, I pushed
harder. Moonlight slid down the silhouette's exterior—a dilapidated
three-story house of hanging boards, missing shingles, and sagging
rooflines buried beneath an ivy mountain. Decrepit or not, if it had a
door, it could keep the dogs at bay and buy me time to catch my breath
and think. I staggered to the top of a gentle knoll, then stopped.

Brazier House.

I'd been in Crest Peak less than two months and heard from at least
three dozen people, *Stay away from Brazier House. Bad things happen there.
Weird things.*

Snapping me from my daze, the barking crept closer. I glanced left,
right, strained to see over the house's roof. Nothing. Forest surrounded
everything beyond the brick wall and rusting gate. Craterous potholes
and fallen debris littered the fractured road stretching past the gate. I'd

never gotten close to Brazier House (barriers blocked the road on both ends), but the townsfolk's fear had curbed my curiosity.

A diesel engine's roar wafted over the barking. I glanced over my shoulder to where the road snaked between the trees. Headlights. Gunfire. Bullets on metal. Crazy Clayton must have shot through the locks to access the road. The barking rumbled dangerously close. I sucked up a breath and tore down the knoll toward the rusted gate.

Better off dead than trapped inside Brazier House, one particularly wiry old man had warned me at the local bar. I'd seen dead. Up close and personal. In Gabrielle's eyes. I'd been running from it ever since. No reason to stop now.

Reaching the gate, I clamped hold and rattled it. A massive lock bound the rusted chains linking the halves together. The barking rolled over the knoll and echoed off the gates. The racing engine barreled closer. Working the gate, I pushed one half and pulled the other. Was there enough gap to squeeze through? Only one way to find out.

My aching arms pried. I squeezed my head through. Chipping rust showered onto my face. I worked an arm and then a shoulder into place. Massive shadows dancing against Brazier House's moonlit exterior drew my attention.

The dogs.

The gate tore my sweater and bit my hands as I pushed and squirmed. Two Rottweilers baying bloodlust spilled over the knoll, rocketed toward me. Moonlight glinted off their bouncing eyes and bared fangs.

I pushed harder. Most of my torso worked through. A leg.

Headlights lit the road where it bent behind the knoll. I jerked my butt and second leg through. The dogs lunged. Their maws pierced the gate's gap, snapped at my legs. The headlight beams swerved and swallowed the enraged canines.

I raced to the porch, toward the door. It had to be open; it just had to be.

Brakes screeched and tires ground into loose pavement beyond the gate. "Francis!"

Gunfire exploded behind me. Bullets shattered wood and ivy around me. I grabbed the door and screamed. Pain cut through my hand, burning it as I turned the dampening handle and ducked inside. I slammed the door shut, fumbled for a lock, found it, turned it. Bullets pelted the door. I dove aside into darkness, scrambled across a dusty floor to a wall, and slipped through a doorway. Thick musty air flooded my nose, gagged my senses. The fire tearing through my palm intensified with each passing second. I slumped against a wall, wrapped my hand in my sweater, and squeezed it with my other hand.

Given the dampness, I must have cut it. Bad. But on what? The doorknob? The tree?

I sat huffing, cringing, squeezing my hand, and working to quell the inferno consuming my lungs. Silence bludgeoned me like a cudgel.

No barking.

No gunshots.

What was Clayton doing now? Waiting for me to peek out the door? Working his way around to the back? Just sitting there with his sights locked on the front door?

As my eyes adjusted to the darkness, unusual forms and lines of walls materialized from the abyss. My gaze followed a light sliver dancing off a wall to a window sandwiched between vines and dust. I slid up the wall and started toward the window, shifting my feet a few inches at a time and feeling around with my free hand to avoid the shadowy shapes. My heart thumped harder with each step.

A floorboard groaned somewhere overhead.

My erratic heartbeat skipped a few beats. I fixed my gaze on the ceiling . . . or the space in the darkness where the ceiling probably hung. That couldn't have been Clayton. He couldn't have found a way inside already.

I inched my head toward the window. A soupy mess of rippling shadow existed beyond the grimy pane. I rubbed a circle clean revealing a semblance of thick ivy interspersed with shifting glimpses of the landscape beyond. Clayton's headlights filled the gates. His driver-side door hung open. But where was he? Where were the dogs?

A gunshot. The window imploded, spewing glass shards. I spun away, squinting and shielding my face with my hand.

I slammed my fist off the wall. "For God's sake, Clayton, I didn't kill her!"

Silence. Why weren't the dogs barking?

"Do you hear me, Clayton?" I stood trembling, glaring at that window. Mist frosted my eyes. He wouldn't listen, but I had to try. "I've told you a thousand times, she was dead when I found her! I didn't kill her. I—" I choked. I always choked when I thought about Gabrielle. "I loved her, Clayton! I loved her!"

Tears rolled down my cheeks and blurred the already distorted scene. I closed my eyes, slumped against the wall, and scraped my sleeve against my face as I slid to the floor.

"Do you hear me, Clayton? You psychopath! I loved her more than life itself!"

More than life itself. I sagged. The house sagged with me—floorboards groaning and dipping with my emotional collapse.

My watery eyes flung open. The house snapped back to normal. I bounced as the floor straightened. I couldn't have imagined that.

Feminine laughter, distant and oddly hollow, trickled through the ensuing silence. No barking dogs. No revving engine. No gunshots. Where was Clayton?

Something dripped down my forehead onto my nose. I jerked, scrambled away from the window, and swatted at my head. Swatted wetness. I stopped and touched the damp hair matted to my forehead. Drawing the dampness to my nose, I sniffed. Curiosity moved my finger to my tongue. Just a touch. Salty. Sweat.

Just sweat.

Frankie, a woman's voice called.

My heart stopped. That voice—gentle, playful. Gabrielle.

Her laughter resounded again—louder, but still oddly hollow and distorted. Impossible, but unmistakable. Problem was, dead girls don't laugh.

"God help me." The words slipped out.

A tremble stole up my spine as arctic air gushed through the fractured windowpane. I hugged myself against the chill. My breath streamed away in misty puffs. My thin sweater wouldn't protect me long in that chill, and sitting around remembering my dead fiancé certainly wouldn't help. I had to move.

KNOCK.

Wood on wood, and close-by. Clayton must've found a way inside.

KNOCK.

I scrambled to my feet. Had it come from the next room? I glanced at the window. Even if I broke the remaining glass, it might've taken an hour to rip through the ivy. I edged right, slipping my throbbing hand free to feel along the wall. I reached the corner with a THUMP.

A breath rattled beside my ear.

I jumped and punched the air. Gabrielle's laughter pricked my ears. Clayton must've found some new tricks. What kind of sadistic nut would use his dead daughter's voice for revenge? Worse, what else did he have planned?

I ran at a dead-sprint toward the doorway's outline. My shin banged something hard and I tumbled over a chair. Floorboards groaned overhead. I scrambled back to my feet, pain splinting up my leg.

Light flooded the room.

I froze. Instead of warm incandescence or a pristine lunar glow, odd yellowish light stretched through the shambled room. My gaze snapped toward the doorway. I couldn't hide from Clayton in that light. I had to find a weapon—anything to defend myself.

Dust streamed atop sagging cobwebs throughout the room and coated the sparse furniture—tattered green couch, cushioned chair, lopsided coffee table, and fringed, yellowed shade crowing the solitary lamp-stand. Only my footprints showed in the dust carpet. If anyone else had visited that house recently, surely some sign would have shown. I glanced toward the corner where I'd heard the breath. No speaker. No signs that anyone else had been inside that room. So how had Clayton done it?

I inched to the doorway and strained to see into the space beyond. Nothing moved in the visible sliver. I moved closer, strained my neck further. The entryway slid slowly into view. My gaze gravitated to the irregular dark line on the far wall—like paint or a stain. With my heavy breathing and my heart thumping like thunderclaps, Clayton had to know where I'd hidden. But if he was upstairs, maybe I could get out. Maybe I could make a run for the truck. I crept closer to the doorway until the stain grew into a letter.

G.

The letter's irregular curve more resembled smearing than art . . . like someone had slopped it onto the wall in a hurry...or in desperation. That color . . . so dark . . . like blood. Sweat drizzled off my brow and twitched my cheek. I jerked my head away, breaking the letter's trance. Trembling worked through my arms. My breathing quickened with the shiver. Was there more?

I closed my eyes and forced slower breaths. I had to get a grip. I'd been running for three years now. A different identity every few months, different lie for every town, different character for every new community, different escape plan for every trap. My escape plan for Crest Peak hadn't anticipated discovery at church.

I'd grown so tired of running though. Maybe I'd let myself get sloppy. Or maybe I'd bought into the preacher's lines about redemption and safety under some wing and all.

I tugged at my collar as sweat streamed off my brow. A shiver danced up my arm. Hot one second, shivering the next. If I got out of that house alive, I'd be lucky to escape without pneumonia. Shaking off the chill, I leaned to the doorway again. The G slid into sight. Still no sound. I leaned more until the rest came into view.

GUILTY!

The sight stole my breath. My hand wobbled forward and clamped onto the doorframe for support. Gabrielle's lifeless body sliced through my mind. I staggered into the wall and squeezed my eyes as if the pressure could strangle the vision. Blood everywhere. GUILTY smeared across the mirror and walls . . . trailing down to her bloody wrist on the floor.

My stomach turned and jumped up my throat. My knees weakened, buckled. The corpse in my head opened her eyes. I opened mine and hurled. The light flickered. GUILTY! flashed between white and black as the house flickered between yellowish light and darkness. I heaved again, but nothing came up.

Out. I had to get out of there.

I jerked to my feet and lunged into the hall. The light steadied and lit the space, lit the massive black stains on the floor. The stench hit me—decay. I rammed into the door and jerked at the handle.

Pain! Wrong hand. I tried the other.

The handle rattled. The door grumbled as I jerked and shook the handle. It didn't budge.

A floorboard overhead squealed. I spun around and stared at the ceiling. Maybe it wasn't Clayton. Maybe he'd expected I would end up here. Maybe he'd set this up, planned it all with the dogs and the gun to lure me here. Trap me here.

I turned and squinted through a bullet hole. Headlights still filled the gateway. But no sign of Clayton, and no sign of the dogs. I retried the handle. I tried it with both hands. Why wouldn't it turn?

Frankie. Gabrielle's voice.

I screamed, jumped, and rounded on the hall in one continuous motion. Sweat spiraled off my forehead, smashing craters in the dust.

The dust.

Just like the other room, only my footprints had disturbed the dust. The ceiling groaned again, then again, and again. Steps. Heading away from me. Toward the stairway. I had to hide. Quickly.

The entryway only showed five exits—the entrance, stairway, a doorway on the stairway wall, and a doorway on each flanking wall. The front door wouldn't budge, I'd already tried the room to my left, and someone would appear at the top of the stairs any second. The room to my right being closest, I darted toward it.

My footfalls clapped off the floor. The creaking steps overhead quickened. I raced through the doorway, spotted bloody words scrawled across white walls, tried to stop, slipped, and crashed to the ground. I hit wetness and inertia propelled me into a full-length mirror.

The mirror—upright on silver legs—toppled onto me, splintering off my body and the tile. I hurled the frame aside and sat up. A stretch of stagnant black water covered most of the floor. The malodor stung my nose and turned my stomach. I worked to avoid the glass shards scattered around and cascading off me as I stood.

Surely, Clayton had heard the noise. I glanced over my shoulder to check the stairs.

I froze.

What happened to the doorway? My gaze snapped in every direction. I'd been in a different room just moments ago. I'd come through a doorway. Entranced, I stared at the wall. Where was the doorway? There *had* been a doorway!

I rushed to the wall, pushed and stroked and pounded the ceramic tiles. Moldy plaster cascaded from the seams. A ceramic chip caught my wound. Pain! I screamed, clamped my mouth shut, clutched my throbbing hand with the other, squeezed my eyes shut. The world spinning, anguish ripped up my arm.

In the yellowish haze, I opened my teary eyes and finally examined my wounded hand—black with dried blood. Fresh blood seeped from a dozen abrasions. When had I done that? Dirt clung to sticky patches around the palm's edges. A thick pine needle protruded from my palm. I loosed my tourniquet grip and the blood oozed faster.

I grabbed the pine needle and an explosion of rapid, stabbing pain danced around it as it shook between my trembling fingers. A guttural groan swelling up my throat, I pulled the needle free. Black ooze trailed from the puncture. I flicked the needle aside and slumped against the cool tile wall.

My vision blurred so that two, no four, no six hands floated back and forth where only one should have been. I squeezed my eyes shut and scoured my sweaty forehead with my sleeve.

The T-shirt under my sweater clung to my skin. My neck itched where the sweater's collar chafed. When had it gotten so hot? A popping noise drew my gaze to the floor. To the ripple in the center of the putrid water. Steam wafted off the water.

Another pop.

More ripples a few inches from the last disturbance.

I tugged at my collar and cringed. It itched. So hot. I jerked and flailed to get it off, sweat stinging my eyes. My stench reached through my nostrils and choked me. I gagged and dry-heaved before I could pull the sweater off and hurl it aside. I gasped and sucked at the air.

"What's happening to me?" The words bounced around the room. Who would hear? With no door, who could find me? Worse, how would I get out?

I looked around the room for some clue to explain my situation. The yellowish light grew off the water, rising off the steam and hanging beneath the darkness blanketing the ceiling. The single bulb on twisted wire hanging from the shadows gave no hint of functionality.

The water bubbled, popped, and rippled in a half-dozen spots.

Nothing decorated the walls. Occasional tiles had fallen away leaving mildewed craters behind. Besides the shattered mirror, a small stand—four rusted legs stretching from the water up to a silver top—served as the room's only decoration. A metal basin sat on the stand. Curiosity drew me toward the basin.

The water gurgled again, faster and with more bubbles.

I moved toward the basin, craning my neck to see over its edge, but unwilling to touch the water. With the pain in my arm diminishing, the room's stench came into focus and I had to block the stink with my arm to lean further. The basin and the stand shimmied. The water moiled faster. The room tilted left. No, right.

I shook my head and opened my eyes wide to stop the chaos. The water offered up a final pop and the room settled.

I moved around the water's edge while craning for the best view. Nothing but glimpses no matter where I tried. Grimacing, I fixed my gaze on the water. I didn't want to get any wetter, so at the edge closest to the stand, I tried leaning one last time.

A hint of color teased me from the basin, but nothing discernable in that haze.

I sucked up a breath, held it, then slid a foot forward. Cold gushed up my back, wrapping around my arms and shrinking my pores. I took another step, hugged myself, and peered over the basin's edge.

Eyeballs. A basin-full suspended in dark liquid. Every one of them fixed directly at me. My stomach fluttered with nausea and I looked away. There, etched on the stand, silvery letters glinted in the yellow haze. I stepped closer and pushed the basin aside.

If you were blind, you would not be guilty of sin; but now that you claim you can see, your guilt remains.

What was that supposed to mean?

Gabrielle's voice. *You're guilty, you know?*

I looked up at the empty room.

Anger boiled inside me. I couldn't handle this sort of torture. Clayton had gone too far. "Where are you, Clayton?"

I kicked the table aside. It crashed off the floor and the basin toppled, spraying eyeballs and black grime. The water bubbled, churned, boiled.

Steam hissed and snapped from bursting bubbles. The churning waves sloshed and spun into a tiny whirlpool at the center of the gurgling stew. The edges receded. A guttural suction noise swelled from the draining cyclone. Gouges in the floor appeared in the receding mire's wake. The gouges stretched into letters. *FORGIVE ME.*

The suction sound fizzled to silence. Gabrielle's voice drifted up the drain. *Forgiveness is an illusion, Frankie.*

"G-Gabrielle?" I dove at the drain.

How long had it been since I'd seen her? It felt like so long.

A hushed male voice behind me said, "Don't let it draw you in, Francis."

I jerked and turned around. Tucked in the corner at the yellow haze's dark recesses, a disfigured boy sat huddled with his arms pulling his knees tight against his chest. His matted fingers were like webbed flippers. His pale skin shone white against the tarnished T-shirt stretched over his knees, much like the tousled, stark-white hair cropped above his uneven ears. Skin hung over his left eye, but his eyes . . . Solid golden spheres. Not yellow like the sun, but a haunting, dark gold.

Even without pupils or irises, his golden glare held me.

"Wh . . . who are you?" I pushed myself away.

The ceiling squealed and groaned. The boy glanced toward the noise.

The drain called to me again. *Frankie. It's so cold, Frankie.*

A shiver shook my body and I hugged myself. "G-Gabby? Where are you Gabby?"

I started back to the drain, but the world teetered left. I flopped onto the ground, but kept my gaze locked on the boy, afraid that he might vanish.

Help me, Frankie. Please. I don't want to be alone anymore. Gabrielle's voice quivered with something like fear. I had to find her, help her.

Was that sadness on the boy's face? "She's lost, Francis. But there's still hope for you."

Hope? The boy shimmered. My head swam. I'd heard something about hope recently, hadn't I? From a tall man with a kind smile…at a church. No, that couldn't be right. Gabrielle had left church and taken me with her. She'd come home Sunday after Sunday weeping from the self-righteous looks all those pretentious women gave her. So she liked black clothes and kept to herself . . . She'd never hurt anyone.

"She isn't real, Francis." The boy's voice snapped my daze.

It *had* been a preacher. What had he said? I'd written it down, memorized it. Something about hoping and waiting for salvation or something. What was it, Lametesions?

A soft smile replaced the boy's sadness. "Lamentations 3:26, Francis. It is good that a man should both hope and quietly wait for the salvation of the Lord."

My pulse quickened. Was he in my head? That made sense. Whatever was happening had to be in my head. I chuckled.

Frankie. Gabrielle's voice, weeping.

I tugged at the drain and it pulled away, leaving a hole just bigger than my arm. I had to see her, had to . . .

A wet, black explosion blasted my face. I flopped away, gasping and flailing to barricade the stagnant water. The unrelenting blast put me on my back. It gushed from the hole, spreading through the room and masking the floor. I scampered away, toward the wall, toward—

A door! The wall where the boy had been. Had been. Where was he? My gaze whipped around, but the geyser intensified and veiled my vision. Dampness spread up my stomach, drew my eyes down. Water covered my body's lower half . . . And continued rising.

I pushed to my feet and sloshed toward the doo—

Something clamped around my left ankle and pulled.

The black pool engulfing me, I pushed off the floor to clear the waterline. I kicked and tugged to free my leg. Clawed at the floor to escape the unseen shackles. Whatever held me, jerked me further from the door. The water swallowed me again. I couldn't find a grip, couldn't grasp anything but water.

I pushed against the floor and gasped for air. Laughter hit me— playful and amused. I looked at my legs, at the grey hand clamped around my ankle. The arm trailed into the water toward fiery hair cropping the gray face half-visible above the surface. The black eyes narrowed and the head plunged under. I kicked at the gray hand, and it loosed. I jerked my leg free, and sped backward.

I crashed into the door and groped for the handle. I froze.

Not the same door.

I looked left, right, left again. No other doors. It had to be the one, but instead of an old, chipped-paint barrier, an elegant door with a stained glass window and golden handle stood before me. Black water splashed off the wall into my face. Gabrielle's laughter redoubled. Hands clamped onto my legs and stretched me toward the center again.

Adding the second hand, I clung to the door's handle. The hands pulled harder. I screamed against the pain. Against the certainty that I couldn't hold on. Against certainty that whatever held me wouldn't let me up again if I went under. The water continued rising, slopping off the wall into my face.

I stretched a thumb toward the release. A hissing howl replaced Gabrielle's laughter. The hands dug into my ankles. My thumb hit the release. Screaming louder, I poured everything into pushing that lever.

CLICK.

The hiss became a roar. The hands dug so deep, I wailed. The door inched open. Pulling me. Pulling me with it. Throwing me into . . .

Light.

I flopped to the floor.

Music hit me—angelic voices resounding reverent chants in some foreign language.

The door slammed shut.

Lights danced across my teary vision. The world teetered through vertigo. I fell back against a wall. I'd escaped. The bright light, the heavenly music . . . I was safe.

Safe. I chuckled and wept.

The music calmed my pulse. I rubbed my eyes dry. The dancing lights focused into flickering candles and a gothic stained glass wall depicting a crucified Christ surrounded by weeping onlookers, Roman centurions, and monstrous figures with blood-red eyes reaching down from orange clouds. A warm and regal scent teased my nostrils as my gaze lingered on the candles. Their flames all flickered to the side as if caught in wind.

I stood and let the room saturate my senses—the sights, sounds, smells, and invisible electricity in the air. So pristine. So immaculate. So . . . majestic. I didn't belong there. I hadn't belonged in a church in a long time, and this place belonged in one of the world's oldest cathedrals. I glanced around, half expecting the pope or a cardinal or something to emerge from the shadows.

Misplaced or not, something had drawn me here. Just like something had drawn me to . . . that church . . . earlier. I had been at a church earlier, hadn't I? My head swam through a haze. There had been a man . . . a preacher . . . talking about forgiveness . . . about grace. Whatever he'd said, he hadn't intended it for me. I just couldn't have certain things. Could I?

My gaze drifted to the crucifixion. To the bleeding feet. Hadn't the preacher shared a story about faith? Something about a woman touching Jesus' feet and being healed. Could it be so simple? What if I touched His feet? I stepped forward.

My footstep shook the room.

Trembling, I stopped and looked around. The candlelight danced and flickered. The window rattled. I stretched my wounded hand toward the wall. Given the room's dimensions, I could reach it . . . just a few more steps. I glanced around me, checked the shadows, listened.

Alone.

No one would hear.

I took another step. Another thunderclap shook the room.

Did the wall move? How had I distanced myself rather than moved closer? Glancing over my shoulder, I checked the door. Farther away than before.

I took another step. The room shook.

The window not only withdrew, it slid upward. Another step. The crucifixion rushed higher and further from my grasp.

No! I crashed to my knees, my lips trembling with the words I couldn't speak. I'd been a fool to think I could touch His foot, foolish to think I could ever find salvation.

A man's enraged voice blasted out of a dark corner. "You don't belong here!" The music died. The illusion of safety vanished with it.

A pale man wearing long black robes and a white collar hovered in the corner between the crucifixion wall and the tiered candles. A priest? He stalked toward me. His bony pointer-finger positioned at my head and his stern look darkening into a scowl, he bent toward me. "Heathen! You aren't worthy to step foot in this room!"

The priest rushed me and clamped his bony hand around my arm. The pain rising from my hand gathered beneath his grip. He jerked me off my feet and hurled me to the door where he grabbed me again. So strong. So fast. How?

He tore the door open and pulled me toward it.

A wall of black, putrid water waited. Specks suspended in the liq-uid sped toward its edge. Eyes. They all stared at me, protruding slight-ly from the liquid. Behind them, a female figure dangled—smiling, her black eyes locked on mine.

"From the darkness you came," the priest shouted, "to darkness you shall return!"

"No!" I squirmed in the priest's grip. I pushed against his side and shifted my feet to keep away from the door.

The priest's grip tightened. "Murderer! There is blood on your hands. Blood!"

"I didn't kill her!"

A voice drifted down from the darkness. "Don't listen to him, Fran-cis."

My gaze shot overhead to find the young male voice. Could it be the same boy? The priest rounded and glared at the shadows above the stained glass window. A silhouette shifted in the shadows. Dull light grew from the silhouette's golden eyes.

"Demon!" The priest released me, rushed to his corner, and dragged a black cross into view. "Foul spirit! You are not welcome here!"

The silhouette's eyes narrowed. Light exploded from his head, ebb-ing from his brilliant white hair and illuminating the shadows. The boy sat upside down on the ceiling. The priest retreated, hefting his crucifix before him as he rushed toward his corner and . . . vanished. The door slammed shut and disappeared leaving only a wall of wooden slats and crumbly plaster.

"You can't trust your eyes anymore, Francis."

I looked up at the boy and trembled. A chill shook me. Sweat seeped from my forehead and clung to my shirt. The room swayed as if gentle waves had caught the house in their tug-of-war. I palmed the floor for support and closed my eyes. I had to stop the vertigo, had to find my bearings.

"Francis."

I opened my eyes. "Who are you? What do you want with me?"

"I didn't bring you here, Francis. You brought me."

Riddles. How were riddles supposed to help me? My gaze fell to the stained glass window. To the weeping men and women. Such sad-ness. Gabrielle's corpse lying in a bloody pool on her bathroom floor flashed through my mind. I knew sadness. I knew remorse.

"Oh, Francis." Sadness hung to the boy's words.

I stared at those weeping men and women. The men became Clay-ton, wailing at the news of his daughter's death. The women became his wife, emotionally imploding and dying inside. Tear by tear, they all became me. Hollow. Alone. Grieving in guilt.

The boy's solemn voice tickled my ears. "Then shall ye remember your own evil ways, and your doings that were not good, and shall loathe yourselves in your own sight for your iniquities and for your abominations."

I saw myself on that wall: my pain and guilt streaming from open wounds, Clayton reaching down with black claws to exact his revenge. I'd never been good enough for him. He'd always looked down at me. Down his pompous nose. The second the detective had spoken the word suicide, Clayton lunged at me shouting "murderer." He'd been hunting me ever since.

Murderer. The word haunted my memories. Woke me from the nightmares ending with Clayton's hands around my neck. I'd killed her.

Tears streamed from my eyes as it hit me.

She'd always come to me for support, depended on me for strength. But I hadn't been there when she needed me most. I'd worked late. All for a chance to spend a few more moments at the office. To spend just a few more moments in a world outside constant sorrow, self-doubt, depression. A few more moments outside a world I'd found harder and harder to endure with each passing day: Gabrielle's world.

"It's just a lie, Francis."

"No!" I glared up at the boy through my tears. Anger warmed the shiver wracking my body in the seconds when I wasn't aflame. "I shouldn't be here." My gaze darted to Christ on the wall. The priest had been right. I'd violated this place with my sin. Was that darkness emanating from me, snubbing the light? "I'm not worthy to be here . . . To be—"

"None are worthy of His love, Francis. But this isn't His house. He isn't the one—"

"Stop it!" I turned back to the wall and pounded my hands off the ancient boards. Blood spattered off my hands with each hammering blow.

"The master of this house is lying to you, Francis. He has distorted your perception. Listen to your heart, not his lies."

The agony throbbing through my hands and arms threatened to overpower me. I had to stop. I slumped forward against the wall and screamed over my shoulder at the boyish monstrosity. "I killed her! If I'd been there . . . If I'd been stronger . . ."

He lifted a webbed flipper-hand to his half-hidden eye and dabbed as if crying. "Gabrielle chose her—"

"Don't you say her name!" I rounded. Spittle flew from my words and sweat from my hair. "Don't you dare say her name! Just leave me alone!"

Was that a tear rolling down his cheek?

His eyes closed. With a trembling voice, he said, "Very well, Francis. But I will leave you with this. The master of this house turns truth upon its head. You shall see this place for what it really is."

The boy's light faded until only his silhouette remained. My stomach leaped into my throat as the darkness rushed down at me. My feet left the floor and I shot skyward, like falling headfirst. I crashed into the ceiling and dust exploded around me. My breath . . . Gone . . . Pain . . . All pain . . . Lights dancing . . . Couldn't think . . . Couldn't breathe . . . needed to breathe . . .

I sucked in air, but dust choked me. I rolled, coughed, sputtered, wheezed, and wept. My head swayed and ached. Lights exploded across my eyes with each fit's pain.

Eventually, the dust and gasping settled. I dried my eyes and focused on the stained glass wall. Upside down. Everything had changed, had flipped upside down. What had I done? Why had I chased the boy away?

I stood and stared at the kaleidoscope wall. Clawed hands reached up out of fiery plumes toward the upended Christ as if to pull him into Hell. Lies. The room was just a lie. There could be no salvation there. Inverted crucifixes, demons reaching out of Hell for Jesus . . . how had I considered that room immaculate? It was evil.

Dread drifted down from the ceiling—the ceiling that had been a floor moments ago. The flames crawling up the candles overhead erupted into an inferno. The fire rolled along the ceiling, consuming it. The music started up again, screeched to a halt, then resumed in a screaming chorus of wailing, distorted chaos.

I had to get out of that room.

Thunder clapped underfoot and the floor to my left exploded. A geyser of dusty wood shards sprayed from the hole. Another thunderclap—no, gunshot! More wood splintered around a second hole.

"End of the line, Francis," came Clayton's voice from the holes.

The fire hissed and crawled down the walls. Scaly, clawed hands extended from the blaze. Another gunshot destroyed floorboards beside me. Orange light beamed up through the hole.

The floor groaned. Squealed. Gave out.

Into a basement, dust and debris fell with me. Something cushiony softened my fall, but the impact still slammed the air from my lungs and sent my woozy head into numbness. I rolled off the cushion—a browned mattress—onto a pile of fractured furniture. Wood clamored and shifted under my weight, but I couldn't stop. I need to breathe. Had to keep moving. Had to—

Clayton's voice thundered over my crawling. "Leave me alone!"

BOOM.

I flailed backward onto my side. Clayton sat huddled in a corner at the orange light's edge with his shotgun aimed at the ceiling where his gaze roamed. The color had drained from his face. His unkempt gray hair clung to his forehead in damp patches. Sweat trails crisscrossed his brow and cheeks. His bloodshot eyes hung sunken behind swollen lids. Cuts and dirt covered his body, with a bloody rag encasing his left hand.

Clayton twitched, snapped his head to the left, swung the shotgun toward the wall beside him, and—

BOOM.

The wall exploded into a spray of dust, plaster, and wood.

Dust, plaster, and wood. A quick survey for an exit showed little else. Sparse cobweb-strewn furniture lay in shambles throughout the dim space. The basement's ceiling beams stretched to walls so thin and weathered that boards showed through the plaster. No door.

"Leave me alone!" Clayton loosed another round at the wall to his right. He twitched again, then squeezed his eyes shut and grabbed his head. A pained, almost maniacal scream rolled off his tongue. "Please. Stop!"

He continued twitching, a pained squeal accompanying each jerk. I'd never seen him like that . . . broken. He looked like I felt. However, for all his twitching and his shifting gaze, he showed no signs of having spotted me.

Perhaps if I moved very slowly . . . very quietly . . .

A splintered table leg shot out from under my hand. It bounced and banged across the floor until it hit the wall.

BOOM.

The wall where it hit exploded. My gaze jerked toward Clayton.

His wild eyes locked onto mine. "They're eating you too, aren't they, Francis?" He shifted the shotgun toward me.

I cowered behind my arms, ducking and shifting to avoid his aim. Eating me? What did he mean? Twitching again, Clayton smacked at his shoulder as if swatting a fly. The shotgun's aim drifted away.

I eased into a sitting position. "What, Clayton? What's supposed to be eating me?"

His eyes narrowed, his gaze taking on a dangerous, almost suspicious quality. His face seemed to melt, then snap back to normal. The room swayed and I had to brace myself for support. How long had I been running? How long had I been stuck inside this house? Hours? Days? Weeks?

"No, of course not." Clayton lifted the shotgun to his shoulder. "They aren't eating you. You got off scot-free. You didn't even cry at her funeral. A heart of stone." He squinted down the barrel with me in his sights. "Not me, Francis. They've . . . been gnawing at me since she died. They followed me here. Followed me here to put an end to it. No . . . not followed me. Led me."

I shivered against the chill drifting across the floor. "I don't understand, Clayton. You're not making any sense." I pushed myself left, right, ducked, dove aside . . . anything to evade his aim. I'd been running too long to let it end there.

"The house." Clayton glanced toward the wall to my left. "It's been waiting for me, drawing me here."

Hesitant to look away, I shot my gaze toward the wall and back. The flash of wall registered through the muck clouding my focus. I looked again. GUILTY showed dark brown in giant letters on the crumbly, plaster wall. Just like the entryway. Just like Gabrielle's bathroom. I looked back at Clayton. A devilish smile crossed his face. He looked the other direction, almost excited. I followed his gaze. PUNISHMENT hovered above a dark stain from which a rusty butcher's knife protruded. The rotted remains of a decaying severed hand hung from the knife.

My stomach turned. "I know you don't want to believe it, Clayton, but I didn't kill her. I swear, I didn't—"

"Judgment time, Francis." His voice trembled. "And we're all guilty. We killed her, Francis. We sinned. And the wages of sin . . . "

CLICK.

A hint of annoyance tightened Clayton's grimace. His sneer bent into a scowl as he looked down at the barrel.

CLICK.

I rolled aside, tumbling through broken boards. I had to find an exit before he reloaded. Pushing to my feet, I ran. Rubble underfoot sent me sprawling hard into a wall, rebounding with dancing lights marring my vision of the spinning world. I dropped to my knees and leaned into the wall.

Everything moved in swirls of sound and color. I had to slow the spinning . . . Find my feet . . . Find an exit.

An unexpected sound cut through the chaos. Was that . . . crying? Clayton crying?

I tried to stand, but vertigo sent me sideways and onto my backside against the wall. "Clayton?"

His head had slumped forward onto the shotgun stretched across his knees. His body shook with weeping. The twitching continued at random intervals.

"I . . . I killed her, Francis. And these blasted rats have been hounding me ever since. Gnawing at me." He screamed, then stood, staggered, took the shotgun by the barrel, and smashed it off the wall. "Leave me alone!" He repeated it like a mantra.

"Leave me alone!" BASH.

"Leave me alone!" BASH.

With each swing, he wavered more and shouted louder. Five or six swings into his tirade, he missed and spun to a heap in his corner.

My heartbeat quickened. He'd lost his mind. The man with the gun had fallen over the edge. Sure, I'd almost drowned in a room with trick doors, and I'd been walking on the ceiling in some kind of satanic sanctuary, and a disappearing circus-freak of a boy kept reappearing to play with my head; but at least I hadn't imagined a horde of rats devouring me.

Clayton's head flashed backward, his hands flying up to tear at his hair. His eyes, brimming with tears, locked onto mine. The shotgun slid to the floor.

"All . . . all of this time . . . " Clayton's voice quivered with remorse. "I tried to blame you . . . her doctor . . . anyone . . . But I've been running from the truth. Hiding it where only those rats could smell it. They came to feed. They've been gnawing at me so much that there's hardly anything left. Just bones . . . The truth is . . . I killed her."

I opened my mouth to speak, but the words caught in my throat. Clayton killed Gabrielle? Anger came and passed in a flash. No, I couldn't be angry with him. He'd become delusional. He'd been home with his wife and a neighbor. He hadn't killed Gabrielle.

My heart fluttered. Ached. My eyes brimmed with tears. Clayton hadn't killed her. I had.

"You . . ." My throat constricted. "You didn't kill her, Clayton. I—"

His weeping broke into a wail. "Yes I did! Oh God, I did. My little baby. My little Gabby. My little . . . " He flinched and slapped at his chest. He cringed in pain and screamed as he swatted. "Leave me alone!"

Clayton's hand darted to the shotgun. A wild look seized his eyes. He jerked the shotgun off the ground, positioned it across his legs, and drew shells from a jacket pocket. The shells clanked on their way into the gun.

"Get out of here, Francis." He fumbled with a shell. It flopped to the floor and rolled away.

A disturbing chuckle grew from Clayton's corner—a chuckle as unsettling as the aberrant look in his eyes. His head snapped up. "Have you seen the boy yet? That little beast almost tricked me, Francis. He tried, oh he tried." Clayton's chuckle warbled between chuckling and weeping. "But the house . . . the house knows, Francis. It warned me to stay away from him. The house sensed my guilt. And now . . . " He rammed another shell into place. "It's judgment time. Punishment for the guilty."

He shoved a final shell into the weapon and his smile spread wider. For such wide eyes, his stare appeared glazed. Was he looking at me, or something I couldn't see? He chambered a shell. His gaze had narrowed, but remained misted. Could he see me anymore?

"Francis, if you see that boy, run or kill him. He's dangerous." Clayton broke into a primal scream and leapt out of his corner.

He loosed a shotgun blast into the wall at his right.

The wall squealed.

Clayton teetered left, crashing into the wall while chambering another shell. He rebounded, swept the barrel toward the ceiling, and fired again. The recoil sent him to the floor and the gun from his grasp. His hands darted to his head, his neck, his chest, his shoulders, his head. He swatted and jerked, twitching and screaming as if under insect attack.

My gaze drifted to the weapon. Clayton's screams pulled at my conscience, but fear set me in motion. The room had gotten so hazy that crawling to the shotgun felt more like crossing a floating dock than a floor—shifting and wobbling every time I moved. Crawling sent fresh fire racing up from my wounded hand. I had to fight to prevent toppling.

With the hand cradled against my chest, I crawled as fast as the haze allowed on two knees and one hand. The orange light had dimmed and shadows seeped into its glow. What remained orange seemed thicker... like a fog. Ahead, Clayton appeared suspended in orange froth.

The shotgun. I had to reach it before Clayton noticed. I latched onto the hilt. Something grabbed the barrel.

Clayton.

Tears ran from his wide, pleading eyes. He knelt at the barrel's end, twitching and wincing with increasing frequency, with both hands pulling it toward his face. I tugged on the stock.

"Do it, Francis." His voice wept desperation. "Please stop the pain."

No. I tugged harder. "No!" He really *had* lost it.

"Please, Francis." His knuckles whitened and his arms shook. "This guilt is eating me alive."

"Daddy." Gabrielle's voice.

We both looked. A dozen steps to my left, Gabrielle rose out of darkness. Dirt and blood covered her white nightgown. Orange light glinted off her eyes and black tears rolled down her cheeks as she approached.

"Why, Daddy? Why did you let me die?"

I cringed. Not Gabby. At least not my Gabrielle. Her shriveled, gray skin hung gaunt on her bones and her eyes shone black. Not the soft blue I loved.

Clayton's watery gaze locked on her. "Gabby?"

"Daddy. It's time, Daddy." She stopped a few steps away.

Gabrielle opened her mouth wide. Wider. A squeak echoed up her throat. A brown rat with beady red eyes emerged and plopped from her mouth. After scuttling across the floor to Clayton, it latched onto his ankle. Clayton jerked and swatted at it. Another rat launched from Gabrielle's mouth. Then another. Squeaking multiplied throughout the room.

Clayton screamed louder, a dozen rats tearing at his pants now.

"Leave him alone!" I jerked the shotgun toward her. "Whatever you are, just leave him alone!"

The squeaking rose to a clamor and Gabrielle erupted into a charging rat volcano—spewing pieces that took vermin form and consumed Clayton. His screams crescendoed.

"Francis!" His arms flailed toward me, rats swinging with them. "Finish it!"

My finger slid toward the trigger. He'd hunted me since his daughter's funeral. Ruined my life. Tarnished my name. Destroyed everything I loved. How many times had I dreamed of such a moment? No matter how much I'd wanted him gone, I couldn't have imagined this demise. He deserved more.

A voice, gentle and warm, spoke behind me. "Francis."

Jumping, I glanced over my shoulder. The boy's brilliant white hair shone so bright it burned my eyes. I had to look away.

The rats squealed. Clayton wailed, his bloody eyes peering over my shoulder. He lunged for the gun. "I told you to get out of here, boy!" Hatred dripped from Clayton's words.

The boy's voice sang like music. "There isn't much time left, Clayton, but it's not too late. There is forgiveness—"

"Death!" Clayton spat, trying to tear the gun from my grasp. "Punishment for the guilty!"

A rat skittered onto the stock and bit my finger, breaking my grip.

After a moment spent holding the bite and staring wide-eyed as Clayton fumbled to turn the gun on the boy, I lunged. I caught the gun again and shoved it away.

BOOM!

The blast deafened me, but I couldn't let go. Clayton's jaw worked muted curses. With the hatred in his eye redirected at me, flashes of my nightmares consumed his face. Still, I refused to release the weapon, refused to let anyone else die. I'd killed Gabrielle, but I wouldn't let it happen again.

Clayton managed to chamber another shell.

BOOM!

My stomach twisted and complained. My head swam in circles. I grappled to keep that barrel away from the boy. Away from Clayton. Away from me.

Clayton stopped. The rats scattered and scampered to cracks in the walls. Clayton hardly resembled a man anymore. So many wounds. So much blood.

The hatred burning his eyes subsided. A tear streamed down from his left eye. He twitched. "I'm so sorry, Gabby. So sorry."

His furrowed brow relaxed, his scowl softened, and his glazed eyes completely dimmed. His jaw stopped working.

"Clayton?" I touched him. No response.

I glanced over my shoulder at the boy. His head hung toward the floor. A blinding tear of light trickled down his cheek. The house quaked.

One after another, violent waves shook the foundation. The tremors threw me to the floor. Dust and debris cascaded onto me. The infested walls squealed. A breaking sound accompanied the most violent shake, and a rift broke across the floor, separating me from the boy. He never moved. The debris cascaded around him, the floor convulsed and groaned, but the boy stood fast. His misshaped head lifted and his golden eyes swallowed me.

"You can choose to leave, Francis." He extended a bloody hand toward me, a thick twisted spike piercing his palm.

Leave? I checked again. No doors. No windows. No stairway. No way out.

My ear twitched. I strained against the rumbling. What was that buzzing sound? It started faint, in waves. Its whisper-like volume grew into a hum.

Voices.

Hundreds of voices.

Surrounding the room.

My disjointed gaze swept the hazy room. Everywhere. Coming from every direction. Were they waiting for me? Did they know? Could they see the blood on my hands? Could they know I'd killed Gabrielle?

I glanced up at the boy's outstretched, bloodied hand. At the dripping spike. *Kill him or run.* Clayton's words. I hurled the gun aside. No more killing. I'd killed enough. Poor Gabrielle. If only I'd been there. If only—

"Francis. The choice is yours. Don't let this—"

A ceiling beam screamed with breaking. Floorboards, dust, and furniture dropped into the room, into a clump above the rift. Squealing and scuttling swelled from the rift. Grew louder, closer. A black-and-brown-furred geyser gushed from the crack.

Rats.

Gnawing trickled from the walls. Holes appeared in the plaster, and in the holes, eyes. Eyes spread along the walls like mold. Every one of them locked onto me. Not rat eyes, human eyes.

The voices swelled. So many conversations going at once, I couldn't make out the words, but I knew the tone—that excited urgency.

Gossip. Accusations.

I peered over the beam toward the boy. His hand remained outstretched. A burst of plaster pinged off my left cheek. An eye filled the hole.

So many eyes. All watching me. Accusing me.

I lowered my head. My stomach lurched. Partially hidden under rubble, a black-and-white crime scene photograph of Gabrielle's bathroom glared up at me. The murmur cut into my haze again. So much noise. So many people talking. They must have figured out what I'd done. Perhaps the boy could save me. I crawled toward the rubble, started over the fallen ceiling beam, and froze.

Below me, down the rift, Gabrielle's lifeless body sprawled on her bathroom floor. GUILTY glared up at me from the walls and mirror. I looked away. GUILTY glared back at me from the basement wall between accusing eyes. With everything so hazy, how did those letters look so perfect?

"Francis," the boy called. "Don't listen to the lies, Francis. Your guilt, your shame, they're lies. You can choose to leave. You called me and I'm offering you hope. All you have to do is accept it."

I tore my gaze from the wall. The murmuring swelled into auditory chaos. Words cut through the anarchy. *Francis. Gabrielle. Murderer.*

Murder. They knew. Oh God, they knew!

Silence. My eyes opened wide and I checked the scene. Where had all the voices—

A thousand voices blasted me in unison. "Guilty!"

The auditory force drove me to my knees.

"Punishment!"

"Death!"

My eyes drifted to the rift. Gabrielle. I might as well have cut her myself. If I'd been there, she would have lived. If I wouldn't have been selfish, relishing just a few more minutes outside her depressing world. How could I have done that to her? How could I . . .

"I killed her." The words rolled off my tongue. My heart shuddered. Tears rolled down my cheeks. The hazy blur worsened. "I killed her."

I didn't deserve to live. The priest's words cut through me. *There's blood on your hands.* I looked at them. Blood everywhere. Gabrielle's blood. What had I done?

CLACK. SCRAPE. CLACK. SCRAPE. Coming toward me.

"Francis." The boy's voice came as a mere whisper.

I couldn't listen to him. He didn't belong there. The way he'd cried for Clayton. The way he spoke with . . . with love. The way he seemed to care when I couldn't bring myself to care anymore. He didn't belong in that house. But I did. I was guilty. And the house knew best.

The house shuddered and showered debris around me. I didn't struggle. The house would finish it. The house would enforce the punishment. The house would bury my guilt and shame so the world couldn't see.

I slumped sideways into a fetal position. Had Gabrielle hurt this much? Is that why she'd left me? Could the pain have been that bad?

CLACK. SCRAPE. CLACK. SCRAPE.

Francis. The boy's voice . . . inside my head. *The choice is yours, Francis. Forgiveness is a gift. It cannot be earned and no man deserves it. All have fallen short of God's glory.*

The house dumped more clutter on me. My leg cracked under the weight. The pain . . . so much . . . pain.

You must choose, Francis.

A blazing light moved into my haze—the boy, gleaming like the sun itself. His spiked hand hung outstretched toward me.

It's appointed once for a man to die, Francis. Today does not have to be your day.

He stepped over the debris and stood only an arm's reach away.

CLACK. The metal spike in his foot clapped off the floor.

SCRAPE. He slid the foot forward, bent as if walking on heels, dragging the bloody nail.

I shied away and closed my eyes. I couldn't bear the warmth and light radiating from him. I didn't deserve to feel that warmth. I didn't deserve to stand in that light.

CLACK. SCRAPE.

Guilty. The house knew I was guilty. I had committed the mother of all sins.

Francis.

I opened my eyes. The boy's warmth and light covered me. His golden eyes captivated me. Such love.

"Please." My dry tongue hardly forced the word. "I have to die."

Francis, Jesus is crowned with glory and honor because he suffered death. By the grace of God, he suffered death so he might taste death for everyone. He died so you could live.

The house shook in protest. The murmuring crowd shouted its whispers.

Francis.

The orange light vanished. Only shadows dotted with a thousand glinting eyes existed beyond the boy's glow. He stood with a pleading look on his face, his hand still outstretched. Could it be that easy? Could forgiveness really be free?

I reached toward the dripping spike. The house dumped a ceiling beam onto my hand, breaking something and redoubling my pain. What had I been thinking? I didn't deserve forgiveness. The house knew best, and it would see me to my punishment.

The voices discussed my sin in snide whispers. Too late for me. Too much blood covered my hands. Too much guilt.

No.

The preacher had said grace knew no bounds. I tried to lift my hand, but the debris and pain held it fast. My mind shuddered. Darkness clouded my awareness, ready to draw me in.

All I had to do was choose. I met the boy's golden stare and opened my mouth to speak. CRACK. A board crashed onto my jaw. The darkness swarmed . . . swallowed everything . . . everything, but . . . but the gleaming tear.

The sun-fire tear plopped through darkness to a white foot just beyond my hand—a foot with a crimson nail piercing its bridge. Hadn't a woman in the Bible touched a foot and been saved? Hadn't—

Pain.

Darkness swallowed the tear.

If I could just . . . reach it . . . just push through the pain and debris . . . just touch . . .

My finger inched closer.

The house screamed chaos—breaking boards, wailing, thunder.

I brushed the foot. Light exploded. The spike in the foot shook . . . spun . . . sprayed blood. The foot grew . . . stretched . . . dirtied. My fluttering eyes roamed up the boy's body . . . no . . . not a boy . . . a man . . . in shredded robes . . . bloody robes . . . with a beard . . . and . . . gleaming suns for eyes . . . beneath a crown . . . a thorny crown. He smiled . . . everything went . . . white.

*   *   *

Francis. A gentle male voice reverberated through the white abyss.

Reality snapped into focus. Lights shone down from the ceiling. Sunlight stretched across me in warm lines. I was in a bright white room. I opened my mouth to speak, but pain cracked down my throat. My head throbbed and my eyes fluttered. Why was I lying down? Where was I?

"Welcome back, Francis," an old female voice said.

A squat nurse with wiry gray hair smiled beside my bed.

She rested a hand on my arm. "Wasn't sure if you were gonna make it. You're quite the lucky one."

My brow furrowed and my dry mouth worked. I needed water. The nurse reached over to the table beside my bed and poured a small glass. She held it while I sipped, choked, recovered, and sipped some more. Each drop, liquid heaven.

"Wh . . . " I had to work my tongue a little. "Where am I?"

"Crest Peak Memorial Hospital. The doctor will be in soon. I'm sure he'll be excited to find you awake." She patted my arm and departed.

My head rolled toward the sunlight. The window framed a Thomas

Kinkade landscape of colorful leaves and majestic skies. Two blots crept in through the masterpiece. At the window's left edge, a charred steeple protruded between orange and yellow leaves. At the window's right edge, Brazier House's battered frame dulled its surroundings. Were those eyes in the distant window?

"How are you feeling today, Francis?" A tall doctor with bright red hair swept into the room.

"Hurt. How . . . how did I get here?"

"Ambulance, silly." He smiled and plucked a chart off the bed.

My gaze drifted toward the window. Toward Brazier House. I couldn't shake the feeling of being watched. My hands squeezed the blanket. Pain tore up my right arm. I relaxed and found a black, blue, yellow, and purple mess of a hand visible around the bandages.

"You might want to be careful with that," the doctor chided. "That's going to hurt for a while."

"What . . . how . . . "

He replaced the chart and set his hands on his hips. "Didn't anyone tell you to stay away from Brazier House?"

I nodded.

"Maybe you should've listened. The sheriff checks that road every night, and lucky for you he did. The toxins nearly finished you off. Another hour and you wouldn't have made it."

Toxins? What toxins?

"I . . . don't . . . understand."

The doctor moved to an olive-green chair beside my bed. His smile died. "I don't know what you were doing out there, you'll have to speak with the sheriff when he gets here about that, but he found you and your buddy on the front porch." He hesitated. "The other guy, the older one, how did you know him?"

He must have meant Clayton. "Almost my father-in-law. Long time ago." Sadness squeezed my chest. "He okay?"

"I'm sorry; he didn't make it."

A tear slid down my cheek.

"I imagine you took one wild trip. Somebody laced the doorknob with a concoction of natural toxins and venoms; the kind of stuff that causes hallucinations, nausea, paralysis, and such. Dangerous stuff. It might even explain a few of the urban legends."

I'd imagined it all?

The doctor leaned closer. "What were you doing up there anyway?"

I rubbed the tear away with my good hand. "I was at church. Clayton . . . the other guy . . . long story . . . came in . . . shooting up the place . . . chased me through the woods—"

"Church?" The doctor lifted an eyebrow.

298 DANIEL I WEAVER

I nodded. "Missionary Alliance."

He sat back, shaking his head. "Probably just lingering effects." He stood and moved to the window. "Jerald Brazier set fire to the Crest Peak Missionary Alliance about ten years ago and stuck around to make sure the place burned down around him. Lucky for the town, he did it when no one else was around. Apparently, he developed a grudge against God when his wife died in childbirth. Brazier House has been a tomb ever since."

I shuddered. How could I have imagined the church? I'd been there before the house . . . before the toxins.

I grabbed my cup and took another drink. "What about the boy?"

The doctor glanced back at me, concern consuming his face. "I think you'd better rest some more. I'll delay the sheriff until tomorrow."

He killed the lights on the way out the door. I shifted my gaze back to the window.

The Crest Peak Missionary Alliance pastor stood in front of the window. I jumped. Pain rippled up my arm as I held the rail. The sunlight caused his outline to glow. Almost as bright as his golden eyes.

Warmth spilled across me. He stepped forward and settled something on my stomach, but I couldn't break eye contact to look.

He smiled. *As promised, Francis. A gift.*

He stepped backward. Mid-step, the pastor vanished and the freakish boy with the blinding hair stood in his place. The same golden eyes. The same loving smile. The child's mangled features melted away until only an angelic boy remained. He winked.

In a blazing flash, he vanished.

Eventually, I checked my stomach. A Bible. I hadn't touched one of those in years. Too many years.

The boy's voice touched my ears. *You have questions, Francis.*

His voice changed to the preacher's. *The answers are inside.*

Then an entirely different voice, but one I was sure I'd heard before. *Old men shall dream dreams. Young men shall see visions. Welcome back, Francis.*

THE TIMESHIP OF SEMACK

Joseph Ficor

Joseph H. Ficor is an avid science fiction fan and daydreamer. He is an almost life-time resident of Illinois (the Marines borrowed him for six years). He has a bachelor degree in Creative Writing from Southern Illinois University. He published a few science fiction stories in a student paper in the fifth grade and another in his high school newspaper. His first published work, *Rocketships, Cherry Blossoms, and Epiphanies*, was published by PublishAmerica in 2005. His short story, "A Few More Seconds," appeared in the Spring issue 2006 of the now departed *GateWay S-F Magazine*. He is working on his first novel, *Starship Chi-Rho*, which should see a publisher's desk sometime in the near future. He currently lives in Southern Illinois. His obsessions are his faith in Jesus, devouring everything he can on Japan and military history, and reading and writing science fiction.

The inspiration for "The Timeship of Semak" was my experience as a foster child during my teen years and a great love of *Doctor Who*. When I first got into foster care, I dreamed that it would be cool to run away and meet an alien who would take me away from my foster home. I believe that if I had met an alien, he would have given me the same advice that 'Ol Bill gives to Joe in the story.

JOE MOVED THROUGH THE woods as fast as he dared, cautiously choosing his footsteps by the light of a half moon. *Nobody heard me leave!*

Escaping his foster parents' house undetected made him smile and walk a bit taller. The Wilfreds were a good family, but they were not his family. Betrayal struck his heart, but he pushed it aside with the thought of his goal: returning to his mother and maybe running away with her to their relatives in Mississippi.

If I go west along the road heading out of town and I stay in the woods, I'll get to the interstate.

The farming community of Douglaston, Illinois, nestled among endless soybean and cornfields, had three public buildings: an old grocery store still selling food that tasted like it had been canned in the 1930s, and two churches: one Southern Baptist and the other Lutheran.

The Wilfreds, Joe's sixth foster home in fourteen months, were prominent members of the former. They'd made him attend services and Sunday School every Sunday the entire time he lived with them.

I hope Mom's okay. I hope I'll find her fast. Members of the Alton Police Department had shattered their home. They'd charged her with drug dealing and child neglect. Joe had fought them. One policeman had tried to grab him, and the boy had sprained his wrist. He hadn't meant to hurt the officer.

The fourteen-year-old leaned against a tree trunk. It was hard to see in the dark. His tears blinded him.

Mother's apology to the cops rang his ears for the hundredth time. "Everything will be all right," she'd promised him. She'd been wrong. Her promise replayed a dozen times a day.

The police took both of them to the station, but they let her go after two hours. Joe never understood why.

He had not seen her since. Mom never showed up for scheduled visits or court dates. He called her, but she was always too tired to talk. He understood. She had to work hard so they could be together. She loved him and wanted him back. Joe just knew it.

Joe never recognized the male background voices on the phone, and he didn't care. He wanted to be with his mother. It was the only life that he'd ever known and Children Services had taken it away. *I'll get back to her no matter what.*

Joe continued through the woods flanking the road but carefully out of traffic's sight. If anyone from the town spotted him, they would try to send him back to the Wilfreds.

The Wilfreds were good people. Joe's one chore was helping take care of the exotic animals on their farm. They raised llamas, peacocks, four-to-six-horned sheep, and other rare animals. His foster mother, Linda, took most of the responsibility for the care of the farm. These were the 1980s and exotic animals were selling like water in Death Valley, but Linda had trouble finding buyers. She was still new to the business. Joe admitted it was fun learning about and caring for the creatures. But Mother . . . it could never be a proper home because his mother was not there.

Dear God, help me to make it back to my mother and get away from these crazy religious foster parents.

He did not think much would come of his prayer, but it never hurt to cover all bases.

Joe had learned about prayer from the weekly Bible studies in the

Wilfreds' home. Joe enjoyed these, especially the story of Joseph in the book of Genesis. He liked to think that he had gotten his name from that character, but he knew his mother named him after her brother who had died. Members of the Bible study talked a lot about getting "saved" and knowing Jesus as a personal Lord and Savior. Joe began to learn what these terms meant, but the whole God thing gave him the creeps. God was that big man upstairs whom you asked for help when you needed it.

Joe walked for a long time.

He'd hoped that headlights would help mark the road, but there were no cars at all, and he could no longer see the road. The moon hardly penetrated the thickening woods.

I'm lost.

A branch cracked behind, and he froze.

Two years ago, according to locals, a little boy had gotten lost in the woods. The howls of a coyote pack echoed that night. The boy's mutilated body was found the next morning.

Joe waited forever, but heard only crickets and frogs.

Finally, he gathered his courage and resumed his trek. He angled toward where the road should have been, but there were only more trees.

I'm lost.

Fourteen-year-olds aren't scared of the dark. Suddenly he noticed every croak, every chirp and hoot. He wiped wet palms on his shirt. Then a distant coyote howled.

Adrenaline overruled his brain's commands, and he ran nightblind.

Then there was nothing beneath his feet.

The falling sensation stood hairs on end. His legs absorbed the shock of landing, but he tumbled down a steep hill.

Pain flared fast and he couldn't stop: arm—rock; knee—log; head—tree . . .

Joe rolled to a stop in a ravine. He landed face-down in a stream, and he sputtered water. He gasped to regain breath, then wiped mud from his eyes.

Something in the shadows moved toward him. Maybe only a tree under moonlight but Joe wasn't about to take chances—his flight instinct screamed. He was up and running.

Joe imagined demon-coyotes behind him as he splashed through the moonlit stream.

In mid-stride, he saw the branch . . .

Joe awoke, fireworks in his head exploding over and over and over. He slowly pushed himself to a sitting position on a dry patch of grass.

The stream was gone. The moonlight shone brighter, but the trees still grew thick here.

He became aware of the figure that stood less than five feet away. It was a tall man, very thin, with a slight stoop.

The man was familiar, but Joe couldn't place him. His head still rang from its encounter with the branch. The hair on the back of his neck straightened when the figure spoke.

"You had a nasty bump, boy. You good?"

The voice cleared any confusion. 'Ol Bill. The locals had given him the nickname. It was said that 'Ol Bill spoke no English when he arrived in town a year ago. Everyone thought him to be a poor immigrant. His English improved quickly. He never gave his real name, so the nickname stuck. 'Ol Bill worked odd jobs to earn money. He never stayed at any of the homes in town, so folks believed he lived in the woods. The Baptist church became his favorite place of worship on Sundays. The old man responded to the altar call to accept Jesus a month ago.

No one really talked to him—even in the church.

"I . . . I'm okay," Joe stumbled. "My head hurts a bit. Did you bring me here?"

"Yeah. Found you in the stream. You were going to get an ungodly chill if I had not gotten you out of there. What are you doing out here in the middle of the night?"

"I'm running away," Joe said sheepishly. "I want to get back to my real family." The boy did not know why he had told the truth. He'd already made up a story about his parents running out of gas. Of course, that was for strangers. He didn't have a story for someone he knew.

"At least you can get back to your family," the bum replied with a sneer. "Mine are all dead ."

"I'm sorry," Joe said sympathetically.

'Ol Bill's shoulders sagged. "I should be the one apologizing, not you. It is not your fault for my people's stupidity."

Joe looked quizzically at the man. *What is he talking about? He shouldn't be talking about dead relatives like that.*

"Don't you live with the Wilfreds?" Bill asked.

"Yes I do . . . sorry, did."

"Those are good folks. Why would you want to leave? They do not seem like people who beat their children."

"They've been very nice, but they're not my real family."

"I can understand that," the old bum said in a matter of fact way. "Are you hungry?"

"Yes, sir."

"Come on over." Bill beckoned him toward what looked like a big drainage pipe. As Joe got closer, his eyes became full moons.

The "pipe" was some seventy feet long and looked like a giant ant that had its legs pulled off. The thing had two short wings and a small hole in the side, from which hung a ladder. Joe couldn't make out any more details in the dim moonlight.

"Boy, come on. I have got things to do and hardly any time to do them in."

Joe realized he'd stopped and stood gawking. He approached and followed Bill up the ladder. Inside, dim lights bathed a small room in soft yellow. A console with a lot of blinking lights sat at the front of the room. The room had three captain's chairs—two in front of the console and one behind.

Ol' Bill grabbed a can of red beans from a cabinet, plopped down in one of the console chairs, and worked a half-rusted hand-crank can-opener. He pulled a fork out of his shirt pocket and stuck it in the beans. "Sorry for the poor fare, but this is all I could get on such short notice."

Joe took that can and started shoveling beans. He'd missed dinner, and hunger had crept up on him. Swallowing whole forkfuls, he watched Ol' Bill working buttons on the console.

"Are you going to turn me in?" Joe asked around a mouth full of beans.

"No," Bill answered without looking away from his button-pushing. "I have too many things to do to be concerned with you and your problems."

"Why are you helping me?"

Bill turned in his chair and gave the boy a curious look. "It would not be right to leave you in the woods shivering in a cold stream. Besides, I don't need the beans. They would have gone to waste if you didn't eat them. You are an answer to a prayer anyways."

"You prayed for me to come?"

"Not for you specifically. But I prayed that I could be a blessing to someone before I left." He turned back to his console.

"Where you going?"

"To die. You are some consolation for a life that was wasted in arrogance." A tear trickled down 'Ol Bill's right cheek.

Fork midway to his mouth, Joe froze. *Die? Did he just say "die?" What on earth do I say to someone . . . who knows he is about to . . . die?* "Um, I'm sorry, I didn't mean to make you cry."

"Do you know what you are in?"

"A camper?"

"This is a timeship,"

"A what?"

Bill shrugged. "It is a timeship—a combination time machine and spaceship—from the planet Semak. I am Njora Taley, the last Semakite in the universe."

Joe's eyes widened even further. He pinched himself to make sure that he was still awake. The pain confirmed it.

"You an alien?"

"Yeah," Bill-Njora said.

"You just look like me, or any other human. Are you a green-eyed monster with three eyes?" Joe asked cynically.

"No. I am what you see. OOOOnly humans inhabiting the universe. In thousands of years of space travel, human civilization has never found a non-human intelligent species. Humans are the only creatures in His creation that have been created in His image. Humans existing as the only intelligent species, is proof of the Creator."

"Why are you on Earth? Do you plan to invade?"

"Weren't you listening?" Njora rebuked him. "I am the only one left of my race. I could not take over this town if I wanted to. To answer your question, I just stumbled onto your planet."

"Stumbled? How does anyone 'stumble' onto a planet."

Njora turned to face Joe and leaned back in his chair. "Semak was located in the Mai Galaxy. I have no idea where it was in relation to your world since I came through a timewarp/ wormhole. Anyway, Semak was the only habitable planet in a system of six worlds. It was very similar to your world—just a bit cooler with less surface water.

"Semakites had been obsessed with time travel for a few centuries. We wanted to alter bad past-choices to see if future-realities could be improved. No civilization had ever achieved time travel, and most experts said the required energy alone made time travel impossible. We even invented an entirely new field of mathematics devoted to the subject. It was called Tramathics. I do not know how to translate into your mathematics, but it makes no difference. Only thirty people in the known universe could understand it—and they all were Semakites."

"Are you one of those math guys?" Joe asked putting a forkful of beans into his mouth.

"No," Njora said. "I am only a test pilot. I was a colonel in the Defence Force. I was selected out of a pool of thirty-six pilots to test fly this ship. Its official name (in English) is the Timeship Experimental One, or just TX-1 for short.

"Back to my story. A race called the Sharei wanted to dominate the galaxy, so they invented a weapon that could destroy a star. The Doisha Sun Destroyer. Somehow the test goofed up, and they destroyed their own sun. Improved the galactic neighborhood, but an aftereffect of the blast created some kind of destructive wave in hyperspace. It slowly destroyed all of the stars in that galaxy.

"Super weapons were used to try to stop the wave, but nothing worked. So most races decided to build an artificial wormhole to send a few survivors to another galaxy to save what they could of humanity.

Semak declined to participate in the program. We thought this would be the opportunity to develop our time program. Funding was appropriated from the planetary congress and construction started.

"It took ten years to complete the project. This experimental ship," Njora spread his hands and looked around him, "was to fly into a sixty-two mile-wide hexagon-shaped ring, straight into our sun, at a very precise angle and speed. In theory, the experiment should have taken me four minutes back in time."

"Well that's stupid," Joe interrupted. "You guys work on something for ten years just to go back in time four minutes?"

"It was an experiment to see if it could be done, you brat. If you don't mind, can I finish the story without any stupid comments?"

"Okay old man," Joe replied, a little hurt. "Go ahead."

"Thank you. It was believed that the ring, powered by the sun's energy, would hurl me back in time before I could be burnt by our star."

"Did you go back in time?"

"I still don't know what happened. Lord knows I have tried to figure it out, but most of the ship's recorders are blown, and my knowledge of Tramathics is far too limited. I was in a dream-state for a long time. Everything blurred. I only recall that the time meter indicated that I traveled about four years into the future."

"How'd you get here on Earth?"

"You can say that I awoke very abruptly. Everything came into focus and sparks flew everywhere. It was only by God's grace that I came out the warp close to your planet. I managed to land right here. I wandered for awhile until I came to one of the houses in town. They fed me and gave me a place to stay. I listened to the locals with my tran-linguist," Njora held up an earplug, "and learned English in a few months."

"Why didn't you tell anyone?"

"Get real, boy," Njora shook his head. Then looked Joe straight in the eye. "Do you think that they'd believe that kind of story from who they perceive to be an old drunk wandering in the woods?"

"But," Joe stammered, "you could have shown them your ship."

"I didn't want them to know. I want to get back home and change everything so that this would have never happened." A tear flowed.

"Just like me," the young man lowered his head trying to fight back a tear himself.

"Do you remember the passage from the Bible that Pastor Stevens used in his sermon two Sundays ago?"

"No. I was too busy planning on how I was going to get away."

"And a fine job you did," the old man smiled.

Both laughed before Joe asked: "So what does the Bible have to do with us now?"

"I can't remember the exact wording, but it is found in Colossians 3:9. Something about putting off the old man. Pastor Stevens said that God wants us to leave the past behind and look toward the future that He has planned for us."

"So?"

"What I am trying to say is that we are both spending too much time trying to change the past instead of concentrating on the here and now. My entire race died wasting all of its resources on a foolish experiment to change the past instead of selecting people to make the journey through the artificial wormhole. I believe now that it would have ensured the survival of my people."

"How do you know that your people did not succeed?"

"Because all of us knew deep down that the time experiment would use up all of the available resources. It was either time travel or the wormhole. We chose pride."

"And you are sure that this wormhole succeeded?"

"I'm not really for certain, but I feel in my heart that it did. I just don't know when it happened or if it has yet to happen."

"You're trying to include me in your mess. How do I fit in?"

"You are trying to run away to change your past. You have a foolish plan to somehow magically make it back to your mother and escape from Illinois to Mississippi. Did you ever bother to think that maybe you were meant to be with that foster family? Perhaps God put them into your life to help you. Just go back to them and accept that they are destined to help you. Running away only makes things worse. You might just be running away from a blessing that God is about to give you."

"What kind of blessing?"

"Well," the old man scratched his balding head. "Maybe God will teach you things before reuniting you with your mother."

"Really?" Joe's eyes lit up.

"Yeah, I believe in my heart that it will happen someday. Just trust God."

Joe desperately wanted to believe 'Ol Bill's words. After a moment in thought he exclaimed, "I think that I'll do that. Boy, wait till everyone . . ."

"No, I won't be going back."

"Why not? You gotta! You don't have to die!" Joe grabbed the alien's shirt and shook his collar before collapsing in tears.

"How old do you think that I am?"

Joe sniffled and wiped his tears before looking up at his friend: "Seventy? Seventy-five?"

"I am thirty-eight of your years old. Somehow the warp aged me several decades. I am dying. I have been preparing the ship so that I can leave and die in space."

"But why not stay here? They have good hospitals in St. Louis. They can find a way to help you." Tears flowed down Joe's cheeks again.

"I sense that my time is almost at an end. My people are gone. I just want to pass into the afterlife amongst the stars, near to them."

Joe nodded slowly, and he relaxed.

Joe stood a barn's length away from Timeship Experimental One as it levitated above the tree tops. It hung in the rapidly disappearing darkness for a few heartbeats, just long enough for Joe to see 'Ol Bill's wave. Then TX-1 shot away into the oranges and reds of the new day's eastern sky.

How can you find and lose a friend so fast? Joe stood watching the sunrise until a distant moo reminded him of goats and llamas.

Njora knew he needed to be among his people and Joe now sensed the same thing. The Wilfreds would have been awake all night. Joe had only been thinking of himself—until now.

An alien had taught both the value of a lost boy, and the meaning of the universe. Joe knew, for the first time, that God was on His throne and all would be well. That throne was the focus of Joe's thoughts.

From the far side of this soybean field, morning light shone off the blacktop a quarter-mile away. Joe ran to the black ribbon and began his walk home. Linda needed help feeding the animals.

SOAR ON WINGS

Carizz Cruzem

Carizz Cruzem is an award-winning author from the Philippines who began writing at an early age. She has had many interesting life experiences as the daughter of a missionary pastor. A 3-year stint at the Institute for Foundational Learning gave Carizz further exposure to the lives of less fortunate people. This rich background provides her with a wealth of information to employ in her writing. Ms Cruzem's current fiction projects are *The Rightful Place* and *Jiyuu*.

All (not just the good ones) things work together for good to those who love Him and are called according to His purposes and plans. A situation may look ugly at the moment. We may not understand why. But time will come when we'll see that the puzzle fits—as crooked as the pieces may be.

SWISH . . .

I wriggled back to consciousness.

Swish.

Glistening leaves rustled under the cold-disk's pale light.

Soft footsteps.

I peeked through my tree-bark crack of a bedroom window.

Humans tiptoed through grass in the dark, cloaked by the shadow of our tree-home.

I guess they don't want to wake the whole zone.

A small girl, whose hair waved in the air, scurried quick steps near the end of the human line.

The man at the end stooped down, scooped up, and carried the girl.

I scratched my head.

A woman in front bent, opened a square of grass and descended into their secret hole.

One by one, they went down the hole.

The last man peered out before lowering himself and replacing the sod cover.

I walked across our fly-tree-house to our ant-chewed front door, leapt out and flew to the sand-sea.

The hot-disk would appear soon.

Anthers!

I'd flown about the sand-sea for two hot-disk and one cold-disk appearances in search of a flower.

I rushed to the shriveled bloom.

Careful now. One foot in the stamen's pollen-bearing shells, a quick pull and a back flip. One anther broke free from its stalk. *Now, five feet to go.*

I backstroked.

The fast rising hot-disk reddened the endless sand-sea and curled up the petals. It bit my heart.

I reeled away and flew towards the human zone.

Father awaited my arrival.

"Father, Father. Look!" I took off the new-found treasures and laid them on the floor for my father to see.

My father smile and winged my head. "Now, Sor, I know you're too excited to give those to Fli right now. But it's buzz-time. You'll only live for a hundred hot-disk appearances, so you'll need to buzz memories as my father buzzed them to me.

Father drew his head closer to mine, and I saw . . .

Ka-boom! The mortar explosion ten feet above, blasted the war-man back into consciousness.

He caught sight of his shuttered legs. "Maggots! Maggots!" His swollen knees stank of rotting meat.

A voice. "There's one over there!"

A Jeep jerked to a stop that had been war-men's home for . . .

Two men with a stretcher . . .

"We're taking fire! Hurry!" hollered the driver over deafening blasts.

They loaded the wounded man, the simple motion evoking more screams.

The Jeep sped toward camp.

The doctor shook his head when they rolled the gurney into the army hospital.

"It's good he passed out again—we're still short on Morphine. By the length of these maggots, I'd say our man's been out there for three or four days before you guys got to him.

"Will he make it, Doc?"

"It's too soon to say. I can't do much for him now. Maggots only eat dead flesh so the best thing to do is let them feed. I'll let him be for a couple of days and see how he progresses."

Father moved his head back. "The lifespan of our kind is very short compared to humans."

I leapt into the air.

"Pay attention!" Father stamped one foot in disapproval. "The one I buzzed is called *The Loud Explosion*."

My wings wiggled.

He looked at me. "Our ancestors." Father flipped a wing with pride. "Those brave warriors who trekked miles of land mines, dodged bullets and ate their way to that man's wounded knees."

I grated my hind legs.

"We are blessed," Father continued. "The wise and observant medicine-man didn't annihilate our ancestors, but even had them eat other men's dead flesh. They got to eat to their hearts' content, and in return, the wounds healed faster." He wing-lashed the air. "Mutualism is a proud buzz."

I clawed the floor.

Father turned his body to look out the window. "But, after *The Loud Explosion*, our whole specie thought things would continue to go well with us."

Both my antenna itched.

"When explosions ceased, humans forgot our partnership."

My stomach got itchy too and I scratched it.

Father smiled at me. "Now, since you can't squat still . . ."

I grinned. "I'll be back after the cold-disk appears." The itching stopped.

"Do be careful." Father thumped my body. "We might have learned to adapt but humans' gadgets' evolution quadruple by the second."

Guilt-smile crossed my mouth. "I will Father, I will." I hastened to the door.

"Your anthers!"

Fli, here I come!

"HUZ, TOOZ, THREEZ, FOURZ; HUZ, TOOZ, THREEZ, FOURZ. LIFT THOSE LAZY FEET, SISSIES." Former General-Commander-Major Zar had his offspring lined up again on a small open space in the dumpsite. "HALT. RIGHT FACE."

The platoon faced their father.

The dumpsite had many smells—apples, chili, molds—name it, the dumpsite had it. All rotten. Yummy!

Former GCM Zar kicked a dust grain. "I DIDN'T RETIRE TO RAISE WEAKLINGS." He circled his broods. "You must get ready for another *The Plague* to punish these ungrateful humans."

"*The Plague?*" I scratched my head.

Fli's antenna twitched in recognition of my scent. Fli—my maggothood friend.

"CIVILIAN." Former GCM Zar turned around and glared at a candy wrapper.

"Who goes there?"

I leapt over the wrapper.

"HALT."

I landed on one leg.

"I should have asked your father to enlist you to the Force." He wiggled a disappointed rear and turned his attention back to the platoon. "ATTEN-HUZ. Private Fli, see me after you're dismissed."

"Sir, yes, Sir!" Fli flipped both her wings and stamped a foot.

"Uhm. Excuse me, Sir." I scratched my head.

Former GCM Zar whirled around. "Now, I have to COMMAND your father to enlist you to the Force." He wiggled a furious rear. "You don't know how to ask permission to buzz. Now, WHAT?"

"Uhm. I'd like to know, Sir, if I can put my other legs down now. I'm getting cramps."

His antenna twisted, but he never smiled. "At ease."

I put my legs down.

"FLIGHT SERGEANT," he said, still looking at me.

His first hatch flew nearer and alighted three wing-strokes behind him.

Former GCM Zar turned around. "Dismiss your flights."

The flight sergeant flipped two wings.

Former GCM Zar returned the salute and flew to their quarters just beyond the platoon line.

The flight sergeant turned to the platoon. "Dismissed."

Everyone flipped two wings, and then flew in different directions.

Fli landed by my side and opened her mouth to buzz something.

"FLI! SOR! YOU TWO COME HERE!" Her father cut her.

She closed her mouth and lifted a wing for me to follow.

Flies living in the dumpsite always changed living quarters. We alighted outside their house—this time, a cardboard box. Wherever they choose to live, it was always damp. One of Fli's maggot siblings high-jumped beside me and wiggled. They had no choice, actually. The place should be called *damp-site*.

"I trust that you two, specially you, Fli, are responsible flies who do their duties inflicting diseases to humans." He pointed a wobbling foot at us.

Fli flipped a limp wing.

He started pacing the whole length of their house. "I want to remind you that humans have been nothing but our species' top enemy."

She flapped another limp wing.

"They have tried everything to wipe us out." He stopped and looked outside. "But we persevere."

He wriggled out of his reflection. "Where are you two going?"

I scratched my head.

"Survey the human zone for your plan, Father," she answered for both of us.

He shook his rear in approval. "All right. I'm not going to hold you back any longer."

She flipped two wings in earnest.

Former GCM Zar returned the gesture.

Fli took off.

I scratched my head, twitched my mouth, wiggled my rear and followed Fli.

We dashed to the left away from their quarters and zigzagged through giant heaps of scrap. The mouthwatering grub distracted me from keeping up with her. At a turn, I flew straight to a gooey thing.

I sat still.

I love banana!

I munched on the oozing banana.

I licked my two front foot and I looked around.

Whoa! Fli left me.

I backstroked.

All my feet got stuck in the banana. I tried again.

One, two, three, fly.

No good. I only sunk lower.

I waded through the slimy banana until I reached the tip. I wiggled.

Freedom! I rolled a triumph's flip through the air, and flew to the dumpsite's exit.

Girl-fly washed her feet in a pothole. She was the cleanest fly in the whole history of flies.

I hovered above her. "I'm sorry. A banana pushed itself on me."

"Yeah. I've heard weirder things than a chasing banana." She rubbed her two front feet together.

I alighted beside her and scrubbed my sticky feet. "I know just the thing to put a smile on your face."

"Just watching you wash your feet is enough." She brushed my left wing.

I grinned. "I know. But this one will put a big smile on that face."

She stared at me. "And what is that?"

"Meet me at my father's house." I sprung up and flew home.

Father came to the door when I arrived. "I put your anthers in your space."

"Thanks Dad."

"I'm going to the dumpsite. Would there be anything you'd like me to bring you?" he asked.

I foot-scraped the floor. "Thanks Dad, but I'm full."

He took off.

Fli came in with her old anthers on her feet. "Where's your father going?" She wore anther feet covers because she didn't want to spread germs.

I shuffled to the end of our house to my space and turned to her. "The dumpsite." I grinned and scratched my head.

"What have you done now?" She whizzed across the house.

I drummed the floor. "Look inside my room."

She crept to my room. "Ok. So what do you want me to see here—a mushy floor, a cluttered bed, your wiggly maggot siblings? What?"

"Look under the bed." I kept my feet drumming.

She gasped and stood still.

"Don't forget to exhale." I tapped the floor one last time.

She jumped up, flew three tight circles of glee and landed again. "You're the best! Wherever did you get these?"

I scratched my head.

She paced left and right and slushed through the length of my room-floor. "I've searched high and low for a few hot-disk appearances and didn't even smell a trace of flower scent."

I scratched some more.

"But here you've gotten me a complete set of anther-foot-covers. Wow!" She stopped and smiled to me. "Thank you."

I jumped. "I know you can't really look for anthers. Your father would wiggle his rear in fury." I backed off. "I'm sorry I had to wear them with my dirty feet though."

She squished out of my room. "Thank you." She brushed my left wing.

I walked to the window and looked out.

"What are you thinking?" She came up beside me.

I faced her. "Your father's at it again."

"I know." She looked out the window. "He's a little stricter and much louder."

"Fli?"

She stared ahead.

"What is *The Plague?*"

"Oh that? Come here."

I drew my head closer to hers, and I saw . . .

Buzz!

A girl screamed.

Flies attacked her hair.

Zoom!

Flies went inside the houses.

People scrambled out.

Whiz!

Zoom!

Buzz!

Flies occupied every space on the floor, on the wall, on the ceiling, on posts, on lights, on beds, on leaves, on tree-trunks . . . everywhere.

The swarm of flies leapt in unison and flew away.

Up above, all their antennas whirred in excitement. Scent of masses of dead flesh hung in the air.

They never stopped. They flew on.

Yuck!

She thumped my head. "Yuck!"

My head throbbed. "What did you do that for?" I scratched my head.

"You're drooling!"

I grinned. "I got carried away with your story." I rubbed my stomach. "All that talk about rotten flesh makes my stomach grumble."

"Now, I have a surprise for you." She whizzed to the door. "Race you to the Port!"

"Wait!" I flew back to my space.

She went ahead and ignored me.

I wore the anthers and flew out of the house.

Fly, these anthers are so heavy! I tried landing on a window glass of a human house but I slid down a ramp. *Not to mention slippery.*

"What are you stopping for?" She skidded back.

I panted. "How do you manage to wear these things all the time?"

"Practice!" she chimed, and flew a few circles around me. Her feet peered through the holes of her anthers.

I smiled. "I'm glad I'm only wearing these until we can reach the waterhole we saw the other hot-disk appearance."

She landed on a leaf and grinned. Her antenna fluttered. "Food."

Other flies rushed toward the scent wafting out the open front door. Each fly exploded in a spark as it neared the door.

"Whoa! That green light shields the door!" she said.

"I knew there was something odd with that open door! Doors are usually closed." I wiggled my rear in fear.

"Finally, they have found a way to open their doors and still keep us out," she whispered.

A boy human stepped past the green light curtain and pointed a stick at us. Green thin lights zipped into the air.

A beam went right past me and nailed another fly.

He shook and spun to the ground.

Fli swooped up and I followed. We landed on the roof.

"What was that?" I gasped. "It almost got me!"

"Something to avoid."

I scratched my head.

"C'mon, let's try for food at the Port," she said.

"You shoulda' shared my banana."

"It didn't chase me."

We entered a mountain-like building that had many smells. We flew up to a pole at a corner.

"Is that monstrous thing a fly?" I jumped back and almost fell off the pole.

"I think she is."

I scuttled back on the top of the pole. "Doesn't he look a little stiff?"

"She's perfect." Fli fluttered to the huge thing.

I followed suit. "He has no hair legs and those two huge eyes shine orange light! He's scary. What's perfect in that?" *Sometimes, I can't understand her logic even though we maggoted together.*

She halted and turned to me. "Well, I think it's a girl-fly."

I lingered.

"Look at how smooth!" She dove down to one of the monstrous legs of the fly. "Without hair legs, she can't drag dirt with her."

I lingered still.

She scooted up to its dreadful head. "Those eyes. I'm sure she can see farther even in the darkest nights."

"You've got a point there." I hovered above it. "And look at those shiny wings!"

Fli flew closer to me.

"I wish I had those wings." I rolled on its head. "Of course, I'd have to have a humungous body too." I looped, spiraled, whizzed, whooshed, zoomed and buzzed around it.

It stood unmoved.

"She's a little odd," she said. "Silent type I guess."

"And look." I took the anthers off and flew to its head.

I breathed in.

I breathed out.

I whizzed across its body and put my feet down. I skidded. "Watch out!" Too late. Fli and I rolled through its rear.

"See what I mean?"

"Yeah, you almost broke my wings!" She stamped her foot.

I scratched my head. "No, not that. I mean, he's too smooth."

She looked at me and shivered. "And cold too."

It trembled.

She darted back to the pole.

I dashed to its head, slipped on the anthers and followed her to the pole.

We turned around.

Lo and behold!

The monster fly's stomach opened.

Several humans went inside.

His low growl became an angry roar.

The humungous fly leapt into the air and flew through the roof opening.

We tried to follow but we couldn't keep up.

If I had live humans inside me, I'd be angry too.

We flew away defeated.

She fell silent.

"I would like to become like that huge fly." She sighed.

"What?" I halted. "You want to get cut up through your stomach so humans could enter your body." I rubbed my stomach. "Way too painful. I don't know how he went through that kind of operation."

"Not that way." She grinned. "But I want to be useful just like her."

"Him."

We landed on a blade of grass.

"I understand how former GCM can prepare you and your fly-siblings for another *The Plague*, but even if he pests this zone clear of humans, how will his germs kill animals?" I scratched my head.

"Don't be too cold to him." She brushed my left wing. "He's still my father."

I rubbed my two front feet together. "I'm sorry."

"He thinks that the dead animals will always come after flies pest a land." She shrugged her wings.

The blade of grass swayed.

I scratched my head.

"Wish I could do something to change his mind." She sighed.

The ground below us rose sideways. We flew up. A man ascended from below. When both his feet stepped on the ground, he scrambled ahead.

We alighted on the blade of grass again.

Another man ran past us and missed the blade of grass by a human step.

We whisked off the grass blade and sat on a tree.

Several men rushed after him. One of them aimed with a stick at the man from below the ground. A white beam zinged out of it.

The man tumbled. "Y'shua!" he shouted.

To my delicious surprise, the man turned red and small holes covered his body.

Other flies buzzed and feasted on the carcass.

The men stared from a distance.

My heart weighed heavier for the man. My stomach grumbled.

Fli turned away. "Go ahead."

I ignored my heart and smiled.

She didn't want dead flesh herself but I knew she wanted me to be happy.

She's really something else!

I glided to it.

No more than a hundred wing strokes away, a flying thing whizzed and hovered above the body.

I halted.

A blinding light covered the body. When the light was gone, there were only ashes.

No flies survived.

A maggot-like thing, only longer, wormed through the air and sucked the ashes.

The onlookers jumped up and down in triumph.

"What are you doing there staring at that thing? Waiting for it to turn and chase us?" Fli shrieked.

We scrambled away the whizz-thing.

Please don't break off! I pleaded to my legs. *Fly!*

Fli stopped and landed on a metal bar.

I tried to land on it too but I slipped down the dirt.

She swooped down to the ramp closer to where I fell. "Let's go to the good humans."

"Wait. Let me make sure my legs are still attached to my body." I lift one foot after another.

She smiled. "C'mon! I'm starving. And let's wash those anthers on our way there."

I smiled back and followed her into the air. The hot-disk began to disappear.

I followed her down to a hole. No green-light curtains, no beam-sticks, and Food Hill always awaited us. Very few flies knew about it.

Or perhaps it was courage.

The passage led down, down, down. Wisdom buzzed not to fly this passage so we would not get lost. But we passed this way many times.

We never thought of it as a maze.

We first reached the pool. I took her new anthers off my dirty feet and together, we washed the tiny pods. She discarded her worn slippers and smiled at the fresh ones.

"Thank you, again." She wiggled her feet.

"You're welcome, little maggot! Now let's go eat!"

This time she followed me.

We reached the small opening to the good humans. Left over food mounted in the hole. We ate to our fill.

"I wish we could live here. We're safer around these humans here underground." I said with a full mouth.

The food room's door opened. Several human men and women entered and closed the door behind them.

Tap. Tap. Tap.

A man opened the door.

The small girl with hair that waved in the air came in. She sat on the lap of a plump woman. The man sitting beside the woman patted the girl's head.

A peaceful sound trickled out of their mouths.

My body became heavier so that my feet swayed under me.

Fli shook me to wake up.

Some of them had their hands up in the air. Others knelt down.

Something like water leaked from their eyes.

A man flipped through some white leaves that had been webbed along one edge. He spoke while looking at the spread leaf.

Some of the heads bobbed up and down. Others continued crying.

The man stopped his lips.

Each one grasped the hand of the human next to them.

The man's voice gushed from his mouth.

Every sound caused more head bobbing and crying.

They said something altogether and went out of the room.

"I will be clean tonight." Fli said.

"Hello?" I stamped my foot. "You're always clean! You're the cleanest fly who ever lived!"

She stared at the closed door. "I mean, as clean as any human can get."

That meant she would kill her every germ. The only way a fly could do that is . . . I stopped buzzing and sat still. The dark hole masked my face. *My friend has gone mad.*

"Come, it's getting late!" she motioned to the exit as if nothing was wrong. "I'm gonna be clean tonight!"

I shook my whole body.

"You must have eaten too much. You're wiggling." She buzz-laughed.

"I'm trying to shake my head, but as it is stuck tight to my body. It just doesn't work!"

"What are you trying to shake your head for?"

I shook my body some more.

"Are you trying to shake your head *only,* again?" She smiled. "Don't try to imitate human signals. We have our own signals. Use those." She whizzed.

I flew without buzzing.

Odd. She is really happy.

We flew to her home by the cold-disk's pale light.

Her dad looked out.

I wonder if he ever stops pacing.

Fli rushed to him and laid her head on his wings. "Dad, I love you! Don't you dare forget that!"

He flipped a surprised wing. Not knowing what to say, he merely buzzed yes.

"Ok." I smiled. "I see this is one happy family. I'll go now. It's been a long day."

"I had fun, " said Fli.

I smiled and turned to former GCM Zar. "G'night Sir."

He, still surprised by her daughter's affection to him, only managed to buzz yes again.

I leapt into the air for take-off and flew home.

I crawled straight into bed.

"I am clean!"

She landed on a tree and leapt from one bark to another. Her wings
shone.

"I am clean!"

She looked at me.

"Don't be sad Sor." She whizzed through the air.

I trembled back to consciousness. My head pulsed.

Weird.

Buzzes trickled through my room. I walked out. My legs shook.

Really weird.

Flies gathered in our tree-home's common room.

I wasn't informed about a big meeting.

Buzzes stopped short and everyone turned to me.

My dad stepped closer to me. "How are you feeling?"

"I'm okay." I shifted my footing. "I guess."

He brushed my wings.

I looked at my dad. "Are you . . . okay?"

"I'm worried about you, son."

"You worry too much." I skipped attempting to whirl. "I'm as
healthy as any young fly could . . ." I flopped.

My father rubbed his front feet together.

My dream?

"What happened to Fli?"

Flies' silence buzzed too loud in the air.

"Last night—" He stopped and stared at me. He turned away.
"Other flies heard her through the labyrinth buzzing, 'The time to be
clean is now.' Her buzzes stopped so some flew into the maze, following her scent."

"That can't be true!" I jumped. "I saw her with her dad last night
and they were happy."

My father rubbed his front foot. "Son, former General-Commander-
Major Zar . . . the buzz was too much for him to bear. He died this morning."

I sat still.

"They saw Fli's body floating inside the bottle of . . ."

My body sagged on the floor.

"... a cleaning liquid—one that kills even by mere smelling."

I stood. "Where is she now?"

"No one knows." My father turned around. "The flies rushed out the hole after seeing her; afraid to lose the scent she left, and be lost in the maze."

I looked out the window. "This is not her end."

Father came up to me. "Whatever your decision is, I'll support it."

"I can't be a common fly anymore." I turned to my father.

"You're old enough. I'm releasing you." He brushed my wing.

"Thank you, Father."

We shook wings.

I walked out.

He followed me to the door.

I took one last look at him.

I leapt and took off.

Humans gathered in the square.

I sat on a man's shoulder.

In the center, four men with similar skins circled a small group of wailing men, women and children.

Other humans, oblivious to my presence, sat around the square and jeered at those who were crying.

I looked up.

A blinding light blasted out from each of the four men's lifted sticks. The beams joined in the center and formed a light-dome over the weeping people.

The wailing stopped. They knelt. The same soothing sound I heard underground flowed out of their mouths.

A flame started on the ground inside the light-dome.

The people sitting around the arena fell in raucous laughter.

The fire didn't stop the people inside the dome from making the peace-sound.

My heart weighed heavier.

The fire slowly consumed the poor people inside the light-dome. They lifted their hands and raised their voices even louder. Their bodies boiled and the peace-sound softened. One body tumbled after another until everyone fell burning.

The people around the square laughed harder. Some jumped up and down and patted each other's backs. Then, the cheering crowd hushed.

A soft small human's voice echoed in the arena. The girl with hair that waved in the air kneeling down in the centermost part of the dome had her both little hands high in the air. She said "Y'shua" over and over again until she fell with the other bodies.

The crowd cheered again.

How do these humans survive with such hatred?

I turned around and flapped my wings to the underground zone.

Did any one of them survive?

I thumped and puffed my chest and flew to the food room. I landed on the floor near the door.

How could I have wished to be huge when I can go anywhere I want with this body? I walked under the door.

Darkness. Bright light came from a distance.

Was that . . . Fli's scent!

I flew to the light.

So this was where she went after I bid her my last goodbye. I sighed.

Insane! I landed on the wall to stop myself from banging my head.

I wiggled my rear. *She is clean now.*

Again, I flew towards the light.

Metal replaced earth.

Whirs and clicks sounded nearby.

A flash. The bright light stole my sight.

I turned away.

Every wing-beat moment showed another angle, another shape.

I turned back into the light.

No!

Wire attached to Fli's hind, sides and stretched around her body. She glittered with green, yellow and red lights.

I fluttered to her. My head bumped something hard. I flew around the glass. *No way in.*

I landed on the glass, above girl-fly.

White-leaf man came in the side door.

He stretched his lips.

"Fli! You get out of there this instant!"

He came nearer.

I took off, and landed on the side of the glass.

White-leaf man leaned very close to us and spoke. Then his lips stretched even wider and his head bobbed up and down.

I stared at him.

He looked up and said, "Y'shua."

The gesture comforted me. *He means Fli no harm.*

I flew back on the top of the glass. *This is what she wanted.*

An awesome sense of purpose swatted me, as real as when she had thumped my head. *I don't want my body to be wasted. I want to be used also. I can't believe how brave I'm feeli . . .*

I wiggled back to consciousness.

The floor shook. My head weighed heavier. Everything moved from side to side.

I started to flip my wings. *Ouch! Did I gain weight?*

My wings fluttered.

I looked around. *Same room.*

I stared in front of me. *Odd.*

The wall in my front doubled to forever.

I angled to the side door.

Whoa!

My view of the door showed in the wall on my right.

I turned to face the dark hole through which I'd entered.

Double whoa!

The same dark hole showed in the forever wall.

What is happening?

I angled to the side door again. White-leaf man came inside the room.

The same man showed in the wall too.

What's wrong with my eyes?

White-leaf-wall man leaned close, and stretched his lips again, wider than I'd ever seen. His wall-face loomed humungous.

Other humans filled the room.

Instinct buzz has told me to fly away. But I'm not afraid.

They circled me.

Some came in front of me and blocked the wall.

They all bore stretched lips.

They lift their hands together and said, "Y'shua."

Each one stretched a hand at me while lifting up the other hand.

They like me.

A different sense of direction flowed from my heart to my wings.

White-leaf man made more of his peaceful noises.

Then I felt a Being—towering over human even taller than humans tower over flies.

Size matters. I can enter any building.

I leapt up and twirled, firing tiny sparks.

My eyes never close. Wherever I turn, the wall will show them what my eyes see.

I rubbed both my front legs.
The hateful faces behind danger sticks filled my head.
The room-full of humans clapped and cheered.
I serve a purpose . . . even if I'm just a fly.

* * *

"And so daughter that is your father's job." I brushed my daughter's wing.

"Dad?" She scratched her head. "Could you help me find anthers, please?"

I smiled. "Have you looked under that dirty thing you call a bed?"

"Oh." She rubbed both her front legs and leapt. "Thanks Dad."

We soared under the bright light of the hot-disk.

My green, yellow and red light glittered.

So did her mother's.

CREDO

Stephen L. Rice

"Sheep Among Wolves," the first story to feature Martin, is set about ten years after this prequel. The original story was written for a genre-bending Western anthology, where one of the examples was an undead lawman. Now, that's been done, but it suggested the idea of a "lawman" divinely appointed to deal with especially bold demonic incursions. The Heralds were born, and Martin and his faithful steed Prophet had their first adventure. "Credo" is Martin's origin story.

MARTIN STEADIED HIMSELF WHEN the carriage lurched to a stop. Todd Jaeger, sitting across from him, sneered as he looked out the window. "There is a reason 'credo' is related to 'credulous,'" he said. "When Catholics meet superstitions and miraculous nonsense, they simply say, 'Credo'—'I believe,' no matter what it is."

Martin could now see the problem: a priest had somehow stopped the carriage and wangled a ride. In fact, he was getting in just as Jaeger finished his remark.

"Please forgive my intrusion," the priest said as he sat down beside Martin's friend. "I am Father Joseph, and I must get to the harbor. It really is a matter of life or death."

"We aren't going to New York harbor," Jaeger snapped as the driver whipped up the horses.

"Neither am I," Father Joseph stated quietly. "I know where you both are bound."

"There are other carriages," Jaeger replied, and Martin thought he detected some fear in his voice. "Indeed, we should have had our own, but the axle broke not long before we left. Stupid luck."

"Perhaps it was an act of God," the priest remarked pleasantly. He added some other comment under his breath—Martin could only make out that it was in Latin—and Jaeger fell silent. In fact, if Martin had been the superstitious type, he would have thought the genial cleric had cast a spell of some kind. Of course, Martin was not the superstitious type. Yet there was something peculiar about Todd's face, which seemed frozen in a mask of rage, and Martin was about to inquire about his health when the priest addressed him.

"I know that my presence has upset your friend, Martin, but it is your reaction that concerns me more."

Martin started, and he almost asked how the man knew his name. But he was not about to concede anything to one simple enough to carry a crucifix. "I am a modern man of science, sir; I respond to facts. I have only the fact that you have boarded our coach and the assertion that it was for a good cause. That isn't much to respond to."

"I respond to truth, myself," the priest replied affably. "It is the substance; facts are merely its shadows, cast this way and that by the fleeting light of circumstance."

"Facts and truth are the same thing. There is no truth that cannot be found in a laboratory. All else is conjecture or superstition."

"Even God? Even love?"

"There is no God. As for love, it is some kind of physical phenomenon, such as Mesmer's animal magnetism. All is physical; all may be observed and predicted. That is the difference between scientific and superstitious minds."

"You believe only in what you can see?"

"Not all observation is sight. Take disease. Superstitious people think it the work of demons; medical science tells us that it is the influence of bad air, or miasma. Once we have learned how to remove such impurities, all disease will disappear—a miracle of science, not of an unverifiable God."

"You seem to argue by time," the priest observed. "Do you reject anything that isn't modern, then?"

"No. Sometimes the ancient ideas were true. For example, Dalton has recently begun arguing for atomism—the idea that all matter is made up of tiny, indivisible particles called 'atoms.' The ancient atomists of Greece knew that everything occurs by physical necessity—simple cause and effect, without divine intervention."

"I think what pleases you is the idea that there need be no god at all—that everything arose on its own. I would agree with Plato: the beauty and complexity we see require purposeful creation, not random mechanical forces. Can you think of an explanation for how plants and animals arose that does not sound as fantastic as any myth?"

"That I cannot does not make it impossible. Others are investigating the matter, and their ideas may prove true, even though I wish they wouldn't talk about 'evolution.' The word refers to the unrolling of a scroll, which invites questions about who produced, rolled, and unrolled the scroll. The whole idea just re-introduces God: the only way it could work would be by divine agency. But I am confident that ultimately modern science will find an explanation."

The priest smiled. "Of course it will. He who seeks, finds—even if what he seeks and finds are merely lies. Despite your insistence on observation, your assertion that there is no God is a personal dogma. You say 'Credo' just as I do—except that I believe whom I have experienced, while you believe what you can neither experience nor prove. Do you really suppose that by denying God's existence you can punish him for letting your grandfather die?"

"He made him die!" Martin snapped. Then he paused, flustered. Why had he said that?

"The non-existent God made your grandfather die? That seems a tall order for a myth."

Martin was silent with fury. Why wasn't Todd doing anything about this upstart? He was the best swordsman, marksman, and all-around fighter Martin had ever seen. He could easily have tossed the priest out the window and thrashed the driver for taking him aboard. But the priest was speaking again.

"Twelve years ago, when your grandfather was still alive and you loved the God you now deny, your grandfather prayed over you, and you vowed to serve the Lord in whatever way he chose. The time has come for you to fulfill your vow—if your sense of honor is greater than your hatred."

"Your God is a lie."

"Your excuse is a lie. Can you even face the truth?"

"I seek after truth."

"So be it," Father Joseph said with a rueful smile. "It is part of your calling anyway: like me, you are called to be a Herald, to proclaim the Kingdom of God to the damned and their followers, to call forth his judgment upon the outposts of evil—to hear the voice of the Almighty and relay his decrees and to know the truth of what you see."

The carriage rattled to a stop, and Martin finally noticed the sea air and gull cries. Todd roused from his stupor, and his mask of ferocious rage melted into an equally terrible grin. But the priest continued speaking, though more swiftly now.

"Henceforward you shall hear the voice of God and obey his commands—your only hope and that of every man. But you shall also see the truth that hides behind the beautiful façade of evil. Like every truth, this shall rescue you if you believe and damn you if you turn to the lie. The Lord has spoken!"

Something happened like the rapid clearing of a mist, and the authority in the voice opened Martin's ears as well as his eyes. The horror of the thing sitting beside the priest sent Martin scrambling from the coach and into the arms of things he dared not believe in or deny.

"What should we do with this one, Master Jaeger?" one of Martin's skeletal captors asked.

"Since the ship has put in, we may as well avail ourselves of its brig.

I am sure that no one on board will object. Take the priest, and bind that young man too—for his own safety," Todd purred. Then he approached his friend and said, "I am sorry about this, Martin. But you remember what Socrates advised in *The Republic*: when a man is insane, it is not just to give him his own weapon back, lest he harm someone. This is just. You shall understand soon."

"It was Plato who wrote that," Martin muttered, "just as he wrote that when a man emerges from darkness to light, those still in darkness will discount what he sees by saying he has gone blind."

"So you trust your eyes. How childish." Todd turned abruptly to the ghastly beings holding Martin. "Lock them both up while I see my sister and find out how she enjoyed her passage."

The ship was large, as it had to be to make the crossing from Europe. Had there been any outsiders watching the boats row out to meet it, they might have wondered how such a vessel came to be moored in a small rural harbor rather than at one of New York's docks. The insiders already knew the answer, and Martin strove to find a purely physical explanation for all he saw as he was taken from shore to ship to brig. What manner of beings were her crew?

"Do you believe now?" the priest asked as soon as they were alone.

"I don't know," Martin admitted. "Saying 'Credo' is easy for you; I'm afraid that like Thomas, 'Dubito' is more in my nature. But one of the things that has drawn me to science is the way it shines light on something I haven't understood. I find myself wondering how I could have failed to see the truth before. This is uncomfortably like that."

"It is a start. But you must believe—and you must repent. God warned your grandfather, but he was too determined to save the girl from the fire."

"And is he damned for being a hero?"

"He is dead because he did not heed a warning. His eternal state has nothing to do with that, but obedience is better than any sacrifice."

"Still chatting, I see," Todd said as he entered the room. "How tedious. I should have told those fools to stuff a rag in the papist's mouth."

"What have you done to the people on this ship?" Martin demanded.

"I? *I* have done nothing to them. I do regret that we came to this part of your education so abruptly. Father had envisioned a smoother transition."

"Transition to what?"

"To the next step, Martin: the next part of your scroll. It is evolution after all. Religion is wrong about many things, but the idea of transcendence is true. Most never go beyond the world of their senses, but some, like you, can understand the unseen without making supersti- tious assumptions about it. Mesmerism is only the beginning: some of us have discovered a whole world outside the range of normal senses. You mentioned what Plato wrote about the cave. The people chained up inside cannot directly see the world, only shadows of things pass- ing by the cave's mouth. But it is we—my Father and I, and others like us—who have broken our chains and gotten outside to see what truly makes those shadows. What you now see is only the initial glare that this terrified religious savage never ventured past. He shows others what frightened him away, hoping it will do the same to them."

"Then how do you explain what I see? If it is at all the truth, I want no part of it."

"Don't you? Remember our anatomy lessons? How horrible the various parts look when brought out of their natural place! But con- tained in a living body, they are necessary and good. Would you forego having a body simply because someone showed you some of the less presentable organs beforehand?"

"It isn't the same thing. Shall I tell you what I see when I look at you? I used to laugh silently when your father called you 'Tott' with his heavy German accent. It sounded like the German 'Tod': 'death.' But now I see that it was his joke all along: 'Todd Jaeger'—'Death Hunter.' You've not only hunted it, you have found it—and it has possessed you. I never used to believe in possession, but I do now. There are too many things that fall into place for me to dismiss this vision."

"Then by all means, let us try another vision." Todd turned and called, "Desdemona, come talk to him. He always listened to you."

Martin closed his eyes, unwilling to see what she would look like now. But some instinctive terror would not let him leave himself de- fenseless. He glanced quickly through eyelids barely ajar—and stared wide-eyed.

There was no apparent difference; she looked much the same as she had before, only perhaps a little more slender. She always had a delicate form, but he knew it concealed great strength for one of the weaker sex. What else did it hide?

"I can't see her properly," he called.

"You are looking with your heart, not your spirit," Father Joseph said. "Believe in what God shows you."

"Believe in me," Desdemona said, and he caught scent of her per- fume. It was almost the same as the one she had always used, but he de- tected some slight difference. He cast about in his mind, but no answer came—at least not from that source.

But if thine eye be evil, thy whole body shall be full of darkness. If therefore the light that is in thee be darkness, how great is that darkness!

Martin knew it was from the Bible—something Jesus had said, in fact. He had only read the Bible through a few times, though his grandfather had read large portions to him long ago. Where had the quotation been all these years?

Martin did not know, but he did know it was a clue. He looked into Desdemona's eyes—those deep, dark eyes he had so loved. The eye is the window of the soul, but when there is no soul to look into, only the Abyss looks back—bottomless pits like the vacant sockets of a skull. A fear beyond reason seized him, and he turned away, his chains rattling. He knew now what was different about her perfume: it was like those used in hospitals to conceal the stench of death. *Miasma.*

"Am I so horrible to look upon?" Desdemona's melodic voice asked.

The simple answer was yes, but Martin felt he owed her more than that. If there was indeed still something human within her frame, he had to seek it. Would it not come forth for him?

"What you have become is not what I once knew and loved."

"What did you know and love? Only an appearance, and it is another appearance that frightens you now. You see death, but it is only the chrysalis. Is not the butterfly more beautiful than the shell where it came fully alive?"

"There is no life in you—no natural life. Were you really like this always?"

"It was my destiny as it is yours. Your spirit was made for greater things—to know a life and power unlike any the people here can imagine. Embrace your future, Martin."

"That is not my future."

"Well, we won't let you return to your past," Todd said. "Do you really want to be another lapdog for God? I thank you for delivering one Herald into our power, but we shall not let another be born here."

"You threaten me, then?"

"Why not? It was in fear and bitterness that you came to us at first—it was so easy for Father to get your idiot parents to place you in our keeping, and you so longed for consolation that you followed wherever we led. Why stop now? But if you resist, perhaps more fear and despair will bring you back. Forget about faith; we took that weapon from you long ago. We immersed you too deeply in doubt for you to believe anything without our help."

"Grandfather said faith isn't something we work up but a gift God grants."

"A gift you have denied too long to accept now. Fear will be easier, and it will lead you back where you belong." Todd swiftly unsheathed his sword and brought it down just beside Martin's left ear, the blade slicing into the timbers of the ship.

"Stop it, Martin—if you can! Only our power can free you now."

I will call upon the LORD, who is worthy to be praised: so shall I be saved from mine enemies.

"Lord, forgive me and save me from my enemies," he prayed. He wasn't sure whether it was silent or out loud, nor did he care. But neither did he know whether he believed a single word of it.

"Believe, Martin," Father Joseph called. "It is the true way of power."

Martin turned to face his former friend, and he found he could actually look him in what should have been his eyes. The creature faltered briefly, then cried defiantly, "So be it! Can you find your faith before my sword finds its mark?"

Martin watched as the thing brought its sword back for a two-handed downward slash. Then something deep inside him welled up and out.

"Credo!"

The sword flashed down, only to be blocked by the iron shackle on Martin's wrist. How or when he had ripped loose from the chain, he did not know. He also could not imagine how he had blocked the blow one-handed—the impact should have shattered his wrist even through the iron. But not only did he feel no discomfort, he found that he had pulled his other hand free as well. He spun away from Todd's second swing.

"Credo tibi, Domine! Conserva servum tuum—" Claws slashed before his eyes as Desdemona interrupted his cry for help.

"Prayer is enough," the priest said. "This is no time for Latin declamation."

Martin dodged another pair of attacks with speed and agility that he found hard to believe. He knew better than to doubt, either, for he was only just staying ahead of his former friends. "How is this possible?" he muttered as he sidestepped a thrust that nearly impaled Desdemona.

"Your strength and speed—all your abilities—are whatever they must be to accomplish your mission," Father Joseph replied. "Don't worry about physics and physiology; this is spiritual."

"Well, I can't dodge forever."

"How true," Todd replied. He glanced at his sister. "Kill the priest. He annoys me."

Martin was only briefly relieved to have a single attacker, for Todd began a flurry of slashes like a windmill in a tempest. "What now?" Martin called, retreating toward the forward bulkhead.

"Faith is breathing in," Father Joseph replied. "Obedience is breathing out. Breathe, Martin!"

He heard a scream that he hoped was not the priest's last breath.

For by thee I have run through a troop; and by my God have I leaped over a wall.

It sounded foolhardy, but he muttered under his breath, "Pareo, Domine—I obey." How he managed to run through the scything attack untouched, he did not know, and he had little idea what came next.

"Oh, very good!" Todd taunted. "Just like your grandfather used to be. Father knew the old fool would steer you to his calling; that's why we had to deal with him. He must have thought there was something in Desdemona worth saving."

Regardless of the sword Todd held poised like a scorpion's sting, Martin gasped and almost turned toward her. "The girl in the fire!" He spotted something like a poker on the floor to his right, and fury moved his hand toward it.

Be ye angry, and sin not. For the wrath of man worketh not the righteousness of God.

"Yes, Lord," Martin whispered through clenched teeth.

Rejoice not against me, O mine enemy: when I fall, I shall arise.

He didn't understand, but the next moment he was crouched down, Todd's sword extended over him, and another scream came from behind him. He rolled away to his right and sprang to his feet. Todd had withdrawn his sword, and Desdemona swayed for an instant, hand to her chest, before collapsing. A cross-shaped scar showed on her left cheek, matching the priest's crucifix.

"Why is there no blood?" Martin wondered.

For thou shalt go to all that I shall send thee, and whatsoever I command thee thou shalt speak.

"Speak, Lord, for thy servant heareth." A message came, and Martin relayed it. "Because ye have said, We have made a covenant with death, and with hell are we at agreement; when the overflowing scourge shall pass through, it shall not come unto us: for we have made lies our refuge, and under falsehood have we hid ourselves . . . your covenant with death shall be disannulled, and your agreement with hell shall not stand; when the overflowing scourge shall pass through, then ye shall be trodden down by it."

"Silence, Herald!" Todd screeched. "If I go down to Hell, at least I shall take you with me." He paused, and a terrible look came over him. "Yes! You might as well see the power you defy." He said something in a language that Martin felt sure had been old before Greek was born, and the timbers between them dissolved into a whirlpool of nothingness. "Come, Herald; defy the Abyss itself if you can."

"He made a pit, and digged it, and is fallen into the ditch which he made."

"You lie, Herald! My covenant with death and Hell stands firm. I . . ."

Todd looked down with a gasp as the wood beneath his feet splintered, and he slid toward the vortex. At the last moment, he leaped, but there was precious little to leap from. He seized the edge of the hole by Martin's feet with his left hand, his right still holding his sword.

Martin knelt down. "Let the spirit go, Todd. The bottomless pit isn't meant for men at all, but for the Devil and his angels."

"Then it is my home. 'Better to reign in—'" The wood beneath his hand gave way, and he dropped, his sword extended as if in salute. Martin fell flat, reaching out his hand, but suddenly another lay beside him, and she reached faster and farther, her fingers barely grasping her brother's. Her impetus and her brother's weight drew her over the side, but Martin seized her arm as she fell.

Whether it was the twisting of her body and of the load she tried to carry or her weakened, wounded state, her grasp on Todd failed, and Martin's physical burden became horribly lighter. She twisted still more, and he could see her face and the eyes that hadn't been there before. She looked almost like a little girl, and for an instant Martin thought he saw what had drawn his grandfather to his death years before. There had to be something salvageable behind those eyes!

"Obey, I beseech thee, the voice of the LORD, which I speak unto thee: so it shall be well unto thee, and thy soul shall live."

She seemed to wilt, and he began to draw her upward. Then she moved swiftly, and only the fact that he was abruptly and rapidly yanked back and up saved him from the fangs and claws that fell away into the blackness.

The priest set Martin down gently. "Obedience truly is better than sacrifice, Martin—especially the sacrifice of your own life."

Martin looked into the pit, which began to fade away and become oak once again. Then he turned to the priest with a question he could not ask.

"The last one out is usually the greatest deceiver, my son. Now let us be on our way—we have nearly overstayed our welcome here."

"Are they truly gone forever?"

"I doubt that was their intention, but it likely is their fate. He did not open the true Abyss: the demons have no power over that and stay as far from it as they can. But it was a demonic realm, and even the Devil's own who venture in rarely return. The creatures there are usually ravenous. Now come."

Martin followed him, but when he saw the chains still dangling from the priest's wrists, he couldn't help asking, "Did you really pull them loose?"

"Of course. Did you think you were the only one whom God grants superhuman strength?"

"Then you could have stopped them yourself?"

"No, my son. They were your mission, as you were mine."

"And the Jaegers' men and the people on board the ship—what will happen to them?"

"Some are dead, but most are alive. They will be dazed for a short time, but we should not wait for them to awaken. The power God grants us is primarily against demonic forces."

Martin tried to break the shackles from his wrists as they descended to the boat that had brought them from shore. He failed: the iron was like iron now, and he could not budge it to save his life. "Credo," he muttered as he tried again—with no better result.

Father Joseph chuckled. "It's a response to grace, not a spell. We do not imitate the damned and their minions. You only have the strength to carry out your mission, nothing more. There is a small smithy at the orphanage where we shall stay, and we can get these irons off soon enough with a little effort. Our Lord is a great believer in work: he came as a carpenter, not as a scribe."

They rowed to shore in silence. Then the priest set out at a brisk pace through the woods, and Martin realized they wouldn't be riding to the orphanage. He would have to get a horse somewhere. Once he got back home, he would—

"You must understand that there is now no return," Father Joseph observed as if reading his thoughts. "Herr Jaeger certainly knows by now what has happened—human science has yet to devise a means of communication as fast as demons—and you are already branded a murderer. Your past is gone; only your future remains."

"But something must be done about Jaeger!"

"It will be, perhaps even by one or both of us. But right now you need time to rest and get to know our Lord better before you venture out again."

"And when will that be?"

"Only God knows. Most of our work involves prayerful preparation. Like any servant of God, we participate in his story through the adventures he sends us every day. It is learning to recognize the adventures that is hard, but that too will come with time."

Martin trudged on, trying to accept the end of his past and the beginning of his future. Already reflexive doubts were rising up. "It's impossible!" he muttered to himself. "What now, Father? If I am to hear your voice, what is your message for me now?"

If thou canst believe, all things are possible to him that believeth. And straightway the father of the child cried out, and said with tears, Lord, I believe; help thou mine unbelief.

Martin bowed his head under the weight of his tears. "Credo, Patre."

CHOSEN OF GOD

Andrea and Adam Graham

In the intervening years between "Frozen Generation" and "Chosen of God," the Emperor executed his former American govenor and replaced him with Donovan the Steward, a young, charismatic political prodigy groomed for office since childhood. Also set during the time of the Empire, "Chosen of God" follows Azura's now full-grown son, A.L. Snyder, as he struggles to overcome the stigma of a disadvantaged youth and find his place in the world.

"COME ON IN TO Snyder's Casino, the best place to gamble without going to Reno. Come on in to Snyder's Casino."

Snyder put his feet up on the chips counter. He could listen to that all night. The dancing girl quit after a mere two hours of singing that, so now he just played a loop from his radio ad. That had been a calculated risk—Idaho had a law against gambling.

He puffed on his cigar. Not much of a smoker; the cigar just projected the right image.

The sheriff sauntered in. "Got my money?"

Most in these parts had a superstition against the international currency, or rather that trading in it required a computerized ID tag embedded in the right wrist. Irrational or not, who could resist the big bucks available tax-free on the underground market?

He pulled out a pile of silver from beneath the desk and slid it across the counter. "Here."

The sheriff pocketed the archaic currency. "Mind if I play a few?"

"Sure." Snyder opened his drawer and handed the sheriff fifty red chips. "First fifty dollars is on the house." He'd have his silver back before dawn.

Thank God Mama Borden still lived in Boise. He'd disappointed her enough without the casino. Still, for a high school dropout who chose enlisting over the pen—and got court-martialed three years ago to boot—he hadn't done half bad. Most twenty-two-year-olds he knew were up to their noses in debt and bussing tables, or something equally glamorous.

Chico ran in. "Boss, someone outside wants to see you."

"Tell them to come in."

Chico frowned. "He refused to enter a place that hires Spics."

Snyder reached under the counter and grabbed his old friend Colt.

The scent of fear poured from Chico. "Hey, Boss, you promised your old woman—"

"—I'll try and be peaceful." Snyder slipped the gun inside his coat. "But it doesn't hurt to be prepared to speak a language he'll understand."

Out on the porch, Snyder approached a White man with a handle bar mustache, and a permanent scowl chiseled on his brow.

The bigot folded his arms. "You A.L. Snyder?"

Snyder took a puff from his cigar. "If you've got magazines, I'm not interested. If you've got religion, ditto. If you're running for office, I like the people we've got. They're willing to take a gamble."

"I'm Hal Specter, Chairman of Citizens for a Better Moscow."

Idaho's worst. Those racist animals would've left Snyder in slavery rather than let a Black woman carry a White boy to term. "Good for you."

"I'm concerned about the undesirables in your employ."

Snyder set his jaw. Hal wouldn't be so polite if he knew about Mama Borden. "I've never hired you."

Hal glanced through the glass door at Chico. "I'm talking about these minorities. Moscow is proud to be a place of White Heritage."

Snyder blew cigar smoke in Hal's face. He put out his cigar in Hal's pocket. "Send my regards to the rest of the committee."

Hal took a swing, but Snyder kicked Hal in the stomach, knocking him to the ground. He punched Hal in the face and placed his knee near Hal's privates. "Everybody whined about me and my men running a gang. Said to do something with our lives. Well, we've done it, and now you're whining about that. Get off my property before I call the police."

Hal smirked. "So, they can arrest me for disturbing your illegal casino's peace?"

Snyder waved at the door. "The sheriff's inside. So's the judge."

He released Hal. "Have a nice day and thanks for coming by. Don't come back again soon."

Snyder walked down the street outside his casino, humming his jingle. So what if Mama Borden wouldn't approve? He'd still proved himself more than a thug. " . . . *the best place to gamble without going to Reno. Come on in to Snyder's Casino.*"

A woman screamed.

Snyder whirled. Inside a parked car, a man with stringy hair had climbed on an Asian girl. She wore the form-fitting, semi-transparent mini-jumper required by law for female slaves in both public and private harems. This unfortunate girl must be in the former. Snyder ran for the car.

The guy called the girl a foul name and slapped her across the face. Snyder opened the car door, pulled the jerk out, and threw him to the ground. The jerk stood and glared. "Who do you think you are?"

The toughest man alive. "What do you think you were doing?"

"Just having a good time."

"Maybe you are. I don't think the lady agrees."

"Who cares? I got her from Francis Baker's."

Snyder smirked. The local public harem, all right. "So, you a pedophile, or a loser who has to pay to get a woman?"

"Why you!" The idiot charged.

Snyder took a step back and extended his leg.

The idiot sprawled on the pavement. Snyder jumped on his back. The idiot stood, trying to buck Snyder off. Snyder squeezed his arm around the jerk's throat. He gasped, coughed, and fell again.

"Had enough?" Snyder asked.

The jerk wheezed. "Please, let go."

Snyder released his grip and stood. "You got your money's worth; now get out of here."

Snyder reached into the car and took the girl's hand. "Come on."

She climbed out. Snyder let go, but walked her past the guy struggling to get up. Snyder shook his head. "How many guys do I have to beat up tonight?" He turned to the girl. "What's your name?"

"Li."

"How old are you, Li?"

"Over fifteen."

Snyder arched an eyebrow. A practiced response. Only pedophiles rented or purchased female slaves that hadn't turned fifteen. Her eyes backed her story, but why didn't she want to give her age? "Do you take appointments?"

Li blinked. "Appointments?"

"Walking around is no way to get business. If I walked down the street trying to carry a casino, do you think anyone would come in?"

An aborted giggle tugged at Li's lips. "Suppose not."

"Meet me at the casino at eleven tomorrow morning. But first: how old are you, really?"

"Nineteen."

He clucked his tongue. No wonder. The average slave lived to thirty, but most harem girls wouldn't see twenty-one unless a private buyer stepped in. "See you then."

Li slipped out of her room, gulped, and approached Francis Baker's desk. He looked up. "Yes, Li?"

She clasped her hands. "No more clients tonight, please. I have an appointment tomorrow."

Baker arched his eyebrow. "Appointment?"

"Yes." A strange flutter stirred in her chest. "The casino owner."

Baker laughed. "So, A.L. Snyder's a good old fashioned hypocrite. He fires his people if they touch you girls. But, where would our business be without hypocrites? I'll notify Father Benalli. He should get over it."

Li took a seat on the couch to avoid the customer still occupying her room. Forget Benalli; Colonel Dread lived up to his name. And owned her future.

Unless she pleased Snyder . . .

Something in those sea-green eyes said he might be the buyer she'd begged the Heavens for. His dark-blond, GI-Joe-in-khakis look usually spelled danger, yet he remained as beautiful as Dread terrible.

Li's lips curled upward and her heart skipped a beat. What would it be like in Snyder's arms?

She jumped a little. When had she ever asked such a question?

Dread marched out from her room. "I had a good time, Baker, but I always do with Li. Now, she's almost reached that age where you ship the girls to Miami to work in your brother's retirement community. That had better not happen."

"No, worries, Colonel. I'll never sell her to my brother as long as she pleases you."

Snyder stood at the cyber café's entrance off the casino lobby. Once Li entered, he sat at the nearest terminal. "If you don't mind, my shoulders are stiff."

Her footfalls tinkled over. Delicate fingers worked into his lash-toughened muscles. Warmth spread over him. Maybe she . . .

He gulped. Only monsters took advantage of a girl who couldn't refuse. He couldn't afford to fall into lust—or the other L-word. "Good enough, you can bill me now." Snyder ran his tag across Li's right hand.

Li stared. "Is that all? You've never done this before, have you?"

"Never touched a girl that had a price tag on her, but I do want to spend more time with you, if you don't mind."

"Oh, well, Baker bills by the hour."

Warmth spread over his cheeks; she still thought he wanted to take advantage of her. She'd learn otherwise soon enough. If all went according to plan, he'd rescue her, all right—but *without* losing his heart. "I want the whole day."

"But, I'm $75 an hour."

Snyder pulled up his computer, interfaced his payment system, and brought up the global link. Shelling out $600 didn't appeal much, but his stint in army intelligence taught him, among other useful tricks, how to hack the "unhackable."

Using his talents always required caution. Best-case scenario, privacy would become a luxury if the army realized what a mistake they made in discharging him. Worst case scenario, his commander-in-chief would once again look the other way, while Donovan the Steward's commander-in-chief—Emperor Herald—hanged Snyder.

His eight favorite enemies had huge debts, though, and wouldn't notice $75 missing. With the tap of a few keys, they paid Li's price.

Snyder whirled around and glanced up at Li. "I'd like you to wear a special costume. It's in the bathroom." He eyed her. She'd pull it on over the jumper. "And take that off, unless the undergarments don't fit."

She returned in the silky pink dress, with a shy sparkle in her eyes. He grinned—the undergarments fit. "Let's get lunch."

After sharing a steak dinner for two at a little place in Lewiston, he took her to a florist shop and bought her flowers.

She stared at the roses. "Why are you doing this?"

He hesitated. Andy. But mentioning he had a brother in her condition would make things too personal. "My mother told me what you people go through. When I saw you in that car . . . I thought you deserved to be treated decent."

"That's very . . ." Li bit her lip. "I don't know the word. You're different from the others, especially Colonel Dread. What are you? You're not cruel, you're—"

"Is it kind?"

She blinked. "What's that?"

Oh boy. "If you're willing to set up more appointments, maybe I can teach you."

Pink tinted Li's olive cheeks. "I'd like that."

"Something's wrong with Li!"

Baker cringed within at Colonel Dread's outburst, but just folded his hands on his desk. "What's the problem?" Li brought in more business than ever, even if she didn't make as much per transaction.

"She acts totally uninterested. That's not the customer service I've come to expect. Maybe she's working too hard."

He could fix this—and earn enough to buy half a dozen of the clearance-aisle kiddies the breeders sold for a fraction of the asking price on the street. "I understand your concern. For a limited time, I can offer you Li at an unbelievably low price. Such a fine concubine sells for $20,000, but for a long-time customer, and member of the Imperial Armed Forces, I'm prepared to offer her for $12,000. I'll even throw in an extended health care warranty and a guarantee for 2000 inter-courses."

Dread shook his head. "My wife's too closed-minded and divorce too costly."

Baker forced surprise into his expression. "What a shame! I'd be glad to board her here for only $800 a month."

"Lovely. Let me sell my rental property. I think not. I'll pay an extra $600 a month to limit her other clients to 4 hours a day."

Sure, that'd only cost Baker $3000 a month. "How about $10,000 and $300 a month for boarding?"

Colonel Dread leaned across the desk. "How about I report that you're renting privately-owned concubines to the public?"

"Half a day then."

While Snyder waited with Li for their food at a local restaurant, Li read aloud from the classic novel he'd used to teach her to read. A smile tugged at his lips. She'd come such a long way in nine months. He sat on his hands to keep from hugging her. "Good work, Li."

Her eyes met his, confusion and longing intertwined in her glance.

A waitress whisked their food on the table.

His breath rushed out. Just in time. Little else could distract him from how wonderful her lips would taste . . . *Stop it!*

Colonel Dread approached their table. "Pardon me."

Snyder kept his eyes on Li. The stripes on his back remembered this creep. He went straight from the flogging post to send a complaint to the Steward's senatorial office. Funny how reporting abusive COs to their commander-in-chief got a guy drummed out of the army.

Dread cleared his throat. "Excuse me."

Snyder flashed a mocking grin at the stewing CO. "Hey, Colonel, haven't seen you since you court-martialed me."

"I remember; you're the private from JD who refused to enter a public harem and thought insubordination a joke. Are you aware this female belongs to Francis Baker?"

Every head in the restaurant turned.

Snyder stood, his fists clenched at his sides. "This woman is my date. We can take this outside, if you're man enough."

Dread stared. "I was making a statement."

Seems Dread chose to forget I'm the one soldier he can't scare half to death.

"So am I. You're less than a man. His Highness should rid himself of fairies like you in his service."

Dread turned purple. "You'll pay for that."

Snyder punched his palm. "Let's collect."

Dread shook his head. "Colonels don't fight in the street. We get our dues other ways. Enjoy your rental, Civilian."

Snyder glanced at Li. The rivers running down her cheeks knifed him. He put an arm around her and kissed her tears away.

Snyder sat on the couch, listening to Mama Borden play the piano in her apartment at the retirement home. He held back the tears. Men didn't cry, particularly men with grandmothers who named them Annunciation and mothers who shortened it to Anny.

At least she'd be happy. Mama Borden inherited him from his grandmother in time to forbid him from dating outside his race. Now that she couldn't stop him, it figured someone else would put the girl off-limits. He sniffled against the tears threatening to steal past his control.

Mama Borden turned from the piano. "Anny, what's wrong?"

He hung his head. "I fell in love."

Mama Borden grabbed her cane and hobbled over. "That'd explain you 'just stopping by.' She dump you?"

Snyder shook his head. "Women don't dump me, I dump them."

"So, you dumped her?"

"Her owner forbade me from seeing her."

"Her owner?"

"She's a slave. I never touched her. I just—" He bit his fist. No crying. Wusses named Anny cried. Not ex-GIs named Snyder.

Mama Borden pulled his fist away. "Let it out, Anny."

Tears flowed down his cheeks. "To start, I wanted to teach her to respect herself, to show her a way out. Then . . . I just wanted to make her happy. I even dreamed . . ."

Mama Borden patted his back. "Anny, for years, your only concern has been you. She's brought out love in you, and you can't let that die; you can't let her go."

Her tune might change if she ever met Li. "What can I do?"

Mama Borden stood. "I didn't want babies to die, and I found a way to stop it. It wasn't legal, but I found a way."

"I offered Baker $40,000 and he turned me down. I could just take her, but I wouldn't want her to live on the run. If Baker didn't have her title—" Snyder sat back. "Maybe he won't."

Snyder sat at the chips counter. Francis Baker sauntered up, his smile too broad. "I appreciate you lifting the ban on your employees doing business with me."

"No problem. The referrals will make us both wealthier." Snyder opened his drawer. "Here, on the house." He handed Baker $1,000 in chips. "Remember, we're serving free drinks." Drunk players made him far more than he lost at the bar.

Tonight, he made an exception about not rigging games. Francis Baker won $60,000 on slot machines, roulette and keno.

Once Baker took his money to the poker table, Snyder pulled the poker dealer aside. "Man the bar. Keep an eye on Baker's beer mug. If it's half empty, send another."

Snyder looked up. One more exception couldn't hurt. "Heavenly Father, give me the right hands. Amen."

On the first hand, Snyder lost $20,000. On the second, $15,000.

Baker laughed. "Never knew I could be this hot."

Snyder dealt a third hand. "I'll bet $10,000."

Baker hiccupped and pushed his whole pile to the center. "I'll raise you $85,000."

"I'll raise you the casino's title."

The pianist stopped on a sharp note. All eyes turned to Snyder.

Baker said, "I'll see that with $15,000 and call."

Snyder put down his cards. "Four twos."

Baker slapped down his cards and snorted, scowling.

A full house. A good hand, but not as good as four of a kind. "Not bad. You almost took my business. Don't let one loss discourage you."

"You're right. Deal me another."

"Sure." Snyder turned to a waiter. "Get Mr. Baker another drink."

Two hours later, Baker scrunched up his drink-reddened face. "I know I can come back; I just don't have any money left."

Or a car, either. So far, all had gone according to plan. "You could bet your business. You just hit a run of bad luck."

Baker wrinkled his forehead. "What will you put up?"

Snyder pushed forward $300,000 in poker chips and Baker's car keys. "Everything."

Baker sent him a drunken grin. "You're on."

Snyder dealt the hands. Baker took a card, and so did Snyder.

Baker laid down his cards, the three, four, five, six, and seven of spades. "Straight flush!" Baker reached for the chips.

Snyder waved his index finger. "Not yet." He spread out his cards. "Royal flush."

Baker collapsed.

Snyder set him back in his chair. "Louie! Get some smelling salts."

Louie obeyed and waved the inhaler under Baker's nose.

Baker sat up. "I dreamt I gambled away my entire personal account and my business."

Snyder waved the title to Baker's building.

Baker covered a gasp. "I did."

"If an outdoor house of ill-repute isn't appealing, you could trade me Li's title."

Baker sighed. "You win."

Outside the courthouse, Snyder shook his head at Mama Borden's crossed arms and stiff posture. Still fuming over Li's Asian heritage, or maybe because they weren't getting married in church. No time for that. He'd signed the paperwork "making" Li a person, but Frances might try suing to revoke it. A marriage license made that near impossible.

Snyder glanced back to his bride. Somehow, it didn't matter one lick that she hadn't been in a position to refuse his proposal.

The judge said, "I now pronounce you wedded spouses."

Snyder grabbed Li and kissed her full on the lips.

Li gasped. "You never kissed me like that before."

"You never could slap me if you didn't like it. You do, don't you?"

She grabbed him and kissed him, sending his blood pumping.

He pulled back, breathing heavy. Oh, man, he couldn't wait to get his bride alone . . .

Mama Borden walked over. The grumble in her eyes denied the smile. Snyder touched her shoulder. "Mama Borden, you accepted me even though I'm not Black. Please accept Li. I love her."

Mama Borden turned to Li. "Be good to my Anny."

Li blinked. "Anny?"

Mama Borden laughed. "Annunciation Leslie Snyder."

Li gasped and covered a giggle. "No wonder. How unfortunate."

Snyder's face grew hot. Li patted his cheek. "Don't worry. I love you even if your mother does call you Anny."

Snyder glanced at Mama Borden. *Please.*

She hugged Li. "I'll love you, daughter."

Baker hid under his desk. Like that would do any good.

A firm hand grabbed him by the shirt and dragged him out.

Dread's breath blew hot in his face. "Where is she?"

Baker swallowed. "I lost her playing poker with Snyder."

"You gambled away my Li! I'll get her back. I'll force Snyder to give me her title."

Baker swallowed hard. "She doesn't have one."

Dread turned red. "What?"

"Snyder married her."

The red gave way to purple. "Are your girls home?"

Baker nodded.

Dread pulled out his revolver. "Then it will be easy to liquidate the business." He fired at Baker.

Everlasting darkness consumed him.

Snyder sat with his men around his boardroom table. "Gentlemen, it's time we moved in a less risky direction."

Louie chewed on a piece of straw. "But the cops are on our side."

"Not the state patrol. It's time we cashed out and bought legitimate businesses."

"Like what?"

"Theaters, restaurants. Anything successful. We'll still live large, but we won't have to worry about paying bribes or getting arrested."

Chico folded his arms. "Why do you want to change?"

Snyder spread his hands like the Steward did on TV. "Guys, I'm a married man. I can't take these risks. Li needs security."

Roger stood. "If you want out, take a quarter mill. We'll buy you out. We haven't become soft."

Snyder leapt up and marched over to Roger. This time, his spread hands invited war, not peace. "You think I'm soft, come take me."

Bill jumped between them. "Wait. Roger, where would you be without Snyder?"

Roger puffed out his chest. "Doing fine."

"Bull! You'd be in your dad's junkyard, and he'd be beating you nightly if Snyder hadn't let you in the gang. We all owe him big. I'd like to settle down someday. Let's try it."

Roger deflated. "Sorry, Snyder."

Snyder patted Roger's shoulder. "It's okay, man. The casino's not closing overnight. I brought along ads of Boise businesses for sale. Let's choose half a million worth. Once we turn a profit on our investment, we'll get rid of the casino."

The men nodded.

Snyder took a note from Li off the fridge.

"Went to visit Mama Borden before she leeves town. Be back at nine tonite." Her spelling needed work.

They must've lost track of time. Mama Borden wasted no time converting Li. Funny how she'd rather he live amongst his own race, even if it meant letting his grandmother raise him a "heretic," something he once overheard her call Catholics.

The clock on the microwave caught his eye. Three a.m.?

At Mama Borden's hotel, he jumped from the car and took the stairs to the third floor three steps at a time. He knocked on her door. No answer. He pounded louder. No answer. He flashed the key Mama Borden gave him and barged in.

Snyder gasped. Mama! She lay on the floor, covered in blood. Some monster had mutilated her face and arms.

Her remaining eye opened. "Anny!"

Snyder knelt beside her. "Mama. Who did this?"

"White man."

"Ninety-six percent of town is White! Who did this?"

"Soldier. Big, with an eagle on his helmet. Jesus." Her eye closed.

An eagle. A colonel. Where was Li?

He stood and gasped. Trembling, he crossed to the bed and covered her mutilated, naked body. Tears ripped through him and shoved him to his knees.

The next day, Snyder reread his statement in the sheriff's office. The sheriff hung up the phone. "The coroner's report backs your theory."

Funny how hanging traitors had seemed the preferable of two archaic practices the Empire revived. "Get Dread. Send him back to Europe; he deserves beheading."

The sheriff shook his head. "If we pursue this, Dread would find an excuse to hang you, me, or even the whole department."

Snyder's jaw dropped. "He can get away with murder?"

"Can, has, and does. You've learned a hard lesson, son. Don't cross him again."

Fury trembled up Snyder's spine. Bad enough Dread laid stripes on his back without cause and no one cared, but this . . . that bloodthirsty nut would rue ever hearing, "Private Snyder reporting for duty, Sir!"

Snyder stood alone at Li's graveside. Nearby, the Bordens amassed around Mama's grave. A hand clamped on his shoulder.

Colonel Dread offered a plastic smile. "My condolences."

Not now. Snyder flashed back a razor-sharp smile. "Some fairy did it, I'm sure."

Dread sneered. "She was so young."

"Yeah. Quite a tragedy, Colonel."

"I'll leave you with your colorful family." Dread walked away, but stopped at his Humvee and flashed Snyder a wicked smile.

Snyder headed for Mama Borden's firstborn. More father than brother, Cerulean never left room for wondering about who fathered him and Andy. His brother he never stopped wondering about. Someday, Snyder would find Andy and free him.

But first, Dread would pay.

Cerulean met Snyder halfway and embraced him. "I'm sorry, Son."

"I know who did this. We can get him."

Cerulean shook his head. "He who lives by the sword will perish by the sword."

Snyder snorted. "Thanks for the cliché, but I need justice. After all Mama did for us, avenging her is the least we can do for her."

Cerulean stiffened. "Don't get uppity with me, Anny. I'm the only Borden who considers you family. Now, listen, Son. Don't waste your life on vengeance."

"They took my life! All that's left is getting Colonel Dread."

"Don't forget the widow of Sidon. She gave up all she had left to feed the prophet Elijah, and God gave—"

"Cut the sermon! Are you gonna help or not?"

"I can't."

"Forget you!" By now, he had all the Bordens staring at him. What hypocrites. "All of you!"

Snyder marched down the sidewalk. Whoever succeeded Dread would unleash fury on Moscow, Idaho. The whole battalion had to die.

He'd whipped tail and even mugged a few people in his wild days with the gang, but he'd never killed. How could he justify this?

Snyder came upon a brick house with people flooding in. Weird. Too clean cut for a party and no Bibles.

The old man herding the crowd pointed at him. "Snyder, right? I heard what happened. Come in. You have the right to know."

Know what? Snyder followed the old man inside, then downstairs into a basement. He sat in the folding chair nearest the exit.

The old man stood before the crowd. "Today's video is banned by the Empire, the usurper of our constitution, whose steward is the puppet master pulling the strings of all three branches of our government. You must swear to never reveal where you saw this."

Puppet master? Maybe, but wouldn't the government collapse without the Steward to make peace between the warring fractions?

Once they had sworn secrecy, the old man pulled on a red, white, and blue cape. "Welcome to the Order of Patriots. Today, we'll hear from the forbidden one, Ronald Reagan."

They played a video of a speech in which Reagan assaulted 20th Century Russia as "The Evil Empire."

Snyder gasped—it wasn't just Dread! All who served the Empire, served Evil. Even nice guys like him, ignorant of the Empire's true nature, or perhaps turned a blind eye to it and went along to gain position. Like the Steward.

Even if His Highness lived up to half the nation's hopes once his crazy old man croaked, how many Mama Bordens and Li's would die in the meantime? If the Steward really deserved the messiah treatment, Dread would have the dishonorable discharge—and Mama Borden and Li would be alive. Evil didn't need reasoned with. It needed destroyed.

At the video's end, the old man turned off the set. "So, we'll meet back next week."

Snyder stood. "Excuse me. What are you doing?"

"Adjourning."

"I understand that. What I don't understand is why. Gentlemen, we're ruled by an evil empire. They murder our families and force innocent children into slavery and prostitution. They take our land, our freedom, and our very lives."

His audience nodded. Snyder grinned. "Are we patriots if we only talk about abuses? This evil lives among us and we must destroy it."

He paused. The nuns who mistook boredom for stupidity would never guess he still had portions of his textbooks memorized. "In the Second Amendment, our founding fathers reserved the people the right to take up arms and form a militia should tyranny ever again find our shores. Brothers, will you sit around and complain as slaves to the crown, or will you stand and fight as freemen of this great republic?"

Silence fell.

The men rose and cheered.

The old man stepped forward. Ancient eyes bored into Snyder. "Son, how bad do you want to take down the Empire?"

"On Mama Borden's grave, whether a thousand go with me or none, I will not rest until the Empire is destroyed, or my carcass hangs in the public square, so help me God."

"If you take this road, it will cost you all that remains, even the deepest desire of your heart. Living by the sword has a price. If you don't pay it, another will."

Andy. Snyder closed his eyes. *Keep your head down, bro. The Empire will kill you if I don't find you first.*

Snyder faced the ancient seer. "That's a risk I'll have to take."

"All right. If it's an army you want, it's an army you'll get." The seer removed a vial from his cloak and smeared oil on Snyder's forehead. "In the name of the God of our fathers, I commission you as the Commander over the Freemen of the Army of the Republic and grant you the rank of Colonel."

Another cheer rose.

Warmth tingled over Colonel Snyder. God chose him? After his failures? His rebellion? His faithlessness? How could that be?

The seer wiped his damp eyes. "I've waited decades for you." His face fell. He sighed. "Son, the Lord says to take care, lest you lift your hand against His anointed. The enemy has him now, but in the fullness of time, the Lord *will* open His Anointed's eyes. The Lord chose you to defend His anointed, not to slay him."

Lovely. A riddle. Not to mention treason. But if this be treason, blessed be traitors. "Taking down Colonel Dread's battalion won't be easy, but we can do it."

The seer's eyes flashed. "Don't change the subject. You must obey this word. Promise me you'll defend the Lord's Anointed."

"Okay, I promise." Snyder cleared his throat. "Now, recruit as many men as possible. Anyone against the Empire is with us and free to join up. But first . . ." He held up his tagged wrist. "Cut this bloody thing out of me or I swear I'll do it myself."

Smoke rose behind Snyder as he marched down Dread's driveway. He pocketed his lighter next to Dread's car keys.

He couldn't treat Dread like Mama Borden and Li had been treated. Only a bloodthirsty nut would. Still, it seemed fair to torture Dread with a tarantula—his greatest fear—and burn him alive.

Snyder sat on the hood of his new Humvee, lit a cigar, and listened to the Humvee's former owner's terrified screams.

Roger marched up and saluted. "Colonel Snyder, we captured 400 men. What do we do with them, Sir?"

Snyder glanced at the officer trailing behind. He wouldn't have let Hal in—if those Bordens had ever owned up to him. "Kill the officers. If the enlisted men will denounce the Empire and join us, great. Otherwise, kill them."

Roger's eyes widened. "But, Sir, they're Prisoners of War."

"And if we ever build a POW camp, I'll consider housing these animals. Until then, anyone siding with the Empire is evil and will be dealt with. Comprende, Captain?"

Roger gulped. "Sir! Yes, Sir!"

Snyder petted his Colt, holstered on his hip. Never again would innocent civilians tremble at the name Colonel Dread. Now, Evil would tremble at the name Colonel Snyder.

The Empire would rue the day it crossed him. Evil would be defeated and America would be free.

THE EDGE OF WATER

Karen McSpadden

Karen McSpadden writes fiction and poetry, with special interest in science fiction and fantasy, and has been published in several small press magazines. She lives in costal Virginia with her husband Josh and her daughter Ember. *Light At the Edge of Darkness* is her first anthology publication.

Light shines the brightest in a pitch black room. That's what I seek to create in stories such as "The Edge of Water"-- places of darkness in which men and women are stripped down right to the very core of who they are and what they believe. It's then that the truth, and the hope that we have in Christ, can shine most brightly, and once again, pierce the darkness through.

WHEN THEY PULLED JOHNNY'S body out of the river, I sat on a bench in the front room of the death house, waiting for the one-eyed woman behind the counter to call my name. If it weren't for his eighteen-story swan dive, I would have erased myself, just as Johnny did, only in a way more calculating than his leap through thin air. I once thought that I would be unable to betray Noah in that way. I was wrong. I ended up in that waiting room easily enough.

Blue-gray curls of incense drifted listlessly under a decrepit fan and sweetened the thick air. Wooden benches lined the walls, except for the back of the room where the woman scratched at her scab-covered arms while she flipped through the State newspaper. I squirmed on the bench and tried to ignore the latest round of vaccine welts that itched like fire ants crawling up my sleeve. It didn't help that my worker's uniform clung to my arms and legs like a second skin in the damp heat.

My eyes flitted between her and the old man across the room who sat rigid as a piece of lumber in his wheelchair. The only signs of life were his sandpaper breathing and the thin line of blood continually dribbling from the left corner of his mouth, which the young woman beside him wiped every few moments. I wondered how many times she had done it before, and if some part of her was relieved that she wouldn't have to do it again.

The orange card in my pocket pressed against my thigh, and I imagined the letters sinking into my skin, like a tattoo. *Notice of Selection for Central Clinic Research Project T11V, to begin 07/13/39. Departure from Terminal B at 0600. Failure to appear at Departure considered a Class I Offense. Please bring Selection Card and all current identification papers.*

The clinicals were part of the survival deal the government stuck on us after the plague outbreak, and I supposed they considered it fair trade. They gave us the vaccines that, in theory, ensured the virus stayed dormant. In return, we lived in their quarantine sectors, worked their factories, and some of us got to play lab rat every now and then. The official storyline was a search for a cure, but we all heard stories of what the bodies looked like when they were piled in the disposal trucks. The smoke from behind the complex was visible for miles. No one came back. If you tried to hide, or run, the black squads found you and carted you back, after a session or two in the silent rooms—although the name was a bit incorrect. Sometimes the screams filtered up from the sewer grates. Noah and I had survived a year, an unbelievable grace. Some people didn't last a week.

I touched the sweaty copper cross resting in the hollow of my neck, my fingers playing with the chain like a rosary. *It's not you, God, it's me. It's not that I'm ungrateful, or that You're not enough, it's that I can't die in that place. Not like that. I can't be that old man, or worse. Hey, You're the all-knowing one, you've seen what they do there. Tell Noah it's not him. It's me.*

"Next." The old woman croaked, "next please."

I walked up to the desk, pretending this was something trivial, like a hair appointment. "Anibeth Darger. I'm here for a consultation."

She adjusted her eye patch without so much as looking up from her paper. "He's in the back. Second door on the left."

I pushed through the heavy orange curtain behind her into a hall-way so narrow my shoulders brushed the walls. The door stood partly open, and the man sitting behind the desk waved me into the room.

I expected a low-budget version of the government doctors, all cold formality and lab coat starch, but this man wore a loose gray tunic shirt with the sleeves rolled back to his elbows, a damp rim of sweat around his neck. His smile flashed against his coffee-dark skin like a camera bulk. He looked more like the janitor in our building than a death mer-chant.

"You must be Anibeth." He gestured towards the chair. "A good name, although I'm sure it's not yours."

"I—"

"No cause for embarrassment. Most of our clients take some sort of precaution. The black squads do a get a bit nasty about this sort of thing. What are you really called?"

"My name—" I took a breath. I had to decide to trust him at some point."My name is Clare."

"Wonderful. I am Lucien Crowley."

"Dr. Crowley?"

"A long time ago, before all this unpleasantness. Now it is just Lucien." He took a drink from a small cobalt glass in front of him. "Would you like some tea? Iced, of course."

Business must be good if he could afford ice this time of year. He produced another glass with ice from a tiny freezer under his desk and filled it with a purple-red tea. "Arjua herb," he said. "You will find it refreshing."

The tea's sweet coolness lingered even after it slid down my throat. A soft tranquility diffused through my body, relaxing muscles I hadn't even known were tense.

"Thank you." I noticed a small painting of a beautiful angel, wings poised for flight, holding the limp body of a man. "It's beautiful," I said. "Who is it? Michael? Gabriel?"

"The Death Angel has no name," he said. "And yes, it is beautiful." He caressed the frame before he folded his hands in front of him. "I assume you have some knowledge of what we do here, but let me clarify a few things. There are a half dozen suicide mills in this sector, offering a quick and painless way out to anyone who can pay. We aren't one of those places. Death, as life, is a sacred thing." He pointed at my necklace. "You wear a cross, you understand that. God sent us Death as an instrument of mercy, and we are here to extend this mercy to those who would truly suffer should they linger. Not to those who merely want a way out. Do you understand this difference?"

"I think so."

"Good." He leaned back in his chair. "I doubt you're here due to viral complications or vaccine reactions. And you don't seem insane. I assume this has something to do with the clinic?"

I took the selection card out of my pocket, sliding it across the desk to him. My throat squeezed shut, and I forced myself to swallow the tea that seemed to congeal in the back of my throat. What if he refused? What if he accepted? *Noah would understand. You're leaving him anyway. How could he blame you for wanting to choose how? How could anyone?*

Quentin examined the card, squinting at it through a pair of spectacles. Except for the blurred noise of the street and my own nervous breathing, the room fell silent. When he'd finished, he set his glasses down, wiping a bead of sweat away from his forehead.

"You have my condolences. It seems to be a genuine selection card. I am indeed sorry, Clare." He was either very good at his job or actually sincere. "The clinics are an evil place."

"Does that mean you'll help me?" I tried to keep the quiver out of my voice, but my hands shook as I dug in my purse to find the roll of hard currency I'd taken from the stash behind our stove. "I have money, I can pay."

"We'll take care of that on the day of your appointment. Just bring what you can." He stood. "Follow me to the front and I'll have Belinda set up an appointment, a day or two before the clinicals start. You'll want some time to say goodbye and settle affairs."

I followed him down the hallway to the old woman's desk, where she produced a grimy calendar and wrote my name in one of the blocks. July 14th. A churning started in my stomach. Perhaps my face grayed a little as well, because Lucien set his hand on my shoulder. "You're being kind to them."

"To whom?"

"The people you're leaving behind. They don't have to suffer knowing what will happen to you in the clinics. They'll be beside you, watching you pass into comfort."

I grimaced. "Actually, I'll be coming alone."

He squeezed my shoulder, gently, and then went to address the young woman and her father.

I stumbled from the waiting room into the humid streets, trying not to think of what I'd just done. Everything was going well. I could catch the evening bus and be home before Noah got off shift; maybe I'd even have time to stop and barter for some real fruit to eat after dinner. Oranges, or plums. Something sweet. Disgust at what I'd done lurked in the back of my mind. But also relief.

*   *   *

When I walked into our flat, a note stared up at me from the scarred plastic table. *At Johnny's. Meet there.* Noah's usual precise script blurred into a barely readable scrawl. He'd been rushed. I didn't even put the oranges down, just turned and walked down the hall, toward the stairs, forcing myself not to run. I tried to convince myself I was being foolish, but a dread I couldn't quite name curled around the base of my spine like a fist that squeezed its way further and further up my back the closer I got to Johnny's flat. My breath and heart raced each other until I opened the rusted stairwell door that led to Johnny's floor and saw Noah squatting against the wall, his face in his hands. I was confused until I saw the body in front of him. Then I couldn't breathe at all.

Johnny. Oh, Noah . . .

The oranges fell from my hands as I stepped forward, staring at the body as if it would vanish if I blinked. Noah crouched beside his brother, close enough so that the edge of his tennis shoes brushed the dark blue of Johnny's uniform, as if to protect him from something. Vaccine reaction scars criss-crossed his face, but Johnny still looked too young to be lying on the floor like that. Or maybe he just looked too much like Noah. Either way, I ached.

Noah snapped his head up when I touched his shoulder, and for the first moment I wasn't sure he even recognized me. His eyes passed through me entirely, as if I weren't even there.He blinked, then reached for my hand, feeling the bones of my wrist as if testing whether or not I was solid. "I was starting to think you wouldn't make it in time."

"In time to what?"

"Say goodbye before the disposal unit comes." His voice was flat, but the muscles in his jaw were as rigid as the old man at the death house. Grief hovered over his words, mixed with an anger that stalked everything he said.

"How?" I slid down to the floor beside him. Part of me still refused to accept what I saw. The body belonged in a dream, in another dimension of space. Anywhere but right in front of my eyes.

"They pulled him out of the river this morning."

"But he doesn't work in that section, why would he—"

"He jumped."

"What?"

"From one of the buildings. They say he was dead two seconds after he hit the water. So at least he didn't—" Noah paused for a moment, and his teeth sunk into his lip. "They don't think he drowned."

An image rose in my mind of Johnny sinking into the dark water, paralyzed, still trying to breath as water filled his lungs inch by slow inch. Bile rose in the back of my throat at the thought. *Thank You for sparing him that.* Someone should've stopped this; one of us should've paid attention. We'd played cards with him just yesterday. How did we not see it coming?

The same questions they'll ask themselves about you.

Johnny didn't have my reason.

You mean your excuse.

"They brought him back here for identification." Bitterness splintered Noah's words. "Before they burn him."

"Burn him?" I knew that was how they got rid of us, but hadn't connected it to Johnny.

"What, you think they've suddenly started putting graveyards here? They're taking him to the incinerators on the next truck." He turned and spat onto the floor.

"But we can do something . . . bribe them . . . we have hard currency, we can offer them a deal."

"Wouldn't work, and you know it. You know the rules. We stay alive as long as we're useful and then we're—"

"Don't, Noah—"

"—then we're garbage." He looked down at Johnny, and the bitterness in his voice faded. "At least I brought a blanket for him. The floor here is filthy."

I pulled Noah to my chest, meaning to comfort him, but he was stiff, as if he were the one who had died.

I don't remember everything about the two hours that followed, but what I do remember I see very clearly. The blanket was too short and Johnny's boots stuck out. We didn't want them to go to scavengers so we gave them to the woman who lived next door to him. She'd once shared her rations when Johnny was sick. The disposal crew that collected the body wore blue uniforms, just like we did, and they even had the same brands on their necks, but they still picked him up and carried him out. Noah watched all of this, without speaking. When it was over, he simply turned and walked down the hall to Johnny's flat. I followed him, but whenever I tried to take his hand, he pulled away. His skin was cold. We got to the flat after the scavengers. The only furniture left was a cot and a rickety metal card table, on which sat a rusted can of baked beans and a tattered notebook opened to the last page.

I didn't get to read this until later, when I pried it from Noah's hands along with slivers of broken glass after he punched through the bathroom mirror back at our flat. I held a yellow washcloth over his knuckles and pressed it between my hands until the bleeding stopped. I couldn't stop screaming at him but then I looked down at the paper. The writing was surprisingly clear—*We are already dead. I am just making it official.*

An emptiness broke out in me that just swallowed up anything else I had to say. I could barely whisper— *does it hurt that much?* He didn't talk, but when he threw his arms around me, his arms shook.

I had the appointment card in my pocket the entire time. That made me cry, so he pulled me closer to him until my ribs hurt, trying to ease what he must have thought was grief for Johnny. I clung to him if for no other reason than to drown out the voice in my head whispering *traitor, traitor, traitor.*

"Is this how we're going out," he said, into my neck, his lips almost touching my barcode. "One at a time? We survived the plague, we survived the camps, are we just going to give up and die now?"

I kissed him. The easiest way to lie.

*   *   *

I woke after midnight, my hair wet with sweat, my body trembling from nightmares of swollen rivers in which Noah stood on the opposite bank, waiting for me to come to him. The current was too strong. In the dreams, I churned and struggled but I got nowhere; in the flashes of lightning I could see Johnny trapped under the water's surface. He was also waiting for me. I woke gasping for air. My hand brushed the damp mattress and I realized I was searching for Noah, on reflex. The bed was empty.

I sat up and saw him across the room, leaning shirtless out the window. Light from a streetlight outside flickered across his shoulders like sparks; I'd forgotten, until then, how many scars he had, how many bones jutted in sharp angles beneath his skin. I could count his vertebrae clearly. From that angle, I barely recognized him. I could've passed him on the street and not even known his name. Another thought struck me—*what is left of me for him to recognize?* I ran my hand over my cropped hair, my gaunt chest, my protruding ribcage. *Not much.*

"Thought you were asleep," he said, without turning.

"Tired of sleeping," I said. "I don't like closing my eyes. Too much behind them."

"Johnny told me he'd stopped sleeping." Noah slid back into a chair and propped his legs on the windowsill. Headlights from a passing transport truck sprayed light across the room, for a moment, and I caught a flash of his silhouette—the lines of his jaw, the lean muscles that factory work had built into his arms and chest, the white of his skin against his blue jeans that still, after everything, left me wanting him.

I am walking away from this man, whom I have claimed is beloved to me. The thought stung. *He'll be sitting here, alone, at this window, with two ghosts. And that's not enough to keep me from wishing that I too had fallen eighteen stories into a river.*

I crossed my arms over my chest and picked at the hem of my camisole. I wanted nothing more than to lie on the floor beside Noah and let all of this heat and grief and hopelessness evaporate off our bodies like steam. These summers lasted forever. Even the faint breeze that drifted in through the window smelled of melting asphalt and the factory smoke. The room was heavy with unspoken things; I had to break the silence before I suffocated.

"It wasn't your fault, Noah."

"He never wanted to come here. He wanted to run, when he found out they were sending us here. He said we could make the border. But I didn't want to risk what they'd do to us if we didn't make it. I was afraid—"

"Johnny was here because he was your brother and he'd cut off his arm before leaving you behind."

"Oh, I've helped us all. You limp now because of the last beating they gave you and I can't even remember where half of the marks on my body came from. I don't even think how humiliating it is when a

sector patrol strip searches us in the street on the way to the food lines."
His hands tightened on the windowsill. "I ignore it because I've figured
out there's nothing we can do. Johnny never got that. He was the one
who fought back. And then he just . . . leaves. They took him. Just like
they're taking you."

"No one's taking me anywhere." I leaned against the wall beside
him, rubbing slow circles in his shoulder and pretending to have no
idea what he meant. "I don't understand what you mean."

"This month's clinical cards came out this week."

"Yeah, on Wednesday. They always come out on Wednesday."

"You got one."

I opened my mouth, but my lie withered on my tongue. When I did
speak, it was with a sort of resignation, maybe even a relief. "Yes. How
do you know—"

"Word travels. That why you have this?" He threw a small square
of paper on the table; my stomach wrenched when I recognized the
death house card. It must have fallen out of my pocket when I changed
for bed. I should've double-checked . . .

"Clare, answer me."

"I just—"

"You're going to leave. Just like Johnny." He jerked his shoulder
away from me. "Because you hate this place. I can read it in every crease
of your face. You hate me for bringing us here."

"It's not like that."

"Just blame me and get it over with."

"The clinicals, Noah." I shuddered even in the heat. "You know
what they're going to do to me."

"And you can't think of a reason worth trying to stay alive, right?"

"You know no one survives."

"You don't even want to try. Because you'd rather choose that than
be with someone who's failed his brother. And his wife—"

"You haven't failed me."

"You planned that appointment for days, Clare. You slept in the
same bed with me, and you planned it. At least Johnny had the decency
to be spontaneous. You were just cruel."

I shrank from him, into a chair, as if I could disappear into the furniture. Silence stretched between us for long minutes.

"What would you do," he said at last, the anger draining from his
words, "if we had a day without all this? And we could do anything we
want, anything normal."

"Normal."

"Think back and tell me if you remember the last time we spent
a day together doing anything besides slaving in the factory lines or
scrounging for supplies or burying the dead? When have we last been

alive?"

A slideshow of the past year clicked by in my mind, rewinding through all the memories of the camps and the barcodes and the first weeks in the quarantine sector, when we were too terrified of the black squads or the rape gangs to even close our eyes. Then the long, slow process of surviving, every day another piece of ourselves traded for another dose of the vaccines, until everything, even sleeping together or making love, rang futile.

"What would you do?" I asked him.

"I would bring Johnny back and tell him he was right. That survival doesn't mean anything if we forget there is something outside all these smokestacks and razor wire."

"I'd find God and ask him where he went. And ask him to give me one good reason to stay alive."

"And if he did?"

I twisted the edge of my camisole around my fingers, tightening the fabric until my skin turned white. "Then I would listen."

He pushed back from the window, his feet disappearing into the darkness abruptly, as if plunged underwater. The humidity thickened, as if the room were filled with liquid and if I wanted to reach him, I'd have to swim for it. My arms refused to work. I was so tired.

After all those months spent trying to hold us together, I was amazed at how quickly I'd put such an unreachable distance between us, even when we were in the same room.

*   *   *

We didn't speak of it the next day. Or the next. We merely existed around each other, as if carefully observing invisible lines that, if crossed, would incite some devastating war. I made him coffee and set it on the table at his elbow, without looking at him. He brought our weekly meat ration into the kitchen and set it on the counter next to me without so much as reaching for my hand. We pretended to sleep in the same bed, although he moved to the floor as soon as he thought I'd fallen asleep. Sometimes, I leaned over and dropped a pillow beside him anyway.

The detente continued until the afternoon of the third day. Heat slid down the factory's corrugated tin roof like butter on a grill, shimmering over the streets and corroded buildings. I slipped down a back staircase on my break to eat the plum I'd carried all day in my pocket. It'd cost me several ration cards and my favorite tube of lip gloss, but I had to taste something besides sweat and stale bread. My eyes crossed the street to the crumbling warehouses and caught Noah walking from an alley between the buildings, his hands in his pockets, coveralls unzipped at the collar. He crossed the street and walked directly to me.

"Meet me at the bus stop for the Market at shift end. Five o'clock."

"We already have our rations."

His hand crossed mine. "Just be there." He took the half-eaten plum from my palm and took a bite as he walked away. I thought he smiled at me, but that might just have been sunlight in my eyes.

*   *   *

We sweated in the sardine-can bus for eight blocks, but by the time we reached the Market, an early evening breeze began to shuffle through the streets. The trade bazaar swelled with the usual crowds—street vendors hawking anything and everything, bored patrols or listless whores smoking joints on the street corners, street children fighting over scraps from the food carts. The omnipresent State anthem blared from loudspeakers attached to every light post and two workers in the white uniforms of the Ministry of Citizen Awareness plastered new political posters onto the wall of an abandoned store. The poster showed a child sleeping in the palm of gigantic hand with fingers alternating in stripes of red, white and blue; the fingers were partially closed, as if to form a cradle or else a fist. Bold blue lettering spelled out: Security Is Freedom.

I'd passed this street on the way to the death house. Guilt and a pang of fear caught me in the back of my throat. Was he taking me there? Would he demand I cancel the appointment or did he just want to hurry things up? Even the warmth of his hand in mine was suspect—did he hold it just to say goodbye?

But we didn't go to the death house. Instead, he brought me to a devastated church. Graffiti curled along the doors and the charred stone walls. All of the windows were broken, even the stained glass above the door that once showed the hand of Adam stretching toward the hand of God; all that remained was God's hand, cut off at the wrist, extended toward nothing. Toward shattered glass. I followed Noah into the cool shadows, amid smells of stale beer and burnt motor oil, glittering fragments of glass crunching beneath our thin soles.

He leaned one shoulder against the cracked wall, beneath a hollow window, and cupped his hands. I put my left foot on his knee and then swung upward as he catapulted me onto the window ledge . . . I slid into the building and landed with a soft grunt. He followed me, landing near a dismembered Communion table now splintered into firewood. Behind him, the fading sunlight shone through the surviving panes of stained glass, the light diffused into colored patterns across his face and hands, across the table's ruins.

He retrieved a kerosene lantern from his backpack and we followed the glow through the sanctuary. We descended a staircase that wound like a backbone through the building's rickety skeleton, past basements and cellars and prayer chapels. The rooms were empty, lonely places, filled with forgotten things—mildewed piles of old hymnbooks gnawed into rats' nests, an iron cross hanging askew from one rusty nail above an altar, prayer candles burnt down to nubs of wax. A sadness settled over my heart. *Oh Lord, what have we done to You? It's easy to say You were the one to leave, but maybe it works the other way.*

Noah led me into a room filled with paintings of the twelve disciples and the Christ, some ruined by damp, others clinging to life. He held the lantern as high as his arm would reach until I could see the bearded faces, the desert-worn skin, the robes now mustard-colored by age and dust. He did not complain of stiffness when I took the time to peer into each painting individually, or when I passed my fingers over the Christ three times in attempt to memorize the face. The decayed canvas was barely recognizable in places, but the eyes fixed me calmly, as if He knew why I was there. I dropped my gaze.

Are You trying to tell me something?

When I looked at the eyes again, they revealed nothing. So much for conversation. We weren't the first to make the pilgrimage; candle stubs and burnt match ends littered the floor. He placed his hands over my eyes and walked me in slow toddler steps across the debris-strewn floor.

"Sit," he said, helping me down. "This will make you more comfortable. I found it in one of the chapels."

I felt a roughness of velvet beneath my legs, a worn cushion stiff with age.

"Noah, I don't understand—"

"Just a minute. Eyes closed, now."

I heard a clink of metal and ceramic as he rummaged through his backpack, then the sound of paper tearing and the flare of a match.

"Okay."

When I opened my eyes, Noah was seated in front of me; light from three votive candles flickered within the lantern glow. A metal flask, empty cup, and partially wrapped loaf of bread filled the space between us. Real bread, not the cardboard ration loaves. Something about the items struck me as intensely familiar, but I didn't grasp what until he took Johnny's notebook from his back pocket.

"I was reading part of this the other night and found something." He shifted it back and forth in his hands. "Thought it might help us remember a few things." He coughed to drive the hoarseness from his throat then began to read. "The Lord Jesus on the night when he was betrayed took bread, and when he had given thanks, he broke it and said, 'This is my body which is for you. Do this in remembrance of me.'"

I closed my eyes as my fingers hovered over the cross at my neck. The painting of Christ flashed into my mind, those eyes pinning me into place. I could see him, standing in front of those he loved, knowing—just as I knew—what would take him from them, what pain waited for him just outside that room. And yet he'd stayed.

Of course it was easy for You, You had that whole Son of God thing going, not to mention a convenient resurrection card up your sleeve. It was easy for You to be brave.

Noah placed a piece of bread in my hands, and covered my palm with his, bending his head so that it rested on our joined fingers.

"Thank You for the bread," he said, slowly. We were both out of practice. "Forgive me for forgetting that You have not forgotten us. Forgive me for letting Johnny forget. Let me—let us—remember You."

He coughed again and I caught a slight glistening in the corner of his eye as he lifted the bread to his mouth. I followed his movement, but the bread hardened on my tongue until it felt like I was trying to swallow cement.

It's not like I want to leave. It's not like I have a choice.

There is always a choice. The words drifted from the back of my mind. I barely realized that Noah was reading again.

"In the same way also he took the cup, after supper, saying 'This cup is the new covenant in my blood. Do this, as often as you drink it, in remembrance of me.'"

The warmth of Noah's fingers closed around mine, holding the cup between us. I looked directly into his face for the first time since we'd been here. He met my gaze and in the moment before he shut his eyes again, I caught a flash of naked hope that left me with a hitch in my breath.

"Thank You for this wine. Forgive me for forgetting the promise you left us. Forgive me for believing that this—" His free hand brushed the brand on his neck. "—is eternal. Let us remember You."

He drank from the cup, then put it in my hands. I too closed my eyes as the bittersweet liquid filled my mouth, and as I drank, the voice again filtered through my mind.

It wasn't bravery.

Then what?

It was love.

When I opened my eyes, my hands were trembling. Noah took the cup and set it aside, then withdrew two more items from his backpack and laid them both in front of me, a plain white envelope on one side, my appointment card on the other. I stiffened.

"What is this?"

"You recognize your appointment card. These—" he tapped the envelope, " — are fake identification cards and a pass that will get us on a rail transport out of the sector."

"Where?"

"The shantylands, eventually, out west. No one out there cares what your official status is as long as you can work and have good teeth." He tried to smile but a strain showed along the edges, like wire pulled taut.

"You really think we can make it that far?"

"I think—" He let out a deep breath. "I think it's a risk. Even with papers, not everyone gets through. And it means no vaccines, nothing to guarantee the virus will stay dormant."

"You don't have to do this for me."

"Yes. I do." His hand traced a circle on the inside of my wrist, setting sparks under my skin. "But it's your choice. You get to decide."

I stared at the envelope, then at the card.

The incense and hush of the death house and Lucien's office came back to my mind—serene, peaceful. Easy. Then a torrent of other images flooded me— Noah and I on the rail together, my head resting on his rolled-up jacket to keep from banging against the window. Noah and I sharing an orange in an anonymous depot, or standing together in the white sun and endless sky of the shantylands, no wire in sight for miles. I saw the other ending to the story—both of us crouching in some alley while black squad flashlights blinded us until we were thrown in the back of a van and final darkness. Dead. Alive. Either way, nothing would be easy.

I picked up the appointment card and held it over the candle's flame until the paper began to shrivel into ash. Noah looked at me through the flame, a sort of suspended relief starting to filter through his eyes and face.

"You sure?"

"Yes. I want to try it, for Johnny. For me. Us."

I moved beside him; he sank his head into my lap, his fists clenching the fabric of my uniform. "I hate Johnny for giving up. I hate him. He had no right."

"Shhh." My hands ran over the back of his head, down his shoulders. "I'm not Johnny. I'm not going anywhere."

We didn't move for a long time. As I sat with him, in my mind I saw the river, but this time both of us swam upstream, twisting hand in hand through the black ribbons of current. Toward the shore.

INFINITE SPACE
INFINITE GOD

Karina & Robert Fabian, Editors

Infinite Space
Infinite God

Karina and Robert Fabian, Editors

SF collection

$18.95 trade paperback
ISBN 1-933353-62-7
available August 2007
from
Twilight Times Books
http://twilighttimesbooks.com/

"...an excellent collection of science fiction short stories. These authors' imaginations are astounding, pulling me into each and every story from the first paragraph... The characters come alive in vivid detail making each story's uniqueness stand on their own merit. Highly recommended, not only to devoted sci-fi readers, but to those who have never read the genre before." ~ *Reviewed by PJ for Scottieluvr's "Chewing the Bone" reviews.*

Come explore the worlds of "Infinite Space, Infinite God." Meet genetically engineered chimeras and aliens who wonder what a human religion holds for them. Share the doubts, trials and triumphs of humans who find their journeys in time and space are also journeys in faith.

Experience spine-tingling adventure. Marvel at technological miracles—and miracles that transcend technology—and meet the writers who made a leap of faith and dared to incorporate familiar religion with fantastic universes.

Copies can be ordered through your favorite bookstore, Baker & Taylor, Ingram, or the publisher, Twilight Times Books, P. O. Box 3340, Kingsport, TN 37664.

PUMPING YOUR MUSE

World-building dills for the seasoned author suffering from writer's block or fledgling writer looking for inspiration and guidance, following these contiguous exercises generates a first draft.

"Donna Sundblad keeps the continuity flowing at an interesting pace and has allowed space for notes at the end of every chapter. Her useful manual also includes a number of excellent writer's resource websites."
—Lillian Brummet, co-author of *Trash Talk*

• **Attention to Detail**: Real World details flood our senses on a subconscious level; exercises hone the writer's skill to furnish detailed information without falling prey to overly descriptive terms.

• **Flip Side**: No matter how bizarre or mundane the story, a writer's thoughts follow a sequence—a thread of logic; exercises force the writer from that path of logic to wander in another direction to explore new concepts.

• **Reconstitute Your World**: These exercises take aspects of 'real world' places and happenings, blend them with fictional ingredients and transform them into believable realms and scenarios complete with flora and fauna.

• **Mapping and Tracking**: Applying these principles teaches organizational skills from the genesis to the last detail of your world, including characters and their belongings; develops logistical smoothness and provides a way to track objects for continuity.

$14.99 print – $5.00 ebook
Publisher: epress-online
Publication Date: June 2005
ISBN: 0970863578
Available at epress-online's bookstore (epress-online.com)

100s of years ago, the Stygian race welcomed disease-riddled Jonnick to their shores despite prophetic warnings. Concealed powers of darkness disembark with the refugees.

Today, Manelin, a social outcast, and Jalil, a lame Jonnick girl find themselves thrust into the midst of unfolding ancient prophecies and a world on the verge of annihilation.

Donna Sundblad's Windwalker
$14.99 print–$5.00 ebook
Publisher: epress-online
Publication Date: September 2006
ISBN: 0977222489
available at epress-online's bookstore
www.epress-online.com

FLASHPOINT

winner of 2006 ELFIE for best sci-fi novel

BOOK ONE OF THE UNDERGROUND

FRANK CREED

**2036:
global government.
The One State's
only threat?
Fundamentalist
terrorism.
A church-bust in
the
Chicago-Metroplex,
sparks Flashpoint
in the Underground**

FLASHPOINT
Author: Frank Creed
978-1-934284-01-8
The Writers' Café Press
June 2007

. . . action-packed, shocking look into a possible future
—MaryLu Tyndall, Legacy of the King's Pirates series

*. . . nerve-racking, breath-taking, heart-leaping action
and emotional attack* —Malin Larsson